DECEIT DESERVES
Revenge II

DECEIT DESERVES
Revenge II

*To Shelia
from Lucy B.
I love you!*

LUCY B. WILLIAMS

iUniverse LLC
Bloomington

DECEIT DESERVES REVENGE II

Copyright © 2013 by Lucy B. Williams.

All rights reserved. No part of this book may be used or reproduced by any means, graphic, electronic, or mechanical, including photocopying, recording, taping or by any information storage retrieval system without the written permission of the publisher except in the case of brief quotations embodied in critical articles and reviews.

This is a work of fiction. All of the characters, names, incidents, organizations, and dialogue in this novel are either the products of the author's imagination or are used fictitiously.

iUniverse books may be ordered through booksellers or by contacting:

iUniverse LLC
1663 Liberty Drive
Bloomington, IN 47403
www.iuniverse.com
1-800-Authors (1-800-288-4677)

Because of the dynamic nature of the Internet, any web addresses or links contained in this book may have changed since publication and may no longer be valid. The views expressed in this work are solely those of the author and do not necessarily reflect the views of the publisher, and the publisher hereby disclaims any responsibility for them.

Any people depicted in stock imagery provided by Thinkstock are models, and such images are being used for illustrative purposes only. Certain stock imagery © Thinkstock.

ISBN: 978-1-4917-0851-4 (sc)
ISBN: 978-1-4917-0853-8 (hc)
ISBN: 978-1-4917-0852-1 (e)

Library of Congress Control Number: 2013917934

Printed in the United States of America

iUniverse rev. date: 09/26/2013

This book is Dedicated to;

Again I'll tell you I dedicate this book to;

CHARLES CRAWFORD WILLIAMS JR.

Attorney, an avid hunter and a courageous, splendid man. No one ever felt as secure and content in a friend's love. No woman ever felt as respected and cared about by her friend as I do. I'm so grateful that our relationship is, and always has been so close and one thing I know for sure, no friend ever loved her friend more than I love you Crawford, courage is what he gives me. Classy is what he is.

Oh! Less not forget my Gary Allen Jackson, my dear friend, singer, songwriter, and entrepreneur. So handsome, he will make your teeth sweat. No drinking, drugs, smoking, or bad language. What more can be said about a fine young man. For sure Gary can fix a broken heart.

Thanks to
Mr. Albert Young, my friend from across the world.

To Lori Keller for helping me with searching the maps to where my men needed to go and for being one of the best friends I ever had.

Thanks to
Jim May
Family man and hard worker
I love Jim

Thank You
Lowell Brook
You light up my life
If this story was true you would be my Anthony
I love you

Prelude

Oh my God! Counterfeit men, are you married to a counterfeit man? That's what I have had all my married life. Don't you think this would blow your mind?

The last words Tony said to me gave me strength. I knew when Tony was able he would help me. Day after day I grew stronger. I did feel the heat from his hands. Tony's mind was still with me, which did make me feel safer and all I have to do is wait.

I really didn't know how much Richard hated me. My family resented me, so bad. Now the whole village leaves me alone. You will see that Richard has put me through a world that I knew nothing about. I learned fast we, the women in my circumstances, will be dead or crippled for life if we don't get away from them.

One thing's for sure if you're married to a male whore you can't keep his knife dull. He's always on the prowl for fresh meat to cut and I'm not one that could turn my head and say its O.K. I know now I'll get my revenge and it won't be a dream.

Chapter 1

As I watched the nurse pack up my things to leave the hospital I was horrified. I wanted to see Mr. Tortomasi one more time.

So I asked the nurse, "Will you take me to Mr. Tortomasi's room? I need to talk with him."

The nurse helped me get into a wheelchair and rolled me to Tony's room and waited outside as we talked. As I sat looking around the room, I couldn't hold back the tears. I breathed deep breaths trying to stop the tears from running down my face. Little Anthony wasn't in the room and Mr. Tortomasi seemed to be asleep. I rolled closer to the bed and he opened his eyes. His eyes are so black, black as coal, looking straight into my green eyes; he lifted his hand and motioned me to come closer. I stood up from my wheelchair and walked to the bed.

He took my hand in his and said, "Dru, you're going home today."

I said, "Yes, I just wanted to tell you goodbye and I hope you'll be well enough to go home soon."

He held my hand tighter and said, "You know you've been in my dreams. I know you so well."

"Yes Tony, you were in my dreams too. How did this happen to us? I feel like I belong to you. I don't want to go back to the world that I came from. Dr. Bradley should have let me die. I don't know what you know, but I'm horrified to go back to Shady Grove."

"Oh no you're not! I give you strength. Do you feel the heat from my hand Dru? You will always have me with you. I don't know how this happened but we are in each other's mind. Our souls belong to each other. When you get frightened, I will come into your thoughts. You may not see me but I will always be close to you. I will never let anything happen to you. Go get well Dru. Let what people say go in one ear and out the other. Don't care what others do. Don't try to fix things for others. Just make yourself happy."

The door opened and the nurse stuck her head in and said, "We must go Mrs. Hallmark."

Tony pulled me closer to him and kissed me lightly. Not another word was said as I sat down in my wheelchair and the nurse wheeled me out of the room. My tears didn't stop and as the door was closing behind me I heard Tony say, "I'll be seeing you."

Back in my room Dr, Bradley came in to say goodbye. He also gave me a prescription to stop me from crying. Dr. Bradley said, "Don't be such a cry baby."

I said, "I love you Dr. Bradley but you don't have a good bed side manner. The only people that would understand how I feel are the ones that went through the holocaust."

Dr. Bradley said, "Bullshit!!! Cry baby."

Without another word he turned and stormed out of my room.

I turned to the nurse and said, "You would have to know this Doctor for him not to make you mad at what he says."

I went on to tell the nurse about Dr. Bradley. I was in this bed for fifteen days without a drop of water. I told Dr. Bradley I wanted some water. He smiled and told me, people in hell want ice water too, but like you they won't get any either. Then I screamed out "I want my head washed." That crazy Doctor ran out into the hallway and started screaming, stat, stat, stat somebody get this girl's head washed. That embarrassed me half to death then, even though it's funny now. Within five minutes a lady was in my room washing my hair and three days later I got a few chips of ice.

Richard came into the room to take me home, home hell, yes that's where he's taking me, to hell. Every person I passed, on my way to Shady Grove, I silently screamed out, "Hey people if you think it is easy to leave a heavenly dream and go to hell! It is not!'

We drove into the carport and Richard helped me into the house. The couch is only two feet from the door and that was as far as I could go. I was cut from can to can't, so sore that I could hardly breathe. There would be no waterbed for me.

Harriet came by to see me. I said, "I have plenty of food. Why don't you cook here and take some home with you, or all of you eat here?"

We have done this many times before but not this time no never again, as I was to find out. Harriet said, "I'll cook you something but we are going off."

She went to the kitchen and started cooking. In about an hour she announced my dinner was ready and walked into the kitchen. Richard helped me to the kitchen table. To my surprise Harriet had boiled five pounds of potatoes and poured three cans of English peas over them. No joke, that was all. I don't know why I was so shocked but I was. After eating a few bites I went back to the couch.

I called Harriet on the phone and asked, "What's this all about? Why would you boil five pounds of potatoes?"

Harriet said, "Drucilla, Richard has money. He can feed you from the deli in the grocery store."

With that I hung up the phone. What could I have said? For the next four months Richard fed me from the deli and Harriet didn't show her face.

I had no one. No one would go against Mama Marselle. Well hell, I wasn't sorry that I had killed DeRoy. After lying on that couch for four months, looking at the dark walls in my house, it almost killed me. I didn't know how bad staying inside, all the time, could be. I promised the Lord, if He would let me get well enough, I'd paint everything white or pink. It wouldn't look like a dungeon ever again.

As the days and weeks passed I felt sorry for myself. I couldn't help but think of all the food I had prepared and taken to my friends and family. Here I am, not able to lift a pan. Richard worked every day from early morning to sometimes late at night. No one has come to wash my body, much less my clothes. Not to change my bed sheets, wash a dish or bring me a bite of food. Not even to talk. My house had cobwebs hanging from vase to vase, dust covering everything. I called a cleaning service. Two ladies came and working as fast as possible it took them seven straight hours to clean my house.

One of the Ladies asked, "Is Harriet not your sister?"

I said, "Yes, on paper she is. But you know those, on paper sisters, aren't worth a dime. As a matter of fact, I have three, on paper sisters and I had to get you to clean my house."

I asked them to come back every Wednesday to clean. Richard never said a word about the house. He seemed to have been pretty happy that I was damn near dead.

The food from the deli was bad enough to kill anybody. I could hardly get past the smell just to eat a few bites. Then I found out about the Alexandria honey pot, working there. I really had to let Tony run through my mind then. But ohhhh, I couldn't let myself think about Tony. Thoughts of him heated my body to the boiling point and I wasn't able for that, just yet.

My friend Phillip Jimez came to see me. He asked, "How's this family treating you". I replied, "They are either afraid that I will shoot them or tell the truth about who their daddy really is." He asked me if I knew who my daddy was. I had never given it any thought but I told Phillip, "I had no doubt my Daddy put up with Mama Marselle just like I had put up with Richard. To tell the truth I didn't want any of these people. They have made it plain and clear that they don't want me. I just wanted to get well so I could take care of myself and get Brandon grown so we could leave here."

Phillip told me to take care and he would see me soon. I did take care and Christmas was coming. Christmas has always been special to me. I am a child on Christmas. I sent Richard to the store with a list a mile long. I spent two days cutting up pecans and candied fruit. I had everything ready to make my fruitcakes. I had the pans ready, the eggs beat, now all I had to do was to stir them together. But my energy was gone. I began to cry. I looked around the kitchen, bowls everywhere, the kitchen was in a mess and I wasn't able to finish. I called Harriet, but she didn't have time. I called everyone I knew and no one had time for me. I even called Richard and as usual work came first with him, never me. I had cried myself sick.

I called Dr. Bradley's office to get another prescription to stop me from crying.

Dr. Bradley's nurse answered the phone and asked, "Mrs. Hallmark what's wrong?"

I said, "I can't stop crying."

The next minute Dr. Bradley was asking, "Drucilla, what's going on? Why are you crying?"

I said, "I can't stir my cake mix."

He said, "Did you say you can't stir up your cake mix?"

"Yes." I sobbed.

Dr. Bradley asked, "Do you have a freezer?"

"Yes"

He said, "Then you take each potion and put it in the damn freezer. When you are rested and able to stir it, then get it out and stir it. But don't forget those damn people who wouldn't help you, when it's time to eat it. Will you do that for me?"

"Yes"

He said, "I'll call you in something to calm you. I want you to go to bed."

I sobbed, "Yes."

He said, "Drucilla, you are stronger than you think. You have a will of iron. Not to mention that temper of yours. Now I want you to stay calm. I know that you are spoiled so take advantage of it and let your body heal."

I asked, "Can I ask you about Tony?"

He said, "Yes, he is coming back to see me in about six weeks."

I asked, "Can I beg you to let me come for my appointment at the same time?"

He said, "You had me thinking you were about half dead."

I said, "I am but I'll stop crying if you say you'll do this for me."

He said, "O.K. I'll see to it that your appointment is changed. That will be good I want to talk to you both myself. Now will you go to bed?"

I said, "Yes sir."

I went to bed and called Richard to pick up my prescription on his way home. In two days, to my surprise, Fed X delivered a box to my door.

Richard opened the box and asked, "How do you rate this?"

I said, "You will never understand. It's called kindness."

Richard hates it that I love my doctors and lawyer. Think about it, both hold your life in the palm of their hand.

Anyway the box contained a five-pound fruitcake, candy of all kind, cheese, wine, crackers and a honey baked ham. The note inside was addressed to "Cry Baby" I want you to have a Merry Christmas. Signed-Dr. Bradley.

I sat in the waiting room watching for Tony but Nurse Alice called me to the back and put me in examination room three and told me Dr. Bradley would be with me soon. Soon I thought, fifteen minutes later he came in and checked me over never saying a word about Tony.

Dr. Bradley said, "Your blood pressure is high."

I said, "Yes, that's what you do to me."

We both burst out laughing. A knock at the door and Tony walked in without waiting.

Dr. Bradley walked out saying, "I'll be back before you know I'm gone."

Tony reached up and helped me off the examining table, took me in his arms and just held me for a minute. He kissed my neck, tenderly. We looked into each other's eyes and both had tears in our eyes. He then gave me a full kiss for the longest time. He slipped his hands into the back of my sweater, rubbing my back while holding me tight to him.

Tony said, "You make me crazy. I can't think of anything without you coming into my thoughts."

I said, "Thank God Tony. I hope to see the day that I'm not out of your sight, for a long, long time."

He said, "That day will come. I promise you. Just keep getting well and always remember, I'll be here for you soon. We have to have everything right. Remember I'm in your mind. I know what you want and if you need me I'm only a thought away. You stay busy and be safe for me."

I said, "Oh, I will! Really I'm O.K. I have a long lost cousin coming to see me. His name is Rex. He told me that he had heard so much about me that he wants to get to know me."

Tony said, "O.K. maybe he will keep your mind off a lot of things."

I said, "Please, be quiet, kiss me. I want to know if you can read my lips."

After a long passionate kiss Tony pulled loose and said, "You should be ashamed."

I said, "Well I'm not. Someday I'll kiss you all over."

Tony said, "Is that a promise?"

I said, "Oh yes!"

Just as Dr. Bradley walked in Tony said, "And I'll pay you back."

Dr. Bradley asked, "What did you borrow from her?"

Tony said, "Just a promise."

Dr. Bradley asked, "Are you still in each other's mind?"

Tony said, "I can even read her lips."

Dr. Bradley asked, "Can you read his lips Drucilla?"

I said, "Oh, yes!"

Dr. Bradley asked, "And when did you last do that?"

I said, "Just before you came back into the room."

Dr. Bradley asked, "And what did his lips say?"

I said, "They said don't stop now, I need more."

Dr. Bradley said, "I want you both to get out of here and come back in six months. You go first Drucilla."

I said, "**No!** We will see you in three months."

Tony said, "I'll be seeing you doll."

I cried, "Yes."

But I really cried when Dr. Bradley left Caraway and moved to Salisbury, North Carolina. Lord did I cry. I cried for a week. All the pills in the world couldn't stop the tears. This doctor could be as mean as a pit bull but he always does the right thing for his patients. He did leave me in good hands, Dr. Bob. And I do love Dr. Bob.

It took me many months to get my body running right. In the meantime I had received many phone calls telling me how much Richard loved me and how he feared for my life. I thought he must have put on a good act at the hospital. Boy could I tell them a thing or two. Look at the time it took him to get me to the hospital. Richard could have driven it in thirty minutes but he called an ambulance and it took them three and one half hours to get me there. The ambulance sat in my yard for hours trying to stabilize me. They damn near let me die. At that time I wanted to die, but that was before Tony.

Jerry, my brother was the only one to ask me what he could do for me. I told him to take my rings off, that I was ready to die, and for him to look out for Brandon. My whole time in the ambulance I prayed to die. I asked God to never let me come back down Shady Grove Road again.

In the trauma unit, at the hospital I heard Dr. Morris say "This girl is dead." Then I heard Dr. Bradley say "Hell no, you do this and you do that, damn if I'll let her die."

God had other plans for me. He gave me Tony. Our minds and souls merged together. From then on I belonged to Tony.

But Tony could take me into an unknown world. I have never gotten heated up in my life; but Tony. Even my teeth sweat thinking of Tony. Oh, how I would love to read those lips while kissing him. How I would love to see me in his eyes. I wish his heart would hurt for me as mine hurts for him. I know it's real love that I feel for him because I've never, in all my years with Richard, wanted anyone as I want Tony. I know it's wrong to break a vow. Today I would break them all.

Richard has never loved me. He has forty-two honey pots that I know about; besides that he killed my love for him long ago. I'm just now realizing that I've been walking around in a coma. All of these years, damn I am awake now. Bright eyed and bushy tailed, a prissy feeling in my tender privates with a sinful wish that Tony would steal me away, all the way to the Gulf to the far end at Fort Morgan. Smooth water, snow white sand, incredible breeze and me with a need for him that would heat up the entire ocean.

His luscious lips, dark eyes, my God listen to my thoughts. I have read it in books, watched it on TV, but now to feel this need! In all my years, why haven't I ever felt like this? When I think about Tony, I could take him in my arms and step into another world.

Chapter 2

"I've been told all of my life that a truck driver has a woman in every city he passes through. Well Richard beats that record all to hell. He is a telephone man and he has a honey pot in every other house. Breakfast houses, fast foods, hotels, trailer parks to fine homes from Oak Mountain in the south to Smoke Rise up north, and west to Walker County. I'd say that covers the better part of three counties."

"I have interviewed dozens of telephone men and they all say the same thing. We check out every crack and corner and when we find thighs we can part, we do it. When we can find a 'lick a dick a day girl,' we are there every day and pass the name and address around to other workers."

"I interviewed some telephone women that work in the field with other men. They all agreed that working with a man is a guaranteed affair. Getting close to one another, the smell of each other and then the touching of hands sets them both off. One told me she had six kids, her husband is a long haul truck driver and is out of town a lot, and when she wanted a man it didn't matter, any man would do. She even had it going with her Yankee boss. To me he looked like a worm but she said he is hotter than a ready to explode cherry bomb. His wife was seven months pregnant, so go figure."

"Some of these stories are so unbelievable. That is why I became an investigator. Richard has told so many lies and dumb enough to be caught in damn near all of them. Like the ghost girl, Kay Chappel, and another time we were at a baseball park, Richard, Brandon and I, when up walked a little dark headed woman about five foot two, no wedding ring and looked to be nine months pregnant, right up to Richard's knee and asked, "How is your hammer hanging?" You should have seen the look on Richard's face. She was smiling, painted up like a clown and rubbing her belly against Richard's knee. I got up and walked away as if I didn't know who Richard was. In reality I don't and here we go again."

"That was in the Spring and now I'm home from the hospital, from near death and my mind is spinning. The tongues here in Shady Grove are wagging. Gossip is running rampant that I'm going to get even with everyone that has hurt me. And that I'll investigate everyone that crosses my path, and I am."

"Now it has been six months and I felt good enough to go to the store. While standing in the checkout line I overheard two women talking behind me. The first lady said, "You know, she is the one that shot her brother-in-law." I turned around and tapped the second lady on the shoulder and told her. His name was DeRoy and there are going to be a lot more where he just went. To hell, you know? Both ladies left the line and went to some other part of the store. I didn't crack a smile but the lady at the cash register died laughing."

"I don't care what the people of this town think about me. They make me sick. I've lived here all my life and I know their between the sheets nicknames, the thieves, the ones that have a dime and the ones that don't. I know the ones that take their mattress off their beds and lay in the woods every weekend. I call them mattress whores. Some of them even have a working credit card machine. I often wondered how sex is written up on their credit card statement. They will take your husband for sure but some will take your jewelry in trade."

"Well Rex, I've about talked myself to death and you haven't told me much about yourself at all."

Rex asked, "What do you know about me?"

"I know your Mother left my Uncle when you were six weeks old and left your older sister in Graysville. And you just turned forty. You said you just flew in from Detroit, Michigan. You say you came here for me, which I don't understand. You look like your Daddy, only taller but you act a lot like your Uncle Louie."

I continued, "Now you tell me. Why are you here at this time in my life, with my whole family nipping at my heels? Why would you have anything to do with me? You may know, everybody that knows me thinks I'm crazy. If that's what you came here to see, I'll tell you all about me. The first thing I'll tell you is, look around you. Go through the house and around the yard, go in my closets and take inventory. You must know something about me or you wouldn't be here."

Rex smiled and said, "More than you think."

I said, "Well, I'm not going to let you believe hearsay, like I said, look around."

Rex said, "No need I already have. Like I told you, I know more than you think."

I said, "Go and invite the rest of your relatives to look. Take note of this, Aunt Drucilla doesn't have what she has by being crazy. You best remember that."

Rex never said a word, just sat there smiling.

"My Daddy gave me this land and I turned a damn near chicken coop into a beautiful home. I drive a new Camaro Z28 convertible. I have nineteen carats of diamonds, two mink coats worth eight thousand each and I co-write songs. My co-writer has a new limousine in which we ride back and forth to Nashville where we have songs cataloged at a major record label."

Rex's ears perked up at that last remark and said, "What you need is a boyfriend."

"Listen old boy, you can wipe that smile off your face."

Rex said, "I could turn you on."

I said, "Listen fool, you're my cousin. Even if you weren't you'll never get to try that and you better be careful what you say in this village. None of these Shady Grove bastards like me, but they don't let their shirt tails hit their back before they're on the phone telling me, who said what about me."

Rex said, "I'll keep that in mind. Do you have another beer?"

I handed Rex a beer as we went out onto the back porch. He sat down and lit a cigarette. I pointed out where Brother Percy lives and where Sister Harriet and my Brandon live, then where Brother Jerry lives.

Rex asked, "Why do you say, your Brandon?"

I said, "God sent him here for me. He just used Harriet as a shuttle to get him here. I thought you said you knew about me?"

Rex said, "I guess I didn't know as much as I thought."

I said, "You can believe me, Brandon is the only reason I'm in these woods. This is a hellhole. I can't imagine why you would come to Alabama. You know, Alabama is known as the hellhole of the United States."

Rex said, "Why Drucilla, are you a racist?"

I said, "Hell yes! That comes tagged to all white people in Alabama. Don't ask me things when you may not like the answers. I call it prejudice but I know the damn Yankees don't know the difference. I'm prejudice against all races that commit child abuse, whores, the people that tell lies, criminals, people that won't keep their yards clean, people that won't keep their homes clean, people with a mouth full of rotten teeth or no teeth at all, people that open my refrigerator without washing their hands, gays, male or female, men that won't support their wife and children, people that eat boogers and the politicians that send our soldiers to war and then put them in prison for killing the enemy. I think this Iraq war came about to give us something to focus on while the Mexicans flooded across our southern border. I don't think the U.S. belongs to us anyway. Obama wants to make North America one nation. Clinton wants to let everyone tip toe thru the tulips, singing <u>I Feel So Good</u>, John Edwards, I think is a communist. I wish I could be president. I'd bring our soldiers home and put them on our streets. Gays and lesbians would be hunted down and a stake drove in their hearts like the vampires they are. The drugs would be gone."

Rex asked, "You don't mind that I came to see you, do you?"

I said, "No, I wish you would get to know me so you could tell me about myself. The good, the bad and the ugly; I'm as good as you let me be and as mean as you make me."

With a wicked smile Rex said, "You said I can't get to know you that well."

I said, "I'll tell you one thing about yourself boy. The Farley's were your great grandparents and they married their first cousins. So are you crazy or just talking crazy?"

Rex was still laughing when he left. He went back to his sister's house and came to see me every week. He found a job and bought a new pick-up truck. He was a sight. The last time he came by strutting his stuff he had a ten gallon cowboy hat, cowboy boots and country music blasting the doors off the truck. I could hear his truck before he turned into my road. But this time he parked across the road and just sat in the vehicle for about twenty minutes. I was sitting at the kitchen table, looking out the glass sliding door, thinking I am not going to put up with him coming down here drinking his beer. I went outside and sat in the swing on the patio. Here he came, beer in one hand and a cigarette in the other.

I asked, "What's this deal, with you sitting in the truck?"

Rex said, "Well, I was writing out my bills. There is so much noise at Sis's house that I couldn't think and I love to come here, it's so quiet."

I had just washed my hair before Rex came and I had my head wrapped in a towel. I pulled the towel off and was shaking my hair out when Rex pulled a camera out of his pocket and took my picture.

I screamed, "You fool, you can't take a picture of me looking like this."

He said, "I didn't know you would look like this. I have never seen you not made up looking like a million dollar baby. I want to know the real you."

He laid the camera down and later when he went to his truck for another beer. I threw the camera across the road as far as I could into the woods. Rex never acknowledged that he even saw me throw the camera into the woods and I watched him get into his truck and leave. One week from the day I received a letter in the mail, no note just a God awful picture of me, wet hair standing straight up, towel flying and me screaming. I thought, "How in the hell did he find that camera, and when?"

Three weeks later I was sitting on the patio, he came two stepping around the house. I didn't hear his truck this time.

Rex said, "Drucilla are you going to shoot me like you did DeRoy?"

I said, "Maybe, but to DeRoy it was a surprise, to you it won't be."

Rex got quiet and just stood there for a minute. Even the birds were quiet. Then he smiled and asked, "Drucilla I want to be a writer and if I can, I want to write about you."

I laughed out loud and said, "Rex I forgot to tell you about my best friends in this whole world. First of all, I love all of the Jefferson County Sheriffs, they are my big brothers. I don't know what you've been told about me but I'll tell you this, I'm very out spoken I'll tell anybody where to stick it when they're trying to stick it in the wrong place. You see this bleached hair? You know what they say about blonds? One thing you need to know about me is, I don't tell lies. I don't have enough sense to keep up with a lie. So I have to tell it like it is."

Rex said, "Drucilla you laugh but let me write about you, after DeRoy? I can't sleep at night thinking about the things I've been told. We never talk about Richard and he acts like he loves you to death. He jumps at your every wish."

I asked, "How many times have you been to this house and me not here?"

Rex said, "Never."

I said, "This is my jail. Richard is my guard. I take a sleeping pill every night and Richard goes out to play while I'm asleep. He took my car out, one night and drove the hell out it to the tune of nine hundred dollars to fix it. I keep my mouth shut and he keeps his hands off me."

"I know there is a higher power and I'll tell you how I know. I'm far from being a bible thumper but I do know there is a God."

"A few years back I was diagnosed with sarcoid in my lungs. It is like moss growing in a pot. I was told to stop smoking or I would die within six months. I did everything to quit. I even went to a hypnotist. I would go from one cigarette a day to one pack a day and back to one cigarette a day."

"One March day, it was beautiful about seventy-eight degrees and a steady wind blowing from the south. I put on a two-piece bathing suit, a glass of tea in one hand and a pack of cigarettes in the other.

I set out to get a suntan. I pulled my lounge chair out in the sun and before I laid down I held my cigarettes up to the sky and said, "If You are up there and You have all that power I want You to take these cigarettes away from me. I don't want them anymore and I can't do it by myself." I don't remember lying down. But when I awoke I was brown as a brick. Every pore on my body was oozing in nicotine and from that day to this I've never wanted another cigarette. I met Richard at the porch that night and told him not to bring another cigarette into this house. We will never smoke again. For a long time after that if I were around people that smoked in my presence, I would pass out for three or four hours. It was like a reminder to never go near a cigarette again."

"I have seen visions. I was going up Union Grove Road one day, about a mile before I got to my turn I had a vision of a white pick-up truck running a stop sign right in front of me. I slowed my speed, sure enough the same white pick-up ran the stop sign and I barely missed hitting him."

"The sarcoid in my lungs didn't get me. God showed me His power. He has watched over and given me the best of friends like Mr. Williams and the whole Jefferson County Sheriff Department. He gave me the power to search out the truth about Richard. I know full well what I'm dealing with and He tells me that Richard is the one and only **Satan** that's in my life. Now, I ask you, do you really want to write about us?"

Rex sat limp in his seat and didn't answer me.

"This village I live in and the counties are Richard's play pen; Jefferson, Walker and Blount.

Have you ever read "Salem's Lot" by Steven King? I have never picked up another book that would top it. You read that story, then I'll tell you mine and if you still want to write it, I'll let you."

Rex said, "Damn, you're not joking are you?"

I said, "No, I'm afraid not."

Rex left and three weeks later he came back and handed me a book, "Salem's Lot." He asked, "When do we start? I work five days and off two days. Sometimes the two off days are during the week."

I said, "You call me the night before. You come here and I'll drive us to Lock Seventeen on the Warrior River. It is quiet and secluded. We won't be disturbed. But, when I start telling you what has happened to me, I do not want to hear you say I should have done this or that. I want you to understand that I know where I am, where I have been and where I'm going. The most important thing to know about me is I know before I leave this world, I'm taking out forty-seven earth polluters with me. Now will you get me one of your beers?"

When he returned from the truck I asked, "Do you mind if I take your picture?"

He agreed so I had him change his shirt and put on a flat cappie, some call it a go to hell hat. The next day I had it developed and studied the picture. I swear I could feel my Uncle Louie looking back at me. I could feel his presence. I kept telling myself that I couldn't believe that Rex would think my story is as good as "Salem's Lot." I'll do it. Besides I have Uncle Louie with me, as sure as I'm breathing.

The next week on the way to Lock Seventeen, I started telling my story. I didn't know how I ever lived through it. But then I'm not through it, yet. I was feeling awful blue so I decided to pick things up. I told Rex I would give him a story line. He could kiss my ass and call it a love story. We both had a good laugh before I started with my story.

I said, "Everyone thinks Richard and I are a real love story. Everyone thinks we are newlyweds. That is just what Richard wants them to think so nobody will believe me when I tell them about the real Richard."

Rex gave me that look and said, "Drucilla, you are past praying for."

Then with a wicked smile he said, "Boy, they don't make them like you anymore."

I said, "So you start your story off with. If you live in Walker, Blount or Jefferson Counties and have whored around with a married man you may be in this story, I want all the judges and jurors to read my story and then they will know why. I for one could kill. Nothing is bad enough for a person that has taken all of your young years, sucking the life out of you and then laughing at you. God, just saying it out loud, I could put an ax between his eyes. As for his whores I could pour gas on their asses and light them up. They are going to burn in hell anyway. I'm just giving them a glimpse of what is in store for them."

"Who knows who you can trust? I can't even go to the hospital without running into one of Richard's whores. I had a light run down my throat to check out my stomach and the anesthesiologist's nurse told me the next time she had to put me to sleep, she would do a good job of it. She was a blond from Bagley. You would think that wouldn't happen in the real world. Think about this. If we catch our mate whoring around, they are the criminals. We are the victims. Remember Rex; if you are going to write my story you must write everything just the way it happened. I want you to realize that you will be stepping on a lot of toes, from sex to drugs."

"The people that know the real me know that I love myself. It's very true that I'm as mean as you make me and as good as you let me be. I'm as good as the best and better than the rest. I'm an excellent example of a fool. Believe me, beauty fades but dumb is forever. I found out where the nurse lives. I will show you one day."

I talked as if I were running on new Eveready Batteries. I tell you I was an embarrassment to myself.

"I stay exhausted all the time. It took two years for me to know the truth. For one thing I'm just a fool for wanting to prove to my family the truth about Richard.

Don't let me leave out the hairdresser that turned nurse, the Fosters, the medical examiner Jeff Jones and the gays. The truth is I wouldn't have ever said a word if Richard hadn't brought them to my home. Those people were running up and down my road and fooling with me on the telephone. Like I said my Daddy gave me, not Richard, the land and I've killed myself working for what I have. That is my little acre, my little world and I'll be damned if anyone is going to come on my territory, causing me trouble and make me like it. **No damn way!**"

"So I sent out three hundred letters offering a two thousand dollar reward for information on whoever came into my home while

Richard and I were in California. Richard left a key with one of his whores or left the door unlocked. I knew something was up because the whole time we were in California, Richard was on the defensive. He was cursing and screaming at me in front of my friend that went with us. The sons of bitches went through my home with a fine toothcomb."

"I had found a token that had been oiled and wrapped in paper and placed in Richard's dresser drawer. I hid the token in the finger of my glove, rolled the glove up and placed it in the pocket of my mink coat. Like I said, Richard had a fit while we were in California to the point of making my friend Johnnie sick. Anyway when we got home, one look and I knew my home had been turned upside down. They got the token, two new bottles of perfume and several scarves that were signed by country singers. They got my drumsticks that the Oak Ridge Boys gave to me. The bastards desecrated everything that I loved. I was so full of hate."

Rex said, "Not was, Drucilla!! You still are. I can hear it in your voice."

"Anyway I'll cut his ass up and give all forty-two of his whores a piece of him. I should have said, forty-two is what I've found on my own. I know there are many more.

Turn, turn, turn!! Go down the hill. Here is the dam. The lock is manually controlled. There is always someone in the control tower."

As we pulled into the parking lot, Rex said, "My Lord, look at all those buzzards. There is one sitting on every post."

I said, "No, look how clean everything is. Park over there, by the picnic tables. The restrooms here are clean, and listen how quiet it is. It's a lot quieter than my house."

I got the pillows and comforter while he got the cooler of food and beer and we walked to the river's edge.

Rex said, "Now Drucilla if you had told me there were grills to cook on, I would have come prepared to have a steak."

I said, "We don't have time to cook."

Rex said, "Well we could have if you would get up and be ready before ten o'clock."

I said, "I won't do that. That's time I give to myself."

Rex said, "O K, you take a minute while I get my thoughts together."

I spread the comforter on the ground and lay down. Rex pulled out a laptop and placed it on a picnic table. He stuck his long legs over the seat, under the table and went to work. To my surprise he started typing right away.

"Let me tell you. It starts getting dark about seven thirty and the mosquitoes get really bad. We need to leave here before seven and if we don't cover everything we can come back. But I wish you would change your off days to the middle of the week so no one would be here. There was no one here when we arrived and look at them now."

Rex said, "My off days rotate every week so that won't be a problem. Are you going to be alright with telling me this?"

I said, "Hell no! But I'm going to tell you anyway. Maybe just maybe, talking about it will make me hate Richard more. That's exactly what I should do, and I don't know why it's so hard to do. I can't believe you want to hear this. My life, its all, bullshit, pure bullshit, I can only say that I let each day pass trying to get the truth out of Richard. I should have done what I tell everyone else to do. Find someone to mend my heart and go on with my life."

Insanely there I sat, telling my story.

I said, "Rex, I'll tell you right off that Richard tells everyone that I'm an ice cube with a hole in it. I just smile. Three months married to him; already he has a whore on the side. After that I couldn't stand for him to put his hands on me. I guess he is right I did turn into an ice cube."

"He wanted a freak in the bedroom and I couldn't be one. **I will not** be one! So he thinks that gives him the right to jump every whore in five counties. To top it all Richard told me there was a telephone man in Shady Grove that had had every whore in my neighborhood. Now that was long before he transferred out here but I came to find out it was him. Telling me, right to my face, thinking I would never find out the truth."

"Shady Grove has about five hundred houses, a volunteer fire department, village store, school buses running, people busy living their lives and little old Drucilla letting Richard put her through hell and she let it pass, time and time again. I went right on doing my garden, yard work and taking care of my home. As you have seen I have everything: jewelry, mink coats, new cars, and always beautiful with a smile. Made candy and delivered it to those, I thought were my friends. Cooking the best meals every day and having it on the table at five thirty. I kept the house clean and never put him in debt. In the winter, I had a roaring fire in the fireplace. The house would be so nice, everything was nice but Richard, when he came in the room there was a cold feeling that spread all over the house. I played my part in life and went on."

I paused and looked up. Rex had been typing every word I said.

I said, "Rex, stop for a minute. If I wanted you to help me take care of some of these people, would you, could you?"

Rex looked me straight in the eyes. Never saying a word he just gave me his wicked little smile.

I thought that was a yes without saying yes. So I went on with my story.

"Richard had fed me from the Eagle Market deli for four months, which is where he met the Alexander thing. She is as big as a refrigerator and would take on any man or men. And another one just up the road, she works in a beauty shop, doing nails. She's the reason all the cocks in Shady Grove have no feathers. I caught Richard at her house. He said he was repairing her phone. She had an emergency and needed it fixed right then. I know what was getting fixed and it wasn't a phone. The next day I went shopping and bought myself a three-carat diamond ring. I called it his overtime money. Richard had met her months before at the deli; she was eating lunch for a change. She was real convenient for him just off Shady Grove Road not two miles from home. She serviced every man within driving distance of her. She had no husband."

"Rex, you know it's hard to keep in mind that women are the victims. The wife is only supposed to hate her husband, the one she married but it's too hard, it's impossible not to hate the whores. I hate Richard and his whores! They know he's married and they should leave him alone. They know most wives will bring hell down upon them and that's just what they deserve but in reality they get away with it. Working wives don't know and don't care. As for me I think a wife should be able to tie the other woman to the bumper of a car and drag her whoring ass up and down a gravel road. Then pour gas on what's left and light her up. **Yes!!** I know what makes one want to **kill!!**"

"The whores pretend to believe the man when he tells her his wife doesn't care. That the wife never has sex with him and he just needs a friend. **Lies, damn lies!!** In reality ninety-five percent do not know about the affair and are devastated when they find out."

"As for myself, I have always known when Richard had a honey pot because he is always mean to me, Dr. Jekyll and Mr. Hyde. **The bastard!** Well let's get back to when this all came about."

"I was busy trying to find someone to put music to my song lyrics. When I'm writing I'm absorbed with it. Sometimes I wake up with a song on my mind. I have to jump up and write it down while it's fresh on my mind. I wasn't paying attention to Richard. He was always at work anyway."

"It was tax time and the lady preparing our taxes needed some papers. We just had a new garage built and our files were in the garage. It is a big garage, twenty-six by forty feet and I didn't have a problem finding the papers but I couldn't believe what extras I did find. Right beside the file cabinet sat a nasty clothesbasket full of junk like someone had moved and filled this basket with things to throw away. Some old clothes, not mine, door knobs with keys, old dish drainer and pictures, all junk stuff I'd never have, cheap and I do mean nasty. When Richard came home I asked him about it. The bastard said he didn't know anything about it. It must be something I had put there. **Hell no!** I don't own junk and nobody else could get into the garage."

"The next morning as soon as I sat down, on the table right in front of me were two wall pictures. I picked them up and went back into the family room. I had two pictures just like them hanging on my wall. One set in my hand and one set on the wall. I thought, "The bastards are trying to tell me something." When Richard came home I jumped his ass. I had the pictures in my hand. I wanted to know where they came from and whom they belonged to. Innocent little Richard didn't know a thing. According to Richard, Harriet must have left them there. I laughed at him. I knew what he was doing, all over again."

"Richard had transferred out of Birmingham to Gardendale. He was working late every night and weekends. The money was good and I was busy. I had started helping a friend take care of his wife, she had broken her leg and one day I needed his truck so I let Richard drive my van. A few days later I asked Richard to take me to the store in the van. As soon as I opened the door I smelled the smoke. I asked him who had been smoking in my van. He hollered out, "No one and don't start your shit". I told him I wouldn't but I wouldn't drive this honey wagon of a van either. Richard screamed out, "Then get you a car." I did and I got what I wanted, too. I didn't let him drive the van anymore either. I searched it and found a cigarette lighter, a child's rubber ball and a small toy car. I went to Dewey Barber Chevrolet and bought a brand new Z28 Camaro. It was a red convertible with a black top and only six miles on the odometer. I still have his honey pot's things that he knows nothing about. He lies, over and over again. He's gutless. I had made up my mind to let Richard live his life and I would live mine. I sold the van for five thousand dollars and used it for a down payment on my Camaro."

"Months passed with the overtime and money still coming in. Richard had his check electronically deposited in the bank. Works for me!! Christmas was not far away, Brandon and I had the tree up and the house decorated. We went Christmas shopping at the Jasper Mall. I had forty three hundred, in overtime dollars in my checking account. I bought everything Brandon wanted. We sat on Santa's lap and had our pictures taken. We came home and wrapped all the presents."

"Brandon wanted to see the new Christmas movie, so I told Richard not to work next Saturday that we were taking Brandon to the movies. I was excited about going to the movie until I received a letter from the bank. My heart sank; one of my checks had bounced. I couldn't believe it. It had to be a mistake. I got out my checkbook and checked my figures. I had plenty of money. The bank must have made a mistake. I didn't want to fight about it here at Christmas. I was frightened and didn't know what to do. I called Johnnie, a friend of mine, borrowed five hundred dollars and deposited it in the bank. I would see about this after Christmas. I was trying to keep it out of my mind but on Saturday, the day we went to the movie, I received another letter from the bank. More checks had bounced. I don't know how I sat through the movie. After we let Brandon out and arrived home I broke down and cried. I told Richard what had happened and I knew I had not made a mistake. He told me not to worry about it. He would take care of it. The next day he told me that he had told me the wrong amounts. He always called me on payday and told me how much to put in checkbook. I never called the bank to check for myself. He said he had given me the amount before taxes. But he was too calm about it. I know he did it just to ruin my Christmas. You see, I always keep a thousand dollars extra in my checkbook and I'm the only one to know that. Richard didn't touch my checkbook."

"Weeks passed, New Year's Day came and went and everything was going smooth until I started gathering up tax papers for the income tax. Richard gave me a stack of bank receipts. I don't know why it took so long for it to dawn on me. They were ATM receipts! I don't have a card for the ATM. Richard, the bastard, had been going to the ATM and drawing out money for his whores and her kid's Christmas."

"Anyway that got me thinking and for the first time in my life I looked back at our bank statements. I found where he had lied repeatedly to me. He had told me the right amount before Christmas. He just forgot how much he had already taken out. **And that** isn't the pisser; he took out ten thousand dollars from the credit union and placed it in a Savings account. Sounds good doesn't it, except he never told me. **And,** he would take every Monday, Tuesday and Wednesday off and work as late as he could on Thursday, Friday and Saturday, if they would let him. He then transferred the money from saving to checking to make up the difference for the days he was off. The bastard never thought I would find the little books of where he kept records of the hours and days he worked. I was shocked to death. He was keeping some whore's kids while she worked three days."

Rex said, "Where did you get, that pisser thing? That sounds as if it came from a backroom in a dirty little bar."

I said, "Where do you think? I've heard Richard say it many times. He has a home away from home and his honey pot has three boys. That's why he donated so much to the boy scouts. This was automatically deducted from his paycheck each payday."

"Oh yes, we had hell when I told Richard. He denied the credit union withdrawal and stopped the Boy Scout money but it didn't matter. I had him and he knew it. I had the credit union send me copies of all his transactions. The missing money had opened my eyes. I'm not the fool he thinks I am and this was the beginning of a war that he would regret. He is not a good liar and again things were stacking up against him."

"I can still see Richard standing there with that stupid look on his face when I confronted him about the Christmas money. I screamed at him calling him everything but a white man. That year the bastard spent ten thousand dollars for puss and another twenty three hundred, in December, making my Christmas a nightmare. I tried to stay calm so my family wouldn't know anything about it. The bastard even took a box of homemade candy to his whore. I made a box of candy special for a friend named John and put a sweet note in the bottom. The note read. "It took Richard and me a long time to stir up this candy." I would have liked to have seen his honey pot's face when she read that note. Well John never got the candy. I told Richard that whoever got that box will know it was not for them. Richard got real quiet and told me I shouldn't do things like that. I thought I could drag it out of him, exactly what he did with the candy. Richard wouldn't fess up so I decided to stick needles in him. I told him John had called me one day and it took me forever to answer the phone. When I finally answered the phone John asked me why it took so long to answer. I told John I was making candy. John said, "I've heard it called a lot of things but never making candy." I told John maybe someday he could help me make candy.

Rex said, "What else do you have to drink in the cooler?"

I was so mad I didn't hear him. I jumped up stomping my feet as I walked around the table. Rex sat quietly as I paced back and forth.

When it dawned on me things were too quiet. I looked at Rex. He was sitting there watching me with that wicked little smile of his.

I snapped at him, "What the hell you looking at?"

Rex said, "I'm waiting on you to get me something to drink. I think we both could use a cold beer about now."

That cooled me off. After a beer I continued with my story. "I had been taking care of Mrs. Hill for about two weeks when I received a call from Mike, one of Richard's co-workers. He was very nice and told me he was worried about Richard. Richard was cursing so bad and acting like a wild man. He wanted to know if he could help us. He knew that Richard was leaving work early and not coming home which led him to believe we were having trouble."

"This really put me to looking at and listening to Richard. It was only a few days until push came to shove. I was home early, sitting at the kitchen table looking out through the glass sliding door. I could hear the car before I could see it. A white Chevrolet Monte Carlo, low to the ground, with a black hood, it stopped in front of my home. I went outside and as soon as he saw me he put the car in reverse and floor boarded the gas but not before I got a good look at him. He was a young man, about two hundred pounds and blond to light red hair with a crew cut. You know my road is a dead end with my Father and Mother living at the end. My parents being old, we all know who belongs here and who doesn't. He doesn't. That was the first time I had ever seen or heard this car. It sounded so fine. It was a racecar, big wheels and all."

"I called the Sheriff's office and reported him and told them I would find the car. The next day I went to the Sheriff's office and talked with an officer who told me how to start my search. I went to grocery stores on Thursday, Friday and Saturday nights, and churches on Sunday mornings during church services and trailer parks on Saturday and Sunday mornings, very early before people were out and about. I found the car in a trailer park on Cherry Avenue. I ran the tag number and it was registered to a Mike Picket. I was right; the car was built for the drag strip."

"All during this time the telephone was ringing off the hook, all hang up calls. Richard was coming in at all hours of the night. He was being a real bastard."

"I was determined to find out more about this car and me having driven a racecar gave me something to talk about. I went to the trailer and knocked on the door. A tall, slender, young, dark headed lady answered the door. I told her I wanted to talk to Mike about setting up a drag car for me, that I was sponsoring a new driver. She told me Mike worked nights and was asleep but I could call later and come back to see him. I called back and talked to Mike. He was very nice and we talked for a long time. He told me to call whenever I was able to come back to the trailer."

"Meanwhile I found out some of my calls were coming from the telephone company's main switch in Graysville. I called the supervisor in Graysville. He flatly refused to admit the calls could have come from there. So I called the head of security with the telephone company. He informed me the calls were coming from that office but I would never be bothered with them again. It wasn't long before that supervisor was transferred out of Graysville."

"Then a Mr. Foshee called me saying I needed to see for myself who Richard was working with. Richard worked on a two-man truck except one of the men was a woman. She was anybody's honey pot and Richard's partner. The phone company not only paid his salary, but supplied his puss fur?"

"Before I married Richard, he swore to me he wouldn't have anything to do with another woman. After I caught him lying about the Shelby Finance Company and the other honey pots he worked with. When he came home I well let him know that I knew about Shelia Nell."

"Shelia Nell came to work one morning telling everyone that she needed the locks changed on her house. She was afraid of her ex-husband. Richard volunteered to take **over all** of her ex-husband's duties. That's where the door locks came from that I found in my garage, plus all the other garbage."

"I started investigating her. Her neighbor said a very handsome man driving a telephone truck had been at her house every day. He was helping her to remodel the downstairs. He even painted the outside of her brick home. He painted the bricks white. Sounds just like him. I knew it was Richard. For one thing, I needed to use our paint sprayer back in the spring and Richard told me it was broken. He said I had broken it. What a lie. I have never touched it. The bastard had left it at Shelia Nell's house."

"My questions were making him crazy. I told my brother Percy and sister Harriet about it and asked them to help me. Neither one believed a word I said."

"Percy couldn't help but to hear the cars that stopped in front of his house. They came day and night and stopped not fifty feet from his front door. All he had to do is stand up and look out the window. But he never saw a single one. Hell, I could hear the cars from inside my house. How could he not hear them? My glassed-in-porch faces Martin Drive and there is a stop sign for people leaving Melissa Lane. This is the only street sign and this is where car after car came, three to four times a week. They turned onto Melissa Lane and stopped as if watching my house. Most of the time it would be an old faded red Mustang. It showed up different days of the week but always on Saturday."

"Richard would call every night to say he was working late for some reason or another. My stupid self would put dinner on hold and tell him to be careful. Well I couldn't get that Picket boy off my mind. So on January 12 when Richard called saying he'd be late. I called Mike Picket and asked him to meet me at Hogg's Barbeque on Cherry Avenue. I had with me all the stuff from my garage. That was before I found out it came from Shelia Nell's house. I wanted to know if Mike recognized any of this stuff."

"Mike drove up and we sat in my car talking. He didn't recognize any of the stuff. So I asked him who was driving his car to my house. I described the other man to him. He didn't know anybody that fit that description. That, if it were his car, his wife would be the one to give him the key. He let it slip that his wife's mother worked for the phone company and even gave me her name."

"As we sat there, a beautiful blue Camaro, with dark tinted windows, drove up behind me, looking at my tag. Then circled my car and stopped at my window for a minute. Then drove off in the direction it came from. Their windows were so dark we couldn't see even a silhouette. The Sheriff had taught me to be observant at all times. I had noticed a nineteen ninety-one or two IROC SS go up the hill beside the barbeque only a minute before the car came down the hill and circled us. It had beautiful blue gray ground effects on it. And then I heard Richard's truck. I looked around and his black truck came flying down the hill with the blue Camaro on his bumper. They both ran the stop sign and took a left on Cherry Avenue toward Richard's work place." Now Rex, "I'll never know why I didn't tell Mike to get out or buckle up. I know I could have run my car up that bastard's tail pipe. I didn't, I just went home."

"I beat Richard home. He came in looking like a sheep-killing dog. He wouldn't even look me in the face that night or the next morning. But there was a fight, I forced him to prove what time he got off work that night. The dumb bastard always catches himself. He printed out his work report and it showed him clocking out at five P.M. and changing it to five thirty. To be so smart he sure is dumb."

"Now I was determined to find that blue Camaro with the black tinted windows. I was mad as hell and determined to find these people. I followed every lead. I found a contract from a construction company to do home repairs on a house in Robinwood. I found it under Richard's jewelry box, in a bureau drawer. It was a bill for forty five thousand dollars. I was very interested in who paid this bill. I called Amanda told her about the paper and asked her to go with me to the house."

"We drove right into the fenced-in back yard. I got out and knocked on a glass storm door on the back porch. A mule of a woman with black hair and a baby jumped up and ran into another room as soon as I knocked on the door. A man, Mr. Oliver came from inside the house and answered the door."

"I made up a lie about why I was there. I told him the company had sent me to look over the work done on the house. He was nice and told me all about the workers and the good work they had done. He gave me a card with his business number and home number and asked me to come by and have a drink with him. The next day I called and told him the real reason I was there. After I told him, he said, 'I'll be damn. You sure fooled me.' I asked about the woman that jumped and ran. He told me her was Patty Sartain. He let her move in with him to help him get over an operation and now he couldn't get rid of her. She worked at a Racetrack gas station on Fieldstown Road in Gardendale."

"The next day my friend, Johnnie, did I mention Johnnie is a lady friend?"

Rex nodded his head yes.

"We went into the gas station to get a better look at her. No joke, she was as big as a mule. Her face looked like the ass of a mule. What more can I say! She didn't look at us when she waited on us. But I was looking! As I handed her the money I said, 'Tell Richard I said hello.' She never looked up."

"The next day I went back to Hogg's Barbeque. I went up the hill that the blue car had come down and talked to everyone I could find. Three different people told me the same telephone man was at the barbeque house every day at two o' clock and after five o' clock the very same telephone man picked up a woman from their road. They would be gone for a while and he would bring her back. Someone would be there to pick her up."

"I talked to Nancy; she worked at Hogg's Barbeque for several years and knew Richard well. She described Richard and his personal truck to a tee. When I confronted Richard, he lied like a dog, up one side and down the other. I, of course expected no less."

"I called Hogg's later and talked to the little black-headed slut. She told me she was dating Richard and she would tell him to his face. I asked Richard to take a sick day from work and go with me to face her, but he refused. After he went to work I called him and asked him to meet me there. He said he couldn't go there. He would be fired if anyone saw him there. He told me to just leave him the hell alone."

"I didn't give a damn if he was fired or not. I would not leave him alone! I called Terry Swindle, at the phone company and the Sheriff's office to tell them where I was going. By this time I had many friends at the Sheriff's office. I was mad as hell, just because Richard was so full of lies. When I stepped in the door at Hogg's Barbeque, two undercover men from the telephone company were right behind me. I no sooner sat down when Richard came in. A big ass blond waitress ran over to our table and told me the black-headed slut didn't mean what she said on the phone. She was just mad and blurted it out. She called me Drucilla, which was her first mistake. I asked her how she knew my name if it wasn't true. If Sherrie hadn't told her my name she would not have known it. The blond looked straight at Richard and screamed out, 'Look at him. He's an old man. No one here would have him.' Richard hearing his blond friend saying that to his face was too much for him. All the blood drained from his face and he got up and left."

"Later that day a little gray car came flying in my driveway and out again. By the time I backed my car out of the carport the gray car was gone. I drove around but I couldn't find it. I did find it later. It sometimes came to the house across from the old Parker Grocery store."

"This started more hell. I was out for blood and the **truth!** Too much had been said and done. I wanted answers! I wanted Richard's head! I didn't know what to think about the men who worked with Richard at the phone company. They said they suspected Richard was on drugs or at least buying drugs for someone. They said they wanted to help Richard. But what they were telling me, I wonder if they wanted me to kill him."

"I called in all the help I could. I had been everywhere looking for the blue Camaro. Richard had gotten so mean. He stayed mad at me. I would show up on his lunch break. No matter where he was. I was under his feet every time he turned around."

"I had written down every phone number that called the house for Richard. I called in and got address on every number. Then I went for tag numbers. If they were on my road I wrote the tag number down. The Sheriff's office told me, living on a dead end road, if they didn't stop and visit someone on that road they didn't have any business driving on that road. So I called in and got addresses on all the tag numbers from Jefferson County. Nineteen tag numbers were from Walker County. That meant a trip to Jasper. At the Jasper

Courthouse, I was told I needed a Judge to sign the order before they could give me copies. I found myself a Judge and came home with copies of all nineteen tag receipts. One of the nineteen belonged to the mule face Sartain woman. That's why she jumped and ran. Her tag number was written down while I was driving on my road . . . My dead-end road."

"I bought a county map and went to every address on my list. I went into areas that I knew were dangerous but I was driven to get the truth. I was going to stop the phone calls and the cars coming into my yard. I continued to find stolen cars, drug houses and many others having affairs."

"Now I set out to find another woman Richard used to work with. Her name was Huggins. My friend Carrie was with me. We had to wait two hours for her to come home. Huggins' husband was a little man. He said being a truck driver had taken its toll on him. I could see that he looked a lot older than I expected. Then he shocked me by saying,' You know child, even God forgave Mary Magdalene. Maybe you could forgive her too.' I told him I was sorry but I wasn't a forgiving person. I didn't know until I got my phone bill that Richard had called and warned her. I guess we were lucky to have only waited two hours. She turned out to be a short, fat woman with big boobs. I told her I was writing a story about men and women working together. She didn't mind telling all about others. One woman would get into a bucket of an aerial lift, which was not made for two people and her being fat made for close contact. You can guess the rest. The men had many a laugh at her expense. It was she in the bucket with Richard."

"Now it was time to talk to Shelia Nell. I called her and told her the same story. She didn't know that I had already investigated her. She told me she would be happy to talk as soon as she had time. She never seemed to have time. One morning I showed up at her front door at seven o' clock. I wasn't going to be put off any longer. As I drove up, her husband was putting his golf clubs in a car. I told him who I was and he said, 'I know you, you're Richard's wife.' I followed him into the house and waited in the living room as he went to get Shelia Nell."

"She came into the living room shaking like she had a chill. She picked up a blanket out of the chair before sitting down. After sitting down and wrapping up in the blanket I could still see the blanket shaking. She tried to tell me she couldn't talk today. I wouldn't take no for an answer. I told her I would drive her anywhere she had to go. I told her to go get ready and we could talk in the car. Her husband spoke up and told Shelia Nell to tell me where Richard spent his time and how he treated her."

"This nasty bitch works for the telephone company. I couldn't believe it. Richard had remarked for years how the standards of the company had gone downhill. That morning I saw what he was talking about. It was unbelievable. She sat in my car seat putting on make-up over yesterday's make-up. Then she wanted me to stop at a quick-mart so she could buy a coke and cookies. She said Richard stopped at this quick-mart for her every day. So help me, you could have taken a garden hoe and scrapped a month's worth of food off her teeth. And I could see dirt under her unpainted fingernails. **God this woman was nasty!!**"

"She showed me all over the city of Fultondale. She told me about the cafes where the phone men took their breaks, to the run down trailer parks and a medical clinic in Warrior. She pointed out where all the known whores and drug houses were."

"I drove her up in front of her house to let her out and she told me Richard was a male whore, a hot male whore. He had left her for another woman he worked with. Her name is Sherrie Loring. She gave me her phone number and address. On my way home I checked out where Sherrie lived. It was easy to find, she lived on Tommy Town Road. I only had to make one extra turn on my way."

"I waited a few days in case Shelia Nell had spilled the beans to Richard about me knowing about Sherrie. I didn't tell Richard until late one night that I knew about her. I told him in the morning the two of us were going to see her. He tried to tell me that he didn't know her. I told him I would introduce her to him. I was up early and ready to go. I knew she was off that day. I went straight to her house but drove by it to see what Richard would say. He screamed 'Where you going? You just passed her house.' Didn't I tell you the bastard was dumb? When I reminded him that he said he didn't know her. He screamed out 'Go to hell.' I told him I probably would but not before I sent him. Richard wouldn't get out of the car so I went in by myself. She told me that Richard is telling everyone that I was dying with a lung problem and we live together in name only. I told her my lung problem was long gone but living together in name only wasn't a lie. What I didn't tell her is I didn't want him. I just wanted for all of them to pay and pay dearly! She told me that she, Shelia Nell and Kay Chappel were all HIV positive and by now Richard and ninety-five percent of the phone company had it too. I left there in a better mood. It served them right and I don't care. I just wanted to share my hell with every one of them."

"I had set things in motion; by the time Friday night arrived I was fit to be tied. Richard had lied about everything and everybody. I gathered up all the things I had found in the garage. I put them in a sack and told Richard I was taking them to let a husband look at them. If the husband told me they were from his home I was coming back to kill him. We were screaming at each other. I called him everything but a white man and left. I took them to Shelia Nell's husband. He looked through it all and went back to the door knob and keys. He fiddled with them for a while, not saying a word. He then told me that I should throw this stuff away and forget it. He told me he was a lot older than Shelia Nell and he had made up his mind to let her have her way as long as she let him play golf. She leaves him alone and he doesn't make any waves. He asked me why I couldn't do the same. I told him I couldn't. I had to prove to my family that Richard was trying to hurt me. Now I knew for sure the stuff in my garage came from Shelia Nell's house. I was going to make both of the bastards pay. I wouldn't kill the bastard, not just yet!"

"I was on my way home when my cell phone rang. Sister Harriet called to tell me to get home as fast as possible. Richard was loading his truck and going to leave me. He was already gone when I got home. Harriet told me that the whole back end of his truck was piled high. I later found out he gave his pistol and some papers to our daughter, went by the ATM, drew out three hundred dollars and left town. He left the washing machine full of wet blue jeans, his company keys and company beeper at home. Everyone said he had to be crazy to leave his job. He only had two years left before retirement. Amanda and Harriet insisted I call the Sheriff's office and file a report on him. Amanda went home feeling that her Daddy would call her and he did. She talked him into coming home. She told him I would leave him alone, **yea right!** Richard called me from a motel in Arkansas. He promised me he would help me find the blue Camaro. I told him to go to sleep and leave the next morning. I knew he would go to sleep while driving if he tried to leave then. The fool he is, he didn't listen to me. He got into his truck and made it to West Memphis, Arkansas where he hit a bridge, head on. The cruise control was set at seventy miles an hour, the bridge pillar was eight feet square and he never hit the brakes."

"A nurse in a hospital in Forest City, Arkansas called me about seven. She told me Richard has had an accident and they were still checking him out. I told her I'd be on the next flight out. She hesitated, and then told me if I planned to drive his truck that it would not be possible. The paramedic told her they couldn't understand how he came out alive. I called Amanda and asked her to go with me to get Richard."

"I couldn't believe that truck. The back bumper was bent forward, all four tires were blown out, all the windows were broken out, and the motor was actually sitting in the front seat and blood everywhere. From the amount of blood in the truck he should have been dead. Hell the taillights were broken out. All he got was a broken nose and a broke big toe. God didn't want him and the devil wouldn't have him."

"After a little talking the company let Richard come back to work. He was put on light duty. His face looked as if he had gone through a meat grinder. What wasn't black and blue was swollen out of shape. Boy I wish I had done it to him. I think I did."

"While I was taking care of Richard, Sister Harriet and Brandon were gathering up the stuff from the garage, Richard's little black books and other papers and took them out and burned them. She told me if I didn't have them, I'd forget. Hell, I'd have to be brain dead to forget."

"Richard was on painkillers and couldn't drive so I had to drive him to work. Everything was fine for a couple of weeks. Then one morning he hollowed at me. He didn't like my driving and before I knew it, I backhanded him right on his broken nose. It couldn't bleed because his nose was packed with cotton. The bastard has never again complained about my driving."

"To show how sneaky he can be, that night when he took off his shoes, he had the whore's footies on. Never in my life would he wear footies. As soon as he pulled them off I picked them up with just my fingernails and put them in the garbage can. The next morning my niece came over to help me clean house. I told her about the footies and we went out the garbage can to show her, well guess what, they were gone. Richard got them out of the garbage and returned them to his whore."

"Then we had a fight over money. I asked Richard to let me see his bankcard. The fool, he gave me the card and I took my scissors and cut the card into little pieces. I told Richard if his honey pot wanted any more money, she would have to ask me for it. Damn was he mad."

Rex, I'll ask you, "If he was going to carry on, why would he come home to me? Why would any man put up with, all that I was doing to him? I was not letting him give these people any more money. I told him if they were blackmailing him or if he was paying for a bastard child, just say so and we would deal with it. He would not talk and I wouldn't stop talking."

"The next Friday night a car came flying into our driveway and out again without stopping. By the time I got outside the car was gone. There were no lights outside and I couldn't see a thing. I called the sheriff's office; they came and made a report on the car. This was only the beginning. The next week the car came on Saturday. For nine weekends it came. I could tell it was the same car by the sound of the motor. Richard never made a move to find out who they were. They would switch nights just to throw me off. I made Richard hide his truck in the woods behind the stop sign and we waited on them. I was behind the steering wheel and if the bastards showed up I'd run them into a ditch and keep them there until the sheriff showed up. They never came on the nights we sat in the woods. A sheriff's deputy asked me if I thought Richard was having it done. I told him yes. Richard is trying to hurt me or have me killed. He gave me the idea of placing a board of nails across the driveway to flatten their tires. That same day the nails were in the driveway. They stayed in the driveway, every night for three weeks and the car didn't come back. On a Monday night Richard asked me if I wanted the board of nails placed in the driveway. I told him no. They never come on a Monday. Well they did! They not only came that night but they went to Jasper and called me on the telephone and hung up, as if to say, 'We got you again.'

"I hated Richard more each day. I was going to find them, all of them! So I started going back to the addresses from car tags and telephone numbers. Two of the numbers took me to Holly Grove Road in Jasper. I was in shock because Richard had been taking me there to play golf for over two years. The addresses were for two house trailers across the street from Arrow Head Golf Course. The people in one of the trailers came from Eleventh Avenue South in Birmingham. The other was named Hadley but she used to be a Higgins."

"It all made sense now, why Richard treated me so bad at the golf course. He would jerk the steering wheel trying to throw me out of the golf cart. We were supposed to share a bottle of water on our way home, but Richard would guzzle it down and I would have to do without. This water deal only happened once. From then on I had an ice chest filled with six water bottles and three bottles of lemonade. I never offered him a thing. Water or no water I still beat him every game."

"I not only found those two trailers, but another one of his honey pot's place just off Holly Grove Road. She has three kids and her name and phone number was written in every golf cart at Arrow Head. She had a light blue Camaro but it was an older model. Her name is Deb Bankston. Keep in mind I only found her because, her telephone number was on my caller ID and when I returned her call, I came right out and asked her why my husband was coming to see her. She didn't beat around the bush. She told me she let men in her rectum and wanted paid for her service. They lived in a big house with a nasty junked up yard. I had asked her what was wrong with her husband. She told me he worked two jobs and was never at home, and with three kids and being so fat she couldn't get a job she decided to be a house whore. It worked out well living close to the golf course. The men advertised for her. Richard also helped her get the car."

"I found another light blue Camaro by tracing the numbers on my phone bill. Richard had called Terry Nix's house on Copeland Ferry Road just off Highway 269 before you cross the big bridge. I pulled into his yard one Sunday morning and there set a Camaro. I got out of my car, with my telephone bill in my hand. Terry was coming across the yard with a bag of garbage in his hand. I asked him if he was Terry Nix, and he said that he was. So I showed him my telephone bill and asked him why his number was on my bill. I explained to him that I knew my husband was having an affair so I had metered service installed on my telephone. I wanted to know who was being called from my home. I put my finger on his telephone number and said here is your number and here I am to find out why. A four minute call was made on Sunday morning while Richard had sent me to the store for milk and bread."

"Terry asked me to come inside and he would see if he could help me. I followed him inside. Was this nuts or what? I wasn't thinking. I wanted answers and I did what had to be done. When we went inside his wife was cooking breakfast. The big fat ass woman was frying bacon. Terry told her what I needed and she never turned around to look at me. She stood at the stove and fried the whole three pounds of bacon. Terry's brother was standing by the table listening to my story but never said a word. I thanked Terry and he told me he would call me in a few days. As I left she still had her head down over the stove, cooking bacon."

"I found another light blue older Camaro on Hull Road in Sumiton. It belonged to a big fat ass redhead named Michelle Wilbert Nix. By this time I was well known by nearly everyone in the three counties of Walker, Blount and Jefferson and for sure every sheriff in Jefferson County knew me. I drove my beautiful red convertible with a black top and my tag number was DRU II. I could be seen from a mile away but guess what. I didn't give a damn! Michelle Wilbert Nix was from Marklund Road in Sumiton."

"Remember the blue Camaro flying up the hill at Hogg's Barbeque? I found one just like it on Highway 269. The bitch was a hairdresser from Holly Grove Road, now living in Adamsville. She was a Barker."

Rex said, "Drucilla, you could have gotten hurt, if not killed."

I said, "I found not only Richard, but most of the telephone men had a honey pot at every other house. One drank whisky on the job and didn't try to hide it. I could do more work in half a day than six of these bastards were doing in a five day work week."

"Richard called one night and told me he was lost in Smoke Rise, a community north of Warrior. He was lost alright, in an ass that worked at the Warrior Clinic. Two of his honey pots lived in Smoke Rise."

"I found another light blue Camaro in Bagley. It belonged to Karen Tucker; only this one was a nineteen ninety one or two model. We will see before this story ends if Tucker bought this car from the Bates in Sayre."

"Rex, let's go home, I'm tired. You know I could talk till the twelfth of never but now I'm tired."

Rex said, "Drucilla you are talking too fast to be making any of this up. It's all true, isn't it?"

I said, "You damn right its true!"

Rex said, "Come on Drucilla lets go. But I'm taking tomorrow off. I've got to hear the rest of this."

I said, "It will take more than tomorrow."

We no sooner pulled onto the road when I spotted a patrol car behind us. I said, "Do you see that Sheriff's car behind us?"

Rex said, "Yes, I saw him the minute he fell in behind us."

I said, "He's one of my big brothers. I love them all. I never go out that I don't see them. At first I didn't know if they were protecting someone from me, or watching out for me, but I soon learned they were watching out for me."

I told Rex about going to the Sheriff's office. "It didn't take the deputies long to get to know the real me. I won't crawl into a hole.

You slap me and I'll slap you harder. You curse me and I'll curse you worse. You shoot at me and I'll put a bullet between your eyes. When I want to know something I'll go ask and that's just what I did. I went to the Sheriff's office and told them what was going on and that I intended to do something about it. I talked to a Sergeant Stone. He was very nice. He even gave me a list of phone numbers to call if I needed someone. He told me if I ever got afraid of a situation to drive to the nearest Sheriff's station, stay in the car and blow the horn. I did drive into their parking lot and till this day I still love them all for being good to me."

"The chief of police in Graysville pulled up beside me at a four way stop in the Daisy City Trailer Park. He told me, 'Someone is going to get hurt, don't you think,' and I told him it wouldn't be me. Then he asked me to come to his office and talk with him. I waited until the next week to go see him. I felt fear when I walked into his office. This man could have picked me up three feet off the floor. I'll bet you he was seven feet tall. The top of my head didn't reach his belt buckle. We talked about forty-five minutes. He is the one that told me about the Barker's on Holly Grove Road and helped me find them in Adamsville. So when I see them around me I know it's for my own good. They are watching out for me."

As we turned off Highway 269 going toward home, the Sheriff's car went straight. As we pulled into my yard I said to Rex, "Don't you dare get here before ten o'clock."

Rex said, "OK, Drucilla, don't you worry about me. You just have your happy ass out of bed and ready."

Chapter 3

At ten o'clock I stepped into the car and off we went. I didn't say much on the way to Lock Seventeen.

"Rex I want to start today by telling you about my friend Johnnie. She went with me too most all the places I told you about yesterday. She even gave me a letter stating, I never harassed anyone at any of the places we went. No one could have been a better friend to me than she was, but I had to give up her friendship to keep her safe."

"I would pick up Johnnie at four o'clock in the mornings to go places with me. This one morning we pulled into the Kelly Trailer Park about five o'clock and a car flew past us and I do mean she was flying. Johnnie said she bet that was the car we were hunting. I didn't try to catch her. By the time it would have taken me to turn around she would have been out of sight. We drove around writing down car tag numbers and getting to know the place. Then we went back down the road to the Breakfast House. Remember Shelia Nell told me about the place. We went inside and sat down. A waitress named Lona waited on us. She owned one of the dark blue Camaros I was hunting. When I asked about the car she told me she only had it for 2 days and let the bank take it back. I think Richard couldn't pay for it. Then she told me she knew that I was looking for Richard's honey pot. She told me to look for a girl named Jennie that worked at the J-J Drive In, just up the highway and that she lived at One Hundred Oaks Trailer Park across the street from her. I asked her to give that to me in writing; she did, and I still have it. The Gardendale police came in and sat for a while. They seemed to be watching us but that didn't intimidate me one bit."

"After a while Johnnie and I went back to Kelly Trailer Park. There were three men standing in a yard as we drove into the park. We got out of the car, walked over and talked to them. I told them we were investigators for the telephone company and wanted to know if they knew which trailer the telephone truck stopped at every day. They told us at first they thought she was having a lot of telephone problems but after months of this they just assumed that he had moved in with her. He gave us good directions, which took us to the three worse trailers in the park. I mean small, old and trashy. A young girl was outside in the yard with what looked to be a fifteen-month-old baby. The baby had shoo shoo running down both legs from its diaper to its ankles. The front porch was running over with trash. It was a very sad sight. I went on with my business, telling her the same as I had told the men. She too wrote a note telling me the one I wanted was Tammy Fields. She wrote it all down. Tammy has three kids, one girl and two boys, her boy friend's name is Bo and the telephone man's name was Richard Hallmark. Richard had just moved them all to the projects in Dora. She had a light blue Camaro but had wrecked it. It was totaled and sitting in a junkyard on Highway 31 in Fultondale. She was now driving a silver gray Firebird and worked at the veterans' hospital in Birmingham. Johnnie and I went to the junkyard looking for the Camaro and were told the car was sent to the shredders last week."

Rex said, "Drucilla can you hold up a minute? I'm getting behind."

I said, "My God, Rex. You just keep typing. I'm going for a walk and do some thinking. You just whistle for me when you get caught up."

About forty-five minutes passed before I came back and Rex was still typing ninety to nothing. So I went to the water's edge to skip stones. Finally Rex whistled and I went back to telling my story.

"Johnnie and I drove back to my house and I got out one of Richard's little black books. I was looking for the telephone numbers of the two men in Dora on Horse Bend Road. A Mr. Wire and a Mr. Shores, I called Mr. Shores and asked him to look at some pictures for me. He told me to come on down right then. I showed him Richard's picture and he told me that was the man who came to see him about renting a trailer but he called himself Tony Hallmark. Mr. Shores didn't rent him a trailer but noticed him heading into the projects. I thanked the old man and went home. Remember the little boy that kept calling our home? I made Richard take me to the address. The little boy's mother was Mr. Shore's daughter."

"It was February of nineteen ninety-six. I asked Johnnie to fly out to California with Richard and me. Richard wanted to go see his Aunt. She had a stroke and was in the hospital. I was afraid to travel with Richard alone."

"The next few days I spent getting ready. My niece came over to help me. I put all of my papers in the trunk of my niece's car for safekeeping. I had found an old transit token under Richard's jewelry box. It was old, rusty and soaked in oil. I rolled it in paper and placed it in the finger of one of my leather gloves and put it the pocket of my mink coat. When I first found the token I asked Richard about it but he wouldn't answer me. For that matter he wouldn't talk to me about any of this. The only thing he would say was he didn't know any of these people and they were all lying about him."

Rex said, "I doubt that that many people would be lying."

"We all flew out to California and we weren't there two nights before Richard started his shit. He was mean, grouchy and smart mouthing. He talked worse to me than he had ever before but I gave it right back. He told Johnnie that I was the coldest bitch in the world. I didn't like sex and I was crazy as hell to boot. I screamed at him, 'What is happening back home? I know you're crazy for some reason'?"

"Somehow I knew he was letting someone search my home. I always know when he is up to no good. His nerves go crazy and his hands and feet itch real badly. He was a real bastard the whole trip. We came home and one look through the house, I knew it had been searched from top to bottom. I went straight to his closet and the extra key to the house was gone. The token, two Auburn quilt tops, two new bottles of perfume, several scarves signed by famous country singers and God knows what else was gone, all gone! I'll never forgive him for his lying; for letting those maggots, those filthy whores and their bastards coming into my home."

Rex said, "I think now is a good time to take a break. Let me walk around and stretch my legs."

Rex walked over to the car, popped the top on a cool one. He leaned against the car giving me time to cool down. After finishing his beer he came back and sat down without saying a word. We sat there for a minute or two before I continued my story.

"There were times when I thought Richard was a queer. He's whatever the game calls for. I remember Richard taking me to a party in Ensley Highlands. It was a big white house but it was just us and seven other boys. I was the only woman there. Richard always said that things didn't happen for the reasons you think. He would scream at me that he didn't have another woman. Well if it wasn't a woman then it has to be a man."

"I can say for sure if I was a whore after a man, I wouldn't torment his wife to death. I'd make him tell her. But these gutless sons of bitches are trying to get me to kill myself. I'll tell you this, Dr. Smith didn't like Richard and he would do almost anything for me. He knew Richard was hurting me. He has taken x-rays of my hands and put one in a brace from where Richard slammed the door on my hands. He has all kind of notes in my file. I asked him to help me lose twenty-five pounds. He prescribed a diet pill called Obenex for me. I didn't tell Richard about the pills. Every morning I had one cup of coffee, two oatmeal cookies and my diet pill. A diet pill wakes you up and gives you energy. This morning Richard knew that I was going to Pleasant Grove and he knew about the dangerous hill I would be going down. If you lose control of your car on that hill; there is no way anyone would survive the wreck. Richard put something in my coffee that put me to sleep. Fifteen minutes down the road I was so sleepy I had to pull to the side of the road. I rolled my windows down to get some air and finally made it to Mr. Hill's home. I went into the house, lay on the couch and slept for two and one half hours. After I awoke I was still sleepy and sick the rest of the day."

"I told Richard that I knew he had tried to kill me again. I should have gone to the hospital and I will if I ever feel like that again."

Rex said, "He may do a better job of it the next time."

I said, "Yes, I know in my heart, the next time he may succeed. So from then on I wouldn't eat or drink anything he gave me."

Rex said, "Drucilla, why in the hell, didn't you make him leave? Why girl? All this makes you sound crazy!"

I said, "I know it does. And I know he's not worth a damn. He's just a piece of shit. I know he doesn't love me. He wants me to shut-up. He doesn't have a family and he doesn't want to give up my family or all that he's worked for. More than anything in the world I want my family to know the real Richard. He has hurt me over and over and screamed that he hates me. He wishes I were dead that he would be better off. Well Rex, the table has turned! I want his ass dead. I hate him and today I don't care what my family thinks. I don't love them anymore either."

"He has made me go through hell time and time again. Mama Marcelle calls him 'Luscious Lips'. She would tell me not to mistreat Richard. He's just looking for love. Well Rex, now I'm looking for love and by God I won't stop until I find someone to love me."

"OK, OK, let's get back to Dora and Sumiton. Sumiton is where I go to the dentist. Richard was working in the area alot. Calls started coming to the house from a Donna Harris when I wasn't home. After a few calls I called back but the number had been disconnected. Then calls started coming from Charlie's Place. Charlie's is a barbeque shack that has a live band and dancing after five o'clock. When I returned the call of course no one knew who had called me from there."

"Eight months had passed, it was September. I called Richard and told him I was coming to have lunch with him. I then called Sergeant Stone and told him where I was going. That means only three people know where I'm going. I was driving down Highway 78 and an old sports car pulled out of the median and up beside me. It was a four lane road. Their car was an old faded out orange color, hood was missing and it had a long front end. I looked over at them and they were grinning at me. They looked like two greasy thugs. The one I got a good look at had his two front teeth missing. Then he started swerving over into my lane. The thugs were giggling and pointing at me. I hit my brakes just as they pulled over into my lane. I gave them the finger and slowed down to get away from them. I gave them time to think they had rattled me. Then I flew up behind them wrote down their tag number, pulled out around them and gave them the finger again as I pulled away from them. My car was too much for theirs by the time I hit one hundred twenty miles per hour I knew I'd never see the bastards again. I called in the tag number and it was registered to an Edward Alexander from Cordova. I was late for lunch but I didn't care. I know Richard had sent them after me."

Rex asked, "How do you know that Drucilla?"

I said, "Because Richard never once went to find the bastards. He just laughed at me. Another time I called Richard to tell him that I was on my way and where did he want to meet me? He told me to come to the Dora City Park. The park is behind the Dora police station. I was driving down the same highway and a small white car drove up beside me. The girl driving had long dark hair and her skin was the color of cream. She had a little boy in the car with her. He looked to be about ten years old. This bitch started making faces at me. I thought what in the world have I done to her. I sped up and she would too. I'd slow down and she would stay beside me. I came to a side road and turned off without using my signal light. She slammed on the brakes and swerved to follow me. I slowed down as if I was looking for an address. The bitch came around blowing her car horn. She pulled back into my lane and hit the brakes and just as fast she hit the gas. She did that about three times. With each time my temper began to burn. I hollowed out, 'OK Bitch if you want me to follow you, here I come.' I sped up and got on her bumper. I bet there wasn't six inches between us. She was going as fast as she could on curvy back roads but I stayed on her bumper. She took me down County Line Road and turned onto Marklund Road, which is a one-lane road, by now, I didn't know where I was. We went past a few homes then came to some house trailers that looked like dumps but the cars looked real familiar to me. We came to a doublewide house trailer and she turned into the yard. She and the boy jumped out of her car, almost before it stopped, and ran into the house trailer. She turned so fast I missed the driveway. I went up the road, turned around came back and wrote down the tag numbers of all the cars in the yard. Her tag was a personal tag, Dana. The other tags were personal tags too, one was Dana Mac and the other was Mac II. These two cars looked familiar. I went back the way I came. At the end of the road there was a man standing in his yard. I pulled up beside him and asked if he knew the people that lived in the double wide down the road. He said they were truck drivers and he only knew them by their CB handle. I asked how to get back onto Highway 78. When I got back on the highway I called Richard and told him I'd be there in a minute. Keep in mind, only Richard knew where I was going."

"When I pulled into the park there set a pretty blue Camaro with a red headed woman, sitting in the driver's seat and a little boy sitting in the passenger's seat. I pulled in between the Camaro and Richard's telephone truck and let my convertible top down. I got out, with shorts up to my butt and went around my car reached into the backseat and pulled out our lunch. I'm a beautiful woman and I was already mad as hell. I looked the redhead straight in the eyes and said, 'Richard if I had known we were having guests for lunch I'd have brought more food but I didn't.' That bitch left smoke from her tires and I could hear her squalling tires a mile away. Even this wasn't the Camaro I was looking for."

"After she left, car after car came into the park, circled my car and parked. I put my pistol under my leg. Richard was screaming at me not to start a damn thing. I told Richard if anyone came up to my car I'd kill the bastards and him with them. As it was I only wrote down the tag numbers. I told Richard that I knew he had sent them there to scare me. It didn't scare me it made me mad as hell. Richard went back to work and all the cars left. I walked over to the police station. I gave them a copy of the tag numbers and asked them to call Sergeant Stone and tell him I needed an escort back to Adamsville."

"Sergeant Stone knew this only made me mean and more determined to find this fool. I was going to find them even if it killed me. What were they trying to keep me from finding?"

"I waited a few days and went back to Marklund Road. I stopped at the doublewide house trailer. I knocked on the door and a woman came out to talk to me. I showed her a picture of Richard and asked her if he had ever been here. I told her he was nothing but a male whore and if I ever found him there I would bring his clothes and dump them out. I just wanted the gutless bastard to tell me the truth. I also told her that I knew that the tag on her little red car didn't belong on that car. The tag belongs on another car. There sat another car and the tag said 'Dana Mac'. She pointed with her thumb over her shoulder toward the door and shook her head no. She pointed to my car and waved me away. She looked like she had been in a fire. Her skin was spotted with big brown splotches. Anyway, I left and went to the trailer that the girl in the Dana car went into. I knocked on the door and to my surprise Hilda McAdams opened the door. She works at my dentist's office. I couldn't believe my eyes. She asked what I was doing there. I told her to let me in and I would tell her. I told her about the girl in the Dana car and asked her who she is. She calmly told me she didn't know who would come into her house or anyone fitting her description or her car. I knew she was lying. I also knew I'd be back. As it was I had other things to check out first. Why would she lie knowing I had seen all the tags, 'Dana', 'Dana Mac', and 'Dana 5?'"

"I went to the Warrior River to check out the Sartain, Hadley and Higgins families. I saw loads of drugs being loaded into boats. I knew the river was running wild with drugs. More drugs moved up and down the river than all the roads in Alabama. I found drug houses, meth labs and more stolen cars than the Jefferson County Sheriff's Department."

"Then out of the blue, at the Village Store where I buy gas, Mr. Jackson asked me why I was moving. He also told me he had heard a rumor that I was losing my house due to foreclosure. I assured him that I was not moving and I owned my home. The next day Mr. Click came to see me and asked if there was anything he could do to help me. I explained to him the rumors were wrong. This was just the beginning of my troubles."

"I received a bill from a credit card stating I owed six hundred dollars to America-On-Line. I didn't own a computer! Richard called them to cancel the card and tell them we wouldn't pay the bill. He asked America-On-Line what address it was sent to. They told him if he would pay the bill, they would give him the information. So they wouldn't tell me. I knew Richard knew."

"Then my mail got messed up. Someone had forwarded my mail out of State. Again, no one knew who requested the transfer. I got this straightened up and two weeks later I go to the post office and Mrs. Tanner asked me why I was moving. I told her that I wasn't moving. She called downtown right then and stopped another transfer. It didn't take a genius to know it was Richard doing it. I told Mrs. Tanner that if I didn't come in and forward my mail, not to do it. She suggested that I call all the utilities and give them a code name for my accounts and if they didn't receive a written letter from me not to make any changes in my service. I don't know what would have happened if not for my friends that really love me."

"Another friend of mine took me to an old church off Republic Road. Just past the church you could tell a house trailer had just been moved. He was told a telephone man had moved a woman's house trailer from there to the Forestdale Trailer Park. We went to the trailer park and he showed me the trailer. A woman named Gooch and her boy friend named Chris lived there. Chris was a truck driver. I checked this out and found that I knew a person whose daughter lived across the road from the Gooch trailer. I went to see her and gave her a picture of Richard. She told me it was Richard and he was at the Gooch trailer often. She told me she would get pictures of them together but I was so mad I wasn't waiting for pictures. I knocked on the door of the Gooch trailer and told her if she would tell me, in front of Richard that he was spending time with her, I would put his ass out the door, and she could have him full time."

"Just so happened Chris was home that day, I told him to make her go with me. I screamed at her that all she'd get was his hot ass, because I owned everything else. Two days later I was told she was moving."

"That night Richard ran into the house. He was on top of me screaming at me that I was just a damn fool and I wouldn't know the truth if it hit me in the face. He stormed out the door. He came back into the house. He said he would cut my throat. He was still screaming he'd turn into O. J. and cut my damn throat. I calmly told him he may but then the world would know him, and Mr. Williams would see to it that he went to Hell."

"The next few days I received calls from Arron Reality Company's office and the real estate woman wanted to talk to Richard. I told her he wasn't home and she said that she'd call him at work. I told her, 'You do just that and I'll talk to your boss.' The next day Johnnie and I went to her office. It was in the basement of a house on Edwards Lake Road. We went in and told the woman why we were there. She looked at her records to see if Richard was trying to buy a house. I could tell she didn't know what to tell us so I didn't pull any punches. I told her that my house was in my name and if Richard was trying to use it as collateral, I'd sue them all. And told her to tell whoever was calling my home to forget my number."

"We left there and went to Sumiton. We drove around until I saw a man and two children out by a big barn. It was at least two good blocks off the road. It looked like a stable in the middle of a big pasture. The man was looking at the back hoofs of a horse. I thought he might be shoeing the horse."

"I knew that whoever Richard was involved with had horses. He had received papers that were addressed to someone else and they had sent them on to him. They were careful to remove their name first. The papers were about wild stallions captured out West and sent to Tennessee to be adopted. If someone kept them under the care of a veterinarian for a year they could sell them. My friend Johnnie and I checked this out. The company's main office was in Mississippi. We went there and were given a list of names of people who had adopted the horses. I crosschecked this list with a list of names that had called my home. There were several names on both lists. Even a veterinarian in south Alabama were on both lists."

"I drove up the drive and up to the stable. Now there were two ladies, two children and the man. He looked older close up. I stopped and got out of the car. One of the ladies walked off toward the stable and the other lady walked over to us. I told her my name, about the blue Camaro at Hogg's Barbeque and about the car that was flying into my yard on the weekends. By this time we were all sitting in my car. She was a very nice young lady; skin the color of gold and dark hair down to her waist. I told her about the car with the 'Dana' tag that had taken me down Marklund Road and about the McAdams woman. She told me that her Grandfather would help me and to my surprise she offered to take me to the house that has the blue car. She told me to go up the driveway and turn left. We stopped beside Sayre Auto Parts. There was a house sitting on top of a hill in the middle of a pasture. We could see the horses from where we were and she told me the blue car could be found behind the house. She then picked up my pen and paper and drew a map from there down Marklund Road to the McAdams' house. She added another house with name and telephone number and told me to call this lady and she would tell me everything about the McAdams because she hates them. One of the girls that I described bought feed from her Grandfather. She had long blond hair and also lived on Marklund Road. I asked her if the girl's name was Odom. She said it was and I told her I knew who she was talking about and it wasn't her. I know her mother and father. I took her back home, thanked her and left. On my way down the drive I noticed my niece's green Jeep setting at the end of the drive but before I got close she backed out and sped away. I drove back down Marklund, didn't see the Jeep, so I took Johnnie home and went home."

"I checked my answering machine as soon as I got home. I had a message from Johnnie to come back to her house. Someone had broken into her home. They stole thousands of dollars worth of jewelry, electronic equipment and some cash. That's not all . . . They had broken the ivory keys on her piano. I was devastated. I knew I was the cause of this. Her driveway is about two miles long and on my way in I had past the Alexander car. The same car that tried to run me off the road on Highway 78. As soon as they saw my car they took off like a speeding bullet."

"I went to Johnnie's house everyday for the next two weeks. She and I painted the whole inside of her house. During that time several cars came down to her house that we didn't know. Even the beautiful blue Camero came in, but we couldn't get out the door fast enough to block them in. By this time I was mad enough to kill."

"The last day I came home from Johnnie's house I had a message on my answering machine from the most precious friend, saying she had just dug the sweet potatoes and needed my help to get them washed and into baskets. Mrs. Birdie asked me to help her and just forget about the blue car and let Richard do whatever. No one could understand that this wasn't about Richard, it was the fact that they came to my home and they called my home. I never wanted to slap them saying to leave my husband alone. I wanted them to stay away from me and leave me the hell alone. I wanted Richard to make it stop. Believe me you can be pushed to the point that you can kill. Anyway we worked for five hours in front of Mrs. Birdie's home and from there we could see a big blue old station wagon with a man standing up against the door. He watched me all day. Also there was a small sports car that came up to her house and turned around five times. We finished with the potatoes and Mrs. Birdie gave me potatoes, tomatoes, corn and peppers, and I left for home. I stopped at the conveniences store. I got out of my car to get a good look at the old man. He said, 'Lady you wouldn't want to get that car messed up, now would you?' He said, 'You don't want to wreck it now do you?' Looking him eyeball to eyeball I said, 'Don't you worry Sir, about my baby, and if someone is going to get hurt it won't be me.' I walked into the store and got me a bottle of water. I got into my car and drove to the Green Top Barbeque on the county line. I went in and sat on a stool. I ordered two barbeque sandwiches and two French fries to go and as I waited I heard someone saying, 'Miss? Miss?' I turned around to see the same sawed off little bastard from the blue station wagon. He said 'You know your friend; you wouldn't want her face bashed in, would you? You know those teeth of hers came from ACIPCO and cost a lot.' He said what he came to say and left. Fear had me now. I took my sack, paid my bill and broke all the speed laws getting home."

"I called Johnnie as soon as I got in the door. I asked her if her boyfriend was still there. I didn't want her to be alone when I told her about the ugly little man. I described the shit head to her. He had to be sixty-seven or eight years of age. He was short maybe five foot at the most because I'm four foot eleven and I could look him straight in the eyes. He wore eyeglasses with lens that are one-quarter inch thick and his teeth were as brown as a brick. His clothes looked as if he had worn them for two months."

"I called her two boys; they lived next door to her, and told them to watch out for her and her home." Now Rex, "You know this is what Richard wanted. Richard knew that Johnnie would go anywhere with me or help me do anything. I let myself calm down for a few days then I went back to Sumiton and Dora looking for the sawed off little maggot. I didn't find him but I haven't stopped looking for him. I do know one thing for sure, I've never told anyone about Johnnie's teeth, except Richard. Richard caused all this. Two weeks later Johnnie called and asked me to get Richard to take us to the Cracker Barrel Restaurant in Gardendale. Richard didn't want to go. It was a Saturday night. He threw a fit. He screamed and cursed me all the way to Johnnie's house. It didn't make sense at the time, but later it did. We were seated next to Mr. and Mrs. Bates. Mrs. Bates' sister was with them, she lived in Sayre also. Richard didn't know that I knew Mr. Bates. I knew him from when I was racing at Dixie Speedway. While Richard was in the restroom, Mr. Bates told us to be careful. Nothing else, just be careful, because Richard was returning. Richard never said a word the whole time. He was real calm. The next day I called Johnnie and told her I was worried about her and it was best if I didn't come around her until all this was over."

"After a few days of taking care of some home things and hearing about old Aunt Bessie dying. I was set free of hating Sandusky. I drank a half a bottle of wine to celebrate. I really did hate Aunt Bessie. My God, Mama Marcelle was mad at me for saying Bessie should have died at birth. Anyway I drove all over Sandusky and stopped to see Mr. Cork. Mr. Cork gave me the cabinets in my kitchen. I love Mr. Cork. He has been good to me all my life. Mr. Cork had company when I arrived, Mr. Weems from Quinton. Mr. Cork talked to me for a good two hours. He told Mr. Weems I was a wonderful girl not like city girls. He said I was pure country and worth my weight in gold."

"I left Mr. Cork still bragging about me. I wasn't a block from his home when I noticed a car following me. Later I found out it was Jeff Black, a tall thin black headed young man from Adamsville."

"Early morning before daylight on the 19th of July 1997, I received a call that Mr. Cork had been murdered and his house was set on fire. I thought my heart would explode. It almost killed me. Did what little time I spent with Mr. Cork cause this? Was Jeff Black involved in the murder? Mr. Cork wanted me to leave Richard and move out of these woods. Now he's gone and it's too late. Now I had to stay. I had to know, even if I was next."

"At Mr. Cork's funeral an old Lady came and sat down beside me. Her name was Bankston and she said Richard and me sure made a nice couple. Then she asked me if I was happy with him. Lying like a dog, I said yes. I never noticed when she left and no one else remembered seeing her or what she was driving. I couldn't help but wonder if she was connected to the Bankston whore on Holly Grove Road."

"Losing a friend like Mr. Cork was hard on me. I wanted someone to pay for this. I didn't have to wait long. My big brothers were on the job. Melinda Sides and two men were arrested for the murder. The men were named Wayne Tolbert and Harry Stone. I knew I had one of them in my papers. I looked until I found Tolbert's address. It took me straight to Sumiton and my dentists' office. Judy looked up Tolbert's dental record for me. He had followed me from the dentist office and I got his tag number. I also told her about McAdams. Remember McAdams works there too. This put Richard deeper and deeper into the mix. I never went back to my dentist even though I loved him very much. I know now that I should have told him but at the time I didn't think he would have fired her. Hilda damn well knew Richard. He has been in that office many times. She lied like a dog. I was told about them selling drugs and her slut daughter sleeping with any kind or color."

"I started investigating the phone bills again. I found that Richard was working in the same area on these days and some of the houses were kin to each other. It was all beginning to come together."

"The older blue Camaro belonged to Michelle Nix. She was once married to a man named Gilbert Nix. Gilbert worked at a casket company on Finley Avenue. I went to the casket company and cleared it with Gilbert's boss to talk to him. He told me all about the Nix girl and he was soon to marry a girl from Shady Grove, my own little village."

"Shady Grove is according to the Sheriff's office full of dope heads, thieves, whores and drunks. I'm ashamed to live there and glad that I don't know any more than I do. I know seven young men that have gone to jail about drugs. The beauty shops are buzzing with the news of what happened last night. My insurance man came by and told me he had come home early and found his wife plugged up to a man that looked like Kenny Rogers."

"When we first moved into Shady Grove we were told not to talk about anybody because everyone is kin to everyone else. The little Baptist Church was ruled by a prominent family, I hate to say it but the church was full of the wrong kind. They can tell you all about the Bible stories and I can tell you all about theirs. Now if everybody is kin, and everybody is whoring with everybody, what does that tell you? The whole damn village is crazy. Right!"

Rex said, "Right!"

Rex asked, "Drucilla, why in the world, are you still here?"

I said, "Rex, why do you keep asking me this?"

Rex said, "Well, for one, you don't belong here."

I said, "Because I'm crazy too. Rex, maybe someone should have told them not to do anything wrong because they might turn up on page forty-three, in someone's book, like yours. Get this Rex, the fire department knows who all the AID's patients are, the village store knows who all the alcoholics are, not to mention the Saturday night beer buyers that teach Sunday school the next morning. Secrets are not kept in a small community, everyone knows that."

"Oh Rex! I just remembered, going with Richard to see a fishing hole that he and a co-worker had found. It was out in the woods, we drove up on a Shady Grove woman buying drugs from a man on a motorcycle. She didn't care that we saw her. She went right on with her business. Three or four months later her house was up for sale. You and I both know a new address won't clean her up."

"Remember I told you, that Richard had told me, that a telephone man had whored with most of Shady Grove? I don't know of any mattress whores today. The Sheriff's all call them house whores. More husbands need to come home early and see who their wives are plugged in to. There is no telling how many men are living with their sister or half sister. One family took their grandson and raised him as their son. Their daughter had gotten pregnant by the neighbor next door. They told him just before he was to be married. His Mother married another man and he just found out he has a twenty one year old brother. My God, Richard should be telling you about Shady Grove. He certainly knows more than I do, if you could get the gutless bastard to talk."

"Let me see, the next thing that happened to me was that I had some friends from our square dancing club. Who's son worked for a movie company. He ran a camera. Steve called and talked to me about my novel and in a few days a Mr. Calwell called and asked if he could read my manuscript, I had Mr. Williams, from the law office, send him a copy. Mr. Calwell was in Atlanta, the next thing I knew he had written a screenplay based on my manuscript and was in Los Angeles to find backers. About a month later I was told that Steve had been shot to death in his car while stopped at a red light in Hoover."

"This was making me crazy. First Johnnie's house was robbed and her life threatened. Then Mr. Cork was murdered, gas poured on him and burned in his house. Now Steve was shot to death with no suspect or motive in his death. Plus Amanda's yard was torched with gasoline, and they had ransacked my house."

"Why wouldn't they just do away with me? I tell you why. If anything happened to me, Mr. Williams would for sure have Richard's ass put away, somehow, someway. Richard knew not to touch me. He knows the Sheriff, police and even the post office was helping me. They knew I wanted proof and was willing to turn over every rock in this town to find it. I've said it before and I'll say it again. Richard is as guilty as a dog in the hen house with feathers in his mouth."

"I got through Steve's death. Richard and I were fighting like cats and dogs. I wouldn't stay home and leave all his shit alone. I told him I wouldn't stay home and if he hurt me or had anyone else hurt, I'd go to the police and try my best to have him arrested. All I could hear was he didn't know what I was talking about and to stay out of his way. He insisted that he hadn't done a damn thing and I had let the phone calls drive me crazy. It wasn't the calls. It was the things he did that convinced me that he was guilty. One morning Richard told me to put my car radio on a new country station 102 Dixie. On the way to work that morning they announced the thirtieth anniversary of Richard and Melinda. I knew who Melinda was and it was Richard's and my anniversary. The next day was my birthday. I asked Richard to call the radio station and wish me a happy birthday. He did, but it came over the radio as Teresa's birthday, not mine. Melinda was the whore Richard was dating when I met him. She has been married seven times. Each husband caught her in bed with another man. I wonder how many times, Richard has been caught by her many husbands."

"Remember the board of nails on Monday? I can tell you one better than that. I had a little dog. He was black and white Shih Tzu. Brandon and I loved that little dog. One day he came up missing. I put up posters from Forestdale to Warrior, Walker County to Shelby County offering a three hundred dollar reward. We couldn't find our dog. I thought someone had stolen him. I was hurt to the bone. It was in the Spring about six months later; Richard awoke me early one morning and asked me to come outside. I followed him around the house where he started kicking in the dirt until some black and white hair came up. He turned and left for work without another word. Richard had killed my dog. After six months of looking for my dog, he was buried in my own yard. I know why some people kill because I could have thrown gas on Richard's ass and set him on fire, or whatever the worst death could be. I hated the bastard; hate that has built up and up. He has done everything to me except take my life and he has damn near done that. I told Percy and Harriet everything trying to get them to help me; but no! It was poor Richard. That he had to live with me."

"I went right back to trying to find the beautiful blue Camaro. I was as mean as a pit-bull dog. I didn't give a damn about Richard! I'd see to it that he couldn't do away with me. And if he left he wouldn't take a damn thing with him. I was out to tack his balls to the wall. I had been working on my list of people with blue Camaros. Believe me I think I have everyone in the state of Alabama that owns one."

"Rex, I've done a few real dangerous and crazy things during this time. I was driving in the rain and spotted what looked like the beautiful Camaro SS. My Z28 will fly and hug the road but on wet pavement it will lose traction and kill you. I was so mad that danger didn't cross my mind. I flew up behind the Camaro and it took off with me right on its bumper. We went down Fieldstown Road and it went around an eighteen-wheeler, so did I. But I spun out in front of the truck. He blew his air horn and hit the brakes. I spun around twice in the middle of the road and without stopping straightened it up and went after the Camaro. It turned onto Highway 31 went half a block and turned into a bank and parked. I didn't take my eyes off of the Camaro the whole time. I followed it into the bank parking lot. I jumped out of my car and so did this big ass man. He asked what I wanted with him. I told him my name and I wanted to know how long he has had this car. He said that he had just bought it off a car lot in Mount Olive three days before and didn't know who the previous owner was. I told him I wanted the tag off his car and I would find the owner myself. He didn't say a word. He opened his trunk, took out a screwdriver, removed the tag and gave it to me. Without a word I took the tag and headed to my car. I could hear him say; 'Damn, she sure is mad at someone.' That wasn't the right car but I still have the tag off that car."

Rex said, "I hope you learned a lesson from that."

I said, "I think I did. He was one big ass man. I won't be doing that again. The Bates in Sayre were the owners of the Camaro I'm looking for."

"Remember me telling you that I knew the Odoms on Marklund Road? Well Percy and Jerry had married sisters and their sister was an Odom. That's how I knew them and that's why I knew that their daughter wasn't the one I was looking for. What's odd is there are lots of these Odoms and this family was the only ones that I liked. Anyway I told Harriet about them and one of Percy's daughters, she and I went to the Odom's house to make sure it was my niece's Uncle and Aunt, in others words the right Odom. Their beautiful daughter talked to me and told me there had been a telephone man down the street so much that she thought the red headed woman had married him. I thanked her and we left. Low and behold the next weekend, my niece and Harriet came to my home telling Richard that the Odoms were going to have me arrested for harassment. The Odoms were accusing me of going to the feed store where their daughter worked and calling there to harass her. I walked to the kitchen table where the last three months phone bills were lying, picked them up, shook them in my niece's face and told her if she could find the feed store's number on any of these bills that I'd kiss her ass. What they were calling a feed store looked like an old barn to me and I had only been there one time. I asked Richard to tell them I didn't do anything. The bastard screamed at me that he didn't know what the hell I'd been doing. I told the bastard, either he was for me or against me, and if he was against me to get the hell out of my face. For that matter all of them to get the hell out of my house. They just stood there and looked at me. I asked Harriet if she knew where she lived. When she said yes, I told her to get her fat ass across the road. That sent my niece and Harriet running. Remember my niece had been watching me in her green Jeep."

I sat down at the table and wrote a letter to the Odoms and told them I was sorry about the misunderstanding. I was not harassing their daughter. I copied the letter and had a notary public witness it. I handed it to Richard and asked him to deliver it to the Odoms. He told me to go to hell. I asked advice from a dear friend about delivering it myself. He advised against it. So I went to the Sheriff's office and Sergeant Stone called Richard and told him it was his place to deliver the package. Richard wasn't home when I returned. He came in and I asked him where he'd been. The bastard had taken

Percy to the feed store. He wanted to prove to Percy that I had been there."

Rex said, "Why didn't you just kill the son-of-a-bitch right then and there? You just told him you had been there one time. So sure they knew what you look like."

I said, "Will I knew he hated me. I just didn't know how much. I'm the stupid bitch that cut off his money, his on line whores and blew up his home away from home. He was always screaming at me that I had ruined him. I would just laugh at him and tell him that I was Rambo and Rambo was going to put him in the cemetery next to DeRoy. After a fight I'd always get into my car and leave."

"I forgot to tell you that to keep the Odoms from having me arrested. Richard had to take me to church. The big Church of God in Adamsville was having a revival; I gave in and went for three nights straight. I had enough. I told Richard, 'No more.' I'd rather go to jail than go back to that church another time. These people stood up to sing and acted crazy for three hours. The church was packed with women; every hairdresser that I'd ever seen was there foaming at the mouth at the handsome preacher. The preacher was acting his part. He was running from one side to the other and front to back, stirring them up. Everyone was raising both arms in praise of him, not God. Most of the women wore short skirts to start with. And when they raised their arms, I've never seen so many assholes and elbows in my life. I had said the wrong thing the night Harriet and Miss Piggy came saying that I was going to be arrested. I said I couldn't be arrested because the worst thing for me is to have to call Mr. Williams to get me out of jail. After saying that, all that I have heard is that they would have me arrested."

Chapter 4

"I asked Richard, one night, why didn't he take me anywhere. He said he was ashamed of me."

Rex said, "Drucilla, you're killing me."

I said, "Rex, do you want to stop?"

Rex said, "No, no, no! But I don't want to think that you're feeling sorry for him. Richard is a piece of shit and you have been a coward. If you tell me one more time that he's ashamed of you, I'll go kill him myself."

I said, "Here's you something to think about. One night I answered the phone and a strange man's voice asked me what I was doing. I told him I was watching television. He said his name was Larry as in Larry the Plumbing Guy. Well poor Larry's wife had left him for Richard and left him with a son that had to be placed in a nursing home. His wife, Karen Wade moved to Tennessee. She and Richard had put my phone number in his beeper. Larry called the next night and I made Richard listen in on another phone. Richard listened to every word and never once did he say don't call my wife again."

Rex said, "What could Richard have said. He had taken his wife."

I said, "Another thing Richard left for me. A note with just, 'Fo ha Fo ha', what does that mean?"

Rex said, "I have no idea. Let's talk about Brandon."

I said, "Well, I see him growing up. He doesn't like people. He's afraid of this world. Being raised in these woods has harmed him. Harriet always kept him under her coat tails except when he was in school and everyone was mean to him. He's a very good person, no drugs, no liquor, no cigarettes and doesn't say bad words. Every job he gets he quits. If anyone raises their voice to him, out the door he goes.

He needs a shop of his own, to do brakes on cars. He can make things run that no one else can. He won't go out and get a job because he is afraid of people, and this is true."

"No one has to tell me what harm has came to this young man. I have begged everyone I know to help him. Just take him under their wing and train him. Teach him a trade. Rex, once I paid his salary for six months thinking he would be taught a trade. When the six months were up the man who was supposed to be my friend and also knew Brandon's mother called and told me the Boss was letting Brandon go because he didn't know his way around town. Needless to say we had World War Three. This old fool knew that before he hired him. That's what I thought I was paying for. Brandon was working with his son. Brandon came home every day telling of the fun he had at work that day. I thought everything was going fine until the phone call. He told me he had giving Brandon enough hours at work to graduate. I believed him until the school called and told us Brandon wouldn't graduate because he didn't have enough work hours in. The reason for the job was Brandon would have a trade and learn how to deal with people. He went to school in the morning and worked in the afternoon. This left me beside myself. Mr. Clay had been a wonderful friend to me. Now I was seeing the other side of this man. He went as far as to say that Brandon was stupid. I tried every nice way in the world to talk to him about Brandon. Then I screamed; 'Now you listen! I told you that Brandon had been sheltered all his life. He has his driver's license but you can't tell him to go across town to get something without telling him how to get there.' This old man took my money to pay Brandon every week and didn't teach him a thing. He didn't even give him the right hours. Well, Brandon graduated anyway but he had to fight for it. He had worked for Winn Dixie for a year. It was only five miles from home."

"Rex, someone makes us what we are and I tried to guide Brandon's life, but it was Harriet's way or no way. Anyway I didn't see or talk to Mr. Clay for a couple of years. Harriet and Mr. Clay hated each other but I do talk to him now. I know he sees Brandon out and about and I know that his son that worked with Brandon at his place was on drugs and knee deep in trouble. I know now that Brandon was just a joke to him. This hurt Brandon more than anything because Brandon really likes them all. He trusted them and made all kind of plans to go hunting and fishing with them but it never happened. What my friend Mr. Clay did to Brandon caused a lot of harm to Brandon."

"Brandon doesn't need anyone to tell him too much. Now he drives any and everywhere. He can shoot a gnat off a bird's tail while in flight. He loves to fish but he doesn't try to have friends anymore. He is a loner. Life has been ruined for this young man unless I find a miracle."

"Rex you have been around Brandon. He is precious. I wish you would spend some time with him. No beers please!"

Rex asked, "And why not."

I said, "Because one thing leads to another and I don't know how strong his brain is. Rex what are you laughing at?"

Rex said, "Drucilla, everything to you is a brain thing."

I said, "Well! Hell yes! If you lift your little finger, it's a brain thing. Man I think you have a brain fart and don't even know it. Now write that in your story."

Rex said, "I will! On every page I'm going to tell that you had a brain fart the day you let Richard come back into your life. I'm also going to tell what you said about lesbians having an eating disorder and that gays don't have a vitamin deficiency because they are full of protein. For that matter you told me that one said he couldn't stand the smell of women. He loves to smell himself."

I said, "Rex you're full of it."

Rex jumped up grabbed me holding me close in his arms, wrapping his long legs around me, fell over on the ground and started to roll over and over and over. He stopped but wouldn't turn me loose.

I said, "You stupid bastard. I bet I've got grass stains all over my clothes."

Rex asked, "You're not mad at me?"

I said, "No Rex! I don't get mad at people I love or people that's bigger than me."

Still holding me tight Rex said, "You know that old saying; keep your friends close and your enemies closer."

Rex slid his hand down my body and grabbed my back pocket. Rex asked, "What do we have here girl?"

I said, "It's a thirty eight Smith and Wesson, snub nose, and yes it's loaded."

Rex loosened his grip and gently turned me loose.

I said, "That's what I call a brain fart. Now, keep your hands off me. I've had enough of this donkey dicking around. Don't ever try to be vulgar with me."

Rex said, "You think I can't disobey you."

I said, "That's damn right Mister! I have something you want, remember, is it my story or do you just want to know if I'm a virgin? What if I say I am? Not a bit has been taken off this candy cane in thirteen years. I am undamaged, with the tightest ass in the USA."

Rex's face turned red.

I asked, "What's wrong big boy? You need a whore? I can give you a list a mile long. Most of them look like they have been rode hard and put away wet. They will give you most anything you want, herpes, gonorrhea, genital warts, and AIDS. Fool, you better marry your left hand and stop thinking about a hairy hornet's nest."

Rex said, "Girl it's that damn perfume you wear. It makes me crazy, those green eyes, and your temper."

I said, "Well if you want you a Drucilla you're out of luck. When God made this piece He broke the mold. I'm an endangered species, one of a kind, and you cousin, you can't have me."

"You have been told that I destroyed Richard. Men like him are an embarrassment to me. Now, Rex, I've given you one more month than you asked for of my time so let's stop pussyfooting around. Will it satisfy you to know that I'm looking for myself a man? A man that I can believe, deep in my soul, that he won't hurt or embarrass me. A man that can give me a thousand acres of land, an antebellum home and workers to raise five hundred acres of okra."

Rex could be heard for five miles as he screamed, "**Okra!** It will sting you to death." I said, "Yes, okra, you tell me how much it costs at the market. How hard is it to get gold, coal or diamonds out of the earth?"

From the look on Rex's face I could tell he had no idea of the cost. I said, "I'll bet you have never been to a farmers market. I bet you don't know the price of a pound of okra. In another two years we the people won't have food to eat. It's going to be pills and more pills. So can't you see in a few years food from the fields will be gold."

I told him, "100 foot rolls pay 3 dollars to the picker and this is every other day. You pay 10 dollars at the market for a 6 quart basket."

Rex said, "Drucilla, food can be shipped in here from everywhere."

I said, "That's true big boy but you take it from wherever, it sits in the hot fields all day then it rides in an eighteen wheeler for a few days. It's now at the store where it sits for another few days then you buy it and it sits in your refrigerator for a few days and then you cook it. Remember it costs gold for this old food. By the time it's cut until it gets on your plate all the nutrients are gone. The only good it does you is to exercise your jaws, your intestines and separate you from your money. There's going to be big money in food. Another thing, when I get through with you and your book, I'm going to start a business of ear piercing for dogs."

"I asked my daughter to help me get it started and she said she didn't have time for my hair-brain schemes. How fast she forgets the shopping trips we went on at Christmas time. In every mall you could buy doggie bones, homemade doggie clothes from fifteen dollars and ninety-nine cents and up. I've seen diamond collars, painted toenails but I've yet to see little diamond ear rings for dogs. This would only take fifteen minutes to pierce both ears. Keep your mouth shut about this exclusive news. I'm really going to do this. Oh, don't worry Rex, I'll do yours for free."

"Are you ready now? I want to tell you about a dream I had last night. In the dream my ass was a potato hill and you were a hog rutting in it."

Rex said, "Well I'm surprised it wasn't Max."

I laughed until I cried.

I said, "Now for real. Let me tell you about being in Savannah. It was a Saturday night and I was the girl Conway Twitty sang about, a tiger in tight fitting jeans. About one thirty in the morning we were in the lobby leaving the lounge when I felt a tap on my shoulder. I turned around and looked into the damnest blue eyes in the world. A very sharp looking man, in a deep Southern voice asked me for a dance. He explained that he had a bet with three gentlemen, pointing to them standing near a wall not far away, for five hundred dollars and if I helped him win the bet he'd give me the money. He then put out his hand and introduced himself as Starr James, an attorney from Savannah. I told him, what a coincidence, I'm also a lawyer from Whoathoughit near Birmingham, Alabama. I'll bet your motto is liquor up front and poke her in the rear. The blood drained from Richard's and Mr. Starr's face. I wouldn't have taken a million dollars for that moment. Richard threw a fit and told me I could stay out all night but he was going to bed. I looked at Mr. Starr and said, 'What the hell let's dance'."

"Mr. Starr and I walked into the lounge arm-in-arm. His three friends stood by giving us a nod. With his magnificent Southern voice he said, help me show them that I can dance. I fell into his arms just like my hands slipping into the softest leather gloves. I thought with his Southern draw, he has to be from Mississippi. My God I loved his voice but when he pulled me into his arms, it was like walking on a cloud. We floated around the dance floor as he softly sang in my ear. He was singing as the piano played, <u>You Have The Right To Remain Silent</u>, <u>Take The Ribbon From Your Hair</u> and <u>Satin Sheets</u>. The last song was <u>The Tennessee Waltz</u>. I pulled away from him to see that we were the only ones dancing. I asked him if he didn't think he'd won his bet. He asked me how he could keep me there. I told him one more dance and asked the piano player to play, <u>You Have The Right To Remain Silent</u>. Mr. Starr was a splendid dancer. When the song finished he again asked, 'How'. I burst out laughing and told him he could keep me only if he had more money than me. With that voice that gives me cold chills' til this day he said he didn't know what his total assets were but if I would tell him how to find me he'd let me know in a few days. I told him, 'Look for the

Williams Law Office on Eleventh Avenue South in Birmingham, Alabama and ask for Drucilla Hallmark. I live in a loft over the First Alabama Bank, and my ass sets over billions.' We both laughed."

"I called Becky to say this was the best vacation I've ever had. I want to live in Savannah and dance for the rest of my life. If Mr. Starr comes looking for me, get me on the phone and I'd be there even if I looked like a rag doll. Hey, I clean up good."

Rex said, "That sounds like a good dream. One I'd like to be in."

I said, "Come back down to earth. I must tell you about Frank. One day I came home and the stereo unit, caller ID box, microwave, telephone answering system and a recorder wouldn't work. This recorder was new and wasn't plugged up. Richard was tearing up everything in the house. I called Mr. Frank. He came over looked at everything and took them back to his shop to repair them. Richard told me they were hit by lighting. Mr. Frank came by four days later with a note for Richard stating none of these machines were hit by lighting. A surge of electricity went through the machines but it wasn't a lighting strike. Mr. Frank told me he'd go to Court with me if I wanted him too. He knew that Richard had the knowledge to send a surge through the machines. I thanked Mr. Frank. I had forgotten that Rhonda Barns was killed in a car wreck after telling me that Richard was at the Gooch trailer. I called Mr. Frank and told him to not to say anything about the machines."

"I told you before that I found a note in Richard's pocket to come to eleven twelve, Second Street North. Go over the hill to the store on Eleventh Court turn right to the door. I'd like to know who lived there in nineteen eighty four."

"Here's a good one. I took Richard to a new female Doctor. I had been in the office with Richard and her a few times. She looked at me and asked who I was. I told her that she must have Alzheimer's disease. I'd been in the office with Richard several times and she doctored me twice before. She didn't answer she turned back to Richard. Richard had his shirt off. He fell on the back steps and hurt his back just above his belt line. When she finished touching and rubbing his back, she leaned her head over his back and let her hair sweep up his back and across his shoulder. She said, 'I'll see you in four months unless you need me before then.' Richard never said a word and neither did I until I got home. I called the Doctor's office and told Sadie to change Richard's appointment to my doctor and if he couldn't see him then we'd both find another doctor. Sadie told me that Richard was pleased with her. I told her Richard was real pleased with her but I didn't like her. She would change his doctor or I'd go to the medical board about her. Richard's doctor was changed."

Rex asked, "Does this have anything to do with jealousy?"

I said, "None whatsoever, the one time I didn't go with him to see her, he came home with that famous Viagra. I put it in the garbage. Remember me! I'm an ice cube with a hole in it. So what does he need with Viagra, gay pills?"

Laughingly I said, "You know four to five hours, they have to have a strong dong to get in that hole. I just out and out asked Richard if he was queer. He jumped up and screamed, he'd cut my throat from ear to ear. He said that he'd cut me up, and asked did I hear him. I got into my car and left. But this time I told myself, this damn house belongs to me. He was damn right. I heard every word he said and I'd had enough It wasn't long after that I divorced him."

"I turned around went back home, called Mr. Williams and told him I couldn't take any more. The next morning his secretary was at my door at seven thirty. I let her in and she strutted those long legs straight to the kitchen table. She laid divorce papers on the table in front of Richard. She had two witnesses with her. Without a word Richard signed the papers and all of them left. I spent the whole day packing up Richard's personal items, put them in boxes and placed them in the carport."

"When he came home that night, he asked, **'What the hell is this?'** I told him he didn't live here anymore. He loaded his things in his truck and went to live with Amanda.

"Now for sure I couldn't see Brandon anymore because my good old family wouldn't talk to me anymore. So much for the saying, blood is thicker than water. Even Amanda wouldn't come to see me. She thought I was crazy and she was ashamed of me. Well that was all well and good. I'm crazy and know it; some people are crazy and don't know it."

"I went to the post office and bought three rolls of stamps and asked if it was against the law to send out letters offering a reward for information. I mailed out three hundred letters and within a week I received a call from Mr. Jake, the owner of the, so-called feed store. He wanted to know if he could help me. I told him my story. He asked if I would come to his place of business, on Tin Mill Road to see him."

"I called Ann, another friend of mine and she and I went to Fairfield to see Mr. Jake. He was a very nice man. He told me that I couldn't have harassed the Odom girl at the feed store because she never worked there. But Richard has been to the feed store many times. He has bought feed in his personal truck and his telephone truck. I asked if it was horse feed and it was. I asked Mr. Jake if he would give me a letter stating the Odom girl never worked there. He did and then took us to lunch. He told us that Sumiton was a troubled city and he was sorry that I had spent so much time there. He told me he had closed the feed store some time ago but if I would call him he would open it up any Saturday so I could bring Richard there. He would tell Richard to his face that he had bought feed there many time and that I hadn't harassed anyone there. He could see that Richard wanted me to stay away from Sayre and Sumiton. Richard didn't care if I got hurt or not. Ann told him that I have a lot of friends that do care and wished I would just leave it alone. I can't, I won't, too much has happened, I have to have answers and I won't stop until I do."

"So Rex, here I am. My subconscious has linked up with Tony Tortomasi. I want revenge, so bad. I know who most of his whores are. I know the Bates owned the blue Camaro and they live in Sayre. I live to see the day they are all dead. I could kill their kids and old Grandmothers. I could skin Richard alive or watch someone do it for me. I'd do anything to hear Richard tell Percy and Harriet what he has done to me. I should say once I would have but today I don't love them. So I don't care what they think of me. I've learned a lot. A wife has no rights. A whore has power and benefits."

"That reminds me. One Saturday, Richard was putting on a show. He was bragging, if that car came back, he would park his truck in front of the house and block them in or at least chase them down. I watched Richard closely. He had a bulge in the front of his blue jeans all day. I knew it was a set up. I even told him his Viagra was showing. Dark came and so did the car. We ran for the truck, Richard got in first and left me standing in the yard. An hour and half later he came back and his bulge was gone. He said he chased them with no luck they got away from him. I later found out he went to a friend's house about a mile away. I didn't let him know I just set him up for another weekend. I told him I was having a dinner party and it would be up to him to catch them. He fell for it. It was Friday night but earlier that day I had went to a yard sale and bought six, tall wooden cabinets and had to wait until Richard got off work to bring them home. We went to get the cabinets and it was eight o'clock and time for the dinner party before we returned. Just as we got to Martin Drive that beautiful blue Camaro turned down Martin Drive from the other direction. She made a u-turn and pulled to the side of the road. I tried to make Richard run into her but he fought me away from the wheel. As we were passing her, Richard hit the brakes several times. She was squalling tires slap out of Shady Grove. I have never hated as bad as I did that night and he knew it. He stayed out in the garage until bed time."

"The next day it dawned on me that she had turned right. It also dawned on me that big nose Joe, Richard's co-worker, lived in that direction and he was also divorced. It must have been his house where Richard was taking his whore. I got in my car and went to big nose Joe's house. I confronted him that I knew what was going on and the next time I'd set fire to his damn house and watch it burn with him in it. I left him standing there with his mouth open and it wasn't long before the bastard sold the house and moved to Mobile."

"I got another response to my three hundred letters. There was a call on my answering machine from the Adamsville police. They wanted to talk to me. I called them on the phone and was told that I was in trouble over the letters. I checked with the downtown post office, the Sheriff's office and my police friend in Graysville all of which said it was OK. Then I checked with Mr. Williams, and damn did he give me hell. He was mad about the letters and the piece in the

Birmingham News. He let me have it with both barrels. He shamed me to death. But when I told him that I had fired four shots at a car, which was leaving my yard. He jumped out of his seat. I swear he almost came straight over his desk. He screamed at me, 'Damn you, don't ever do that again.' I screamed right back, 'I'd shoot the bitch right between the eyes, if I got the chance.' He told me to go see the Adamsville police and tell them the truth. This time he didn't say call me if you need me. My heart sank. I thought he would have been there for as long as I didn't kill somebody. I prayed he'd be there then. Mr. Williams did call saying, 'Dru, you must get away from these people.' I replied, 'But that is **my** home'."

"I went to see the police and explained why I had sent the letters. The officer said I could get into serious trouble with the letters. I told him that I had checked with the post office before mailing them and that the post office had said it was OK. If it were against the law the post office would not have OK'ed it. And according to the postmaster it wasn't. He was nice in a business manner. He told me to leave it all alone. I could tell that he knew I wouldn't and I won't. Not until my last breath leaves my body."

"I said it a million times, Richard is gutless and so are his whores. Richard wants me dead. He doesn't care a thing about my family. If I was out of the way he'd sell my place and move to Bagley, Alabama. Bagley is next door to Sayre and Sumiton where drug money has built many a beautiful home for the crack whores to live in."

Rex said, "Drucilla, what do you want done about this mess?"

I said, "That's simple, kill the whores! I have found forty-two whores that Richard has been with during our marriage. I know their whereabouts and I want all of them killed and put into the same grave. I want Richard's ass in there with them."

Rex said, "Damn girl, that would be a massacre."

I said, "Don't ask, if you don't want the truth. You could take them one at a time and nail them to the wall of an old barn. You could put them all in a building and set it on fire. Take them on a cruise and feed them to the sharks. I don't care just as long as you get them off the face of this earth. Oh yea, don't forget the one that helped them torment me. I want them gone too. I want everyone to remember why they all died. For as long as the holocaust will be remembered."

Rex said, "You want all this done, because of one man?"

I said, "Damn, you have not been listening. How many times do I have to tell you this is not a slap on the wrist to leave my man alone? It's because they came to my damn house, my damn phone, and my damn mailbox. It's because they tormented me to death. It was my money that I raked and scraped to save. It was my stupid ass that stayed at home cooking, sewing, cleaning and raised a damn garden to feed his whoring ass. For years, I never said a word. Hell, I didn't even know about the incentive check he received every year. He spent over ten thousand dollars in just one year. All the overtime money he stole from me. Hell, the bastard stole my life, now I want payback. **I want paid in full!** I want the ones that have hurt me. I want them to lose the rest of their lives. I can tell you one thing. All of them best be watching their asses. The older I get the less I care about living. One damn thing's for sure, I'll not leave this world without Richard and you can bet your ass on that!"

Rex said, "Drucilla you do know that the cars being the same color and make, means that Richard helped buy every one of those cars. You have come up with several Melinda's, Sherrie's, Deb's and Jeanie's. Does Richard pick women with these names so he won't get them confused? There are so many of them."

I asked, "Rex do you envy him for being the stud he is?"

Rex said, "Hell no! If he hated you this bad, he should have walked off and never come back."

I said, "No Rex, I was a game to him. He is gutless, like I said. He's not smart enough to live with another woman. No one else would have been so stupid. He couldn't do to them what he has done to me."

Rex said, "Drucilla, Richard is the only one you need to get rid of."

I said, "They all knew he was a married man. They knew others would be hurt. They knew the wife hangs on until the end. But they didn't know Richard was married to Rambo. I intend to kill them one way or another. The end is near, for them. I'm really after the bastards that ran in and out of my drive way nineteen times."

Rex asked, "Drucilla, how long has this been going on?"

I said, "About four years now. It started two months after I came home from the hospital. Richard would come in acting crazy and was badmouthing me. A few nights later I invited a couple to the house to play cards and when they left I couldn't find my car keys. I always put my keys on the back of a rocking chair beside the carport door. It took me two days to find them. They were inside a hutch in the dressing room."

"That same night I picked up my shampoo bottle and poured shampoo in my hand. I didn't even have to open the lid. It poured out from the neck of the bottle. Someone had cut the neck on the bottle. I got out of the bathtub wrapped a towel around me and went to find Richard. I told him, he must have done this last night. I started looking to see what else he had done. I found fingernail polish poured out in my makeup drawer and a big bleached out spot on my new bathroom carpet. He said my dog peed on the floor and he thought it was carpet fresh. He had to have kicked my dog or he wouldn't have wet the carpet. Richard hates everything I love, even to the people, and he never failed to let me know. He would tear things up and blame it on my friends. He ran most of my friends off and I quit inviting others. Rex, I wonder how many couples go through things like this? I guess no one will ever know."

Rex said, "Don't wonder Drucilla. Don't even worry about anything outside your world. You can't do anything about it. Don't even listen to the news on television. Just keep the world inside your little circle as safe as you can and forget the rest."

I said, "Hell! I do try that. Rex, do you hear me! Those bastards came into my world. I didn't go looking for them until they came to my home causing trouble."

Rex said, "Yes, Drucilla! Do you hear me when I tell you that if, you didn't have Richard, you wouldn't have any trouble."

I said, "Damn! Richard would have to be dead to go away and stay gone. You just keep typing. I'll deal with Richard; he's out for now."

"I just thought about this little episode. One night I received two telephone calls. My caller identification listed the calls from a Pizza Hut in Hoover. I called back thinking someone in my family might have had car trouble. A man answered the telephone and I asked if he knew who called me. He told me there were two women using this telephone a minute ago but they were already gone. Later that night I received another call from a number I didn't know. I called the telephone company and got a name and address on that number. It belonged to a Mr. Robert Lacy. I called Mr. Lacy and asked who he was calling at this number. He said he did not call my number but he had a birthday party at his house and had invited a few friends over. He'd ask them and call me back. The party was over and his friends had gone home. He called back and we talked a long time. Mr. Lacy was a truck driver. One of the women at the party was a truck driver named Sherrie Post and she told him that Richard Hallmark had helped her get her CDL license. The other woman was a wife of a truck driver and she raised horses. Mr. Lacy said Sherrie lives close to him but she had just moved from the Kelly's Trailer Park in Morris, Alabama. He said I could trust him and to prove it he gave me his father's telephone number, his sister's number and his daughter's address. He said he knew Richard. His Uncle was Richard's boss at the Gardendale work center."

"I made Richard call Sherrie Post while I listened in on an extension. She answered and Richard told her who he was and she said that her mother had told her that he'd called the other day. They talked a minute and hung up. Richard looked at me and said that he didn't know her. I told him he was telling the wrong person. I asked him why he didn't tell her he had not called her mother. Why didn't he tell her that Mr. Lacy said she knew him? I asked Richard why didn't he get us all together and see who the liar is."

"I walked off. I knew Richard was lying because I found a sample test for CDL license in Richard's drawer. I made several copies of it and stapled my telephone bill to it. The phone bill listed call after call to several states, as if someone was tracking a truck driver. Calls made from my home! It was Richard tracking his whore."

"I called the bitch and she said it wasn't her that I needed to talk to. I needed to understand that Richard was born a male whore and he would die one. Later Mr. Lacy called me and told me that Sherrie came to visit him with a bottle of whisky in hand. She wanted to call a truce. She didn't want him to tell me anything else. It was too late. Mr. Lacy did not realize how much he had already said. Remember Richard's boss, Uncle D. F. Tucker and Karen Tucker at the Carraway Clinic in Warrior; it's all beginning to come together. Karen also had one of the light blue cars."

"I was in the bathroom one morning putting on my make-up. The phone rang and I answered it. It was D. F. Tucker wanting to speak to Richard. Richard was still in the bed so I laid the phone down, went to the bedroom and told Richard he was wanted on the phone. I went back to the bathroom but I didn't hang up the phone. I listened as Tucker asked Richard if he wanted to come in to work. I was about to hang up when Tucker asked Richard if he was alone. Richard said, 'Yes'. Then Tucker asked if he was sure no one was listening. Richard said he was sure. I told you the bastard was stupid. Tucker told Richard the woman called this morning that he was trying to get a hold of. Richard needed to call this woman. I never let on that I was listening to his conversation."

"I got in my car and was half way to where I was going when I spun my car around in the middle of the road and headed back home. I was getting madder by the minute. Richard was still in the bed. I was so mad at Tucker and his unethical telephone call to Richard that I made Richard take me to the plant in Gardendale. We were told he wasn't in, but would be back in about thirty-five minutes. So we waited for him inside the fence. Tucker got out of his truck, so did Richard and me. Richard said, 'Wait a minute Tucker, Drucilla wants to talk to you'."

"Tucker said, 'I don't have a damn thing to say to her'."

"I screamed, 'Well, I was listening this morning to your call to my home and I'm going to whip your ass'."

"Rex, do you believe this old man ran from me, ran inside and locked the door? I went home and called Terry Swindle. The phone company put Tucker on leave. But I'll tell you even to this day; I want to punch his lights out."

"Before we left home, I threw the phone at him and told him to get her ass on the phone. He pulled a card out of his billfold and dialed a number and left a message. In a matter of minutes she called back. Richard said she was an analyst for the telephone company. Tucker had sent him to her. She advised Richard to go see a psychiatrist. She made the appointment and I had to go with him."

"This call was a lie. There was an analyst, but this was Helen Beasley. I knew the bitch was calling Richard at work. She left Birmingham to get Richard out of her system. Richard moaned and groaned over her leaving. I was fed up with this shit. A friend of mine, named Mike at the telephone company gave me her phone number and address in Montgomery. I knew she was calling him at work. I called her and told her she could come and get his ass if she wanted him. She never came after the bastard."

"He wanted a doctor, so I got him one. We had an appointment with a psychiatrist in Wildwood. I told Richard if I went that I'd go with both barrels loaded, and I did. I went to a flower shop and had the lady make me a pot of yellow silk roses in a pot just like Richard had given me on Mother's Day, a damn grave yard pot!"

Rex asked me, "What are you talking about?"

I said, "Richard asked me what I wanted for Mother's Day. I told him I wanted yellow silk roses. When he brought them home they were in a clay pot with gravel and foil wrapper and a big bow. **A damn pot for the graveyard! Not a living wife!** I pulled them out of the pot, placed them in a vase and set them out so he would see them every day. I went to a shoe store and bought a pair of penny loafers just like the ones Harriet had burned. I took them to the garage and used a grinder to wear down the heels of the shoes. Richard has a peculiar walk and wears down the heels of his shoes in a special way. I bent the toe of the shoes to look worn and got a paper sack and twisted it up to look old and used. Richard kept a similar pair of shoes on his company truck to change into when he went to see his honey pot. Richard didn't know that Harriet had burned his shoes and now he won't be able to tell the difference. I was ready to go now.

I took all my papers and all the other things I had found and met Richard at the Doctor's office."

"We went in to see the Doctor and he asked me what I did with my time. I told him we must have all day. I summed it by telling him I'm an author, songwriter, homemaker, that I raise a garden and preserve the food, and that I sew, quilt and wash my car every Saturday. He asked Richard if this was true. Richard told him I enjoy staying at home. He wanted to know what all the fighting was about. Richard opened his mouth but I cut him off. I said it was over his addiction to whores, whores coming to my home aggravating me. I dumped out all the things I had with me. I picked them up one at a time and explained them. These papers are my proof of everything I've said. Richard is so stupid he thinks I'll continue to let things slide by while he lives a double life. I won't!! Especially him trying to kill me! Richard tried to blame all the items on Harriet's yard sales. I got in Richard's face telling him now is the time to fess up. His lies won't hold water against my evidence. The Doctor saw that I was getting hot under the collar and tried to change the subject. He asked me to bring him some of my songs to listen to and he wanted to read my novel. I told him I would but I was too busy for Richard's bullshit. I told him that if he couldn't make Richard come up with the truth, not to bother me anymore, and that he wouldn't talk because he has a yellow line up his back as wide as my ass."

"I took the Doctor a copy of my songs and novel. Two weeks later he called and asked me to come see him. He wanted to keep my songs and novel but he had something for me. He handed me a letter that stated after talking to me I was one of the most perfect people he'd ever met. I was beautiful inside and out. It got me to thinking about what other people thought of me. I asked many people to write a note with the good, bad and ugly, just what they thought of me. I was not surprised, all were positive. I know I'm good. I'm good all the time. Well, I was at one time. Now I'm as mean as hell. I'm as good as the best and better than the rest. You remember that!"

"Richard didn't talk Doctor to me anymore. I had sent Richard to live with Amanda but that didn't last long. I let him come back.

He put his things in my garage. We had a few fights but they weren't bad."

"I bank at Regions Bank and Richard banked at Colonial Bank. He had gotten another ATM card. Well he came storming in one morning, beating my door down. As soon as I opened the door he started screaming at me, what the hell I'd done with his bankcard. I told the bastard I haven't seen it. His whore probably had it. He just kept screaming at me and stormed out. He rounded the curve on two wheels. About an hour and a half later he came back and apologized. He left the card in the bank machine. I told you he was a dumb bastard. That same day he received an overdraft from the bank. Richard had come back a full blown screwball."

Rex said, "Drucilla I want you to tell me about Amanda. How did she treat you when you came home from the hospital?"

I said, "She was married to Jeff at the time. Jeff was in my dream. That was the best part of my dream. I took Jeff's ass fishing. I gutted him and left him in a slough. Too bad that part of the dream wasn't true. Anyway Amanda almost killed me when she married that thing. I raised her to be a professional skater and New York model. She met Jeff and lost her ever-loving mind. She had always been an earth angel. But she gave up a new Triumph Spitfire convertible for that piece of shit. The worst she ever did was leaving bath towels in her room. Jeff convinced her that an eighteen year old doesn't have any rules. The first few times Jeff came to my home he was nice. I guess he was sizing me up. Richard was never at home when Jeff was there. He didn't have a prissy walk but he primped worst than any woman I've ever seen. He wore a gold necklace and couldn't pass a mirror without primping with his hair. I was sick from surgery and wasn't able to fight with Jeff and he pushed me to the limits."

Rex said, "Like what, Drucilla?"

I said, "Like telling me that Amanda's car should be taken out and burnt. Jeff was jealous of everything she had. So this made me tell her that he was not to drive it anymore. He would keep her out past midnight on weeknights. My car radio was taken apart and laid on the front seat. Five or six beautiful light green moths were pulled apart and thrown all over the porch. He would do anything to aggravate me. One day I had company over for lunch and Jeff came into the kitchen and asked if we wanted a glass of tea. I told him I would if he was making it. He got a full pitcher of tea from the refrigerator walked over to me and poured it all over me. Almost the whole pitcher! It was such a surprise that it took my breath. This is one time I would have killed this fool, and I should have but I didn't. I asked my guest to excuse me and went to change my clothes and clean myself up. When I returned to the kitchen Jeff was sitting in my chair. I went straight for the pitcher and to my surprise there was about a glass full left. All I remember was looking in the pitcher and then next thing I knew I had thrown it in his face and told him to get his ass out of my house and not to come back until Richard came home. I forgot he didn't have a way home but then it would not have mattered if I had remembered. He sat outside for two hours before Amanda came home. Amanda was furious with me. She tried to pass it off as an accident. That was a bare face lie. The tea pitcher had a pressure button on top. I could have turned the pitcher upside down and the lid wouldn't have come off. I have the same pitcher at home if you want to see it. It is what I say it is."

"There are other things Jeff tried to pull on me. I rode to the car races with him and Amanda. During the races he made a steady trip between the beer stand and his seat. After his fourth or fifth trip I told him that was all. If he drank another I wasn't going to ride home with him. He turned it up, gulped it down and went after another beer. He came back with beer in hand and a shit-eating grin on his face. I grinned right back but I didn't ride home with him either. The next day I had to go to his house to get my purse out of the trunk of his car. I told his Daddy he'd better have a talk with Jeff before I put him six foot under. Jeff walked up with a baseball bat in his hand. His Daddy was reading him the riot act but Jeff just stared his Daddy in the eyes and twisted the bat until his knuckles were white. I told him I wanted my purse. He didn't say a word just staring at his Daddy. His Daddy told him to go get my purse now! I told him not to come back to my house drinking and if he drank while he was with Amanda, she wouldn't be with him anymore."

"Amanda graduated that May and went to work. Jeff still didn't have a job. I tried to get rid of him. It was one thing after another. Amanda was supposed to be at my home at nine o'clock to help me get prepared for my brother's wedding shower. I had finished cleaning up, when they arrived. I had written a note for Amanda that she wasn't going to stay out late anymore. Jeff picked it up and read it. He told me the nights were his time and I didn't have any right to demand this. I told Jeff to go home and not to come back and I'd call the law if he didn't leave. Amanda started crying and I went to get Richard. I told Richard to get him out of my house. As Richard walked into the kitchen Jeff stood up and reached out to shake Richard's hand and told him he was sorry to bother him but he hoped he'd help get this misunderstanding straightened out. I told Richard to get him out of my house that I was going to take a bath. As I was leaving the room I heard Richard say, "She'll be all right tomorrow, don't worry about her.' I walked back into the kitchen and told Jeff to pick up Amanda at the door and leave her at the door. If he ever came back in my house someone would haul his dead ass out."

"Do you hear what I'm saying, Rex? Richard didn't care one damn thing about me. He let Jeff walk up one side of me and down the other. The fight with Jeff went on and on. Amanda wouldn't listen to me. Jeff had convinced her that being eighteen years old; she didn't have to go by my rules."

"It was New Year's Eve; Richard and I went to bed early. I heard Amanda answer the door and Jeff ran into my bedroom shouting for me to get outside that Amanda's real Father was outside and wanted to talk to me. I came out of the bed, reached for my purse and ran out the door behind Jeff. Jeff was smart enough to leave his car running with the door open. I told Amanda that he was **not to ever** come back to this house."

"I just thought of another time. He has pulled so many things. One morning I received a call from Fritzie, he is a drummer and singer in a nightclub. You'll hear a lot more about him I'm sure. Anyway he said Jeff was at the nightclub last night and was asking a lot of questions about me. It sounded to him like Jeff was trying to dig up some dirt on me. Fritzie told me to tell Jeff that I knew he was there asking questions about me and if he ever came back Fritzie would stomp his guts out. A few nights later I had a house full and Jeff was standing in the doorway to the kitchen. As I passed him, he whispered in my ear, if I didn't start being nice to him he would spill the beans on me. I stopped and called everyone's attention that Jeff has something to tell everyone. Jeff just stared at me so I told everyone about my call from Fritzie. I never took my eyes off him as I told him to take his happy ass back to the club and my big brother would teach him what war was. Amanda ran to her room, and Jeff, well he slithered out the door."

"Another time, in nineteen ninety-three we had an ice storm that lasted for days. I called Fritzie and left a message for him to come stay with us if he needed to. I later found out that Jeff had called Fritzie and left a message that I had died. The next day Fritzie called and when I answered the phone there was a long silence on the line. Then Fritzie asked, 'Drucilla, is that you?' I asked him who he thought he was calling. He said damn I've called every funeral home in this town looking for you. Then he told me about his call from Jeff. I told him not to worry about me. Jeff and all these other bastards would be dead before me. That was the day I took all the telephones out of my house and put them in the trunk of my car. I told Amanda now, if Jeff talks to you he'll have to come here and then I'd kill the bastard. Amanda cried for three days and nights. She threatened to sneak out after I went to sleep."

"Harriet and Betty, friends of Amanda, talked me into putting the phones back in the house. The very first thing Jeff called and Amanda beat me to the phone. Jeff said he would come and talk to me. I told him to come on. Harriet and Betty wouldn't let me out of their sight. Amanda insisted that Richard go to Mama Marcelle's house. Lord knows Richard wouldn't help me anyway. Jeff showed up with his Mother and step Daddy. All three sat on the fireplace hearth. Harriet, Betty and Amanda sat across the room facing them. That put five of them between Jeff and me. If I could have only gotten to him the world wouldn't have had to put up with him. All I could do was try to shame him but how do you shame a shameless twit. I asked Jeff if he was drunk the night he came into my bedroom. He admitted that he was well aware of what he was doing. Betty told Jeff if he loved Amanda and had planned to marry her he should leave me alone. Jeff blurted out that he wasn't going to marry anybody; all he wanted was his ring back."

"Amanda jumped up screaming at me that it was all my fault. She was heading for the door; somehow I beat her to the door and slammed it shut. I grabbed Amanda by the arms and sat her down. I turned around telling Betty to go get Richard. I looked around and the three bastards were gone. I asked Harriet where they went. No one saw them leave. They slithered out like the snakes they are. The telephone rang and like before Amanda beat me to it. It was Jeff calling from the Village Store. With me on the line he told Amanda if she could get away they would give her a place to stay. We argued for over an hour when Amanda said, 'Why should I stay, you're dying anyway'. That was when I had my lung problem. Anyway it took the wind out of my sails. I told her if she left it would be with the clothes on her back. She took off her rings and gave me her car keys. I opened the door and she left. I really thought Jeff's Daddy would make her come back home. She wasn't in her right mind. Those bastards kept her hid from me for over a year. I didn't see her face or hear her voice and she was only five miles up the road. I asked everyone I came in contact with if they had seen her. Finally an old boy friend of Amanda's came to see me. He told me she was at Jeff's Mother's house in Graysville. I had called that home many time and never got an answer. I thought there must be a code so I called, let it ring twice, hang up and call right back. It worked! Amanda answered the phone. I told her if she didn't meet me at the church in five minutes I'd drive my brother's dump truck through the front door of that house."

"She came to the church looking like death. She was wearing rags and was bones. I talked nice to her. I just had to make sure she was still alive. There is no telling what those bastards were doing to her. That night I called a friend who ran a business in Graysville and asked her to help me get my daughter away from there. I told her if she let Amanda live with her I'd pay her rent and her salary to work in her business. My friend went to see Amanda. She got Amanda to leave there and she wouldn't let me pay her a dime; what friends! This girl was a good friend to me and I'll never forget her. Amanda stayed with my friend until she married Jeff. She sent me an invitation to the wedding and put on it that I would have to behave myself. Of course I couldn't see her marry him."

Rex asked, "Drucilla why didn't you just leave? All of this would have killed me. I don't know how you stood all this."

I said, "I can tell you one thing Rex. Children can make your heart hurt and men will make you crazy. You know all my folks say I'm crazy and I'm ready to show them just how crazy I am."

Rex said, "Drucilla no one can spit all this out as fast as you do. No one could keep the stories straight over and over again all these years and I know you have."

I said, "Rex you barely know me at all. How could you know if I've lied?"

Rex said, "I've got your records from the Jefferson County Sheriff Office. I've talked to your Sergeant Stone and many others. I know you're not lying and I also know you've been in more danger than you've said. Drucilla I fully understand why you had that dream. You want revenge! I went to see your Doctor Bradley but he wouldn't give me a copy of your records. You have to get them for me. I want the records from the doctor in Adamsville. The one you were going to when Richard had his wreck. Also I want a copy of the letters your friends gave you, copies of your phone bills where someone was tracking the truck driver and everything else you can think of."

I said, "Rex what do you want all this for? You don't need all that just to write my story."

Rex said, "No, but maybe through searching all this out I'll be able to help you in more ways than one. Now let's just get back to Richard."

I said, "Rex, I don't want to talk about Richard all the time. It makes me nauseated and makes me feel more stupid than I am. I think Richard has a bastard child and all these people are making damn sure I don't find him. I think that is where all the money is going."

"Anyway Harriet and the rest of the family, except for Jerry, wouldn't even talk to me. It was me, not Richard that took care of them all these years. I assure you Richard wouldn't even pull them out of a fire. Like I said it was me, and now, the hell with them all."

"I was writing songs and I did go to some clubs asking musicians to help me put music to my lyrics. Every time I found someone to help me; in a couple of days they had changed their mind. I blamed Richard and he blamed my friend Carol. I knew she didn't have anything to do with them not helping me. Now there was one other friend that I told about the clubs and who I talked to on the phone. She was house bound because of a stroke. At least I thought she was a friend. I talked to her every day."

"I had been introduced to a young singer. He was handsome and with a voice you wouldn't believe. I took this young man to Nashville and introduced him to the president of a major recording studio. We no sooner were home before he asked if I knew this woman. I knew of her but I didn't know her. He told me the girl told him that he would be crazy to get involved with me; that I was a nut. I asked him how many nuts could introduce him to the president of a recording studio. He said this person told him, he should make me go away. I asked him if he wanted me to go away. He stuttered but before he could get it out I told him to tell her to take him to Nashville and get him a deal. Tell her you can't deal with me anymore. Then you tell her to keep my name out of her mouth or I'd kick her ass all the way to Nashville. I called my home bound friend and asked if she had told this girl about my music deal. I told her about my call but she defended her friend. I've never talked to her again. I'll tell you when I find Richard is not guilty of what I accused him of; I'll fess up unlike that bastard!"

"Rex, you know I have songs cataloged in Nashville. They may never be sung on the radio but they are there. It's sad but you best keep your mouth shut about your hopes and dreams. There is always someone out there waiting to screw things up for you. That boy has a wonderful voice but now I wouldn't help him if it meant a million dollars overnight. I had done exactly what I told him I'd do. He had no reason to doubt me. I'm sure Richard told that Alexander bitch about my music but he didn't stop all my deals in this town. My home bound friend did."

"My friend Jean started helping me with the phone calls. One call took us to a used car lot in Jasper. They had called and asked to speak to June. I told them a few time not to call back but he insisted that he had the right number. He told me a little about the deal. Someone had bought two vans and still owned on one of them and he wanted his money."

"The next day Jean and I showed up on the car lot. We were dressed to the hilt, briefcase and all, dripping in gold and diamonds. I told him I was June Randoff and wanted to know the pay off on the vans. He came up with the files and told me everything I wanted to know. June has a beauty shop in Sumiton and lived in West Jefferson. I wrote down every word and told him thank you. As I was going out the door he asked about the bill. I told him that I was Drucilla Hallmark and he had my phone number and that he best find the real phone number for June and not to call my house again or the next time I saw him would will be in court. The next morning at six thirty I was at June's address in West Jefferson. There were several mailboxes in a row. There was no way to tell which house she lived in. A woman and three children came to the mailboxes at the road. I asked which house June lived in and she pointed out the yellow house. I asked which mailbox was hers. She told it the one on the end. Then she asked if she could help me, was there anything wrong. I lied and told her we were giving a friend a surprise party and wanted to invite June and was making sure we had the right address. The man at the car lot did call back and I hung up on him. I took Richard to the car lot and asked the man if he knew Richard or if he had ever seen him before. He said no so I told him it was his last warning not to call my home, to find June. There is no June at that number."

"Armed with June's address I got her telephone number. I called her and a man answered saying June was not home. I told him about the car lot and wanted him to put a stop to it. He asked was I also getting calls from Lacy Road in Quinton. I said yes, from a girl that told me that his house was lined with computers and he was selling time on X rated web sites. I told him to answer my question and I'd answer his. The bastard hung up on me but I was never bothered by them again. I wondered how he knew I was getting calls from Lacy Road. Was Richard going there to buy time on sex web sites or maybe this was where Richard had American Online installed? I have found names and address of whores from Florida, Georgia, and Mississippi and all over Alabama. I found business cards from party strippers. This really pisses me off. I'm at home dealing with Jeff and Amanda, Harriet and Brandon and Mama Marcelle. While Richard is up every skirt he can find. He comes home when he takes a notion, then he takes a bath and goes to bed. He looks under me, around me, over me but never at me. He is a professional liar. He passed a lie detector test because they asked if he did this to his wife. He doesn't consider me his wife. Richard has a way around everything and whores just play along with these type men."

Rex said, "Drucilla do you think, if Alabama legalized whore houses and gambling would some of this, would not have happened?"

I said, "Yes, now they have to sneak around with the neighborhood whore or your best friend. People go as far as Mississippi to gamble and when they lose, they whore around to get more money. I think they would feel free to do whatever if they legalized everything. It would give them a place to go instead of their neighbor's bed."

Rex said, "Are you saying it's O K?"

I said, "Hell yes, as long as they leave me, and my home alone. Richard told me one night, every time he finds someone he likes, they wind up being crazy. I asked Richard who he was talking about but he wouldn't answer. He didn't have to say it I knew it was those Sartains. But the one I want the most is Tammy Fields, after the Bates in Sayre. Richard and I were watching television and the movie, <u>Three Men and a Baby</u> was on, Richard started crying. I asked him what the hell was the matter with him. Did he have a baby out there that I didn't know about? He said no, but he cried like a whipped child. I've never believed Richard. I think he will take it to the grave with him. I'm waiting for the Fields' child to get old enough to talk then I'll take Richard to see them and a few others. Some day he is going to be confronted."

Rex said, "All you need, Drucilla, is to be taken away from all this bullshit, and these people. You see now that Brandon is grown and still does what Harriet tells him. He doesn't stand up to Richard. You and Richard are always going to be at each other's throats. With no happiness in your life, ever, why don't you just disappear?"

I said, "Hell, Rex, why don't I just die. I'd have to be brain dead to forget all that has happened. I'll never be right until Richard tells the truth. I know in my heart that he is too big of a coward to do that. He rubs it in my face but the truth isn't in him. Like the day he was putting up a light on the dollhouse. A green Camaro or Firebird stopped and talked to him at the dollhouse. When he came in the house I asked him who was in the green car and he said he didn't see any car. Damn Lie!

"I received a call from the Steel Plant in Fairfield. An unidentified man said I should look for the Johnstons and go down Alexander Road in Quinton. The Johnstons live close to the old Adamsville School. I checked them out and they could hold for a while. I went down Alexander Road and stopped at a cabinet shop. It was run by two brothers. I told them I was an investigator for the telephone company. I gave them the number of Richard's phone truck and description of his personal truck. One of the brothers told me Richard's truck was there all the time, working behind the building. He also saw him riding up and down the road with a child and a redheaded woman. He noticed Richard was wearing a cowboy hat and glasses. I asked what else he could tell me so I could tell if we were on the same page. He told me to turn around and look out his front window at his truck. He had Confederate bumper stickers on both sides of the bumper. He said there isn't a truck or car that passes here with one of those stickers on it that I don't see. This man has Confederate bumper stickers on his front and rear bumpers. He told me to be careful on this road as it could get rough. I left knowing he was talking about Richard."

"Get this Rex, Mr. Weems, the man I met at Mr. Cork's house was from Quinton also. It wasn't long after talking to the cabinet men that Mr. Cork was killed, too."

"A child is the only reason Richard would act this crazy. I do believe Richard has a bastard child."

Rex said, "No! Drugs! You said yourself there was a lot of that going on."

I said, "You're right! A Sheriff's deputy told me that the car coming to my home every weekend could be a drug drop. One morning Richard took me out on the porch and showed me a cigarette carton lying on the side of the road. I told him I'd pick it up later but after he left I went out to get it and it was gone. No one on this road smokes and it's a dead end. So who put it there and why? Makes you wonder doesn't it? I believe Richard picked it up but he never said a word about it. It must have been a drug drop."

"Richard was acting so crazy I decided to call one of Richard's cousins to come here and talk to him. This cousin had raised about fourteen foster children and I thought he could see through Richard. The first night he was here Richard had a fit on him. Richard was screaming at me for getting a wet coat out of his truck and hanging it up. He told me to stay out of his truck, his garage and leave his shit alone. Then he got in his truck and was gone for a long time."

"Sister Harriet came to the house and by the time she got through telling them what a bitch I was, they took Richard's side and everything was my fault. You can bet your last dollar those stupid bastards won't be back to my house. To top it all they stayed a week and the man didn't take a bath or shower all week. Water never touched his hands the whole time he was there, so it was good riddance."

"I don't know what I would have done if not for my friends Betty, Johnnie and Jean. Jean even gave me a key to her house in case I needed a place to get away. It didn't matter if she was home or not. Johnnie showed me where to find the key to her house or find one of her boys who would let me in. Betty worked at the hardware store with her brother and both were very good to me. Her family was like my very own."

"Once I went into the hardware store for something and Robert grabbed me and held me tight. He told me he knew that Richard had broken my heart. He said I'd be all right because I was one of the strongest women he'd ever met. I tried to pull loose but he held me tighter. I cried as he held me. He told me they all loved me and if I needed anything just come to them. I can't tell you what this meant to me or how it made me feel. I didn't need anything but I just needed to know that I was loved. He made me feel loved. Betty's family is my family and I love them all."

"Mr. Williams has told me many times to build a fence around my world and not to let bad things come into it. Not to deal with things I couldn't do anything about, be good, think good and live happy. Rex, this is all I ever wanted but with Richard, trouble comes to my door constantly."

"Once, I had to go into the hospital for surgery. Richard stayed with me the whole time. I thought, how nice but one week after I came home, calls started coming from the hospital. Four months after that I went to the hospital to have a light put down my throat to check my stomach. As I was leaving a woman in her thirties, short blond hair and lived in Bagley told me the next time I came in she would really put me to sleep. Needless to say I never went back for anything that required me being put to sleep."

"I had a wreck on my bicycle. The handlebars bruised my ribs and I had a bad sprain on my right ankle. I didn't know if it was broken or not but Richard wouldn't carry me to the doctor. I called Jean, she took me to the hospital and I came home with a large foot brace. Richard wouldn't even help me take a bath or to the potty. I knew this man wanted me dead. He still had his fits even though I wasn't able to fight back with him."

"I was in the hospital on one of my many surgeries and asked Richard for some ice water. I got it, all over my chest and the nurse had to change my sheets. Richard made his excuses, but I know he had me down and was taking full advantage of it. I watched Richard just to see how stupid he would act. He put his fist through a lampshade and hung it outside for everyone to see. Remember his whores drove up and down my road. He put his fist all the way through the bathroom door. I put a mirror on both side to hide it. I bought a new lampshade, new carpet throughout the house, new living room furniture, new tires for my car and a new four wheeler, at the tune of ten thousand dollars, and then I made him leave and took him for half of all his stock certificates. I told everyone that crossed my path just what a whore hopper he was. I wanted all the men around to know that they were licking up Richard's leftovers."

Rex asked, "Drucilla, how do you think Richard was able to take on all this?"

I said, "Maybe it's the Cherokee blood in him. This man's anticipation gives him a temperature of one hundred six and I found out his female doctor was supplying him with Viagra. When I found it in his sock drawer, I dumped it in the garbage but he dug it out. She was giving him office samples but I found his prescription and tore it up. That's why I made damn sure he'd never go back to her. There needs to be a law that the wife must agree that her husband needs Viagra or he doesn't get it. If you ask me it was invented for the gays."

Rex asked, "Drucilla, don't you enjoy sex?"

I said, "Boy, it makes me sick to even talk about sex. It's not just me; many wives are made sick of what their husbands are doing. Rex, a man should be yours alone. He should make you feel, that he is yours alone and safe in his arms from day one. That's not too much to ask."

"Richard is just a male whore and I know of two more just like him. Both live in Graysville and like Richard have serviced everything in three counties. Mostly on telephone company time. I can tell you this, his whores are women that no one else would have. Go look at some of them and see for yourself. Try Melinda, one of my hairdressers, Richard helped her pass her nurse's training. When I caught them she moved out of State. Richard made fun of her feet. He said her feet were as wide as her ass and always dirty. He said you could park an automobile up her ass. I couldn't believe she would whore with Richard but trash runs with trash. So why can't I turn this piece of shit loose."

"I have done everything to emotionally turn him loose. I went to see Father Cross. He told me to get rid of Richard. I went to see Father Ray. He told me to have Richard put out by a court of law and put in jail."

"Richard is the happy man, dancing, talking and outgoing but when he's with me he doesn't say two words to anyone. All of Richard's co-workers told me he has always danced to the music."

"The blacks get on television and tell about their hardships and struggle. I know what they are saying. I was given away to a man when I was still a child. We were poor. The poor knew only hard work and didn't have time for luxury, like reading. Richard saw this and knew he could have a slave in me and that's exactly what he did. I was his Toby, while he lived a single life, a whoring life, **the bastard!** He never looked at me to see my hurt."

"We went to a songwriter's seminar in Mussel Shoals. My eyes got infected so bad I couldn't see and Richard went to a drug store and paid thirty dollars for medicine. When I could see, my eye drops looked like urine and smelled just as bad. The date on the medicine was outdated by four years. I knew this was a joke on me. Richard tried to smooth it over by taking me to a jewelry store. We went in and looked around and a tall, thin man with black hair from behind the counter said, 'Drucilla knows what she wants.' I asked him if he had seen me at the seminar. He said no and started walking toward the back. I asked how he knew me but he didn't answer. A woman came out to help us. I walked out with Richard behind me. I asked Richard if he was queer. Richard didn't answer. It was another slap in the face, right?"

Rex said, "It sounds like it to me."

I said, "That isn't the only time. I was in Fairfield, in heavy traffic, and a beautiful new, white and black Camaro pulled up beside me. A man rolled down his dark window and screamed telling me they were going to kill me. He was laughing like crazy with his hand over his mouth as he was rolling up the window. I let him get ahead of me so I could get his tag number. No luck the tag was covered with duct tape. About two weeks later the same car was beside me again but this time it was a different driver. He screamed at me that I was fooling with a pack of gays. You guessed it, the tag was covered with duct tape. The traffic wasn't as bad and I tried to follow him but I lost him on Weibel Drive. My nerves were so torn up I was half crazy."

"Just when I thought they had done everything they could to me, my Amanda called on the telephone and told me someone at the Gaines Gas Station had driven off with the hose on the ground. Gas ran into the gutter and into the storm drain and it ignited and blew up Amanda's yard. If Amanda had been in her yard it would have killed her. It rings in my ears, Sergeant Stone telling me these people won't stop until you get hurt. This just keeps getting worse."

"Rex, I worked for two months getting Richard's resting place ready. While riding my four-wheeler in the woods I found a large tree that had fallen years ago. I chiseled down the side of the log and split it long ways. I used the winch on my four wheeler to lift the top up and propped it open. I cleaned out enough of the middle to put Richard's dead ass in it. That's what you can help me do!"

Rex said, "Drucilla, you're not kidding are you?"

I said, "Hell no! I'm not strong enough to do it myself or I wouldn't have told you about it. When we get home I'll show you where the log is. I have it hidden and we'll have to walk about two blocks."

Rex said, "O.K., girl, seeing is believing."

I said, "You better believe it! You'll see!

Let's stop for today and I'll take you for a ride."

Chapter 5

As soon as I backed the four-wheeler out of the garage it started to rain.

Rex said, "Drucilla it's raining, we can wait until another day."

I said, "Oh no! A damn little rain won't hurt you. You'll see, Rex. It's the perfect place. It will hold two people and it will never be found until I've been dead for thirty years."

"Rex, You'd never tell on me would you? You know I've got to get this bunch before they get me. I will, with or without your help. I think you were sent here to help not to just write this bullshit. No one has believed me about this but I'll show them it's all-true. If I even thought you'd tell I would kill you myself."

It didn't take but a few minutes to get to where we parked the four-wheeler and another ten minutes to reach the log.

Rex said, "Damn, who were you planning to put in here with Richard?"

I said, "A slut named Robin Pitts. I talked to her about singing some of my songs but she wanted to use Richard for a microphone, if you know what I mean. Robin, the one that thought she had hurt me the worst, is the only one I felt sorry for. She ended up with genital herpes that tortured her for the rest of her life."

Rex said, "I got a pretty good idea."

I said, "Then the bitch got mad because I wouldn't take her to Nashville. She made Richard act real crazy. She was known all over Birmingham as 'Deep Throat'. She couldn't remember a complete song. She told me if I could get her in the door she could make it the rest of the way on the flat of her back. Her Mother and Dad were the ones that told on her. Her Mother talked too much at the western store where we traded. She also had a light blue Camaro and lived in Sandusky."

"After a while some of the cars that came to the corner didn't run from me anymore. I drove my car up there and got their tag numbers. One belonged to a van owned by Mr. Seals. I got his telephone number and called to ask why their van was watching me. The Mother told me she had two sons working for the telephone company and one was a queer. She has disowned him and wouldn't talk about what he was doing on my road."

Another old couple from Leeds called me after I had mailed out the three hundred letters and told me the car I was looking for was involved in a death in West Jefferson, Alabama. I didn't have time to go see them yet, because all this happened about the time my Daddy died."

Rex said, "Tell me about the day your Daddy died."

I said, "Well, it was a Tuesday. I got up that morning and decided to go get my hair done. I never go to the beauty shop on Tuesdays. As I was driving out of the yard I thought I should go see Mamma and Daddy but decided I'd see them after going to the beauty shop. As I was leaving the beauty shop in Adamsville a sheriff's car fell in behind me. I thought he must be going home with me. When I turned onto Martin Drive my cell phone rang. It was my nephew telling me to come home and not to be upset because of all the fire trucks at Pa Pa's house. I drove out to Mama's house with the sheriff's car right behind me. It was Sergeant Stone. I asked him if anything had happened to one of my parents. He said we should go in and see. Daddy was dead sitting in his recliner. Mama said that Daddy asked her not to turn the television on; that he just wanted to rest. The nurse had come to bathe Mamma earlier and both were tired. They went to sleep and Daddy didn't wake up. I called Richard's supervisor and he said he would send Richard straight home. It took Richard five hours to get home. Sergeant Stone stayed with me until two forty-five P.M. Sergeant Stone told me I'd be alright and he would see me tomorrow. The house was full yet I had no one."

"I know one thing; Daddy loved Richard more than his own sons. Daddy's death released me from caring so much about Richard.

It was like Richard said, 'Now do what you have to do.' I saw Richard as a real son-of-a-bitch for laying up with his whore while my Daddy sat dead in his chair. But I guess it's no worse than him laying up with her for half a day on my birthday or any other day."

"Hell, here I am in a world of gays and whores. It was a week later that my oldest brother, the one that lived in Sumiton, took too much insulin and was placed in the hospital. From there he went to a rehabilitation hospital. They were moving him to a nursing home when he died in the ambulance. What was strange about this was that I passed his house and saw someone backing out his front door. The very day he was supposed to take too much insulin. I believe that person went there to kill him. So, see this is all my fault, too. I'm going to get them all. If it takes me until I'm ninety-nine years old."

"Harriet moved in with Mama Marselle and Gertrude has married again. Brandon is grown up and I'm just a sore ass, trying to stay alive until I'm through with Richard. And that won't be until he has told me the truth or his ass is dead! I want the truth about Michelle, McAdams, Tammy Fields, Robin Kirkpatrick, the Sartains and Miss Melinda. I want to know what part Mike Denard played in this. Did I tell you about Mike?"

Rex said, "No, that's a new name for me."

I said, "I met Mike at a songwriter seminar in Cullman. He called me and we became friends. I took him to Nashville a time or two then I didn't hear from him for a long time. Then he called and told me he had met this band that wanted to do some of my songs. I fell for it and he came over to get a copy on tape and written song lyrics. Richard went to the computer room to print out the lyrics. He was gone a long time and when he returned he said the word processor wouldn't work. Mike took the tape and left. I got a call the next day telling me the joke was on me. I went to the computer room where I had many of my papers and tag receipts. Well, three tag receipts from Walker County was missing. The joke was on Richard, I have other copies of the tag receipts but now I know which ones he's trying to protect. Richard stole the papers and Mike helped him. Never again has Richard tried to help me find these people, nor care what happened to me. Mike worked for a bakeshop. He lied about the band. He called the next day saying Richard had given my word processor away".

"Richard took my word processor to AAA Typewriter Service to be repaired. Or so he said! I called about it and was told there was nothing in for repair for a Richard Hallmark. I drove over there and showed him a picture of Richard. He said that man brought in a word processor but his name is Gary Williams. A woman has already picked up the processor. He described her but it could have been any number of his whores. I went and bought a new word processor."

"One day I called Richard's beeper number and a child answered. Richard had his beeper number transferred to the Stano house. But wait, the one I'm interested in is a Baker. She drives a dump truck. Her husband works for our famous potato chip company. Her family comes from Shady Grove. Her number was on my telephone bill. Also on my phone bill was a call to Joplin, Missouri. It was a skating rink of all things. I found drawing of guns, cowboys and cats in Richard's pants pocket. Things children draw."

"Then out of the blue Johnnie called. She told me she could not be left out until my mess was straightened up. She wanted for the three of us, Richard, her and me to go to Double Springs to have our fortunes told. By the time we got there, there was a long line ahead of us. Johnnie went in first and by then it was two in the morning. She was told the love of her life had just died. She would have many friendships but would never know another love like the one she had lost. Richard went in next and wouldn't talk about what she told him. He just said she was a phony. I was last and we talked about my song writing. She was once a singer in Nashville. She showed me pictures of her and famous country singers. She said in time I would get what I wanted but it would not be overnight. Then she blew my mind. She told me about Richard. She told me to remain calm. She said she wouldn't blame me if I killed him but not to do it. He wasn't worth it. He's a pile of shit. I asked her to spit it out. She said Richard was a queer. Hell I laughed at her. I told her he was a male whore. She insisted that Richard was bisexual. If he has a woman it's for blowjobs. They will hurt you and your friend. Get him out of your life! I did stay calm. I told Richard and Johnnie what she said. Richard said she was a phony and full of lies. He acted as if he was asleep all the way home. She was on the mark with what she told Johnnie and me so I didn't doubt her. This put me to thinking about the women that are married to this type of man. What kind of dangers are these wives in? I had things happen to me that were in question."

"Life was hard on me. I asked Doctor Hudson for some Ambien sleeping pills. They worked all right! It knocked me out to the point that you could have put me outside, naked as a jaybird, in an ice storm and I'd not wake for eight hours. Fifteen minutes after taking that pill, I'd be in a coma. I'd go to sleep talking on the phone. I'd get up in the middle of the night, go to the kitchen eat and talk to Richard and never remember it. I wanted to be dead so I couldn't have to listen to the loud television and Richard screaming at me. I wanted to sleep day and night just to get away from the torment."

"There were many months I'd come up short on my Ambien. I know I wasn't taking two at a time. I guess Richard was giving me another pill after I went to sleep. I found many signs that others had been in my house. I put them up and never told Richard. I was told that Richard was leaving the house at night for three or four hours. I didn't care about him going out but to find out he took my Camaro Z28 and drove the hell out of it was more than I could stand. Richard had lied big time. We got into my car and backed it out of the carport. The transmission sounded as if it was falling out. I made the bastard pull it back into the carport. I called a friend to come and look at it. It turned out to be gravel between the muffler and heat shield. But a week later it really was broke down. The distributor shorted out and it cost over nine hundred dollars to replace it. This stopped my taking the sleeping pills and the fight was on. Richard was mean and was getting meaner. My hurt turned to anger so I got meaner with each day and it was tit for tat. Whatever bad word he'd say, I'd say it right back to him. I told him if he didn't stop saying the F word and the G D words, I'd use them in public, in front of his friends. It didn't take but two times and he quit. The more I thought about Richard being off in my car with his whores the madder I got. I needed a truck to go to the nursery for a few bedding plants.

Richard smarted off that I better not wreck his truck. That only pissed me off. I've never had a wreck in any of my automobiles and he has wrecked damn near every one he's had. After I picked up my plants I went to the grocery store and bought sugar and syrup. In the grocery store parking lot I put two pounds of sugar cubes and a bottle of Karo syrup in his gas tank. Do you know it didn't hurt his truck? I was told it would stop a motor for good. Well that damn motor is like Richard's belly. It can lap up anything and pass it on through. I prayed every day that it would get him to his whore's house on Holly Grove Road in Jasper and he'd have to have it towed in. He knew if I ever caught him at one of their houses, I'd have set it on fire. And by God I would!"

Rex said, "It sounds like you're jealous."

I said, "No! I'm not jealous! I just can't stand being lied to. Richard keeps saying he has a twin out there. He's a piece of shit!"

"Beth and I were putting up pear preserves and Beth wanted some peaches. We went to the peach orchard. She was so funny, being born and raised in Shady Grove by a bunch of white trash. She tries hard to be classy, rich and a goody two shoes gal. She couldn't stand the heat in the peach orchard or the bees. Then we spotted the hornets' nest, she went wild. I was taking pictures of her. She was running back and forth hollering at me not to take her picture. She got Richard's Confederate flag from behind the seat of the truck, to wipe her face. She finally settled down and we picked five baskets of peaches. We came home washed, peeled, cut up and canned them."

"It was weeks before I put the film in the shop to be developed. Richard was the only one that knew where I put them. I picked up the pictures and every picture of Beth was gone and the negatives were cut out. I knew Richard had gotten them for her. She said she didn't want anyone to see the pictures. Did she make some kind of deal with Richard? Or did Richard do it just to aggravate me? I stopped taking her calls. Maybe it was my loss because I loved Beth but I was eliminating everything that caused me pain or worry of any kind."

"Richard's Aunt in California died. We had gone to see her many times through the years. She willed Richard seventy thousand dollars and in the divorce he had to split it with me. She is Richard's Mother's only sister. Aunt Pauline was a wonderful person and I loved her very much. I had sent her cards and had written letters to her. I made her a beautiful high heel shoe pattern quilt for Christmas. One winter I sent her a fifty-pound box of lighter knot pine, cut in twelve inch finger strips"

Rex said, "Lighter knot!"

I said, "I forget you were raised in Michigan. Lighter knot is heart pine where it has a concentration of pine tar. Do you know what pine tar is?"

Rex said, "Yes, I know what pine tar is."

I said, "This lighter knot was so rich you could wave a match under it and it would catch up. This sounds crazy but she had to buy her firewood from Nevada. But they don't have any kindling wood. The temperature in Newark, California averages seventy-eight degrees but in the winter the rains make the air damp and she liked to have a fire at night. She loved Richard and I didn't tell her anything bad about him."

"When she passed she left me all her jewelry. A beautiful platinum watch with diamonds, her wedding rings, and much more. The first thing I saw was a diamond heart pendant. I call it Aunt Pauline's heart."

"The first thing I did with her money was to build myself a writing room. This is where I learned never to deal with relatives. I signed a contract for to build a room fifteen by twenty three feet with five glass sliding doors. He said he would start on Wednesday and I'd be using it on Sunday. He asked for the seventeen hundred dollars to buy materials. Well I did, knowing better. Monday he started delivering some lumber and Wednesday no glass sliding doors. I called his wife and was told all the material was on the trailer at her house but, there's always a but, the transmission on their truck was messed up. I told her I'd send Richard over to pull the trailer over here. She flat out said no, she'd get it there tomorrow. I hung up the phone and called Home Depot and was told he had never placed an order for the doors. The damn butt was on the other end of the phone when I was talking to his wife. I called the bank to see if the check had cleared. It cleared the day I gave it to him. He went straight to the Radio Shack store and bought seventeen hundred dollars worth of music equipment. For my money I received a pile of lumber. I spread the word on him and found out I wasn't the only one he'd cheated. This scumbag talked an old lady out of seventeen hundred dollars to buy siding for her home. He never came back. He conned money to build his own two-story house, in Oak Grove just off Lock Seventeen Road and pay for a new Lincoln automobile. He and his wife went all over doing benefit singing to raise money for churches. These people are crooks."

"Months later my sister Gertrude moved to Maytown. I went by her house to introduce her to one of her neighbors that is my friend named Jean. Jean was with me and she walked on the neighborhood walk track three days a week and I thought Gertrude might want to join her, plus they could go shopping together. The door was open and I could see the house was being worked on and she wasn't moved in yet. I started to leave when this young boy came through the house and asked if he could help me. I told him I was looking for my sister. He said he was working for her and it would be a long time before she could move in. I started backing out of the house and he asked who I was. I told him who I was and by that time I was out to my car. He pointed to a truck in the yard and told me anytime that truck was there the boss was here. I'm so stupid I still didn't put two and two together. I drove up the road to Jean's house. I wasn't there but a minute when sister Harriet came in the door screaming at me. She said I didn't have any business going to Gertrude's house and they were going to have me arrested. Hell, look at me. I'm a little girl not big enough to take on a big ass man. When I pulled up in front of Gertrude's house, the thief that had taken my seventeen hundred dollars ran out the back door and hid under the floor. He was the boss the young boy was talking about. I told Harriet to tell the son-of-a-bitches, I'm glad to know that, next time I'll bring a gun with me. Then they'll have a good reason to have me arrested. And while you're at it tell that queer, child molester that I want my money back and he best keep hiding from me the rest of his miserable life."

"I waited and waited to see if Richard would make him give my money back. But in my heart, I knew, Richard was enjoying this. I just went on doing things to my house. I had my porches bricked, windows put in my carport and two big mirrors in the family room. I painted the kitchen and dressing room a light pink. Richard and I walked around each other as if we were paint on the wall. I had central air and heating put in the house. Richard did pay for half of that. He sat his sorry ass on the glassed in porch with his feet propped up for three years. He wouldn't do a thing around the house. It was so stupid of me to let him move back in. Thank God he's gone now."

"I was too lazy to get out of this house and make a life for myself. I didn't realize it but I was helping these people torment me to death. That's all changed now. I've come out kicking ass."

Rex said, "Yep, I can see that, and what you don't kick I will."

I gave him a big smile and didn't comment on his remark. I continued with my story. I said, "Richard was sitting on the glassed in porch and I went out there and unhooked the telephone. Damn he went off like a rocket. He ran outside and cut all the telephone lines. He was making sure if he didn't have a phone I wouldn't either. I told him he had ten minutes to hook it back up or I'd call the phone company to fix it and the sheriff to fix him. I asked him why he had done that when he insisted he didn't use the phone anyway. He never answered and I didn't put the phone back either. He was making calls from this house. The phone bills proved that. The telephone men he worked with told me he was bragging about making me crazy. Mr. Foshee told me all Richard had to do was to find an access point between the cross box and my house and there were many of them. He also told me, that he overheard Richard telling another worker that he took on a Big Brothers job for a little boy in Tarrant City. Foshee didn't know that a little boy was calling my home and asking for Richard. One time when I told him Richard wasn't home, the little shit told me to stick Richard up my ass and pull him out my nose. That's all it took I made Richard go with me to see the boy's Mother. When we got there the ex-husband was with the child. He told me the Mother wouldn't be home for another two hours and Richard wouldn't wait. I told the ex-husband to tell the

Mother, if the little boy called my house again I'd be back to see her without Richard. The little shit never called again and Richard denied everything. Just another of his many lies! Tell me how the little boy would know my telephone number and know to ask for Richard."

"Tell me why someone hasn't collected the two thousand dollar reward on Richard. It ought to be easy to get a picture of Richard and one of his whores. Damn there are so many of them! Someone out there has proof and I want it! Alexander Road and Lacy Road in Quinton, someone knows there too."

"Richard worked at the downtown plant for twenty years. Foshee told me the plant manager order the janitor to put a bed in a small room in the basement. A woman splicer was servicing the plant manager and the first line foreman got sloppy seconds. It wouldn't surprise me if Richard wasn't in that mix."

Rex said, "Well, Drucilla, I think that's what they call swinging your way up the telephone ladder."

"OK, Rex, you have me going now. I'll tell you something I shouldn't. After Richard was moved to Graysville plant. I had the heat put on them all. One of the guys couldn't be found but I knew where he was. I had seen his truck many times in the Daisy City Trailer Park. I put the word out that I was taking his wife to find his honey pot."

"My friend at the Sheriff's office, still to this day, bursts out laughing every time he sees me. I let him listen to a tape of a telephone conversation between Richard and me. Richard called home fussing about me turning all the men in for swinging on the job. The fight is on! I had told Richard that I was taking the guy's wife to find him. Richard sent McCoy to get the guy out of the trailer. Richard said I had caused him to get hurt. He went on to say that McCoy knocked on the door and no one answered. It was unlocked so he went in. No damn wonder he didn't hear McCoy knocking at the door. He had a lip lock on her crotch and she was holding him by both ears. McCoy grabbed him by his ankles and tried to pull him loose. He was holding on, for dear life. McCoy's friend grabbed one leg and McCoy grabbed the other. Both of them yanked and his hands slipped to her knees. One more yank and the crazy ass hit the floor face first and busted his lip. The Nut sat up on the floor naked as a jaybird and a dazed look on his face. McCoy was screaming at him to get his clothes on that his wife would be there any minute. He just sat there with blood dripping on the floor. His honey pot was sitting there with both legs spread wide waiting for McCoy to take over. I was laughing so hard that Richard hung up."

Rex said, "That's what I call being in another world."

I said, "If his wife had caught him, he'd be in another world. It's called hell! I could tell you all kinds of tales on these male whores. Another co-worker called in saying he had a flat tire and his spare tire was flat, too. He just happened to have his flat in front of his slut's house on Tommy Town Road. She also worked for the telephone company. Another had gotten off into a wooded area, siphoned off the gas from the company truck and poured it into his lick a dick a daygirl's car. He called Richard to bring him some gas. The telephone company has gone to hell because the supervisors sit on their asses playing video games on the company computers. They have no idea what their men are doing. Back in the seventies the company hired the good, bad and the ugly and most couldn't do the work. Then there were some like Richard. He did his work in record time and paid dearly in money for his honey pots. Richard helped the honey pot living on Tommy Town Road to rebuild her house, inside and out. He met her working for the phone company."

Rex said, "Damn, this is what I call a friendly company, a home away from home. Here and there."

I said, "I wouldn't call it that! These cripple minded, so-called men have let their wives, children and their homes go lacking. That is why they should legalize prostitution. Then those cripple minded jerks could go in and pay for the kinky stuff and then go home."

"One wife, named Doris called me to inform me her husband had came in and asked for a divorce. They had two boys. She took care of her home and boys and never worked during her thirty-five years of marriage. She fought the divorce tooth and nail, until she found out the bastard had spent all their savings and cashed in all their stock certificates. It broke her will. She just let the bastard go and was left with nothing out of a thirty-five year marriage. She got herself a job. A few months later she found out that her husband had put their entire saving in a bank account under his whore's name. His whore ran him off in six months and kept his money. Doris wouldn't have him back. I wonder if it's the same, getting screwed after thirty-five years or getting screwed after six months. There is no limit to the stupidity of men. I have many stories just like this one but I want to get back to Richard, and I know we should know them before we marry."

"Richard had seven suits of work clothes. They were faded so bad that I was ashamed for him to wear them. Even the pants hems were ragged. He was only shaving his face every other day. I thought he was doing that so no one would recognize him. Then I found out he was going to Charlie's strip joint in Sayre. He was seeing Diane, Sandra and Rose. Then there was Donna Harris. I'm talking Sayre Mining Camp, all of them! Richard had to dress like them, smell like them and looked like he came out of one of the shacks in the camp."

"But remember, when Richard worked downtown he always looked like a mannequin from head to toe. He had three pairs of work boots which he spit shinned, a pair of penny loafers which he kept on his work truck and Smitty, a co-worker of Smitty, told me Richard wore rubber gloves to keep he hands clean."

"Mr. Cannon, another co-worker of Richard, told me that Richard had never given up Melinda Brewer. Richard has been her sugar daddy for forty years."

"Remember me telling you that Richard went to the Doctor twice just to get Viagra. The first time the Doctor gave him a sample and I threw it in the garbage. The second time the Doctor gave him a prescription. I tore the prescription up as soon as I sat down in the truck seat. I told him, if he didn't service so many he wouldn't need Viagra."

"I can tell you telephone calls came in from one end of this county to the other. The one he met at the airport lived in Oak Mountain area, the Parkers from South Park and the Sartains from Gardendale and Jasper. I received calls from Robinwood, Jasper, calls from Higdon's in Forestdale and another set of Higdon's in Shady

Grove, different Wade's from Forestdale to Tennessee, and from several Parker's from Jasper, West Jefferson to Adamsville."

"There is a cosmetic lady running loose in this town. She's medium build, brown hair and in her forties and it isn't cosmetics she's selling. She sells mouth service. She gives quickies for thirty bucks a shot. She told me that she services on average five men a day and will do women for fifty bucks. Men are easier to find so she gives them a lower rate. You see sex is easy to get."

Rex said, "Yes, I'll vouch for that."

I said, "Yes, I bet you can, I hate this. I hate sorry people. I hate nasty low down people. I'm in the wrong part of this world. I want to get away from these people and I don't want to know any others like them. God is coming back and I wish He'd hurry up and get me out of this mess."

Rex said, "Drucilla there is another side to this. Don't you think you should get past all these feelings and live a little? Let me ask you a few questions. Better yet, you, tell me about yourself."

I said, "Sometimes I'm happy go lucky, fun loving and a realist. My mind never stops. I listen to people; I watch people and I did love people before I ran across all this trash. I've raced cars on an oval track, I garden, I make jams and jellies, I quilt and sew, I go fishing and play golf but most of all I love sitting on a sandy beach listening to the ocean waves. I like my men to open doors for me and pull out my chair. I love country music and have written many songs. I'm a pink and red lady. I drink sweet tea with lemon or a mix of Canadian Black Velvet, Royal Crown Cola with a twist of lemon. I love roses and day lilies. I'm a petite model for Model Creations, I love my home and yard and to dress up and go out on the town. I love fast cars, beautiful jewelry, fine firs and fine crystal. I think that about covers everything."

Rex said, "So Drucilla, what you are saying is you're an all around person. You will do almost anything twice, if it doesn't kill you the first time."

I said, "But, Rex, do not include sex in that statement and you will be right. OK Rex you're twenty years younger than me. Are you willing to talk sex with me?"

Rex said, "I sure am."

I said, "OK, why do you think girls get their toot toot waxed?"

Rex said, "So they could wear a skimpy bathing suit."

I said, "It started out with a swimsuit thing but there is the herpes thing. With all that free love crap, out comes herpes. Love is not free; you know the wages of sin. Women with herpes have an outbreak once a month. Each sore has pus seeping out and it mats in their hair. So, they wax it all off and wear loose clothes. Have you have ever seen infantigo, on a child? That's what it looks like. You can be infected from a toilet seat but for sure if you have sex with someone who is infected. What do you think about oral sex? Have you ever seen that old woman on television that talks about sex? She says it OK to slurp up that semen."

Rex said, "I know who you're talking about Drucilla. She needs to be taken off this planet. At least, made to tell the truth."

I said, "If you have a sore in your mouth, a cut from biting your tongue or the side of your jaw, a cut on your gum from biting a potato chip or even a sore throat that's all it takes. Semen is body fluid and whether it's in your mouth or up your toot toot, it means AIDS, there is a small string of blood in that semen"

Rex said, "I wouldn't ever ask my wife for this kind of service. If I needed it I'd pay a honey pot. That's what honey pots are for. They'll do what a wife wouldn't or shouldn't do."

I said, "Well, what you're telling me is I should count my blessings that Richard leaves me alone. I do, believe me."

Rex said, "Yes, that's exactly what I'm telling you!"

I said, "You are so right. After forty-two women and not long ago I heard that seventy percent of married men are gays. What do you think about that?"

Rex said, "Sad to say but that's my guess. I see it in all the restrooms, young men selling their services."

I said, "There's no shortage of stupidity! Its sits on the shoulders of parents, our government and our schoolteachers, parents are too busy to raise their children and the others are too busy tearing down America. Hell they brazenly make speeches on television that the end justifies the means and America doesn't get it. America turns a blind eye to everything when it comes to sex. America's backbone has deteriorated to jelly. Evil has prevailed. All that needs to be said is here's a rubber; go do it, do it and do it."

Rex said, "What did you tell Amanda?"

"I told her I'd kill her if she came in pregnant. I told her about the snake with one eye and a turtle neck sweater. This world needs to get back to the <u>Leave It To Beaver</u> and <u>Father Knows Best</u> days, the days when people were clean. I'd never say roll with the flow or if it feels good do it. I don't care if the year is twenty twenty. I'll never say it's OK for a man to stick it to a man or for a woman to do a woman. It's true insanity! Yet, these people are in high places, smart people. I don't give a damn who it is, if their brains can't control the lower half of their own bodies. They are too crazy to run this country. For those who think they could control their needs and don't, it just makes it sorry, insane. They are worse than drug heads and drunks."

Rex said, "But, Drucilla, I think I'd like to see two women going at it."

I asked, "What are you, half lesbian? Do you want to stick your head between a woman's legs?"

Rex said, "Damn, Drucilla, picture another woman doing that."

I said, "Shut up Rex! I know you're a fine piece of art. Tell me what you think about a preacher that would stand before one hundred fifty two women and tell them it's a sin to cut their hair. I can still see him on the pulpit with his pants stuck up the crack of his butt. His hockey pot pulls the back of his pants up, its obesity, insanity to weight four hundred fifty pounds. Remember I'm the girl that God our Heavenly Father gave a miracle. Short hair, long red nails, two-piece bathing suit and all. I'm not perfect. I know I have a bad mouth, sometimes. But, I'm one of God's chosen people. He let me know, for sure, that there is a higher power. You best believe He will make you pay for going against Him. Hey, sometimes I wonder what I do to make Him so mad at me that I get a beating every day. From Richard and his friends."

"That preacher is a chocolate milk hockey pot and a scalawag to boot. I asked him to preach on gays. I even gave him a copy of what is written in the bible about gays. He told me he couldn't preach on gays because half his congregation would leave."

Rex asked, "What does it say Drucilla?"

"Well that I can tell you. Do you think this feel good thing is worth going to hell for? Better yet, do you think there is a hell? When I was growing up the word gay meant happy and the word queer meant strange. That shows how times have changed. It wasn't long ago since these words changed to fit the times. My child knew exactly what a gay person is and what queer really means. It's really something when people are proud of being a degenerate. It's sad to me that these people have become so proud of themselves and came out of their closets in such a way that my grandchildren, someday will look at straight people as being strange."

"This is all signs of the times; sin is becoming the way of life. Righteous living is becoming history and our nation's leaders are so blind to the real problems in this country. Problems like hunger, poverty and homeless children on our streets. Their focus is on getting all the gays and lesbians, that will, to come out and serve on the white house staff or teach our children in public schools. Even serve in our armed forces, to fight our battles. See, they feel this will really improve America but according to the Bible there're dead wrong. In Romans 6:23, they'll pay the price of sin someday. It takes all we can do as Christians to raise our children not to be like the world. In John 17:15, Jesus said we'd be with them but not like them. It's a privilege to serve the Lord. He's given us all an awesome responsibility to be the best we can be for Him. This requires a day-to-day walk and a trust in Him that when we have done all we know to teach our children right from wrong. He'll do the rest as He promised in Proverbs 22:6."

"In Romans 1:26, for this cause God gave them up unto vile affection. For even their women did change the natural use into that which is against nature. And in verse 27 He said 'and likewise also the men'. Leaving the natural use of woman turned their lust one toward another. Men with men working that which is unseemly and receiving in themselves that recompense of their error which was meet. And verse 28 and even as they did not like to retain God in their knowledge, God gave them over to a reprobate mind, to do those things which are not convenient. So verse 27 explains the act of homosexuality and the rewards of it. Receiving in themselves means in their bodies. That recompense of their error means rewards for a bad mistake or departure from the truth, and which was meet means due them. What is due them is AIDS. Verse 20 of the same chapter tells before hand, they are without excuse."

"See, God laid down the plan from the start in Genesis, Chapter 1 and 2. He created Adam. He saw where man needed a helpmate. He no longer wanted Adam to be alone in the garden so He created Eve not Steve. Then He told them to have children. This was His master plan for the family. He ordained the family even before He ordained the church. It's the oldest and strongest establishment in the world. When you go against God's plan you're going against nature and sinning against your own body which is the temple of the Lord; that's in First Corinthians 6:19."

"Parents haven't taught their children to fear God. I spent one day in a Wal-Mart Super Center parking lot asking children, ages from twelve to twenty, question about Christ. Fifty percent didn't know Christ. I asked one little girl, what her cross, meant to her. She replied nothing my Grandmother gave it to me. I explained Christ to her."

"Once I met a lady and her husband for lunch at Shoney's to pick up some papers. I asked to say Grace before lunch. They had their grandson with them. He was about ten years old. When I finished Grace the grandson asked his Grandmother what was that all about. She told him they would talk about it later. I explained to him that we should always thank God for our food. He blesses the food so it will nourish our bodies so we can do good things for Him. He lives in Heaven and He watches over all of us. His grandparents were very quiet during the meal and left right after the meal."

"See, Rex, this world is sad. I can't do anything about it and life goes on. Anyway let's call it a day. I'll call you in a couple of days. That will give me time to sort things out. Give me a few days to think about Richard, and my Tony. I've got to have him, my Tony! That's what I pray for."

Chapter 6

I was on the patio waiting for Rex, with a cup of coffee in hand. I said, "I've had a few days to reflect on my story. I've only just started on the tricks that Richard has pulled on me, but I have a few of my own."

"The lampshade that Richard put his fist through, I hung it outside at the end of the carport. The next day the dark headed Goode, woman and her two kids came around the road. Remember now my road is a dead-end. She came around real slow but when she saw the lampshade she flew out like a flash."

"I had taken all I could stand so I called a friend in Alabaster and went to stay with her for a few days. The second night the Nesbitts called my friend's home and left a message on the answering machine. I called them back and a lady answered and said her husband was a preacher but wasn't home then. The next day a car backed into my friend's driveway. It has a personal tag spelling the name 'Nesbitt'. He stopped long enough for us to read the tag and left without getting out of his car. Richard has known the Nesbitts all his life. They know Richard is lying and they can carry his dead ass to the cemetery. As a matter of fact I'll send a limousine out to pick them up along with Melinda. It was a Nesbitt that was driving that Monte Carlo."

"Another thing Richard did to me. He went into the carport and threw cola all over my car and by the time I found it the cola was dried and was hell to get off. It had to be Richard because no one came to see me that entire week. The next morning I took my car and had it hand washed and laid the bill on the table in front of him. Normally I wash my car every Saturday. Putting cola on my car, cutting the buttons off my clothes, pulling the shoulder pads off my blouses and putting his fist thru the bathroom door. I just let my temper build. I hit back by spending his money. That's the only way to hurt Richard. I spent five thousand dollars on crystal and new cookware. I bought towels and anything else I could think of. I think the meanest thing I did to Richard was to sell his fishing boat. He gave me hell but I didn't care. He was the one that got my mail and tormented me to death. I never bothered a soul."

"I was getting ready for Y2K. I had food stacked in the poolroom, from floor to ceiling and three quarters of it was stolen. Every drop of my blackberry jams and jellies was taken off. I didn't say too much about it because that bastard bunch I have for a family just made fun of me. Harriet was loving it all."

"I finally had had enough on July 10th, I awoke early to go shopping. I left a note on the kitchen table for Richard. The note read, 'you can go north, east or west but get the hell out of the south'. I put a P.S. at the bottom of my note, it read, 'Roses are red; violets are blue; our love is dead; why aren't you, get the hell out of my house!' By the time I returned home that afternoon, Richard was on his way west. I can't tell you how free I felt. I wasn't afraid anymore. I didn't have to wonder what was going to happen next. During the time Richard was gone my keys were never missing. I repaired my clothes. I didn't even lock my doors at night. I called my friends and many came to help me in my yard. We cleaned the garage out. I even had an electric door placed on my carport. But peace wasn't to last long."

"The beginning of the fourth month that Richard was gone, Brandon came to me and wanted Richard to come home, Brandon needed Richard to help him with his schoolwork. My neighbor up the street told me he had talked to Richard and Richard had hurt himself and wanted to come home. Percy told me the same thing and wanted to know if I thought I'd hurt Richard enough. Then Richard started sending me money, gifts and love letters. He said he'd get to the bottom of it all. He'd leave no stone unturned. Now I can see that I was too lazy to live. Too lazy to get out and find someone to love me. I lied to myself. I had the answers! All Richard wanted was my home, my family and to see me dead, and by then I wanted to die. Well I let Richard come back and he ran this place. He screamed at me and I'm sure he didn't live without whatever it was that made him crazy."

"Brandon and Richard would go fishing every Saturday. If Brandon didn't want to go then Percy would. Then Percy told me he wasn't ever going fishing with Richard again. I asked him why. Boy did he tell me an ear full. He said Richard goes to the bank of the lake and off into the woods to take a dump, every time and the last time Richard was gone for forty minutes. I thought he was exaggerating but then he said that's why Brandon won't go with him. I'm talking about Walker County Lake, Richard got mad as hell because Percy wouldn't go fishing one Saturday and I hated to leave the house. Things had started happening again. I made eighteen jars of blackberry jam, the week before, and every jar walked right out of my kitchen, while it was still hot on the stove. My heart was broken but I didn't say much. Anyway Richard was heart set on going fishing so I told him I'd go with him. He jumped to his feet and went out to load the truck. I packed us a lunch and off we went. We were the only ones fishing that day. We fished up and down the banks and never got a bite. Richard paddled the boat into a slough. He hadn't said a word about taking a dump. We went to the far end of the slough and then Richard started paddling out of the slough as fast as he could. We didn't get but a few feet when, all of the sudden, a young white boy and a black girl walked out of the woods. The black girl ran to the water's edge and was jumping up and down screaming, 'Here I is, here I is!' I asked Richard who she was. Hell we were the only people on the lake. I never saw another person on the lake that day. Richard never said a word. He just paddled as fast as he could. I swear on the life of everyone I love that is the truth. Now I knew why Percy and Brandon had to wait in the boat and where my blackberry jam and other foods had gone. If I'd brought my gun that day I'd have shot the bastard right there and then. I don't think there is a judge in the world that would have found me guilty. Hate has caused many a murder and that is why I'm so vengeful and why I'm going to look hard for a man that will love just me. I swear to God I was looking around for the gas can when it dawned on me we only had a trolling motor and battery. Richard is the luckiest bastard in the world. I can still hear, 'Here I is!'"

"I can't wait until Judgment Day. I know I'll have a front row seat when it's Richard's time. I have acted so stupid. I've looked over lie after lie, as my young years past. It all goes back to education. It's better to be dead than to feel like one must stay in a life of hell."

Rex said, "Drucilla you no longer have to feel that way. You have friends, powerful friends. I've met a couple since I've been here."

I said, "Rex, be true to the people you meet, have friends and more friends, and always shoot straight with them. In other words, never lie. I ask you, what could I have ever done, to get a DeRoy and a Mama Marcelle combined.

"Telling you all this has made me understand that I should have gone to my friend and had him move me away from this place or I should have took my life and got out of all this. This home and all the goodies in it, is sure not worth all that has happened to me. I keep telling myself, over and over again what Mr. Williams always told me. We make our own luck. I tell you even though I don't believe in running from man to man. If I had it to do again, I would. This shame is on me. I let this happen to me. After my third marriage to Richard, Mr. Williams told me that I didn't want to divorce Richard, that I just wanted for him to behave but he's never going to do it. He would always be what he is and nothing else."

"Rex, take a look at my home inside and out and then look at me. People think I have it all. What I have is, memories of hell, just hell and torment all of my life. Will these memories ever leave my mind?"

Rex said, "I've heard that saying it out loud helps it go away and telling me your story is saying it out loud and if I can do anything to help it go away well, I'm your man."

I said, "I'm so disgusted with myself! Look, at all my family! Just where the hell are they? Look at Brandon. Richard hates Brandon. He didn't help Brandon with his math. Brandon told me all Richard did was have his screaming fits with him. Brandon is like me. He thought Richard loved him and would someday stop all the hurt. Well he hasn't and never will. We know Richard will never grow up. Both of us have given up on him. What is he! He doesn't want sex from me! He told me more than once that I would never stop him from getting what he wants. You write this damn story and tell me what is it he wants!"

"I know what I want and I'm going after it! So Rex, hurry up and get through with me. Write this story and do what you want with it. It makes me sick! I really do think God is punishing me for not listening to my soul. God gives us a whisper now and then but do you think we do make our own Heaven and hell."

"I can tell you this, the next time Mr. Right walks into my life, it will ring in my ears, I love you but I don't like you. Richard told me that many a time but the table has turned. I can now say there are worse things than living alone and that is living with someone that hates you. Richard makes everyone think he loves me but that's just a joke. I'll say it again. I'm in prison! Death couldn't be as bad. I see death as a peaceful sleep. Like being asleep at three thirty in the morning, when most of the world is quiet. When you're asleep your brain is at rest—and I want to be at rest."

"I've always felt like a jewel that no one in Hollywood would ever wear. I have always been Miss Glamorous. Only Tony has ever made me weak in the knees and that was only a dream. Life is just a big joke—cause you can't get out of it until you die."

"I sit here telling you that I hate whores, but I should have been one. Richard didn't want children and I did. I should have had six of them with highly educated men. I love to laugh out loud, Richard didn't. I was a joy, and Richard was unpleasant."

"The most handsome man in the world told me once that I was a slow burner. I didn't know what a slow burner was and still don't. Maybe I should ask him."

"I know now that it's Tony that I could love. I swear when I think about Tony, my teeth sweat. I would be his, once a week lovers in some hide away. Even now I can hear Conway singing, 'I know you've never been this far before.'"

Rex asked, "My God, Drucilla, is this you talking to me? Do you want the world to spin for you? The stars to shoot across the sky? Do you want to win the lottery?"

I said, "No, Rex! I just want the man that thinks I could charm God off His throne, a man to give me a day of love that I could hold on to, forever. I know it would be wrong. But it would be so good."

Rex said, "Drucilla look at me. Is this you?"

I began to cry. Rex walked over to me and held me in his arms.

Rex said, "It's OK, everything will work out."

I said, "Yes, it's OK. I'm just so sick of this. Going back over what Richard has done to me, hurts so bad. Normally he can't make me cry."

Rex said, "Drucilla maybe it's not Richard. Maybe it's just talking about it. We have covered the people and the cars that have hurt you. You know where they all live. I think I've got it down enough that I can let you rest for a while."

I said, "Alright just don't forget about the time I thought I was in a dream, but I wasn't. I was almost asleep from my sleeping pill and Richard put me in a chair with rollers and rolled me up to a propane gas heater. I barely remember trying to push myself away from the heater. It wasn't hot it was just the raw gas and it was burning my nose. I don't remember getting into bed but for three days I couldn't get out of bed and I could hardly remember anything. My head hurt so bad for so long. I didn't tell anyone about this but I stopped taking the Ambien sleeping pills. Rex you need to talk to Amanda about this pill. No one needs to take this pill."

"You know I've been looking for what had caused this problem since January 12, 1996, when the light blue Camaro at Hogg's barbeque circled my car. Then went up the hill behind the barbeque and came down with Richard, in his truck, right on their bumper. I had a close look at Richard in his truck for four good blocks. They were heading back toward Gardendale. I headed for home. I arrived before Richard and he came in looking like a sheep killing dog. I caught him in a lie that day. He changed the time he got off work and the bastard didn't think I'd catch it. I went back to Hogg's and drove every route between there and Richard's work place in Gardendale. It only took four minutes on the longest route."

"I made Richard go with me looking for the blue Camaro. We went up Mount Olive Road toward Corner as we got near Kendrall

Blackmon's home, there sat an older blue Camaro. Richard went into hysterics, his hands and feet broke out with nerves. He was scratching from head to toe. Then he went into a crazy rage shaking his fist at me. He screamed at me that I was going to get him shot in the face. I told him I hoped it would be soon."

"I turned up the pressure. I left a sheet of paper on the kitchen table with Mike Pickle and Pete Pickens names on it, nothing else. Richard went into a depressed state and his nerves broke out looking like the measles. Then I found the name Patricia Pickens. I hired an investigator to find her. She was a bank teller. I confronted Richard. He denied knowing them and wouldn't discuss it with me. I knew better. I found their name and number in his book."

"I want to stress the fact. This has been very nerve racking, keeping my feelings tender and my nerves on edge. Hell, my Doctor recommended me to give him more sex than he could stand. I did for one week and at the end of that week Richard came home from work and told me, with the meanest look on his face, he couldn't give me what I wanted and left the room. When he sat down for dinner I asked him if he didn't have anybody that he could enjoy life with, why was I living in hell here on earth? Then I was told he wasn't going to do without what he wants. He leans over, our faces almost touching and says he wasn't going to do without what he wants. I asked the gutless bastard 'Just what is it you wanted?' He claimed up and didn't say another word."

"I asked him, who made the call to a mental health help line in Milton, Florida. It was on my home phone bill. The call was made from this house. He wouldn't answer me so I called the number. A recording told me if I needed assistance to call a beeper number. A man named Billy Jackson returned my call. I asked whom he had talked to from the Hallmark house and what it was about. Mr. Jackson told me it was my spouse or a family member. They wanted to know how to have someone committed. He explained that they would have to take me to a Doctor, then to a Judge and prove to the court that I was not capable of taking care of everyday affairs. Then the court would turn me over to the state and place me in a mental facility. I believe that is just what that bastard, Richard was trying to do to me. If this is not true, I want answers to my questions."

"I'll give you two more examples and then try to wind this up. I wanted him to take me to his foreman, when he worked in the central district, and talk about his vacation in nineteen eighty four. I wanted nineteen ninety-four, ninety-five, and ninety-six vacation schedules given to me. I wanted him to take me to face the Sartain's, Becky Holloman, Terry Nix on Copeland Ferry Road, the Parkers, Drummonds, Donna Turner, Barbara Aaron, Barbara and Melinda Vines the Estes, the Byrams and the Knoxs. This could all be done without causing a scene."

"The Knoxs for example, a friend told me to watch what was going on Republic Road. I drove down to the end of this road and found a telephone truck in front of a house. I sat there a few minutes and Richard walks out the front door and standing in the doorway was a woman in a see through nightgown with a baby in her arms. It was four thirty in the afternoon. Richard walked over to me and asked if I was lost. Talking to me as if I was a stranger. I said, hell no, I know where I am, where I have been, where I'm going and I know who she is too! I drove away remembering that on Richard's voice mail beeper, the week before, the message read Personal, Urgent. If this was not to tell Richard that a baby was being born, then I want Richard to let his boss tell me who would put a message like that on his beeper. Also to explain all the overtime he works that he did not get paid for. I knew he wouldn't, no man would."

"I'm so tired of being told that I'm lying about these things, like the smell of perfume in his truck, cake wrappers, sticky items that a sticky child's hand had been playing with and finding the middle seat belt adjusted to fit a small child. When I asked Richard about these, he screams at me to shut my damn mouth and stay out of his truck."

"That reminds me about the call I received reminding me to watch out for Richard going to work early. As he was going out the door I told Richard I wanted to use his truck that day. We were about half way to the work center when Richard turned into a wild crazy man. He screamed that I was going to have to leave his truck alone. I told him I'd drive the damn truck anytime I took a notion. We were about three blocks from the work center and there she sat. An old blue Camaro sat beside West Hardware Store. I could now see her. She had short blond hair. I did know her, Nix was her name. I knew who I was looking for because the week before she was sitting there. I let Richard out and drove off but I didn't go far. I sat watching the work center. A man in his early seventies, driving a green Jeep, stopped at the work center and sat there as if waiting for someone to come out. Everyone had left the work center except for Richard. I cranked up and started toward the Jeep. He left too fast for me to get his tag number. After that they tried to run me off US Seventy Eight Highway. It was the crazy woman in the white car from the park incident who threatened to arrest me. I want to put all these bastards behind bars or six feet under with dirt in their mouth."

"Richard once said that I had destroyed him but looking out of my eyes I'm the one that has been destroyed. I am the one this is being done to. I have been the target to everything I've told you. I'm not worried about these bastards because I'm being watched over by the Graysville Police, the Brookside Police and now what I call my big brothers, the Jefferson County Sheriff Department. Richard hates me and I can prove it to any Judge. Richard is not as smart as I am. He's not as handsome as I am pretty. He has no morals. He has no conscience. I'll bet he's licked more shit off a whore's ass than I've ever flushed."

"Melinda, the hairdresser, clawed Richard's back up, just so I could see. She bragged, at the beauty shop that wives should know and that was her way of telling them by clawing their backs up. Richard said he got caught in some bushes but his shirt didn't even have a pull on it. The only bush he was caught in was another Melinda. The Amazon woman has two grown kids and a seven year old, brain damaged boy. Her daughter is a tall, slim woman, with wheat blond hair, and a bastard child, like Mother like daughter. Mamma whore had her hair braided with beads. She was trying to be his Indian squaw. Guess what? Her neighbors thought she was dating a black man. It was just Richard."

"I wouldn't have believed it but my Jerry told me that Richard has had many a glass of tea with them on his hot days out working.

The Hollomans down on the river were once Claytors. The Bakers and Watts and don't leave out Rosa, she's from Sumiton. She was Richard's dancer and then I'm told about Sandra, she's the daughter of one of Richard's whores in Pleasant Grove. Rex you won't believe this. Richard had a whore thirty five years ago and this whore had a seven year old daughter. Now the seven year old is grown and she is one of Richard's whores. Mother and daughter fight over who is going to dance with Richard."

Rex said, "I wonder what he does to put a spell on so many women. It can't be just sex, they could get that on any corner."

I said, "Don't kid yourself we know it was drugs. Go find Norma Jean Harris and ask her. She's one of the bitches that drove the beautiful blue Camaro registered to the Bates in Sayre. Oh, let's not forget Diane Langford. Sayre looks like a dead town but you can believe their women are horny. It looks trashy and the people are raunchy. Cordova is a clean little town but this place turns out more red headed whores than any other. Jasper in Walker County, Jefferson and Blount Counties are running a close race. I went to different Wal-Mart stores in each county and interviewed people in the parking lot. I interviewed fifty men from all walks of life. Men say women have something they want and they won't turn it down. One man said he kept a douche bag under the front seat of his truck. All my life I've believed that if you're married, you do not have sex with anyone else. You don't even put yourself in a spot to think about it."

"Rex, I've been hit on by many men and I have always joked it off. Now, if sex, has nothing to do with love, I'm waking up a little too old, or maybe I'm just in time to teach this roll. Say for instance, if my man isn't listening to my needs or I need new tires or the power bill is due or I just want a shopping trip for the kids. I find myself a man with a need and take his money. There's one thing for sure, no one will climb between my sheets and part my thighs if it doesn't mean money, big money, not pocket change. Do you see where I'm going? If you could get rid of this Angel that lives within me I could have that home in the Hamptons plus a vacation home in Salt Lake City, Utah."

"Do you realize that Richard has bought or helped to buy all these look alike blue Camaros. He has paid dearly for his whores. If Alabama would legalize prostitution I could hire them all and get a percentage of Richard's money."

Rex said, "Drucilla do you know its hell to know that you're an Angel?"

I said, "Do you know there's going to be hell in Heaven when I get there? I'm going to find my Guardian Angel and kick his ass."

Rex said, "Get off my back, Drucilla. Remember I'm a man."

I said, "I'll get off your back and in your face. To be honest with you Rex, I'm ashamed of myself. God will forgive all these things that I haven't forgiven Richard and his whores for. It wasn't any fun working in the garden, canning, sewing and quilting. It was hot as hell in the kitchen making jams and jellies. Not to mention being home alone all my life. All the food I've cooked and threw out is money I don't have in the bank. The septic tank is the richest thing I have."

"I am able to cope with Richard because I know I have my medical insurance. I have Angels like Johnnie, Mr. Williams, Jerry and Becky just to name a few. These people are as near to as the phone. Even you Rex, Telling my story has made me feel different. You have me wanting to investigate you. You are Uncle Louie's son, aren't you?"

Rex said, "Yes, you know I am."

I said, "Somehow, someway my Tony sent you here for me, didn't he?"

Rex said, "Come off it girl. What was it that you said to me when I first met you? Let's see, oh yea, 'Ask me no questions and I'll tell you no lies.'"

I said, "Fool, I also said that I didn't tell lies because I'm not smart enough to keep up with them. So I'm telling you now, I don't want to save Richard from going to hell. I want to send him to hell. I know more of the truth on him than I need to know. His sins don't sit on my shoulders. I don't even feel sorry for him anymore. I don't pity him and I sure as hell don't love him."

"You know I'm sick of hearing people say, I love you with all my heart. The heart is just a muscle, an organ like the lungs or kidneys. This love thing is just a brain thing. I'm a different girl right now. I'm my favorite person. I know now, in time I'll get what I want. Don't you think so?"

"Girl, I know it's time to go now. Just a little while ago you were showing me some one's deathbed."

"Oh yes! You want to go back. I'll let you rest in his deathbed, if you like. It's real cool, too."

"No, no, no I don't want to go. Girl, you're freaking the hell out of me."

I stood there just looking at Rex. I was thinking, "Tony didn't send you, I take it all back you don't belong to my Uncle Louie nothing would freak him out."

I said, "Cool down, I wasn't going to take you there again. Let's get real I'm too smart to let anyone know a secret on me. That is, anyone I don't trust. I assure you, what I do, I do alone until I'm with Tony and you can rest assured I will be someday."

"Rex, please let's not start back on this story until Wednesday about ten in the morning. Meanwhile, I want you to go over the part about the car at Hogg's Barbeque in case I missed something."

Rex said, "Now, something new to ask you, I've talked to my son Charlie about you. He thinks you're real cool and he wants to know if you will let him e-mail you."

I said, "Tell him sure; also tell him to have patience with me. I'm not at all smart on these computers."

Chapter 7

I couldn't go to sleep for thinking about Hogg's Barbeque. Half asleep I remember saying to myself, God won't give me more trouble than I can handle but does he remember that I'm just a little girl.

The next morning I awoke and went into the bathroom. Looking in the mirror, I said out loud, "Good morning Mrs. Stress I can deal with you today."

With pen, paper and a glass of tea in hand I walked out onto the patio. I wanted to make notes on what I was to tell Rex. I wanted most of all to make Rex understand just what I want. I had a long list by the time Rex arrived.

I said, "I know you said you had enough information on Richard but I think you'll want to hear this, and I'm going to give you some of the same names because I don't want to leave out anyone."

"Give me a moment for my laptop to warm up."

I said, "We were driving around a little subdivision when I noticed a little red car following us. I parked in front of a house and the red car parked. When I moved, he moved. I turned around and chased him down to get his tag number. Richard was really pissed. The car was registered to a medical examiner named Jeff Jones. I may have mentioned him before, but what I didn't tell you happened the next day. I didn't wake until one forty-five that afternoon and I had blood on my left hand. My hand was burning as if on fire and even today the vein in my left hand looks pinched. It still burns every once in a while. I was sleeping by myself but I had started taking Ambien again, that's the sleeping pill that many times I have had a sore spot on my hips, with bruising, and feeling drugged all day. I decided to stay in the house and keep quiet until I got back to normal.

Remember I found the Mental Health Center's phone number on my bill. You might need the number; it's area code 904-983-0494 located in Milton, Florida. I talked to Billy Jackson, his beeper number is 904-435-0168 and he told me that someone was planning to put me away. Believe me I got in the know about what was going on around my house."

"After that blew over I called and we went to check out the McKeever's at One Hundred Oaks Trailer Park. I caught her on my road and by this time I had a long list. We checked out the Estis, Mary Hayes, a black and white Monty Carlo, Knox's and the Nix. What a story the Nixs are. I received calls from Robert Nix wanting to be paid for building a porch on Tammy Nix's house. I thought I had Richard then. I told him to bring Tammy to my house at five thirty that day, my husband would be home and we would talk about it. They never showed up, that day or any day."

"Then the Shoemaker's in Center Point drove down here to my road and told me that the blue car I was looking for was involved in a murder in West Jefferson. Then a whore called asking for Richard. She called two times from a Pizza Hut and then from Langley's home all the same night. I talk to him for a solid month before he told me her name. He said her name was Sherrie and Richard had helped her get her commercial driver's license. I made Richard call her while I listened in. Sherrie told Richard that her Mother had told her that he had called yesterday. Richard didn't make a denial not even that he didn't know her. Sherrie hung up saying, 'I'll see you around'. I sat there remembering the Alessio calls. It was really weird. I returned a call from caller identification. I called 591-991-9423 and the person that answered told me I had called a pay phone at the airport. He gave me the number on the pay phone, it was 591-9423. I dialed the 991-9423 another day and Alessio answered the phone and said it was his home phone. I asked him about the pay phone at the airport and he denied knowing anything about it. I received calls from Donna Marks, Rosaline and Becky Peivee all asking for Richard."

"Two weeks before Richard was retiring from his job. He told me the company was sending him to school for a week. Get this, two weeks!! Ask the President, why would the company send a man to school one week before he retires. Anyway, a day or two before Richard was supposed to go to school I made him take me to the Brookwood Mall. He parked right beside a blue Camaro with a tag number that I knew. I walked over to the car and Richard went wild. He acted like a bastard the whole time we were in the mall. It was only Sherrie Wilson's car and she lived about four minutes from the school that Richard was going to. I can't imagine a man retiring from a company being sent to school with one week to work. I guess it was whoring 101 classes."

"Then there were the Bakers, McCartys, Hollomans and the Sartains. Good old Robinwood, Sandusky, Pell City, Kelly's Trailer Park in Kimberly and Scaley Bark Drive in Adamsville where Miranda Cooper Nix lives. That Kelley Drive in the Kelley Trailer Park was a place to remember, from Kimberly to Mount Olive to Holly Grove Road in Jasper to my dead end road. And don't forget Sumiton. I know the list goes on and on. I know of forty-two women that have called for Richard at my house."

"Stupid! That's what I am! Yes but I wouldn't let Richard touch me with a ten foot pole. He sure must have some tool that I don't know anything about. I've gone through a hell of a lot with Richard. I was too stupid to know he was living a single life style. On my birthday he took a half of a day off work but didn't come home until 7 pm."

"I want to make sure I've told about the Turner car. It was an older black Camaro with two red stripes on the hood running from front to back. It followed me two times before I turned around and ran it down. I ran the tag number and went to their house. The Camaro was in the yard, I beat and beat on the front door of the house and no one would come to the door."

"A Glassco boy in a little white truck parked at the stop sign for thirty minutes looking at my house. I drove up to his truck and asked if he was looking for someone. He said he was just sitting there. I told him if he wasn't visiting someone on this road that he didn't have any business being on this road. He asked me if I owned this road. I screamed back at him, you damn right I do. He wasn't as stupid as he looked; he tucked tail and ran. I've found five different Jeff

Jones: a drug head, a drunk, a whore, a whore hopper and a medical examiner."

"I had planned a wonderful night for Richard and Brandon. I even hate to tell you about this night. I cooked a grand dinner just for my two boys. As they sat looking over the table I asked them how it looked. Richard shocked me to death by saying He didn't know about Brandon but he was used to eating shit. I walked out of the kitchen, picked up my keys and left the house. To this day I can't stand to cook. Later I told Richard that I hoped he lived to be an old man so I could feed him shit, and so help me I will. Speaking of shit reminds me of the Vines, McAdams, Roberts and the Walls."

"Richard went to have me a sign made at Vital Sign Company. Week after week I asked him if it was ready. Richard said, 'She said for me to come back in a few days.' Two months later I went by there and got my sign plus I found the cars that had been on my road. The day I picked up my sign the girl asked if my brother was OK. I said he sure is, thanks for asking."

"Lord I want to make sure you know about Rose, at the Pit Stop and Sandra and Donna Harris. Richard and I were married for three years when he had an affair with a whore named Faye Wilkerson. It lasted for seventeen months, the affair. The whore was from Pleasant Grove. How unreal could this be but it is so true. Sandra is one of Richard's whores and the daughter of Faye Wilkerson. This is the best example of monkey see, monkey do. I can't help but wonder if I tell this out loud, would anyone believe that one man could take on so many women. Now Sandra, Donna and Rose have the same nickname of 'lick-a-dick-a-day-woman'. But who will tell me how much can one man take."

Rex said, "Yes, Drucilla, you have told me all about these people and I think you've had one beer too many."

I said, "Richard has had many women with the same names and has helped them all buy Camaro's and Firebirds the same colors, a light blue, two dark blue and two red. He has helped some of these whores pass their test to become nurses and two that I know of to pass their commercial driving license test. He has paid for three boys to be in the boy scouts and has helped a whore's Daddy for over a year when he almost cut his arm off with a circular saw while working on a porch."

"As I sit here telling my story to you I couldn't help but think that I was talking about a man that doesn't have a family. He is a very quiet man around me. He doesn't want to hear me or see me. In our last thirteen years of hell he hasn't put his hands on me and very few times in our whole life together. He's calm and quiet and gives me what money he thinks I need and doesn't care if I spend it or keep it. Like I've said a hundred times before he wants me to leave him alone and I do until trouble comes to my home."

"I know how Richard passed the lie detector test ten years ago. He didn't consider me as his wife and he has no conscious. He has had a few close encounters. Once while driving downtown a city bus ran a red light and hit Richard's truck in the driver's side door and he came out of it without a scratch. One of Richard's co-workers told me about the accident two years later. Another time he was up in the bucket of the bucket truck and was hanging out over the street when a tractor-trailer came by and clipped the bottom of the bucket. He came out again without a scratch. Something broke and the bucket spun around like a top. Usually the bucket turns upside down and the person inside lands on his head in the street. Richard has the devil in his pocket looking out for him. It was months before I heard about that, too. He was receiving an incentive check for years before I found out about it. I was with Richard when one of his co-workers asked him what he was going to do with his incentive check. During that time I found out about the bedroom in the basement of the central work center. I must say I've learned more about downtown Birmingham, Gardendale and Graysville than a new street reporter for a newspaper. Like the Shelby Finance Company, Richard said it was a cubby hole with one old man in it. He neglected to tell me about sweet little Teresa and the queer club on the next floor. You should have seen the look on Richard's face when I told him the guys were harmless. They love us girls because we buy their silk flowers, crystal figurines, we let them do our hair and we let them play with our men. But I'm sure one of them could be real mean if someone was trying to take away his lover. One of those would never have any trouble out of me because if I found out Richard was one of them I'd give him two sleeping pills, tie a fishing line around his privates and the other end to the ceiling fan and when he awoke I'd turn it on. I wonder how many women are sleeping in the same bed with a queer or maybe like us sleeping in different rooms for years and years."

Rex asked, "What did you say? Drucilla, Drucilla!"

"Sorry Rex, I was off in a daze. Now where was I? Oh yea, with a slip of the tongue the truth can jump out. I can't leave wrong alone. Some women can act deaf, dumb and blind. God knows I can't."

I handed Rex a hand full of letters. Rex opened one and read.

"To whom it may concern;

I've known Drucilla Hallmark for at least fifteen years. I've never heard anyone speak ill of her. Her actions, in my presents, have always been that of a Lady and in my opinion her morals are above reproach.

Francis S. Key
3 August 1995"

"Drucilla whatever you do girl, don't lose any of these letters."

I said, "Don't you worry. This is just the start. I have letters from Richard admitting that he lied about the Shelby Finance Company, the garage girl and admitted that I was not important to him. He also stated that he did not enjoy it but he knew it was wrong. I took these letters to Father Cross. He told me to take out the nots and read it back to him. It pays to have friends in high places. They can see what you have overlooked."

"If you get your book out maybe this will help someone else that is caught up in a situation like mine. I'll just get some sun, on the lounger here, while you finish up. I couldn't sleep last night so it's all down on paper for you to go over."

"Wake up Drucilla! You're red as a beet. I think I've caught up with you. Anyway I want you to tell me about Hogg's Barbeque again. I think I missed something. What was that Camaro?"

"OK Rex, it was a beautiful blue Camaro IROC, Super Sports. It was very sporty with ground effects and every window was so black you couldn't see inside. Now just up Cherry Avenue there are two dark blue Camaros, just alike, one belongs to a young queer boy and the other belongs to the girl that works in Hogg's Barbeque."

Chapter 8

"One of the Graysville police called me one day and asked me if I would consider speaking to a group of battered women living in a home for battered women. I told him I would but I wouldn't baby them. We set a date and time for the speech and I went to writing my speech."

"I arrived at the Center and was shocked to see so many women there. I didn't expect more than a hand full. I went straight into my speech. Here is a copy of it . . ."

"What do you have hidden in the compartments of your brain? Have you injured your pride? Have you wrapped your feeling up in self-pity? Do you grieve because you can't be your real self? Are you surrounded with people that think you're the happiest person in the world? Do you laugh when you really want to cry?"

"There's one thing I know. You do not have to struggle alone, if you have a respectable Father or a for sure best friend. One that will not pity you, one that will tell you what you need to hear, not what you want to hear. Go to them and spill your guts. Just say I'm miserable. It doesn't matter if it's mismanagement of money or some company or some fool trying to jerk you around. Whatever it is that gets you down, tell it. I don't care if you're five foot seven, weighting two hundred forty pounds; you may just need someone to hold you while you cry. Don't wait until you are pushed to the point that you wished you could get a Doctor to say you're bipolar just so you can kick ass for a few days. You know you can't do that! So Ladies! Stay calm, go see that special someone and talk. You need help. It's a lot easier to go through things with someone's help."

"If you have been all used up and think maybe you're not worth saving. Then keep searching until you find a friend like I have. I really mean what I say, because I do have a friend like this. I call him my Equalizer. I've yet to find a man that's equal to my friend. First I'm not a whiner and I tell him the truth, the good, the bad and the ugly. He doesn't put up with beating around the bush. He asks what is it you really want. I'm the first to say I'm a mover and a shaker. I talk back. Hey, I don't talk back to this friend. If he says get over there and sit on your roost. I find a roost and sit down. But I love him and I know he will take care of any problem that I can't. So far it's been without leaving his desk."

"Once I was mad because my husband was running around on me. I told my husband, I'd have my friend erase him from my life. He screamed back my friend couldn't hurt him. I told him if my friend had to put his hands on you, you'd never have another erection and if you keep running your tongue you wouldn't have that for a sex tool either. I want each of you girls to take out pen and paper and write me the reasons you're in this place."

"I thought, The girls were getting pumped up by now and after a fifteen minute break I was shocked, reading the reports, nine out of twelve were ashamed to go home to their parents. The rest of the parents lived out of town because they met their man on the Internet."

"Two wanted to know how I felt. I went back on stage to answer their questions. I don't look like I belong here, do I? Why, because I outsmarted my husband? He had money and I wanted everything money could buy. You have to know what it is you want! Do you want love from him or do you want money. I want you to use your brain. Money is freedom, money is power!"

"Think back at the things your Mother may have said or your old Aunt or even a neighbor Lady. First I'm going to tell you that my Mother gave me away to a sorry ass man when I was still a child. I was a child having a child. I moved from house to house, half starved to death and I was in misery but I got out of that. Even as a child I knew what I wanted. Then I married the same man three times because I wanted his money. Oh yes! I know how you feel but I don't feel sorry for you, none of you. All of you have an education. One of you has worked for a bank for thirteen years. All of you had good jobs. What's wrong with you? That stuff called love or is it really called being too lazy to live. The room got quiet. When I told you to get yourself a friend, I wasn't talking about people less than yourself. What was it your Mother said? Girls you're known by the company you keep. Think about it. Girls you're known by the way you look or by the way you talk. If you lay down with dogs you'll get fleas. You can't do drugs or drink and love yourself. That, is number one on your list, love yourself first."

"I asked my friend to get me a divorce. He looked me straight in the eyes and told me I didn't want a divorce. I wanted my husband to straighten up and act right and he was right. I had to face that. He said, 'You and I, both know he won't.' What I needed was to live the life that makes me happy and stop giving a damn what he does. Let him live his life and for me to do the same. I couldn't stop his words from running through my mind, over and over again."

"A girl friend of mine and I went to Cordova, a small town southeast of Jasper, to buy quilt batten. The owner of the store was the nicest man you'd ever want to meet. He owned most of the town and was eighty-eight years old. Mr. Tatum gave us not only a good deal on the merchandise, plus a silver dollar to remember him by but most of all some good advice. Mr. Tatum asked me as we were leaving, 'Honey, does your husband tell you that you're beautiful and he loves you every morning.' I always tell it like it is and said. 'No.' He said, 'Then cross your legs and keep them crossed until he learns to say it.' You know that old man gave me more than money could buy. He told me I was worth at least a good morning, I love you. Now, what are you worth!"

"We have laws. You can either get your good morning I love you or his money for not saying it. We can have true good friends and we can all pull together. Now, for those who don't like their jobs, get a better job, a place to stay and get out of the hell you're in. Pull yourself up by your boot strings and get a life. Tell the ones that made you run in this door that you're not running anymore. Tell him you don't need his type."

"My best friend told me to draw a circle around me and let it be my world. Don't even listen to television news if you're going to worry about it. You can only take care of so much so start with yourself. That's what I do. I make some of my clothes, I work in my yard, I make quilt tops and quilt them and I help young people. I don't smoke, it cost money, I don't do drugs it controls your mind, it costs money plus makes you crazy. Drinking liquor messes up your mind. We don't need that. All these things cause trouble it doesn't help to cope with trouble. These are things that sick, weak people do. None here are sick or weak or you wouldn't be here. My Grandmother use to say, 'We may be poor but we can be clean.' Clean of all things that makes us wrong. Clean of all things that control us. You can be the bug or the windshield. Now I'm coming back day after tomorrow and I want you to listen to a tape I've made for you and I want you to tell me what you're worth."

"Before I go I'll leave you with something to think about. I could tell you to go back to that hellhole and feed him a bucket of lard every day. Light him one cigarette after another and mix his drinks stronger and stronger then give him a laxative every time he roughs you up, but no, I'm telling you to stay here a few more days and think about what I've said."

"For those of you that need a job I know of a new restaurant that's about to open and they need fourteen workers. All of you have jobs if that's what you want. Now make a list of everything you want from the place you were living. I have a Sheriff friend that will go with you and get whatever it is you want but it must be your personal things. All things disputed must go through the court system. If you want to start over then now is the time. But before I leave here today I must say if you don't take this time to better yourself, well, don't come back here whining. Suck it up girls, spend his money or get the hell out."

"Call your Mother and tell her you love her and that you wished you had listened to her ten years ago. Talk to your Father; tell him you want to see him face to face. Don't get in a conversation about your past life. Tell him you need help in taking some steps in a new direction of your life. Tell him you're coming over to talk to him."

"Now, you listen to me. No one owns your brains! No one is going to heaven or hell for you. Only you can decide if you're going to be an earth polluter, or a first class citizen. Be the first class person I know you can be. I know what you're saying, that I make it sound easy, don't I? Hell, life is not easy but tomorrow is coming, like it or not. So what is it going to be? A different tomorrow or do you like your yesterdays. Think about it and I'll see you soon."

"The next time I went to see the girls I had applications for jobs in my hand. I told them the main thing I see is wasted time. I want all of you to start a day calendar. The first thing on your calendar, write in two days a week to go to a library and tutor a child. You can almost choose your time. Do something every day for someone else even if it's just to hold a door open. Give smiles to everyone, put a spring in your step, this tells everyone that you know you're somebody. You already know you're somebody. You just have to keep reminding yourself. Every morning after you've washed the sleep out of your eyes, look in the mirror and say, 'I love you.' I'm going to do something for you today', and do it! Take a good look at yourself. Some people never do. Go to the mall and watch other people. If you don't like what you see, then make the effort and look to see if you're doing the same. I'm here to tell you if a woman has a lick of sense, the heels of her feet will be clean and soft and not looking like a pan of cornbread. Her hair will be clean. Her nails will be clean. Another thing, I cringe at some of the clothes. I do not wear fad clothing. I wear what I feel good in, what I look good in."

"God gave you a brain now use it. Please leave a speck of decency in the minds of the little ones. I wrote a poem about the children and I'll read it for you, it's named . . .

The Children Are Watching You

>
> The children are watching you
> Be careful what you do
> For what you do
> Want escape their eyes
> They'll think it's OK
> To try it too

Don't injure their minds
With doubt and despair
Fill them with faith hope and joy
Fill their lives with love

Today do you do what
You heard and saw
Do you remember
The good and the bad
The things your parents said
What will their children hear
See and say someday
Are you teaching
Your child better ways

Choosing your partner
You choose the color of their eyes
And the shape of their body
And their size
Do you know that when
Your children are born
God gave your life to them

Don't injure their minds
With doubt and despair
Fill them with faith hope and joy
Fill their lives with love
Fill their lives with love."

"All in all I've said is don't be foolish. It's called mental deficiency, mental retardation when you waste your young years. I want you to think a lot about love. Yes love! First of all you can learn to love anybody that's good to you. Ask yourself, what is it you want. What do you want to be worth? Then where would you like to live? Do you want to fit in to the upper class, middle class, low class, or so bad you'd have to climb a ladder to be white trash."

"Now, I may be the first and only person to tell you this but if you say anything less than middle class well, my advice is to find a way to put yourself to sleep for good. You and everyone else should be trying to set a pattern of perfection to everyone in your midst."

"Hey, the first thing that comes to mind is the baggy ass boys running around with one hand holding up their pants. Do you think for one minute that they have anyone that loves them? Hell no! They don't even love themselves. I know of three brothers and their Daddy would have yanked them up by the nap of the neck and told them to look decent, act decent or they will stop breathing because he'd beat them to death or at least make them think that he would."

"You make your own luck in this world. You can get out in this world and be whatever it is you want to be, it only takes work. Or you could look like, act like and even be a criminal just as easy as being a good person. I may be the first to tell you if I had my way I'd give all criminals a shot and put them to sleep. I'm not a bleeding heart. I'm sick of hearing this and that happened to me when I was a child. Well I've got news for them their not a child anymore. It's time to act grownup. Girls, if it was past right now, then forget it. Get a life, go back to school, do what it takes to get where you want to be."

"None of you could have been any worse off than me. I grew up nasty, naked, snotty nose, hungry and barefooted. Living in a nasty house with sorry people but I didn't end up that way. I didn't want that life. But I suffered a lot to have a home. Many times I didn't think I could take anymore, but I did, time and time again. I made friends in all walks of life. Not rainy day friends but very good people. Be good, be decent, work hard, don't tell lies and help others especially the elderly. You could put their Christmas trees up, do their hair, help them in their yards, help them cook and clean just to name a few. There are many ways to help someone."

"You need a home, go to a church and put a note on their bulletin board stating you are willing to stay with them at night while working a daytime job, and do their shopping, run their home or some may need someone to watch after them twenty four hours a day. You do not have to put up with a sorry way of life; work, work, work and stay away from trouble."

"If your parents didn't teach you a good way of life then watch the <u>Andy Griffith Shows,</u> they teach you good things. <u>Leave It To Beaver, Father Knows Best</u> or talk to your grandparents, ask them what's wrong with this world. I can tell you myself. No Mother or Father with guts will sacrifice their children for a fine home, drugs or alcohol. The second car in the family meant the Mother had to go to work and giving their children to the devil's day care centers."

"The leaders of this country said it was OK to have love children. The government will pay for them. The government is the taxpayers not the recipients of government handouts. They said abortion is fine. Then they let gays and lesbians out of the closet and their population skyrocketed. Our schools are running wild with these people and only a few decent people could afford to home school them. The government has sorry assholes watching over our country and decent people get blown out of the water. They send our best off to war while they let the Mexicans sneak across the border in droves. They turn their heads while the blacks are killing each other by the dozens. Our military should be here on our streets taking care of this country."

"They pass laws to protect child criminals. Yes, Ladies, there is a place for these teenagers, it's called Fort McClellan where they can be locked up. They are criminals because they didn't have a Father and Mother. The fathers should be put in jail with them for not teaching them better. They have put marriage in the crazy house and act like our children can't be given a switch to make them mind. Washington can get rid of the communists. I don't care what anyone will say about how I feel which is, our world has gone to hell. We can be brought back to being decent but it will take a lot of work by our people. We the hard working God-fearing people will have to insist that our government be cleaned out and do something about the trash running loose in the United States. Or we will have to do it ourselves. Our government, what a laugh."

"Have you or do you know anyone that has not been too busy to understand how all this human stupid pity has hurt our young people. Our people are so hungry for money they will do anything for it. Even at the expense of our children. Our people! Our young people are being turned loose to run the streets at twelve, thirteen and fourteen years old, running wild to rob and kill. Our government has made it too easy to have illegitimate children that no one wants. WIC being given out. Our teenage girls have found out if they want government money just spit out a love child. I know of one girl gets six hundred dollar a month just because her child has acid reflux. An unmarried Mother, how many others are there? How much is this costing the hard working taxpayers? Kids having kids, what do they care. It's so easy to have them. Welfare will feed them or they'll just give them away. They get WIC for five years. No child left behind. No child would be left behind if they had a Mother and Father fit to live."

"I'm telling you today that you have a friend. It's me! But no drinking! No drugs! Now, let's go to work and make a change in our lives. Remember yesterday is gone."

"The young ladies stood up with happiness all over them. They lined up to bring me papers they had filled out asking for me to help them. I had just made about twenty six new friends."

"Then I had read a piece in the Jasper newspaper one day about child discipline. A doctor John was telling parents that he just didn't have any single answer to make children behave. This blew me up. He was talking about doing time out in a chair and standing in the corner. Well, I sent him a letter about my Mama's eyes. Here is a copy of the letter."

"Doctor John, where have you and your readers been? I'm past fifty years old and I remember full well that my Mother worked her magic on the disciplining of her seven children, to the point of giving you that look, cutting her eyes at you with a raised eyebrow. We all knew what the consequence would be if we didn't do what those eyes told us to do. And **No Sir!** It wasn't just my parents. It was all the parents I knew."

"We never got three strikes and you're out. We got a slap on our hand with her saying, 'No No!' She knew how to shake her head from side to side. This started when we started walking. She didn't put away her pretty things, she said, 'No!'"

"Now if her child didn't take heed to this, the child would be introduced to a bush called a hedge. A long skinny limb, we had to go out into the yard and break it off and hand it to Mother. She held one of our hands while switching us with the other. From our knees to our ankles, the string from the switch would make us dance. It would make you behave. If not, she would send us out to get two switches the next time. She would twist them together and make us dance and never leave a mark on us. This is discipline for our children and it has been for all our grandchildren. If parents have a discipline problem, they need to look in the mirror. They need to have a discipline talk with their Grandmother."

"Introduce your readers to the magical hedge bush. Also tell them I will sell them three for a dollar. After that it only takes that look."

"Doctor, have you ever heard of a hedge bush? What about a hickory tree or a peach limb?"

"Even my three brothers didn't need but two or three and she never brought blood or left a mark but it did give my Mother those magic eyes. That is the right communication."

"New Mothers of today don't realize that God gives them these children but He also gives their lives to the children. It is a Mother's responsibility to deal with her children before they get out of hand. It is for sure we have a world full of earth polluters and it is sad. Earth polluters is what we have running Washington now. In five or ten years what will it be like?"

"Don't forget three for a Dollar."

"I never heard back from the Doctor but I never saw his name in the newspaper again. I did put an article in the newspaper but it wasn't about child discipline. I offered a reward for the fools that were harassing me. Here is a copy of that article . . ."

"Reward for information leading to identity of person or persons who has tried to ruin the lives of the Hallmark family of Shady Grove. Someone took one of our credit cards and had the address changed to an out of state address and charged $600 to AOL on that card. The credit card company refused to help us because I refused to pay it, I didn't even have a computer. They broke into my home and stole a valuable token, three Auburn quilt tops, and several bottles of perfume that hadn't been opened among other articles. They drove into my driveway twice a weekend for nine weeks. They called my house saying Richard had children by other women, that he was moving out and that he hated me. The past two years have been unbearable. We wish these people no harm but for our own peace of mind and safety we need to know who hates us this bad. We were offering a Two Thousand Dollar reward to find these people. We ask everyone to pray for them. Richard said, 'The love I have for my wife and home is seeing me through this. I love my wife. I have not cheated on her with anyone. I am not guilty of any wrong doing. If you have any information that would help us solve this problem please send it to the Hallmark family in Shady Grove.'"

"He opened a P.O. Box for this."

Rex said, "You don't believe his lies do you?"

I said, "No Way! I know for a fact he's been with forty two whores."

Rex said, "I should be so lucky."

I said, "Oh God! Rex you stay so horny you and his sluts would make a good match. There's one you wouldn't want to forget."

"I had a poem book I wanted published so I went to talk to Mrs. Malviene. She agreed to publish my poem book. She and her husband came to meet my family. I had cooked dinner for us. They came back time after time. You know I have strong morals. Sex wasn't talked about around my home. That's all Mrs. Malviene wanted to talk about. They said that I was tops on their list and we were going to take a vacation together. We would go to the Hamptons, Salt Lake City, Paris and London. I got Richard and me passports. She hired me to be a freelance writer for her new magazine. I got interviews and did write-ups on college students. I wrote articles on beauty and gardening. I bought film and had it developed at my expense. I worked all summer writing articles for her magazine."

"She called one day saying she had four tickets for the ballet to see <u>Sleeping Beauty</u> and wanted to know if Richard and I wanted to go with her. She giggled and said she had us the best seats in the house. Then she wanted to know what I was going to wear. I told her I had a beautiful suit that was gold and black in tiger print. Well

Saturday came, she came to see if we were ready hateful as she could be she informed me that I was not wearing what I said I'd wear. I told her that when I put it on, it was too tight so I changed. Rex, I was beautiful. I had on a black sweater with black feathers around the neck, a black skirt with slits all around the bottom. Yes it was short and my shoes were black velvet plus, now get this, I had enough gold and diamonds on to outshine a Christmas tree. Her husband Rufus started taking pictures of me. He told Richard if I was his girl, he would keep me under lock and key. Mrs. Malviene was mad and getting madder. She turned toward Richard and asked if he and I had oral sex, that she and I had been talking about sex. When Richard said, 'No', Mrs. Malviene said she felt sorry for him. I chimed in and asked her if she really swallowed his semen. I asked her if she knew that semen has a string of blood in it. She informed me that semen was pure protein. I asked her if she knew where AIDS came from and I'm surprised that she was not eaten up with it. That didn't slow her down. Right in front of Richard and Rufus she said that sex was to enjoy and before she met Rufus she had three kids to raise and if she or the kids needed anything she would find a man with a need. It was good for new tires, the light bill or a house payment. There is a man on every corner with a need and she would do whatever they wanted. Besides she loved sex and I was suppose to give Richard whatever he wanted."

Well, I said, "Whatever he wants is none of your business."

"Now, Rex, during our sex talks she even asked me what size Richard was and if it had a mushroom head. I told her I've measured a lot of things in my life, but that wasn't one of them. Richard said it was time to go or we'd be late for the theater. Her best seats in the house were in the balcony and three fourths of the lower levels were empty during the whole show."

"On the way to the theater, she wouldn't stop this BS sex talk. I had heard all the sex talk I could stand, book or no book; I told her I didn't want to hear another work about sex. I didn't have a toilet on my shoulders and I wouldn't lick a Lillie or be a lick-a-dick a daygirl. When I was growing up these love children were bastards and a woman who had sex outside of marriage was a whore, and I would never be one."

"Then she said her daughter would call her and tell her she was stripping for one man after another. My daughter would never talk to me about her pregnancy much less how she got that way. We sat through the ballet not talking, but on the way home she started again. I asked her if she had any morals. She said, 'There should be any such word.' Believe me that night I went from being called Mrs. Hallmark, to Drucilla and back to Mrs. Hallmark. She asked Richard how he felt about what I had said. He suggested that if she didn't want to know, then don't ask because she won't lie to you. Then she asked Rufus what he had to say. Rufus said, 'Not one damn thing'. Needless to say my book was a mess and I had to find another publisher. The last thing she said was for me to remember that she was a card-carrying member of the ACLU. I couldn't' help but ask if she knew the ACLU are liberals and communists. She found her lawyer online, a Mr. Bill Romit."

"Rex, do you remember O.J's dream team of lawyers? Well I only have Mr. Williams but I assure you he's all I need. He would make the dream team look like a bunch of first year law students."

"Oh Yes! She did tell me for someone that hates whores I sure looked like a hooker that night. I burst out laughing and told her if times ever got hard I'd have a big book of very classy men cause I knew I was the most beautiful hooker in Alabama, with the tightest ass in town. It had no wear and tear."

"So, Rex, I'll give you her new address. Mrs. Malviene is one ugly thing. She is the twin of an intoxicated hippopotamus with a hoggish character. Her publishing company was for her book only. No one else would publish the trash. It is not historically correct. Any Southern historian should sue her if possible."

"The story tells of a Southern man on a plantation home in the eighteen fifties whose son brings home his wife-to-be and flaunts her around like a whore. In her story she lets you believe that was accepted behavior at that time."

"Rex, Mrs. Malviene knows nothing about the South of the eighteen fifties. A father would have shot his own son for bringing that kind of shame into his home."

"I gave five of her books to my lady friends before I had read it. We all trashed the books."

"Mrs. Malviene gave me a lot of advice about the IRS. She would buy a pair of shoes or a pack of panty hose; she would claim a deduction on her income tax. She admitted she would steal every dime she could get her hands on. She run her business out of her home, but there is no company sign in her window. I do believe she is much more stupid than she knows. You can see that by the pictures on the cover of her books, her camera was no good to do that type of work."

"Rex, I was just kidding about you going to see her. The last time I saw Rufus his head had been shaved and he had sores all over his head and in the corners of his mouth. Looks to me like he had his head up her skirt one too many times. Anyway, she made me feel like a college educated woman."

"I know she printed some of my books out of her house and sold them. Some of the books were smaller than the others and the ink rubbed off the covers. Anyway, I was never paid for the books she printed at home or any of the free lance work on her magazine, or the candy I sent over to her house for her to sell."

"I have a dear friend that has thirty-seven years of psychiatric experience, whom I told about Mrs. Malviene being raped by her father. He raped her one morning in the kitchen floor with her mother and siblings looking on. The doctor explained that when, a little girl is raped by her father, from then on she thinks that sex is the most important thing to a man. Thinking, if it is so good that a father would do this to his daughter, it must be an OK thing in her mind. So she spends her life eaten up with sex. I really feel sorry for Mrs. Malviene all her talk about sex has no romance. Sex without romance is dirty and ugly. Her disorder has caused her to be a dog-eat-dog person. You could dress her up in the finest clothes but, unfortunately she would have to climb a five-foot stepladder to be on the level with white trash. Believe me there isn't a ladder high enough to put her on my level. She's a bitch dog."

"Now Rex, let me tell you about another lady this doctor introduced me to. Her name is Nora. She was raised in church and had a wonderful family. When she graduated from high school, she went to work for a fine company making good money. She married her first sweetheart. He went to the same church. Everyone thought he was a good man. A couple of years into their marriage he began to act as if he was bipolar. When he would have his fits, Nora would beg him to be nice. She loved this fool and was too ashamed to let anyone know how much he was tormenting her. After a few months of this he would stay out all night. Nora would be up all night walking the floor, worrying about him. This would make her almost too tired to go to work. Nora knew he needed treatment but couldn't get him to give in and go see a doctor."

"To her family and church a divorce was a disgrace. Besides she loved him. But this love almost took her life and in some ways it did. She finally divorced him, but the damage was done. Nora was afraid of men and wouldn't marry again. She could hardly bring herself to go to work, but somehow she did."

"I'll begin at the beginning. Nora was eighteen when she started dating him. Her parents were very strict on her and she lived by their rules. Joe was his name and when she married Joe, she was still a virgin. Right from the start, Joe began to show extreme jealousy and possessive behavior. He was a nut so she broke up with him several times. He had frightened her to death. He told her if anybody came to her door to pick her up he'd shoot them. Then he would cry and become depressed. She felt sorry for him so she married the bastard."

"He would take her for a ride in the car out on back roads and drive like a crazy man. Joe was insanely jealous, yet out of the blue he would ask her for a divorce. Nora was beside herself, her Bible told her to obey her man and she did. If he told her not to get out of that chair for two hours, she would sit in that chair for two hours."

"Many nights Nora would roll her hair on curlers for the next work day. She would no sooner get into bed than Joe would tell her to get the rollers out of her hair. That he wanted sex and she would obey him. Then one night he told her to take her clothes off and get into the bath tub. Then he urinated all over her and laughed like a crazy man. He sodomized her several times and chocked her until she passed out, leaving bruises on her neck. One night he drove her to the beach. After getting drunk he pushed her out of the car and ran over her with the back tires. When she tried to get up he started shooting over her head and around her. She didn't know he owned a thirty-eight revolver."

"Things continued to get worse, one night he sat her in a chair and played Russian roulette with the revolver to her head. He would say, 'Baby you don't know which chamber the bullet is in', and then would pull the trigger. Then he would lay the gun down and sing, 'You Always Hurt The One You Love'. She was in shock frozen to the chair. In a matter of two weeks Nora's weight went from one hundred eighteen to ninety-eight pounds. Her nerves couldn't take anymore. Church or no church she was only twenty-four and so ashamed but she called her mother to come and get her. Nora lived in Foley at the time when her mother and sister came to take her home. Her mother took her to a family doctor at home and because of the stress and trauma; she didn't menstruate for eight months."

"Rex, she is a wonderful person, so kind, clean and would give her shoes away, in the snow, if someone needed them. He is a first class son of a bitch that I want taken out of this world. As a matter of fact, I'd like to take a nail gun and tack his ass to the side of a country out house, and then set it on fire."

"After Joe, Nora was so sick she wouldn't have another man. She was cheated out of a home, children and any happiness for the rest of her life. When a young girl leaves her father, her father should make it his business to see what kind of stress his baby girl lives under. But I love Nora and I'll see to it that no one ever hurts her again. Remember me telling you about the group of ladies the Sheriff had me talk to? It was one of those ladies that introduced me to Nora. She said Nora had helped her a lot."

"What a job you could do for me, find each one of those ladies a good man."

Rex said, "Drucilla, I 'm not built right to find any man. Besides I have never met a good man in my life. I think Courtney would do a better job with that."

I said, "Courtney, why didn't I think of her. You are right, she could have them lined up for miles. I really enjoyed talking to that group of ladies. I know they will do good with a little guidance. I'll see you tomorrow Rex, I need to check my email from Charlie."

Chapter 9

Miss. Drucilla,

    Would you like to go deep-sea fishing?

Charlie

Charlie,

    You'd probably laugh at me, but I think it would make me sick.

Drucilla

Miss. Drucilla,

    I would never laugh. Some people do get sick. First I'll take you out on a big river to get you used to the water. Dad tells me that you do all kinds of things, but you love to dance best. Guess what? My school is giving us ballroom dancing lessons. Today we learned ten tips in ten minutes that results in ten times better dancing.

Tip #1 Perfect the correct closed dance hold
Tip #2 maintain posture
Tip #3 learn where your head goes
Tip #4 maintain frame and connection

Tip #5 learn the correct single hand hold connection
Tip #6 maintain the big top
Tip #7 dance to the music
Tip #8 learn the dance walk
Tip #9 leading turns with the cup and pin system
Tip #10 stopping the stutter stepping

This is two whole pages to learn, but it's important. Some of the guys were laughing at me.

Charlie

Charlie,

Don't let it get to you. The girls will love you for it. Do you think you can teach me what you learn from school on the computer?

Drucilla

Miss. Drucilla,

Yes Miss. Drucilla, and it will also help me.

Charlie

Charlie,

OK then, it's a deal. Now you have me all excited. I love the clothes they wear. I love the swing, foxtrot and the salsa. Gosh, the Tango.

Drucilla

Miss. Drucilla,

    It's also good therapy.

                                  Charlie

Charlie,

    Boy you already have my heart beating ninety miles an hour. Just think, maybe someday we could win the amateur dancing championship. I can just see us a young man and an old lady, ha-ha.

                                  Ducilla

Miss. Drucilla,

    I'm going to send you some DVDs and videos. I f you want more Google dance vision.com, they offer over four hundred titles and you can listen to them online before you buy them.

                                  Charlie

Charlie,

    I'll look at them and get back with you.

                                  Drucilla

I called Rex on the telephone. I said, "Rex, this is Drucilla. I hated to call so late, but Charlie is going to teach me ballroom dancing. Just think the hustle, the Lindy Hop, the tango and"

Rex broke in and said, "Drucilla, you can dance."

I said, "Oh well! That's just the Waltz, the Two Step, Old Twist, the Jitterbug and the Charleston. That's not what Charlie and I are going to do."

"The reason I called is you will have to help me. Like with the dips and drags." Rex said, "I'll drop you on your head, in other words, I've got to learn this too."

I said, "Why sure. It's also going to help Charlie."

"Durcilla, the next thing you'll want is a Latin lover."

"Oh My God Rex!" That's just what I need. Where could we rent me one?"

"Shut Up Drucilla!" Rex said.

"Damn you Rex! You got my hopes up. You call Doctor Bradley and tell on me. Tell him I'm not going to be a crybaby anymore. I'm going to look for love. No more candy making for me. Tomorrow when I get up, I'm going to the fabric store. I'm going to make a beautiful dancing dress and cover a pair of shoes to match. Good bye and good night."

I turned on my computer to email Charlie.

My Dear Charlie,

> The other dance that I couldn't think of was the 'Shagg'. I was watching the public broadcasting station on television last night. It will come on again and I sure won't miss it. I can't wait until my book gets here. Poor Rex, I'll make him help me. I'm sure it will be fun fun fun.
>
> Drucilla

Miss. Drucilla,

OK, we aren't doing this just for fun fun fun. What about your computer lessons?

                                                Charlie

My Dear Charlie

Well my little schoolmaster. Can't you read my emails? Yes, well I guess I'm doing fair and I keep working on it anyway. I don't want to talk about my lessons. I want to dance so, and you tell Rex to get his dancing shoes on. You and Rex keep my heart pounding. My feet are dancing under the table right now. Remember the man in my dream, Tony? Its Tony I can't wait to dance with. Maybe you're too young to hear this.

                                                 Drucilla

Miss. Drucilla,

No, no please tell me.

                                                Charlie

Charlie,

OK dancing with Tony in my dreams. It's four legs, two bodies, and two hearts beating as one. When the two of us dance our hearts beat as one. It was ecstasy, the passion, and the chemistry. When we danced the tango, we danced as one, partner's two halves of one. I can still see the audience; they could feel love in the air. My Charlie, I'm going to tell you I think that your dad is keeping me locked up, so to speak, me telling him this God-awful life of mine. I hate everything about it. I just wish that everyone that has hurt me would fall into hell and be forgotten and I could dance and never give them another thought. My Charlie, I hope you will always love music and dancing. It is so wonderful for you. For you to be able to teach me the computer, and dancing its magic. Oh yes, I have ordered me some dancing clothes. I may have to kill Rex. Oh my gosh, I just remembered I have a friend that lives up the road apiece. Boy can he dance. I swear, I had forgotten about Jean. I'll call him the first thing in the morning. Good night Charlie, someday I'll dance with you.

Oh No! Not good night Charlie. I have to tell you something. You told me you wanted to be sure you know how to do the Waltz.

The slow waltz come from European courts about Seventeen hundreds. It's like an off spring of the faster Viennese Waltz in three quarter time. You will whirl around the floor enjoying the thrill of the waltz. I think it started in Austria. I know you will just love it.

You must also learn the Jive, a very fast lively dance. I've heard PaPa say the men wouldn't have made it though World War II without the swing music. You know Charlie; I have all the music of Benny Goodman, Tommy Dorsey and Glen Miller. I love the jive, bouncing with very sharp kicks and flicks but especially the east coast swing jive, the faster tempo swing music. Wait, wait Charlie you know we talked about the swing. I'm a dumb blonde baby. I want the single time swing without the triple step taught to me first. You know child, I'm very worried about your daddy.

Drucilla

Miss. Drucilla,

That's a laugh, he can dance, don't let him fool you.

Charlie

Charlie

That's not his story, but I'll take your word for it. I'll go find him and we will start with the Charleston. This dance I do know and the Blackbottom. He will see that I am a born flapper. Good night baby.

Drucilla

I turned off the computer and reached for the phone.
I said, "Hello Rex, Can you take me dancing tonight?"
Rex said, "I'll take you anywhere you want to go. But I can't tonight."
I said, "Well, I'll call around and see if I can find Jerry. Hopefully he'll be at home. I'll call PaPa and Mama Jackson, maybe even PaPa Anderson."
"I promise you, you'll be doing the Charleston in no time, maybe even the Salsa. But the swing is more important to me and I know the doll of Forestdale can teach me that."
Rex said, "Drucilla, Charlie sure has gotten you all wound up, hasn't he?"
I said, "Yes, but that's a good thing. I don't think so much about Richard's whores. When I do think about them I just want them off the face of the earth."
"Rex, about a month ago, Charlie told me to make a mental list of all the people that had hurt me. Do my yoga every day and while doing my yoga to repeat their names in the same order and to start at four o'clock every afternoon. He asked me once if I still believed that

my friend Mr. Tony Tortomasi was still connected to my brain waves. The answer is a very big yes. I told Charlie that I tell Tony every day how much I need him and love him, but I never hear from him. I told Charlie that I was going to the Gulf to see if I could find Tony. Charlie begged me not to go. He wanted me to wait until you and he could go with me. Charlie wants to meet Tony. He said Tony must be super special. Tony is my special everything. I told Charlie that it was time I got Richard out of my life for good. I don't like living here anymore and I would give it all up for Tony and Anthony. Charlie assured me that Tony was getting things ready for me and when he's ready he'll come for me. It sounds to me as if Charlie already knows Tony. That would be nice."

"Charlie said it wouldn't be nice for me to go looking for a man. Charlie said, 'Make Rex, I mean Daddy, take you to a chicken fight. I think he told me they have one on Saturdays in Winfield, Alabama.' Rex, Charlie knew that I square danced. He suggested I do something humorous and learn to belly dance."

"But I changed the subject and told him that someone had told him that I love the chicken fights and I wanted to know who that someone was and come to think of it, just why did he call you Rex, instead of Daddy? Are you talking behind my back?"

Rex said, "You know I would never say anything to hurt you."

I said, "That's just what Charlie did."

Rex said, "What did Charlie do?"

I said "Just like you, he changed the subject. Said he was just clowning with me. I told him I wasn't clowning and when I do see him that he had better know how to do the turkey trot."

"Me, I've seen a lot of men do the turkey trot but I didn't encourage them and didn't do any belly dancing. What I'd be doing would be for Tony's eyes only."

I hung up the phone and slipped into a bathtub full of bubbles but once there, I felt I needed to hurry and get out. I washed everything, dried off, rolled my hair and polished my nails. I then went to the kitchen, fixed myself a fruit dish and sat under the hair dryer for thirty minutes. I took the rollers out and ran my fingers through my hair a few times.

I knew I wasn't healed inside from being shot, and it would be months before I would be in good health again. I was tired and climbed in bed between two soft blankets. All of a sudden I felt like I was being held by someone, someone was holding my hand tight. I went to sleep thinking Tony was in my dream again. I knew Tony was there with me in my mind, just as if he was actually there. I could feel the strength from Tony's hand and I felt warm all inside. I heard myself say, 'We are twin souls. Tony, I feel the need for romance. I feel the need for passion.' I rolled over to find Tony, and when I opened my eyes Tony wasn't there and I was staring at the alarm clock, it said it was nine thirty in the morning.

I laid there thinking it's hard to believe, I found my love in the trauma unit at Carraway Hospital. How sad it made me feel when Doctor Bradley moved to Salisbury, North Carolina. As soon as I could I would go see him. I knew Doctor Bradley thought I was crazy because I didn't want to live but now I do. I wanted to thank him for saving my life. I wanted him to be my friend and wanted him to see me marry Tony.

I wasn't out of bed long before the door bell rang. Richard was at the door.

Irritated, I asked, "What do you want?"

Richard asked, "Are you up to going on a cruise? It's just seven days and somehow we were selected to have this cruise free."

I replied, "**Free, Hell!** That's a joke."

Richard said, "Oh no, I checked, it's because I signed forty eight friends up for this cruise."

"Oh yes, I remember that. You sent in about fifty-five names for the cruise to Yucatan. Are you telling me that forty eight people are going?"

Richard replied, "Yes, Drucilla, all forty eight have sent in their money and now Chris at the cruise line is waiting for you and me."

I said, "There is no you and me! Besides you know I'm not well enough and my doctors wouldn't let me go anyway. You can go. They are **your** friends."

Richard said, "I sure can because all your time goes to that Rex, and now that new computer friend you have."

I said, "Oh yes, Richard, his name is Charlie and he's so smart he is teaching me to dance and teaching me so much about the computer. Now you go and pack for your cruise."

Richard said, "You really don't care, do you Drucilla?"

I said, "**Good Lord No**! If I need anything I'll call Rex. He is good to me, you know. And my Charlie, he is sending me DVD's and everything I need for my dancing lessons. Rex doesn't know it yet, but he is going to be here a lot. Maybe its best that you have somewhere to go and Richard, I do hope you have fun."

As I closed the door behind Richard, I hugged myself and thanked God.

Chapter 10

I sat down at my computer to check my email.

Hello Miss Drucilla

I need to talk to you about how to cut and paste on the computer. Also I hope you know that just because you do away with your email as in deleting it, it never really leaves your computer. So please don't ever put anything on there that you wouldn't want someone to see someday.

Charlie

Hello Charlie,

Thanks to my doll, that I did remember. It was one of the first things you taught me. Yesterday I ordered shoes and they will be delivered in three days. Also I have dishes with the Desert Rose pattern and I found some pieces that I don't have online and ordered them. This online shopping may get me in trouble.

Drucilla

Hello Miss Drucilla,

    I only have about two weeks left before I go on vacation with my Grandfather, so make a list of the things you may need to know and I'll get right on them. And don't be buying dishes.

Charlie

Charlie

    I'm going to miss you Charlie. Why don't you take a laptop with you?

Drucilla

Miss Drucilla

    Well, we are going hunting and a laptop is just not part of our gear.

Charlie

Charlie

    It should be, and a cell phone.

Drucilla

Miss Drucilla

We'll be out of range of any cell tower so no need to carry either of them. Don't worry Drucilla, Daddy is going to keep you busy, remember, dancing. When I get back I want to hear how good the two of you are.

Charlie

Charlie

Us two? I'll probably have him killed before you get back. Charlie, even on the computer you don't seem to be anything like Rex. Rex is mean and cold. Charlie, you seem so sweet, kind and loving. You are so full of knowledge. When I read your emails, I can almost hear your voice. You are smart, you dance and you have taught me so much about this computer. Not only telling about the vacations you have been on, but showing me how to bring them up on the computer makes them come to life. You have shown me the world right here at my fingertips. Computers really are a miracle. Charlie, you amaze me, but I also want you to remember that you can get into a lot of trouble if you do stupid things. So hear me, I am asking you to be very careful. Charlie, let me tell you a funny story. You know I'm a blond and I do think we blonds are a little crazy. The other day, your dad told me I'd better check my mail because you were going to send me something. I jumped up and ran outside to my mail box, looked in, found nothing, shut it back then in maybe two hours later I went back out to look again. This time your Dad came from around the house and asked me what I was looking for. I said 'The mail you fool, the mail from Charlie'. Your Dad laughed and said 'Email, you blond.' I picked up some rocks and put him back around the house.

Drucilla

Miss Drucilla

Don't worry about me, I'll be faster than anything, besides, Papa watches after me with a thirty ought six and I have one of my own.

Charlie

Charlie

What kind of gun is that? Are you strong enough for that gun? Lord I hope it doesn't knock you out of your shoes.

Drucilla

Miss Drucilla

Thirty ought six is the size of the bullet, it's a high-powered rifle and I shoot it very well. Dad told me about Brandon. Does he go hunting?

Charlie

Charlie

No he doesn't. I hoped he would. I started him out with a four ten shot gun when he was seven years old. Then he got an automatic rifle at age twelve. But remember, there are no men in his life that like sports. He only has me and I try to teach Brandon everything that my father taught me. He is very careful and he has a very good aim. As a matter of fact, he can shoot a gnat off a bird's tail feathers.

He does love to fish. We would wade the creek behind the house and catch three to four pound bass. We can stand in the creek and watch catfish swim between our feet.

This young man has never had many friends. His mother won't let him out of her sight, not even to go on vacations with me. Sometimes he tells me he hates her and she needs to leave him alone. I know this is true. I don't see how I can ever help him. If he comes to my house, she calls on the phone and tells Brandon to come home, she needs him to do something, just any excuse. I just don't want to fight with her any longer. I have bought him everything money can buy. Charlie, you can't buy brains or guts. Somehow I lost Brandon these last few years. He comes to see me every day and I know he is girl crazy and he does love his computer work. He graduated from Minor High School here in Alabama. I don't think that any child that graduated from that school got an education.

Brandon loves mechanic work. He can do brake jobs on any car. For that matter, I was given an old truck with the motor and transmission in the truck bed, and in three days Brandon was driving that truck around the road. He had another truck pulled in with a wrecker that was setting in a field for two years and he got it running. I have pictures of this and it's all true.

You may not know what a phobia is, but Brandon is afraid of people. Why? Because he has stayed in these woods for so long that he has this fear that won't turn him loose. Brandon has had many jobs but when a boss or anyone screams at him or talks bad to him, he just comes home and won't go back. He also has a pea size tumor on the stem of his brain. I do not know if this affects him in any way, but it doesn't seem to. He's good on the computer and can do anything with his hands. For that matter, maybe you could email him sometime.

I'm gone now baby doll. Be safe and let me hear from you soon. Love you doll.

Drucilla

Miss Drucilla

I'll tell my Dad to help Brandon. You don't worry about all that. We will take care of it all. I'm gone.

Charlie

Chapter 11

I lay down to take a nap and was almost asleep, when the phone rang. Rex was calling.

I said, "Hello?"

Rex replied, "What were you doing Drucilla?"

I said, "Well, Rex, I was day dreaming about night things in the middle of the afternoon and, **NO,** you were not the man."

Just thinking about my dream I slipped back into my dream of Tony. I was put several aromatherapy candles around the bedroom and lit them for a sensuously romantic atmosphere. Tony, I want three hours of lovemaking. I want us to explore each other in many ways. The communication between us will be natural and easy. There is no question about it; I've loved you for so long.

Rex said, "Drucilla, Drucilla, did you hear what I said?"

I replied, "**What!** Oh, I am sorry Rex. What did you say you wanted?"

Rex said, "I asked you if Richard was going on that cruise next month."

I said, "Yes, he's going on a seven day cruise. I think he knows he has lost me for good."

I slipped back into my dream of Tony. Oh, how I wish Tony come to see me while Richard's gone. Making love to Tony will be pure heaven, sensual and passionate. It will be like that all the time with us. We are completely compatible and our souls are one.

Rex asked, "Drucilla, are you there? Can you hear me?"

I replied, "Yes, I'm here."

Rex said, "Drucilla, you have changed. When I first met you, well you hated Mrs. Malviene. You were mean and cold and now?"

I said, "**No, No, No!** Rex, I still feel the same about Mrs. Malviene. She's just a whore. Richard never loved me and now I'm in love with Tony." (Pause) "You son of a bitch, if you are insinuating that I'm in any way like Mrs. Malviene, she would screw a squirrel if she could catch one. Just like Richard. What more do I need to say, I'll kill you myself, do you hear me?"

Rex replied, "Hey, hey, I am sorry."

I said, "You need to be sorry. Maybe you need to go on that cruise with Richard."

Rex said, "I'll call you tomorrow."

I said, "Don't you hang up on me, you bastard, you Yankee carpet bagger. You damn well better be here at 10 in the morning and eat before you come because we'll dance though lunch."

I hung up the telephone thinking that bastard messed up my thoughts of Tony. I laid back down thinking of Mama Marcella and Harriet.

That red headed niece would be on the cruise but not Harriet. Harriet had taken good care of Mama Marcella until she died. Harriet became good friends with a Bible thumper from Maytown. At once she became my friend too. That is until the day we had a Bible study class here at my house. Thumper said that once saved, always saved, that she could steal my jewelry, my drugs, get drunk, get into her car and hit a tree and die, and she would still go to Heaven because that's what Jesus died for. She said our lives are predestined by God before we were born.

That's not what I believed and I asked the others if they believed in that. They all agreed to that belief and it was the teachings of the Southern Baptist Church. To me, this meant that when a seed is created, God says this one is mine and that one is going to hell. It's a free pass to be as sorry as. If you were a saved person, those things wouldn't even enter your mind. God gave us free will, but made us responsible for our actions. I called our pastor and to my shock he told me he could get drunk, cuss a blue streak, hit a tree and die and still go to heaven. I assured him not in this lifetime and I wouldn't be back in his church in this lifetime either. My pastor was not the smart man I thought he was. Having heard my conversation with the pastor, Harriet and Mrs. Bible Thumper were crying and ready to leave. One of the ladies on her way out said her mother was seventy seven years old and had taught Sunday school all her adult life. If she taught once saved then she is teaching her way into hell along with all the ones she taught. She was right, I didn't understand predestination. Maybe I don't, but I just stay focused on the Ten Commandments. Like I said, once saved bad things don't cross your mind. Bible Thumper's Sunday school of nineteen people was lost and Thumper changed churches so she could sow her seeds of evil to others. It wasn't long before the rumor was out that Bible Thumper and the preacher were having an affair. Pastor's wife was size five by five. She had stomach surgery and lost all her weight and that was the reason Thumper changed churches. The Bible Thumper didn't lose a pound. She's still as big as a mule, but not the size of the chocolate milk preacher. He still drinks a gallon of chocolate milk every day. Just listen to me, pure stupidity giving my thoughts to the likes of them, when I could be dreaming about Tony. Come to me Tony. I need you. Remember the song <u>In The Still Of The Night</u>'; that is a lover's song. You and I, Tony will need no lessons to dance to that song. Come to me Tony. I can't be here much longer. Yes, I feel the warmth coming over my body. The dream was so hot when I awoke my hair was wet. I felt wonderful and I was even wet between my legs. I was fully focused on myself and stretching like a cat.

I looked at the clock. It was a quarter till nine, just enough time for some yoga, a good thirty minutes.

Rex will be here at ten. I'll teach him a sizzling salsa. I wonder if Rex will really let loose. I'll bet he can't resist a spicy salsa mix, the Latin Lime Twist and the Mucho Mambo Combo. I'm going to burn up the dance floor and have some fun out of him.

Charlie was helping me to grow a soul and teaching me to listen to my soul. This is called your instinct. If you can really keep in touch with your soul, you will be right in most everything you do, because God shows you the right things. Always remember you make your own luck he would say. I have just enough time to e-mail Charlie.

Charlie

>Good morning.

Dricilla

Miss Dricilla

>Anyway, Miss Drucilla, what is your favorite color, flower, how do you wear your hair and what color is it? Do you have a young mind? My dad said he couldn't tell how old you are, he said you're about five foot and weigh about 115 lbs and he thinks you're beautiful. He tells me that you can be mean, but you had rather be a joy. He said you tell jokes, pull pranks, you love fast cars and you love the nightlife. As a matter of fact he says you are extraordinary.

Charlie

Charlie!!!

Drucilla

Miss Drucilla

>Well, is it true that you owned and drove your very own race car?

Charlie

Charlie

Well yes, but it wasn't like one at Talladega. Did he tell you that I'm just a country girl? Red and Pink are my colors, blond hair/green eyes.

Drucilla

Miss Drucilla

Oh! Yes Miss, he told me all about your garden, he said you have enough food to feed my whole school. He said your jam is so good that he eats it right out of the jar. He said your home is beautiful, your yard is also. But Miss what about your 4 wheeler and he said you're not afraid of anything. That you go fishing and hunting. Is all this true?

Charlie

Charlie

Well yes, Charlie. I love living, but I don't like to be in a large bunch of people.

Drucilla

Miss Drucilla

Well I don't buy that because my daddy said you're a born entertainer. He said you can get on the lawn mower and cut your grass in 45 minutes with your hair in rollers, clean your house, have everything neat, cook dinner and walk out your door at 7:00 pm looking like a queen then dance all night. Is it true that you have lots of diamonds and mink coats?

Charlie

Charlie

Yes Charlie, I have everything but things don't always bring happiness. Remember what you said about listening to your soul? I didn't understand that too well until you explained it to me. I have always lived in a hurry. Talking to you has been good for me. You have me thinking and listening to myself and listening to my soul.
Now, are you laughing at me Charlie?

Drucilla

Miss Drucilla

No Mam! I would never laugh at a lady that likes to hunt, fish, race cars, ride 4 wheelers and dance.

Charlie

Charlie

Someday you can come to my home with your dad. I'll plan a day for us to run the woods. About a mile behind my house is a fishing hole. We can ride the 4 wheeler right to the water. Then wade up and down fishing and no joke, we can get 3 and 4 lb bass and you can see big catfish swimming around our feet.

Drucilla

Miss Drucilla

I hope you make Daddy hurry up with your story.

Charlie

Charlie

OK Charlie, times up, I'll hurry him up if I can. Rex is here now to pick me up.

Drucilla

I answered the door bell to find Rex right on time.

I said, "Rex, I just love Charlie, he is so sweet. He wants to come see me so you better be working night and day. Are you ready?"

Rex said, "Sure, and look at you in that tight baby blue flexible doll outfit."

I said, "Boy, you know the word salsa means sauce, hot? Listen to that Puerto Rican music. This sound was defined in New York. On this DVD it has the Latin Lime Twist, Spicy Salsa and many more."

The doorbell rang as Rex told me that he had invited Courtney and Harriet and two friends.

I told Rex, "This is no party, its dance lessons."

I pulled up my yoga mat as Rex let Courtney and Harriet and his two friends in the door. Just a few minutes into the dancing I knew that I would half kill Rex. He danced like a professional. Three hours of dancing and they were all dead tired.

The guys wanted to practice every other day. I agreed but only for two hours.

I asked Rex, "Why didn't you tell me that we girls would have professionals to dance with? Professionals that look like rag heads!!"

Rex said, "Drucilla, shut up, shut up! They are fine boys. They just work under cover."

I replied, "Rex King, you just remember they'll be no lice in my covers."

Rex said, "I've just about clawed myself bloody."

I said, "Boy you better call Harriet and ask if she needs a rub down."

Rex yelled, **"Go to hell Drucilla."**

I remarked, "Hey, I have been thinking about that."

Rex said, "What woman?"

I explained, "Going to hell. If I can pass through Heaven a few times with Tony, I'll be so hot that hell won't bother me."

Rex said, "Good day fool."

I blurted out, "You'll think fool when I turn Max loose on you."

I lay on the floor thinking, Brandon has not been to see me today. I know it must be those television games; games and more games are making all the children brain dead.

The telephone rang and I crawled across the floor to answer it.

I asked, "How are you Courtney?"

Courtney said, "I'm almost dead."

I said, "Yes, they sure could dance."

Courtney said, "I'll bet they think we don't know what fitness is. Those guys were sizzling and fun."

I remarked, "Let's practice tomorrow. At least it will get some of the soreness out of us."

Courtney said, "Just don't tell Rex."

I responded, "Courtney I've got to go to the tub. I'm so tired and I've still have to do some work on the computer. I can't get behind on that or I'll be in trouble with Charlie. And Courtney, don't show up until ten please. And call Harriet, I want her to start having some fun. Just maybe she'll stop hissing at me. You know sister Gertrude won't come within miles of me? Oh well, they don't know the fun has just begun."

Courtney said, "Drucilla, you have to tell me what you said to Harriet about your rose bushes."

I explained, "I told her I was going to cut some limbs and beat Percy with them. Tush and he have cut my roses on their side of the fence. You are only supposed to cut the dead limbs out of running roses. Anyway, they have cut the rose bush so close to the fence on their side that the rose bush fell off the fence on my side. If the rose bush didn't fall completely off it would be so heavy it would pull the fence down with it."

"He's a damn man, he knows there are three things you don't mess with and that's a man's woman, his dog and his land. In this case, it was my rose bushes. Percy thinks I'm crazy and I'm just about to show him just how crazy I am."

"All you hear from Percy is he's moving from here. He wants to move to Clanton on a farm. He wouldn't even work in Daddy's garden, there isn't any way he could run a farm."

"Now if he cuts one more limb on my roses I am going to hook that big ass Kubota to his trailer and pull it out onto the road and tell him. Now I've got it started so get your ass to Clanton."

Courtney said, "They'll put you in jail Drucilla."

I said, "I don't give a damn, Mr. Williams will burn the tires off his car to get me out. He knows I'm crazy and he knows I know just how crazy I am. Good-bye, I'm gone to the tub and then to bed. I'll see you tomorrow."

Chapter 12

The cell phone was ringing, the house phone was ringing, I rolled out of bed and the doorbell started ringing. I answered the front door and there stood Courtney.

Courtney said, "Harriet and I are ready to Salsa."

Both were dressed in what looked to be witch's bloomers and top. I let them in and answered my cell phone. Rex was at the back door wanting in. I opened the back door and there stood Rex and the same two men from yesterday. All were dressed in tuxedos with rags wrapped around their heads. I calmly let them through the house to meet the girls. I was still dressed in a cotton tee shirt and silk lace panties.

Courtney said, "Drucilla, I thought I told you not to call Rex."

I exclaimed, "**I didn't, I'm as surprised as you.**"

Rex said, "Drucilla get your hand on your chin and your ass in the wind or you'll be dancing in that get up."

I looked Rex up and down and said, "My get up you say."

I let my eyes roam over to the girls and burst out laughing.

I asked, "Alright, come clean, which one of you bitches called these three clowns?"

The look on Courtney and Harriet's faces told me they didn't know what I was talking about.

Rex with a weak smile on his face said, "I got a mental message from you sometime during the night."

We all laughed. I finally put on sweat pants and shirt. We got the Salsa down, maybe not precisely, but good. The shag is wonderful. We practiced until I couldn't move. Rex sure can Jitterbug too.

I said, "Rex, you old dog. You must have been around here in the thirties."

I walked into the front door, opened it and with a smile said, "**Now get out! All of you!** And I'll tell you now you can find yourself a fox outfit. The foxtrot is next. It's one of the easiest dances to learn in the American style."

"In nineteen thirteen on a New York stage it became an overnight success. We are going to do this one."

Rex leaning against the door frame asked, "Who told you all this?"

I replied, "My Charlie. Did you not know he is teaching me a lot of things on the computer?"

Harriet and Courtney at the same time, with one hand on their hips said, "So you've been taking lessons without us?"

I replied, "Good bye, you pray for a Charlie of your own."

I took a nap and then checked my email.

Miss Drucilla,

Good Morning, I hear through the grape vine that you've been dancing. I better make something more clear. The one you need to learn, the foxtrot, may be a little more difficult than I led you to believe. Since nineteen thirteen, it has gone through many changes. The move of soft and fluid linear movements to a very quick and lively dance comprised of hops, skips and kicks. You should begin as a quick version of foxtrot mixed with the Charleston with musical jazz influences. I tell you Dad can do them all. Don't let him fool you.

From what he told me about your workout, you will love the jive. It's very fast, acrobatic and lively. In the time line of World War II Benny Goodman and Glen Miller was helping to rock the world. It was a shame that Benny Goodman's plane was shot down over the English Channel.

Miss Drucilla, it won't hurt you to practice some everyday or have four good workouts a week. I hope you will get the best shoes and just let your clothes be loose.

We have a long way to go. We have the Cachucha. It was first created in Cuba though it is now considered a Spanish dance. It was first made popular in Vienna in the eighteen hundreds. And you're going to love the waltz. It's romantic slow to a faster Viennese Waltz in three quarter time. My bet is you will stick to the slow romantic waltz.

Charlie

Charlie

Hello my doll. It's so good to hear from you. But what have you gotten me into? Just joking, I love it! If only I had someone to rub my feet.

Harriet and I are going to surprise Jerry on Friday night. He goes to a little club down here in the backwoods. He's always after us to come with him. He has a date and we plan to take him away from her.

How was your hunting trip?

Drucilla

Miss Drucilla

My hunting trip was awesome. My best friend came on this trip. He is an avid hunter. But I was the top dog on this hunt. I killed two turkeys with one shot. I didn't even see the second turkey. But that has never been done at this hunting lodge before and you know I was on cloud nine.

Charlie

Charlie

Gosh! I can just see you dancing in the woods over that shot. That's better than a hole in one, ha-ha.

And you tell me your just twelve years old. When did Rex ever have time to teach you all you know?

Drucilla

Miss Drucilla

I have been taking dancing lessons since I was four and I have watched Dad teach a few girls. But my Papa has taught me to be a hunter.

Charlie

Charlie

Well doll, someone has taught you to be a very fine young man and I thank you for taking your time with me. I can't wait to meet you. You have been a joy and you have put breath back into this body. You have been a wonderful friend. I'm gone now, good day.

Drucilla

Friday night came and Rex with his two rag headed friends, Brandon, Harriet, Courtney and I walked right in the club where Jerry was dancing with his date.

I told everyone that I was Jerry's sister, but I didn't' know that crazy bunch that came in with me.

Everyone got settled down when the music started again. Jerry took his darling to the dance floor. I told Harriet to take Jerry away from her. She did and after a few seconds I took him away from her. Harriet stood in the dance floor shaking both her fists at me and told me that if I didn't want a bar room brawl, I best go and sit down. Jerry backed off and I pointed my thumb at Harriet and told her to get the hell out of there. I took Jerry in my arms and continued dancing. Jerry told Harriet to behave. He was shining. His head went up two hat sizes and he was on cloud nine. When we finished the dance, the people gave us a standing ovation. I heard Harriet tell someone that Jerry was our brother and we were just playing with him.

Jerry later told us that we sure surprised him, but he had the time of his life. To my surprise, Harriet and Courtney were fun to have around. But, by damn, when Harriet is mad at me, she is vicious, so Lord knows I am trying to keep her happy for as long as I can.

We all went home. I took my bath and lay in bed for the longest unable to sleep.

I prayed, "Lord you know how hard it is to keep smiling and laughing when I really want to cry. I beg you to please do with me whatever it is you have planned for me. Here I am crying into my pillow like so many nights before. Brandon is at the age now that I can't take him away from Harriet and this place he has grown to love. Harriet loves him and she depends on him."

"I just want you to take me away. It's me that so miserable. Richard has never known love so he will never understand nor miss me. You know Lord, I can't save Richard. I have talked to him, tried to teach him what real love is. I'm begging you to let me know so I can let him go. I want to get him out of my brain. I don't want to remember the love I had for him. Thank You for Jerry, my dear friends that have danced into my life and forgive me for the sins I do that I don't even realize I've done. You are a wonderful Father and I love you. Please take care of Tony and his family. And a big thank you for Rex and Charlie."

Then I recited the Lord's Prayer out loud just like my Papa King every night so long ago.

The morning sun got me up at eight thirty the next morning. I had my oats and began opening yesterday's mail. **Oh my**! July Twenty first, that's Amanda's birthday and that doll of a mayor, Mr. Doug Brewer is having the third annual Mayberry Day. Twenty dollars for a show and dinner including some of Mayberry's original cast or impersonators Barney, Otis, Floyd, and Opie. I wish I could sell everyone in the city a ticket. The show alone is worth the twenty dollar ticket. It's the most fun day this world has ever seen.

Mr. Brewer has tried hard to bring the City of Graysville alive. He brings in wrestling or boxing once a month. He sponsors one or two events every month and it's all great family fun. He is without a doubt the best Mayor in the state of Alabama.

Thinking about Doug, I remembered what happened at a beauty shop. Doug was in his second term as Mayor and a lady in the beauty shop was badmouthing the Mayor. I told her she didn't know what she was talking about. The lady asked me how I knew so much about him. I told her that Doug has been my lover for two years, three months, one week, and looking at my watch, five hours and fifteen minutes. Everyone in the beauty shop let out a gasp. Mrs. Gray, who had just told me that I looked like Marilyn Monroe asked me if that was true. I told Mrs. Gray to ask the old gray headed heifer, she seems to think she knows him real well, but she would do better to keep up with her own husband. He drops her off here and goes to Jack's café and everyone knows that's where older men go to meet their next wife.

Out the door went the gray-headed heifer. It wasn't true about me and Doug. He is a very good man, he stands his ground and he never fails to set the record straight about any rumors that the old bittie starts. When I said he was the best, I knew what I was talking about. The previous mayor did what was best for him and his family, not for Graysville. He was a little white headed puke. He ranked with Mr. Pretty Boy the mayor of Adamsville, where the judge was so old; that he didn't know what was happening in his own courtroom. His clerk ran the show. She told him every word to say. I wondered why this was allowed to happen. Some of the people working for the city need to be behind bars. Hell, the whole city needs to be behind bars and Graysville needs to take over Adamsville and Shady Grove.

The mayor has all the old folks busy at the senior citizen community center. This mayor is on his feet doing things and making things happen for his city. He just might be Governor of Alabama some day.

This beauty shop deal is a good example of what was once called busy bodies that could only do the hustle and bustle of running their mouth. My God, I thought I couldn't go to the beauty shop without running my mouth either. Lord knows I had to take up for Doug.

I went into the house and called Rex on his cell phone.

"Hello Drucilla."

"Rex, let's go play goft this afternoon."

Rex said, "We can't, we have to dance. We could go in the morning. I'll set up a tee time for eight. That way you'll have time for a nap and we can dance at about seven."

I said, "Why in the world did I call you? Good Bye."

I turned on my computer to see half dozen emails.

Hello Miss Drucilla

I didn't know if you have thought about it but I don't want my email address to get out to everyone. You may already know how to stop yours from being forwarded to others, but if not here it is, there are several easy steps.

1. When you forward an email, delete all of the other addresses that appear in the body of the message, on top of page. That's right, DELETE them. Highlight them and delete them, backspace them, cut them or whatever it is you know how to do. It only takes a second; you must click the forward button first. Then you will have full editing capabilities against the body and headers of the message. If you don't click on forward first, you won't be able to edit the message at all.

Charlie

My Doll

Thank you; I didn't know how to do that. Charlie, tell your Daddy to get busy on writing his story because I'll be going to the Gulf for a few days.

Don't get me wrong. He has been good to me but it's not my imagination, he has taken over my life. It's as if this dancing thing is some kind of competition. I'm so fed up I could stick the one half time and three quarter time up his ass and send him two stepping down the road.

Anyway Doll if at some time you don't hear from me, I'll just be at Gulf Shores and I'll be fine.

Drucilla

Miss. Drucilla

Please don't go anywhere. I need to be able to talk to you.

I know it won't be long until Dad is through. I'm sure he doesn't mean to wear you out. He just wants you to be able to dance and have fun.

He said you love jokes, that you're a lot of fun and when he's with you, time flies by. He really does like Courtney, but don't say I said so.

Please don't go anywhere. Didn't you hear the news about that cruise ship? It's missing everyone on board. Everyone on the ship is gone. It makes me think that terrorists are all around us. I don't believe in UFO's and I don't know yet if the ship was near the Bermuda Triangle but promise me you won't leave town without my Dad.

Charlie

My Charlie Doll

If you feel so strong about this I won't go anywhere at this time.

I'll turn on the news and see what's going on in this world. But you listen up, if this is going to be my place of confinement, I'll go nuts.

Drucilla

Miss. Drucilla

No you won't! You can get busy on our genealogy. You said one time you have fifteen or sixteen Confederate soldiers. Now is a good time to find out about them.

Charlie

Charlie

You're right doll. I can get back into that. I'm very proud of my ancestors. I'll tell you this; my Daddy Robert Lee Brown was named after General Robert E. Lee. General Lee was one of the greatest Americans and for sure the greatest general in the War Between the States. God, honor and country are everything to the Southern people. I honor General Lee to the highest esteem. I have no doubt that he walks the streets of Heaven with our Lord, Jeb Stuart, Stonewall Jackson and Nathan Bedford Forrest. For sure being a Southern girl, I must say, I love all our soldiers. Our men have been soldiers for the past two thousand years and I love each and every one of them.

The men that fought this war are just as important as any soldier who fought in any war. But the government wants this one erased from all memory. Alabama does not teach history in its schools. They want the people of America to forget the War of Northern Aggression. They do not want the truth to be told.

Charlie, ask your Papa what we would do if we didn't have people to pick the food from the fields. Who picks it today? Should they be called slaves? They are paid very little. Anyway, that's beside the point. The War Between the States was not about slavery. The war was about economics. The North knowing the South would secede because of the fifteen percent tariff passed a bill raising the tariff to twenty percent. At this time forty percent of all federal monies came from Southern states. Even after the South seceded, Lincoln sent word to all seceding States that if they would return to the Union, he would pass a law guaranteeing that slavery would be preserved forever. Even the Missouri Compromise wasn't about slavery. It was about Northern states being over populated. They wanted all Western land to be settled by Northern white people. When Lincoln was in the Illinois senate in eighteen fifty-four, he made speeches about saving the Western lands for free white men. He also voted for a bill that prohibited a free black man from living in Illinois. This is all historical fact. All anyone has to do is look it up. But because the North invaded Virginia, well history is told by the victors and the North used slavery as their moral high ground.

Look at the Emancipation Proclamation. It never freed one slave. It was a military ploy. Lincoln was very careful to exclude all lands already in the hands of the North. He was trying to incite a slave revolt, but it didn't work, why from the words of a former slave in the nineteen thirties. We didn't know who owned whom. The blacks and whites took care of each other. The only bad feeling between blacks and whites came because the North during reconstruction used the blacks to blame on their dirty work.

General Lee never owned a slave. He inherited some from his wife's side of the family, but he freed them soon after and that was before the war. Now General Grant, he owned a slave before, during and after the war. When asked why he didn't free his slave, Grant said that good help was hard to find. Grant's slave was not freed until eighteen sixty-eight with the passing of the fourteenth amendment to the Constitution. Slavery could have ended without a war like the rest of the world settled the issue. The federal government could have bought every slave for less money that the war cost. But that was not about to happen. One man bought one hundred twenty acres in Ohio and made a deal to buy five hundred eighteen emancipated slaves to settle in Ohio. The Governor of Ohio got wind of the deal and ordered the Ohio National Guard to stand guard on their side of the Ohio River to stop the freed slaves from entering Ohio.

Reconstruction didn't end until President Roosevelt needed the Southern soldiers to win World War II. After we won the war, they started reconstruction again in the nineteen sixties.

The North won the war for three reasons. The North had more men and supplies. We were fighting two or three men to our one man to start with and toward the end we were fighting ten or twenty men to our one.

In the Lincoln, Douglas debate of eighteen fifty-eight, Lincoln stated that he did not want equality between the black and white races. Not only then but in eighteen fifty seven Lincoln being a Illinois legislator urged his colleagues to appropriate money for the removal of all free blacks from the state of Illinois. An Illinois law stated any white who encouraged blacks to enter the state were subject to a five hundred dollar fine.

As President Lincoln made plans to deport all blacks from America.

If you are too lazy to look up the proof yourself, get the book, 'The Real Lincoln' by Thomas J. Dilorenzo. He has recorded what and when all this and more were said.

Not only Lincoln but the newspapers the Concord Democrat Standard, of New Hampshire, the Philadelphia Inquirer of Pennsylvania, the Providence Daily Post of Ohio, the New York Times of New York, the Daily Chicago Times of Illinois, and the Niles Republican of Michigan were all against abolition.

Drucilla

Miss Drucilla

I know what makes you so mean.

Charlie

Charlie

Remember I'm only mean when someone makes me be. It's in my blood. I'm a Scot from the clan of MacDougall. I am a child of a MacDougall. I have a blood relationship with the founder of the MacDougall clan. Clan people have an immense pride in their race. Their relationship with the chief was like an adult child to a father and they have real dignity.

The MacDougall clan dates back to 1164 when Dougall was the eldest son of Somerled, King of the Hebrides and Requlers of Argyll. Somerled led an uprising against the Norsemen. Hell. We have fought the Vikings, the Romans, and the English and damn near every other country in this world. The MacDougall clan at one time controlled the entire west coast of Scotland and a huge fleet of galleys.

So you see, fighting is in my blood. You can pick any war and I've had a soldier in it. My Uncle Louis was in World War II. He was the most decorated soldier on Onawa Beach.

He was in the first wave on June 6, 1944 with the First Army and by August 25, he was in Paris kicking up his heels with the French women, and by August of forty-five, he was in Berlin with the German women. He almost didn't make it to Berlin. In the Battle of the Bulge, he was sitting in the snow without food or ammunition. He sat there for two days waiting on supplies and when it didn't come, he went behind the German lines. He killed a German soldier and swapped uniforms with him. He went behind their lines, sat down to supper with them, ate, joked and drank with them. He re-supplied himself with their weapons and ammo, killed about two dozen of them and came back to his fox hole in his uniform. When his supplies came he told them he didn't need anything. They were amazed at the food and supplies he had in his foxhole.

Oh! But there was my Great, Great Grandfather that fought in the 'War for Southern Independence' some call it the 'Civil War', but there was nothing civil about it. The Yankees made war on innocent women and children. It should have been called the 'Economic War'.

My Great, Great Grandfather, Isaac Monroe Brown, fought with the 28th Alabama Infantry. He fought at Shiloh, Chickamauga, and Franklin, Tennessee before he was captured on hill 16 in the 'Battle of Nashville'. He was in Atlanta defending the town when General Hood ordered the whole Army to Tennessee. This was November and December of 1864. By now, most of the 28th were without shoes. The Southern Army received most of their supplies from captured Yankee wagons and if you're on a defensive line, there is nothing to capture. He walked from Atlanta to Franklin, Tennessee sometimes in the snow, without shoes and then went into battle. General Hood had a lot of nerve, but lacked strategic ability and he lost his entire Army. While my Grandfather was in prison camp, the Yankees burned his family farm, stole all their food and provisions and left his wife and children to die. But being Southerners they all made it through the tough times. We Southerners are as hard as nails, I have found out.

He was pulled off the front lines and ordered to drive a wagon of ammo to the top of hill 16. When he arrived on top of the hill, there was no one there and before he could get off the hill, a cannon ball hit the wagon. He was blown about 50 feet from the wagon, and when he awoke, he was surrounded by Yankees. He is now buried at the McDonald Chapel Cemetery along with seven other brave Confederates. I placed a monument to commemorate their bravery and sacrifice.

I am blood relation to seven of the eight Confederates buried there. It includes both my great great Grandfathers. My Grandpa Capps had three other brothers in the war. I can feel the heartache of his mother. She had six sons and four of them went to war. Not all returned, her youngest son just turned eighteen, was shot in the arm and the Yankee doctors cut his arm off and placed him on a wagon the same day and sent him to a POW camp. He lived for three days. They placed him in the general population instead of a hospital bed at the POW camp. They murdered him in other words. He was buried at Point Lookout, Maryland.

Their generation was the only ones called upon to put their family and fortune in jeopardy for freedom since the Revolutionary War.

I have or should I say we have a Grandfather in the Revolutionary War, too.

One of my Grandfathers owned several hundred acres there and the first person buried there was his Grandson. He was thrown from a horse and was killed and Grandpa started the cemetery. My Grandpa McDonald was also a Mason. He was born in 1803 and received a land grant from the government because of his father's service in the Revolutionary War. He was a Methodist preacher and his church was four miles away at Crumbly Chapel. It took him six hours to travel by horse and wagon to Crumbly Chapel. After a while he decided the trip was too much for his family and he built McDonald Chapel Methodist Church and it still stands today. There are eight Confederate veterans buried in the cemetery of which I'm related to by blood ties they are; Private Isaac Monroe Brown, Company "D" 28th Alabama Infantry, my Great Grandfather; Private George Washington Capps, Company "F" 21st Alabama Infantry, my Grandfather's Father-in-law. The rest married cousins; Sergeant James E Blackwell, Company "F" 38th Alabama Volunteers; Private Johnathan Westley Blackwell, Captain Truss' Battalion; Private John Polk Capps, Company "B" 21st Alabama Infantry; Private William Newton Holmes, Company "C" 12th Alabama Cavalry; Private William McDonald, Company "F" Smith's Legion Georgia Infantry; the one not related is Private James A Goolsby, Company "D" 28th Alabama Infantry all in all I have twenty three relatives which fought for Southern Independence.

My Great-Great-Grandpa Brown was in the Revolutionary War also. He received five thousand acres on what today is TCI ground. He has his name on a monument in Woodrow Wilson Park in Birmingham Alabama. John Brown was his name and his son William Brown received the grant in 1805. He invited Davy

Crocket of the Alamo fame to spend a month hunting with him. He offered Davy some land to settle here but I guess Davy didn't like Alabama. William had several sons and they were founders of several small towns in this county. They were very prominent schoolteachers, planters, politicians and adventures. Some left here and settled in Mississippi, Arkansas, and as far as Texas. But they all loved freedom and when time came, they were all there to fight. I'll say it again; I'm only as mean as you make me.

Drucilla

Miss. Drucilla,

Yes, I know what you're saying. You don't start a fight, but if it comes into your world you will finish it. I'm only twelve, but I can take on four men at a time. I can kick 'em out and you can shoot them.

Charlie

Charlie,

Another Union General of fame, a man named John C Freemont was in charge of Union held Missouri on a 30 August eighteen sixty one issued a proclamation of marshal law and anyone resisting the occupying Union Army would have their property confiscated and their slaves freed. You get the picture I could go on and on.

Drucilla

Miss. Drucilla,

You really do know about the War Between the States.

Charlie

Charlie,

Not just the war for Southern Independence, my GGGG Grandfather was one of the first three men to receive the badge of Military merit later to be known as the Purple Heart. I have grandfathers in every war from the beginning of time. The Irish love their freedom.

Drucilla

Miss Drucilla,

Sorry I didn't know the proper name for the war. The government schools teach only the yankee version of history and sometimes we don't even get that much.

Charlie

Charlie,

If I were a black person I would be doing everything in my power to go back to Africa and scream here I am. I'm back and I'm much better off than when you sold my father to the white man. I don't know why they aren't pissed at their own people for selling them. It's all part of the communists' big Lincoln lie.

We needed workers to pick cotton, strawberries, tomatoes and peaches in a hundred years will the Mexicans hate whites and say they were our slaves too? I wonder how the communists will arrange that lie.

I have had people to work for me at my home. They had much less than me and needed the work. I gave them clothes; food and sometimes-medical help and they love me for it, till this day.

I wish the blacks would be thankful that we did need them. Their own people didn't want or need them. They sold them, why be mad at us? The black mayor of New Orleans wants a chocolate city. I can understand him wanting that to be true. I've talked to whites and blacks alike and both say the same thing. The government makes us go to school with each other and work with each other, but thank God we don't have to go home with each other. Blacks move into white communities because they are afraid of their own kind. Very few go to mixed churches and for sure nightclubs are not mixed. I think if they really check out their own hearts, all their problems stem from the yearning to be in their own homeland.

Did you see on television where Oprah went to Africa and built an all girls school? It was wonderful; they need many more schools, hospitals and homes. They need better health care and today, with all the blacks having all the big money jobs that they would build a country for their people. But they won't. Why??? Look at the African countries in Africa that gained their independence from white rule. All the plantations were taken over and destroyed within ten years, most of the population was starving and gangs of war lords starting appearing and killing everyone in their way.

Just listen to the news. It wasn't ten years ago that the news was tracking a slave ship off the west coast of Africa.

I've heard some say this is where I was born. I'm here to tell you, it has nothing to do with where you were born. It's where your Great great great great grandfather and mothers' roots are from that's where your yearning will stop. They need to go home and build them a world and see to it that all their people learn and have all they need and want.

I was just reading the Birmingham newspaper; it read that thousands have traced their historic steps. These people don't need to keep walking these steps over and over again. They want to be loved and respected by all. They need to build their own empire and then and only then will they have the respect of the world. Tearing down what the white man built will not earn them respect.

From the street corner to the radio talk shows, people are saying Mrs. Hillary came South and walked the walk and tried to talk the talk. She did everything but spray on a tan and call herself black. Mrs. Hillary isn't smart enough to know that there was nothing she could have done. By staying with the likes of Bill Clinton she lost all of her credibility. He does nothing for her but remind all of us what a scumbag he is. He even wrote a book and called it "Because I Can". You can't get any worse than admitting in print to the public how you hurt and disgraced your wife. If communism means it's ok to be a trashy man like he is then our world doesn't need this liberal way of life for our future. Ok Charlie, I'll get off my soapbox and get back to my own people.

Goodbye my doll. I have to be ready for those dancing fools tonight. You know I love it and I thank you.

Drucilla

Miss. Drucilla,

I thought you may like this. You got me in the wind, searching. I was in a chat room with an older friend of mine. He said many will recall that on July 8, 1947 witnesses found the wreckage of an unidentified flying object with five aliens aboard that had crashed on a sheep and cattle ranch just outside Roswell, New Mexico. As you know, this is a well-known incident that many believe has long been covered up by the United States Air Force and federal government. However you may not know that in the month of March 1948, exactly nine months after that historic day, Albert Arnold Gore Jr., Hillary Rodham, John F Kerry, William Jefferson Clinton, Dianne Feinstein, Charles E, Schumer and Barbara Boxer were born. See what happens when aliens breed with sheep. This piece of information may clear up a lot of things. HA HA

Charlie

Charlie

Oh My! So young to be so smart Charlie, are you sure you're not an older man?

You have taught me how to use this computer. You have me dancing like I can't believe. You hunt, fish, and know all about guns and now Washington and the Clintons? Already you know the changes of liberalism. You do know doll, humor is good for us, sometimes and we have people in Washington that need to be laughed out of office. I never got a belly laugh out of anything that's said about them because its truer than most think and they have our world in a dangerous mess.

Learn all you can, learn Charlie and keep your world full of goodness. We must know what judges to vote out. We had one judge here that was a juvenile court judge and when needed, he would step up to regular court. He didn't believe in the death penalty and when called on a murder trial he would not recuse himself. His first murder trial the jury gave the death penalty to the murderer and he changed it to life with parole. There was public outrage but being a good liberal he thumbed his nose at the public. Then he was called to judge another murder trial. This was an especially horrendous crime and again he refused to apply the death penalty. He ran for re-election soon after and was over whelmingly defeated and never heard from again. That's the type of judge that needs to be weeded out. They are on the bench to administer justice according to the law, not their personal feelings. Something else doll, there needs to be a stop put to judges being appointed for life. There should be a clause to take a judge from the bench when he becomes unable to perform his duties. And most of all take the political correctness out of the selection process.

Just maybe you could be a politician and I'll run your campaign. If my dream comes true and I end up with Mr. Tortomasi, just maybe we can groom you to be President someday. I think you would make a great President. You would know exactly what to do with the funky chickens, the turkey trotters and surely the howling horn blowers and whistle blowers. Maybe they will all be out of office by then. You just be sure to check out all the hiding places you know Clinton may still have a few belly dancers stacked somewhere to this day. Maybe that's why Papa Bush is one of his best friends.

The American people should have made sure that the Senate impeached Clinton. He is a real freak. The people running this country are supposed to be leaders. God fearing leaders with morals, but they are just brain farts.

From nineteen forty-seven on this country has turned out nothing but a world full of polluters.

I can see it now. Large billboards advertising Washington's amusement, "Come one, come all, buy your tickets from Mrs. Hillary, see Bill do his cigar tricks." Can't you just see it, a big piggy bank on Mrs. Hillary's desk with the name Sherrie written on the pig. You know Mrs. Hillary could sure use Billy boy to make herself some big time money and just think Miss Sherrie just got paid pocket change, piggy bank money.

I'll tell you something else, if all that had happened to Mrs. Laura Bush, she would have had George's favorite whore's head cut off and his oil wells would have been on her side of the field. She would have tied a knot in his butt worse than a pretzel.

Drucilla

Three in the afternoon I ran to answer the telephone.
Rex said, "Hello Drucilla. How are you?"
I replied, "How are y'all, I 'm fine."
Rex said, "I'll pick you up at seven so we can go dancing."
"I'll be ready, but I want to stop at Dave's Pub for a drink or two. I want to tease Jim a little then we can go over to the Barking Kudu."
Rex said, "Drucilla, the girls want to know what you will be wearing tonight."
I told him, "Levi's, leather and lace, and Rex, I want to stop at Stir Crazy to see Gary for a while, my Gary Jackson, I love him."
Rex said, "Ok, Baby, whatever you say. See you at seven. Drucilla, don't drink too much."
"Don't worry Rex. Gary watches after me. He'll bring me home in that long limousine."
It was late by the time we arrived at the Barking Kudu.
Buddy asked, "Drucilla, what are you doing here?"
I replied, "I'm here in hopes Crawford has heard from Tony. I told Crawford if Tony comes to this town he'd come here. If he comes

here you'll know and Crawford will tell me. Did Crawford tell you to look out for him?"

Buddy said, "Yes Drucilla. Come on in my office, I have a note for you."

I followed Buddy into his office and he said very quietly, "Go through that door and when you're in there, lock the door behind you."

I went through the door and switched on a dim light. I noticed a note on a small table and ran over to pick it up, but hesitated before opening it. I really thought Tony would be here tonight. Then I heard two little knocks on the door. I opened the door and there he stood. So-oo-oo damn gorgeous, Tony looked me up and down saying softly, "Kiss me, and kiss me right now."

I could feel his chest rise and fall as if we were one.

Tony said, "Your perfume makes me crazy. Come with me."

Tony and I went out another door where a limousine was waiting.

Tony said, "Rex has an apartment not far from here."

Tony unlocked the apartment door and took me by the hand.

Tony said, "I know you've never been this far before."

We entered and Tony went straight to a closet door and removed many blankets and pillows.

Tony said, "Come to me."

I softly wrapped my arms around Tony and asked, "Do you have any soreness anywhere?"

"No! And with all that dancing I've heard about I'll bet you don't have any either."

Tony unbuttoned my lace blouse and lay me up against the pillows while he was pulling off my leather boots. I reached to unbutton and unzip my Levi's but he pushed my hand away.

Tony said, "I'll take care of that."

And he did. He got down on his knees took my pants legs and eased my Levi's off. He was so gentle I never knew when they came off. He then removed my blouse, bra and panties.

Tony stepped back and said, "Damn, my Lady, you're beautiful!"

Tony took me into his arms and kissed me and yes I could read his lips.

I turned loose saying, "I think it's my turn."

I loosened his tie while he was unbuckling his belt. He slipped off his loafers, his jacket was off, every stitch, and there he was, my golden God. Tony took me into his arms as if I were a baby. He kissed me tenderly all over my face and both sides of my neck. My God, his skin was getting hotter by the second as if he had a fever.

I said, "My God, Tony, I'm ready for some action."

Tony said, "Don't get too anxious doll. I want to enjoy every second."

I was thinking of the song, 'I've Never Been This Far Before'. I pushed him over and jumped straddle of him, my body sliding down his body, kissing every inch as I slid down. We made love like there was no tomorrow. I made him say "Uncle" three times. It was real love like I've never known before.

Tony said, "Drucilla, time out, time out, my turn."

Tony rolled me onto my side and said, "Now relax those muscles."

Tony was on me kissing me all over. Teaching me about places I never knew I had.

I said, "Stop, stop!"

"No, you're wonderful and you've waited a long time for me. Just for me. I know, with every step I have taken today I've had you on my mind."

With an immediate sensation in my crotch I said, "Yes! Had I known you were here my clothes would have been held together with Velcro."

Tony rolled me over and over again looking at me, kissing me.

I said, "Wait, you have gone far beyond anything I ever intended."

Tony asked, "Didn't your dreams of me ever take you to those places?"

"No Tony! But obviously you know that you have totally aroused me. A fantasy something I couldn't ever have dreamed about. You are the answers to my prayers."

Tony said, "Dru, just be still, please don't move."

I said, "Anything! Oh my, our feelings are so in touch, so intense."

I couldn't wait, my need was too powerful after resting briefly, still naked on our pallet, we were both limp and depleted but I couldn't resist moving my hips, letting Tony know that I was still hungry for his love. Tony came alive and didn't' turn loose of my lips until he heard the moans of pleasure.

Tony held me ever so softly as I said, "I had feared that I wouldn't be good enough to completely satisfy you."

Tony said, "No! It was me that had a fear. I wanted and needed to satisfy you. To show you the passion I feel for you."

I said, "We now know that we're going to be very, very good together."

Tony said, "We know we are together in our minds. There will never be a day that I don't need you."

"I must say Tony; your love making has left me a esthetic."

My mind was racing a million miles an hour. My heart was pounding until I thought it would burst. I'm on top of the world.

"When, Tony, when can I see you again? Please don't make me wait long."

"I won't Dru. I need you to tell me if you remember any of my family. Were they in your dreams?"

"Yes, Tony, your brother Michael, he's thirty four, then there was Papa Perricotti, Max Tombrello, oh my I love Max, are they for real. How is our Anthony? Let me see, Sandra the house keeper and Roger Tommynacker."

Tony said, "Yes Dru, they are all for real, and I've told them all about you. They think I made you up. That is all but Anthony; he knows you are coming home to him someday."

I said, "I sure am Tony, the sooner the better."

Tony said, "Yes, and I'll be right here to get you whenever you say the time and day. But now we must get cleaned up and dressed. All your men are waiting on you in the lounge."

I asked, "Even Papa Perricotti and Max?"

Tony said, "Yes, but only one kiss for each one."

"Tony, I may cry."

"No! Dru, you belong to me now. Your crying days are over."

We cleaned the room and ourselves up and were ready to go downstairs. Tony took me into his arms and kissed me very wet and tenderly.

I begged, "Do we have to go?"

Tony said, "I'm afraid so, but someday soon you'll have me forever."

As we were entering the lounge, Tony said, "I'll go this way and you go to the right and come directly across the dance floor and I'll meet you in the middle."

The singer on stage said, "Here comes trouble in Levi's, leather and lace."

We met in the middle of the deserted dance floor. Tony took me in his arms and we melted into each other arms, dancing as if we were meant for each other.

I looked over Tony's shoulder and saw Courtney was dancing with Max and Harriet was sitting at a corner table talking to someone.

"**Oh my God!** Tony, don't tell me that the two rag heads that were with Rex were Michael and Max."

Tony smiled saying, "I have them taking care of you."

First I felt angry, then weakness and a light-headedness. Tony was all but holding me up when Max ran over picking me up.

Max said, "Now Miss Drucilla."

"**Now hell!** Why didn't I see through that beard and your hair? I know you didn't know me, but I should have known you. This is a dirty trick. Put me down!"

Max and I walked over to Papa Perricotti's table.

"My name is Drucilla Hallmark and it's a pleasure to meet you sir."

Papa Perricotti said, "The pleasure is all mine and my Grandson tells me that you will be coming home to us as Mrs. Tony Tortomasi."

I said, "I hope to very soon."

Papa Perricotti said, "It's amazing how you two met."

"Yes sir, it was. One day I'll tell you about an Angel that made it all happen."

I kissed Papa and winked at Max as we walked back to Tony's table where he was talking to Michael.

Michael said, "Come on Duriclla, Let's show these fellas how we dance."

I said, "Michael I don't know if I can. This night has been too much for me."

Michael said, "You want me to tell Tony that?"

I said, "Do you want me to kill you?"

Michael led me to the dance floor where we danced the Salsa and the Shag.

Then Tony took me away from Michael. Holding me close in his arms we waltzed around the room.

I said, "Tony, you are a wonderful dancer."

Tony said, "Sure I am, but how did I score on those love techniques?"

I kissed him and asked, "Did you read my lips?"

Tony said, "I did. That tight ass of yours is going to drive me crazy."

I said, "No, no, no its not, cause I'll give you plenty of it. I've been a virgin way to long."

Tony said, "Girl, you give new meaning to sleeping single in a double bed. But for now I have to go. I'll be back when you call. Tell the boys what you want and they will take care of anything."

I told him, "But Tony, I want you. Richard is gone forever. You have me the courage to leave him. We have been seen in public now and I don't see any need to wait. I don't want to wait any longer."

Tony said, "Be patient my love. Now is not the time. Everyone here is your friend; no one will talk about us. It won't be long now. I'm just as anxious as you, but we have to wait. By the way, I had your dream home built, the one you told Dr. Bradley about. See dreams do come true."

I said, "Call me soon Tony."

The next morning the cruise ship was on all the news stations and in the newspapers. An abandoned cruise ship was found in the

Bermuda Triangle. What a mystery, no people, no sign of a struggle. They didn't find a dirty dish. No food cooked or in the freezer. No luggage or personal belongings to be found. They found the Captain's log with the names of everyone that boarded the ship. All computers had their hard drives erased not even a finger print on any of them. The gambling machines were empty of money. The ship left Port Canaveral, Florida on Monday, sailed to Nassau in the Bahamas when it laid over for eight hours of sightseeing and then left for Cancun, Mexico and was found Friday in the Bermuda Triangle when another ship almost collided with it. It still had almost a full tank of fuel. The ship's log does not account for the three days at sea and it was found only four hundred fifty miles from the Bahamas. That ship could have traveled that distance in twenty hours and would have been seen if it was dead in the water where it was located.

I turned off the television and went to the computer to see if I had an email from Charlie.

> Hi Miss Drucilla,
>
> Have you had time to read the paper? Turn on CNN; they said fifty-seven of the people on that cruise ship are from around Birmingham, from Walker, Blount and Jefferson counties in Alabama. I do believe that is close to you. I'm glad you weren't on that ship.
>
> Charlie

> Charlie,
>
> Yes my child, I'm glad too, but my ex-husband was on that ship. I think he said about fifty-seven others around here were going with him.

If I ever get to go on a cruise I want you to check out the people that are going with me. I don't want to go the same route as these people did.

Have you ever thought that if there are UFO's just maybe they live under the sea and not in the heavens? Don't let this ship upset you Charlie. It's not the first and won't be the last ship to disappear in the Bermuda Triangle.

Drucilla

The doorbell rang and I cut off the computer and went to the door. Harriet, Percy, Jerry and Brandon were at the door asking about Richard.

Percy asked, "Drucilla, what are you going to do about Richard? You know he's on that cruise ship and he's lost."

I said, "Well he's always been lost to me and remember he doesn't belong to me anymore. I'm sure Harriet has told all of you that I'm leaving. I'm going to marry Tony. If you want to take care of Richard, fine, but I don't want any part of it. I'm marrying Tony on the Fourth of July."

I shut the door behind them and went back to my computer.

Charlie,

I'm sure your Dad has told you about me being shot and while in the hospital I met someone that I love with all my heart and soul. Well I got to be with him last night for about five hours.

He has built me a new home near the Gulf here in Alabama. I haven't known him long but someday I'll tell you all about him. For that matter he has a son about your age, his name is Anthony. I met him first on the beach at the Gulf and to tell you the truth it was Anthony that I fell in love with first. Just think someday soon I'll be his Mom.

Now Charlie, I will always be able to talk to you and for sure I love you too. I must go now, someone's at the door again.

Drucilla

I answered the door and said, "Hello Rex, come on in. I want to talk to you about Brandon. I know in my dreams Brandon was with me at the Gulf, but I know he won't come to stay with me. If he was still six or seven, he would have, but at age twelve he won't. Now he is torn between Harriet and me. With Daddy passing away and Harriet moving in with Mama Marcella. I care for her, and I knew Brandon would never leave here. I want you to make him your friend. Get him out from under Harriet's coattail. I can't do any more as you know I'm leaving this place. I've been here too long already. Rex, have you really been writing my story?"

Rex said, "Yes Drucilla, Sergeant Stone told me much about you and I'm surprised you didn't get yourself killed."

I replied, "I can tell you now boy, I was too mad to let anyone kill me. How long have you known Max?"

Rex said, "Not much longer than I've known you."

"I'll tell you one thing. You are no Max. I'll tell you that straight up."

Rex asked, "Why do you say that Drucilla?"

"Because I know him real well and when I ask Max to help me take care of a problem, he won't be a worm."

Rex jumped to his feet and said, "Well I've done what I was told to do."

I said, "Oh yes, and that was to baby-sit me. Well I don't want a babysitter. I want the bastards that hurt me to be hurt."

Rex said, "Drucilla, we babysitters go over this house inch by inch every day to see if anyone is listening or watching you. I'm sure your telephone men are recording everything you say. Now with Richard missing on that cruise ship it's time to get a new computer and I've seen to it that Charlie has a new computer today. You know whatever you think you've erased can still be brought back."

"Yes, Charlie has told me that much."

Rex said, "In the trash bin, so to speak, it's still there so I need to take yours and set you up another computer."

"Do you mean I can't talk to Charlie?"

Rex said, "No you can't. Charlie knows and it's OK with him. He knows it won't be long until he will get to meet you."

"Fine, take what you will. I'll call Mr. Dasher and he'll put together everything I need and I'll go pick it up."

"Drucilla, you have to be more careful what you type on the computer, or write at anytime and for sure what you say on the telephone."

I asked, "Where is Max? Tell him I need to see him. Don't say it Rex! Just get Max for me."

Rex stood up, his chest stuck out as if it would make him a big man.

Rex sharply said, "That may take a while."

"Then I'll wait awhile."

"Drucilla, you are so spoiled."

I asked, "Boy! Do you smell anything that stinks?"

Rex said, "No."

"Well, spoiled things stink so that leaves me out."

It was about four and one half hours before Max came in. I could have jumped straddled his neck.

Max asked, "Are all these things true that I heard about you girl?"

I said, "Yes. Now I'm going to ask you something and I never want you to lie to me. Not even a little white lie. A lie is a lie even little white lies. Rex took my computer because I can't be connected to Charlie because that could lead to Tony. Is that right?"

Max said, "Yes Drucilla, you can't. You can't write it. You can't type it and you can't say it over the telephone. You have to marry Tony or maybe marry me and get all this behind you."

I said, "What a bargain you offer me. I love you Max. You may never know how much but believe me I love you. I'll do whatever you say when you say it. I know I can trust you. I'll never lie to you either."

Max said, "I'll always be here for you."

I asked, "Anyway, what took you so long to get here?"

Max said, "Well mam, I had to drive here from the Gulf."

I asked, "So if I call for you and you're at the North Pole, you'll come to me? You'll be my partner in crime, my soul mate?"

Max said, "Yes I will. But you knew that before you asked didn't you?"

"Yes I did. So you think the mulcher will make a good reef deep down under?"

Max said, "No I don't, where it's dumped its three thousand feet deep."

I asked, "How is Papa doing? Does he still go to the cock fights?"

Max said, "Yes he does and he has a pair for you."

I asked, "Oh my, does Tony know about them?"

Max said, "Yes, Papa told him that you may become his wife, but you would be going with him to have fun."

Max said, "Tony let us see that film of you singing with a Johnny Cash impersonator. I'll tell you, Papa saw you bouncing across the stage in the little black skirt with slits all around the hem. We heard Papa say, 'Damn, damn'. Tony asked Papa what was wrong. Papa said he had just downed three beers before realizing it. Then he started singing to Tony. Tony had let Papa see his beautiful girl because he knew papa was no threat. All Papa could do was just hang loose. Tony told Papa that he would ask you to send Mrs. Malviene to see him and Papa said there wouldn't be any use and we all burst out laughing."

I said, "That's what I want, a fun family. I want the rest of my life to be happy. Why are you trying to change the subject Max?"

Max said, "Remember, we can't talk about it at all."

I asked "Will you help me find Harriet and Brandon a home in Clanton or maybe someday she will move closer to Gulf Shores?"

Max said, "You just need you. Tony and I and our family need you. You come home to us. It's where you belong."

Chapter 13

"Drucilla, now that you know your destiny, I'll tell you about Charlie. Charlie is your Anthony. He didn't want you to know."

I fainted, and when I awoke I was lying on the floor and Max was holding a cold cloth on the back of my neck. I couldn't hold back the tears.

Max said, "I'm sorry, we couldn't let you know before now."

I asked, "Max, Charlie is Anthony, Tony's Anthony?"

Max said, "Yes Drucilla, the one and only."

I said, "Good God! Max I have talked to Charlie I mean Anthony almost every day. He is so full of knowledge. Good Lord we have talked about everything under the sun. He has taught me so much about the computer and how do you think I knew so much about dancing. My Anthony, I can't believe it. Does Tony know?"

Max said, "This has really got you going. Yes, Tony knows, nothing happens without Tony giving the order."

I said, "Yes I . . ."

Max broke in saying, "Don't say it Drucilla! Remember we don't say anything out loud. We have to keep all of us apart so the law couldn't connect you with Tony. The ship is gone. Everyone knows you were here and not in contact with Tony. You gave Rex a lot to work with and we have screened everyone on your list. I'll tell you girl, I couldn't believe some of this stuff. I had to see for myself and you're right Richard's friends are rubbish."

"You mean Richard and all his whores are rubbish. Don't ever leave him out. He's a male whore."

I paused a minute and then asked, "So Max, you're telling me that I can't talk to Anthony?"

Max said, "That's right. Your computer along with his, was shipped out to be dumped into the ocean."

"Max, I must tell you I don't want anything to happen to Percy or Harriet. Someone makes us all what we are. This bunch was raised by Mama Marcella and now she's half dead. Harriet has to take care of her. She's been going downhill fast ever since I killed DeRoy. Max, why do I feel so sorry for all them? Tell me, do you think I'll be alright with Tony's family?"

Max said, "Yes, they all love you."

I asked, "Do you love me Max? Will you protect me at all times? Will you be my best friend just like in my dreams?"

Max said, "Yes, I'm in love with you with all my heart. I'll be whatever you want me to be. And most of all, I don't' want Rex taking my place."

I said, "No one could ever take your place. I don't even want you to go back to the Gulf without me. To tell you the truth, I'm in shock that Tony would want me. I've been half crazy and down in the dumps for so long. I'm praying I'll be ok with all this. I don't want to wake up and find out this is all another dream."

Max said, "I assure you, this is no dream. I'll ask you again, are you sure you didn't know Tony from somewhere else?"

"I didn't Max, only in my dream. But it is so unreal that our minds got together the way it did. We aligned our lives together in that dream. I know Papa, Michael, Ross, Roger Tommynocker, Charlie Perricotti, and you, baby do I know you."

Max said, "Do you know that Tony had the exact same dream as you. Tony says an Angel made it happen. Two brains, two souls and that the two of you will never be separated till death. I can tell you a few things. Tony has you a new V16 Jaguar and has you all set to play golf. I can't think of anything that you won't have. You will be protected by the best. Most of all, you will have love."

I asked, "Now you swear to me that Charlie is really my Anthony and he knows all about my dream?"

Max said, "I swear to you Drucilla and he loves you."

"Max, do you know if the boys are coming to dance tonight?"

Max said, "Yes, and I know you've got to take a nap."

I said, "Lock my door on your way out, and I'll see you at seven."

Max started toward the door and I said, "Max, come back here."

Max walked back to me and I hugged him saying, "You are special to me. In my dream you and me had a bond and I want that for us now."

Max looked into my green eyes as if searching for my soul and said, "You have me wrapped around your little finger. Only death will break our bond."

With a light kiss on my lip, he was gone.

I sat down thinking, I know we have unseen angels and I know I have a few real ones. Yes, I'm going to be the very best I can for my new family. My dancing will be spectacular. First of all, I'll get out of bed before ten in the mornings. I'll fry pies at three in the morning if that's what he wants.

For Tony, I'll be the best I can be. That will be easy. I'll just be myself. A bath and nap at three and dancing until eleven.

Before Max left, I asked him to go to Center Point and find Phillip Jimez. Tell him I wanted him to come see me. Then find Sergeant Stone and ask him to come see me. Both men came the next afternoon, Sgt. Stone came first.

As I welcomed Sgt. Stone into the house, I said, "I am leaving Shady Grove, will you have the deputies make extra rounds down Melissa Lane to check on my folks and especially Brandon?"

Sgt. Stone said, "Drucilla, your story would make a great movie. You have been a fighter. You didn't let any of this hold you back."

"No sir, because I have friends like you and I'll always need you in my life. You and all my big brothers kept me from going crazy."

Sgt. Stone left before Phillip arrived.

Phillip asked, "Drucilla, is it true that you're leaving us?"

"No sir, I'm leaving Shady Grove, but I'll never leave you. You will always be in my heart, on my mind and just five hours down the road. You're a fine man. I'm thankful that I've had you as my friend. I've had days of doubting myself and wondered if you all thought I was just a nut. I can't help being me. I couldn't leave it alone. I had forces behind me making me get to the truth. Remember what you said to me about the whores I found? You said, 'Tell their husbands'.

Some I did, the other I will. Remember the whore in Sandusky? Before he left, he spray-painted a whore lives here on the front of her house. You had to send three cars out there because she was out in the yard shooting at anyone that looked at her house. That just made sure a picture of her house made the front page of the newspaper. We had some laughs. Anyway, I just want to tell you that I'm moving to Gulf Shores and I want you to come see me anytime."

Phillip said, "Drucilla, you need to stay here and help solve a few cases or are you moving to the Gulf to work on Richard's missing case?"

"No, I'm through with Richard now and forever. But I am the girl that found all those stolen cars and house whores. Come to think of it, there is one house whore married to a detective that lives in Westwood. She drives a dark blue Yugo. The last one I met was Mrs. Malviene. She's the freak of all sluts. Tell all my big brothers she has herpes from head to toe. Her sisters call her the Larva girl. You know I've never lead you wrong on anything and I never will."

"You remember the lady lawyer that has never been found? I'll always say her husband had it done. The young girl that was shot in her driveway, you need to look at her sister's husband for that. One more thing, I want you to pass on. There are more drugs running up the Warrior River than on Seventy Eight Highway."

"I told Sgt. Stone that I'm not going to say a word to Brandon about going with me, I want it to be his decision. When I leave this place, I won't be crying. You know the old saying; the only thing to mend a broken heart is another love. This is the truth, the whole truth and nothing but the truth."

Phillip said, "You're really OK now Drucilla. You have lived through hell and now you're fine. You know we never did get to play that round of golf."

"Well, I'll tell you what. I'll meet you at eight o'clock this Saturday morning."

Phillip said, "That's a deal. Tell me again, where that Mrs. Malviene lives. You said get on Fieldstown Road and turn right onto Shady Grove Road and she's in a new subdivision, right? Is her husband's name Rocky?"

I said, "One in the same."

Phillip said, "You won't ever have to worry about them again. They were both on the cruise ship with Richard. There were a big party on that cruise ship from Sumiton, Dora, Jasper and Blount County."

I stated, "I heard the ship was found in the Bermuda Triangle. My God that must be the dumping ground for hell. So Richard may never come back. That means Jeff, Amanda's ex won't come back either. Well, I'm speechless."

Phillip jumped up saying, "You won't do my lady. I'll see you Saturday."

I said, "OK, just remember, I'll be there to win."

Phillip turned to face me at the door and said, "I know one thing. Golf is the only thing that will get you out of bed before ten o'clock."

Phillip looked deep into my green eyes and asked, "How are you really?"

I responded, "Never in my life have I been better. I thank you from the bottom of my heart for all you have done for me. You being my friend means so much to me. If it hadn't been for you men behind the badges, Richard would have put me in the crazy house. You know that and I know that, maybe even six foot under. Anyway, a lot of good came out of it all. Most of all, I don't love this place any longer. I love my people that I have left. I can leave this place and never look back, and I'll do that very soon."

I let Phillip out with a hug. After Phillip left, I got to thinking about all the things Richard said to me. About the things he would do to my family if I left him. Well, the devil has got the devil in the devils triangle. That's where he belongs. No, no, no, I want to think about Tony. I ran to the bedroom, got under the covers and on the verge of crying, I called to Tony. "Tony I need you. Yes, I'm breathing deep. Yes I'm getting calm now. Yes I feel the heat from your hands."

Almost asleep I thought, thank God, a comfortable relationship, twin souls, so perfect for each other. The hottest and most passionate love that's ever been joined together. Here we are Tony, for all eternity. When I awoke, I was one hundred percent better.

Chapter 14

Harriet called me on the telephone. She said, "I just got home from carrying Mama to the doctor. The doctor is sending hospice out. Mama is dying."

I asked, "Is there anything I can do to help you?"

Harriet answered, "**Hell no!** I asked you to keep Mama for me when she could have enjoyed being with you. Now it's too late. I just wanted you to know. I don't want you to do anything."

I hung up the telephone and thought about Mama Marcella. I did not go to see Mama but once or twice a week because Harriet stayed mad at me because I couldn't take care of Mama while she went out to party. I tried a couple of times and Harriet said she'd be back in a couple of hours and never came back until after midnight. I wasn't in good health at the time and Mama wasn't able to get out of her chair without help. By eleven I was so exhausted I couldn't get out of my chair. I just wasn't physically able to lift mama and that didn't seem to matter to Harriet. Daddy gave each child a plot of land to build a house on and all that was left to the child that was taking care of them in their old age. Harriet made the decision to care for them but soon tired of the job and tried to put it off onto the other kids. She would have a doctor's appointment for herself at two o'clock and not get home until midnight.

When Mama Marcella was put into bed I did go see her every day. I was thankful that I had sent her flowers from time to time. Now I saw to it that she always had flowers by her bedside. Brandon told me later that after I left, Harriet would throw the flowers in the garbage.

I tried to help Harriet, but she treated me so bad in front of her friends and the hospice nurses. It was all I could do just to keep my mouth shut. Then Harriet found Sherrie. I just couldn't take this fat ass trying to take over. I already had one run in with her. She messed up a project we were both on and then lied about it trying to place the blame all on me. But I had a paper trail on her and that pinned the tail on the mule face. Anyway, she came in lingering over Mama like she had known her all her life and even tried to order the nurses around.

Mama was still alert some of the time and I didn't want to upset her so I went home and wrote a note. The note read . . .

> You are not hanging over my Mama's deathbed. She has four daughters and two sons. We are a big family and I understand that you have a Mother of your own. So get your fat ass out of here and stay out.
>
> Drucilla

I placed the note under the wiper blade on the windshield of her car. I didn't tell her to her face in Mama's house, because I didn't want to upset Mama. Mule Face didn't leave until ten that night. Lord did she ever put on a first class show. She screamed and hollered, crying so loud it would have awoke the dead. She acted as if fainting, but she knew nobody would be able to pick her lard ass up. She kept on her feet until her wiener husband dragged her back into Mama's house. Harried called me threatening to call the Sheriff if I ever came back to Mama's house. I told Harriet to kiss my ass and call the Sheriff right now because I'd be there in the morning.

Harriet should have nicely put her up the road. She knew I didn't like the lying gossip. But that's why Harriet brought her down here, just to stick pins in me. I mean, under these conditions, she should stay away without being told. This is a family thing. That makes Harriet and Mule Face, two peas in a pod.

I was still mad the next morning so I called Mama's doctor and told him that Harriet had Mama in a back room where it was dark and Mama was not comfortable. Harriet was also sending someone to a fast food place to buy Mama gravy and biscuits every morning and it was too heavy on Mama's stomach and making her sick.

The doctor called Harriet and told her to move Mama to the living room and feed her light food and less of it.

Just like Harriet said, she called the Sheriff. The Sheriff called me to come out there. Harriet must think I'm afraid of the Law. I'm not afraid of her lies, just like I wasn't afraid of Mule Face's lies.

I took my happy ass in her front door and winked at the Sheriff. Harriet thought she had me. She took out her deeds and put them out in front of the Sheriff and me.

Harriet said, "See these papers. This is my house."

I said, "Harriet, I know all about those papers because they were written up at Mr. Williams' office. Remember he's my attorney and it didn't cost you a dime. This house won't be yours until Mama draws her last breath."

I turned toward the Sheriff and said, "You can come here every day, and walk me in here and stay until I get ready to go home. I'm telling you and Harriet that I am going to be here every day, sometimes all day and as Mama gets sicker I'll be here around the clock."

I turned back to Harriet and said, "I hate to waste Mr. Williams' time about this, but I will! You better keep her away from this bed, or you'll need a Sheriff."

I turned back to the Sheriff and said, "Sir, if that's all you need me for I have food in the oven and I need to get back. If you want to take me in, I'll meet you out by the road. If not, tomorrow come to my house and we'll both come to see Mama."

He winked at me and left and didn't come back but Mule Face did a few times but she sat on the porch sulled up like a opossum. I can just picture that fat ass, Mule Face opossum sitting there.

As Mama got worse, all her kids were with her. My brother Jerry was so hurt. He had loved Mama, he loved us all. I was there almost all the time. The church people came with bowls of food. The nieces and nephews all came.

What I'll never forget is Brother Jerry Alexander. He's one of my sister's preachers. He pulled his chair up next to mine and started talking to me.

He said, "I see and feel the situation you're in here, but just stay focused."

I replied, "How do you know? You don't even know me."

He said, "God lets me see into other people's hearts. Believe me I know. You just stay focused and ever thing will be fine."

He stayed with me as long as he could. I felt like I had an angel on my shoulder. He came to see Mama every day that he could and if he couldn't come, he called and asked to speak to me, telling me to stay focused and that he'd see me tonight.

The hardest time I had to stay focused was when Virginia, my oldest brother's daughter came to see Mama. It was her husband that cheated me out of seventeen hundred dollars. I was sitting beside Mama's bed and had to go to the bathroom when I returned Virginia was sitting in my seat.

I said, "You have my seat."

Virginia said, "Harriet said for me to sit here."

I said, "Well, my name is Drucilla and I'm telling you to get up. You haven't brought yourself down here to see Mama in four or five years so get out of here with your false face. Mama doesn't know you're here, and wouldn't want you here."

You could have heard a pin drop in the room, but she moved and I took my seat. From then on everyone knew not to sit in my chair. By that time, Mama was almost gone. I wiped her face and put lotion on her. Hospice had stopped feeding her many days before. I hate hospice.

I knew Harriet was almost killed over Mama. She had been up day and night. It was hard to see Harriet hurt so much.

Brandon loved his Grandmother. He had never watched anyone pass away. To me it is the worst thing, your last few days on this earth and a room full of people staring at your chest, waiting for that last breath. The wait was over at five thirty in the morning.

Now it was time to take care of Harriet and I did. She is my baby sister and I love her. I know sometimes I don't like her at all. But

I can say, no one could have taken better care of our parents than Harriet.

Mama Marcella has been Harriet's little girl since Daddy's death. I do whatever she lets me do for her.

Brother Jerry Alexander was with me every step of the way. Every once in a while, even before I knew I was getting upset he's lean over and say 'Stay focused.' He was the brother, the husband, the friend I never had, I could tell him everything.

I had to throw five sticks of dynamite into the Warrior River just so I wouldn't be tempted to throw one in Mule Face's car.

Rex was still running in and out my door. I sometimes tell him things I've remembered. This little tale is funny now, but it wasn't at the time.

I had let Sherrie use a very important book and after her bipolar crazy person came out she wouldn't give it back to me. I wonder if Harriet can catch bipolar from Mule Face. Anyway, she gave the book to Harriet. When I found this out I called Harriet and told her I was on my way out there to get my book. I went into Harriet's house and asked for the book. Harriet said she wouldn't give me the book unless she had a witness that she gave me the book. I didn't see the pattern then, but now I know that was Mule Face's idea to cause trouble in our family. Later I found out she does this to every family she comes in contact with. I tried to tell Harriet that the book belonged to me. But Mule Face had her primed and ready, she refused to give up the book. My temper flared and I told Harriet to keep the book, it only cost thirty-one dollars and I spend that much on her child every day. Thirty-one dollars is nothing to me. As I was walking out the door Harriet was screaming for me to get back in there. I walked to my car, got in with Harriet still screaming at me. I hit the gas, spun a three sixty and drove around the road into my carport.

I told Richard if the telephone rang, not answer it, and not to answer the door either. Sure enough the telephone started to ring. She called every five minutes for two hours and she was beating on the door. She didn't bother with the doorbell. She beat the door until I thought she would break the door down. I waited until she left and went into the kitchen, cut on the light and sat at the table.

I was sitting less than a foot from the glass sliding door. I had my back toward the door and Harriet came beating on the glass door. I had just unloaded the dishwasher and wiped off the table and was setting the table with fine Fantasia crystal ware. Harriet was outside screaming, "I know you can hear me." Over and over again she screamed. I didn't even look her way. I finished setting the table, turned out the lights and as I walked through the house I heard her scream, "I'm leaving this book on the picnic table."

When Richard got up to go to work he found the book in pieces all over the yard. The dogs in the neighborhood tore the book all to pieces. Richard cleaned up pieces and blamed me for the book being destroyed. I ordered another book. Expect me to have a witness for those two liars. Not in this lifetime. The liars have another tale about the book. But liars will be liars and I've proved them to be one. If only I could have gotten Harriet on film, I know she was a sight pounding on the glass door. I really felt sorry for her and her goofy friend. That bipolar bitch will always be a bipolar bitch and Harriet will always be my baby sister. I can't pick her friends and she has chosen three sets of losers. Let me tell you about them.

The first set is Andy and Jean Sutler. Jean left her husband for Andy. She had four children with this husband. She left another husband before that. There ain't no telling how many children she has out there. Anyway, those four wound up with her, and Andy made them walk a chalk line. Andy is like a woman; he wants the very best of everything. Jean tells everyone that she can't get any sex from Andy. All she talks about is sex. I love Jean, but she isn't playing with a full deck. Once while they were at Harriet's house, I came in with rollers in my hair. Jean was playing with her new digital camera. She took my picture and told me she was going to put it on the internet. I told her I would put her six foot under with dirt in her mouth. She erased the picture and put the camera up.

I've already told you about the goofies, once saved. Then there's Geraldean and Whitie Black. What kind of Mother would name a child Whitie Black? Well he fit the bill. These two are a trip. Whitie can out pray the preacher then turn to the next group of people and tell his nasty jokes. This is no joke; these people think this is okay.

Once Harriet talked me into going bowling with them. Geraldean and Whities' daughter was there and she started telling jokes. She stood up in front of God and everybody telling sex jokes even adding in the motions. She patted her ass, patted her tits up and down and then shook them in every direction. The whole place got a good laugh. Most everyone at the bowling alley was drinking beer. She walked away and when she returned she said 'Boy do I feel better now.' I asked her if she had drank a beer. She looked at me in a funny way and in a loud voice said she wouldn't offend her Lord that way. I said, "You offended your Lord when you patted your ass and your tits for everyone in this building."

Harriet isn't like the people she's friends with. I believe she enjoys them. They give her something to laugh about, maybe. I can't laugh at them. They make me sick. Whitie cheated Harriet's husband out of about eleven hundred dollars. Harriet gave him hell and didn't speak to them for months. But Geraldean wormed her way back into Harriet's life. The bad thing is, they all have to pass my house to get to Harriet's house. I need the pitching arm of Tim Hudson and a few hand grenades. I'd blow their damn cars up. Here I am thinking how bad these people are and me, Drucilla Hallmark would kill them. What do I think about myself? Am I bad? **Hell No!** I have better sense. No! I'm no put on. What you see is what you get. Oh my God, I don't have time to think about them. I've got to find Max.

I got Rex on the telephone begging him to take me to buy a few dancing dresses.

Rex asked, "Drucilla, did you say Fort Myers, Florida?"

I responded, "Yes, so what! It will only take about four days. They can fit me and then mail them to me."

Reluctantly he gave in. We flew in and rented a car. I stepped out of the car on Crawford Street in Fort Myers. Shop after shop of gowns, original beautiful gowns. Rex sat in leisure while the lady took me into a fitting room. She pinned my hair up, gave me a pair of gold tone three inch heels and I slipped into the most beautiful deep rose pink dress. I rushed out to show Rex. I pranced out into the show room making a spin right into the face of Max. I lost my breath and Max almost beat me to death until I could catch it.

I said, "Damn Max, you about broke my back."

Then I stopped and turning around and around looking everywhere I asked, "If you're here, my Tony is here right?"

Max said, "He said to tell you, he will meet you in the shower at nine a.m. in room four zero nine."

I told the sales lady which three gowns I wanted and gave her a check for sixty seven hundred dollars. I gave her Courtney and Harriet's addresses for her to send them a catalogue.

I turned back to Max and said, "Max, take me to him now."

Max said, "I can't, he won't be in until later. We are to deliver you to your sweetie when time comes. Now we can drive you around to sight see and then go to dinner."

I said, "Then, you will take me dancing. Do you know of a good place?"

Rex pulled into the Sanibel Harbor Resort and Spa.

I said, **"Oh! My word!** Talking about paradise, this is world class."

Max said, "My Lady, you have six restaurants and lounges to choose from."

Rex and Max saw me to my suite, which was pure paradise.

I said, "Isn't Fort Myers beautiful. I've never been here before but talking about a place to escape to. This is it."

I asked, "Max, please get Tony and me on a sunset cruise."

"I'll do that first thing in the morning.

I said, "Well, don't be at my door until after lunch."

Rex said, "We know, you're having Tony for lunch."

I said, "That's right, smart ass."

Rex said, "Drucilla, you beat all I've ever seen. I've watched you dig new potatoes out of the ground, ride the four wheeler down the middle of the creek, be gorgeous by seven, dance till daylight, come home and sit in the swing listening to the beagles run."

I asked, "Max, do you think Tony will take me hunting with the beagles? I'm going to bring them with me."

Max said, "I'm sure he'll do whatever you want him to. Well, if I were you I'd ask Tony about that, in the shower. I'm going to check out the lounges."

I asked, "Max, will I really be okay with Tony's family?"

Max said, "Yes doll, I have no doubts about it. If not I'll run away with you myself. But there is no hunting at the Gulf you know. But we'll find a place."

I asked, "What about all my Confederate pictures? Can't you just see me doing my heritage thing, hoop dress and all in a house full of Italians? I have always had Italian friends. They made a big impact on Birmingham after the War Between the States. But they couldn't identify with the war because they weren't here. I'm going to make it understood that I'm going to be myself. Or I won't be at all. I'll tell you again, there are worst things then being alone. Anyway Max, what do the others think about me?"

Max said, "I will never lie to you Drucilla. They love you. Tony has movie film of you fishing, playing golf, Tony knows your history. Papa loves you, but most of all Anthony loves you."

I said, "Yes, and I'm going home to him and I'll never look back. Okay Max, let me have some time to rest and get dolled up for you. Then you can wine and dine me. We'll dance till the cows come home. You know Max, I think I'm going to love you, like I love my friend Henry."

Max said, "I want you to love me and I love you. Was I not in your dreams too? Was I not totally yours?"

I said, "Yes, but you can't know that."

Max said, "Well I do know that because your Doctor Bradley gave Tony a tape recording of you telling him your dream. If you ask me again if we love you, I'll say No."

I said, "You wouldn't dare."

Max said, "He also gave Tony a tape recording of Tony telling him his dreams. So, see you have no secrets from me. I know all your wishes and I'll tell you now, all you have to do is tell me what your wishes are. From now on and I'll do my very best to make them come true. Now that you know for sure that you can trust me, I have to help you understand that Richard had a curse on him. What he wanted you could not do and he wasn't going to do without. Men like him can't love a woman. We have a saying for his type. They came out of a vagina and they're not going back into one. Tony said many times that you believe love is a brain thing. That's true. So get it in your brain. Richard never loved you! Never did!! He wasn't going to do without, that's why he kept you sick. Sick to the point of almost killing you, more than once. And he would have died before he would tell you what it was that he just had to have."

"You're right Max, it became an obsession with me. I wanted to make him say it out loud."

Max said, "Believe me doll, that's in the past."

I said, "Now I'm looking for a sensual man. His name is Tony."

Max said, "How well I know. I wish it were me. What did you say about a Henry?"

"He and I were like you and me. Till he married and was too busy and lived too far away. I've always missed him so badly. I'll tell you more about him some day. Now, get your sweet self out of here. Oh, find Rex and tell him he better limber those legs up. We'll do the 'Swing Time Boogie'.

Max said, "Yes, and you and I are going to dance to 'It Takes a Lover to Know One'."

I said, "Get out of here. I'm saving that one for Tony."

I sat in the bathtub thinking of Max and how special he had been to me. Plus he is a very joyful person. I laughed out loud at the things he and I did in my dreams. Yes, I do know that Max loves me, but not the love Tony and I have. Oh my, what was that line he used on me? Oh yes, that sounds like a good song.

Me	Can you read my lips
	When I kiss you
	Do you see you in my eyes
	Does your heart hurt
	When I don't call you
	Do I have you
	Stuttering your words

Duet With Max	It takes a lover to know one Our twin souls are Perfect for each other Hot passionate love That explodes when we touch A desire that I've never known
Max	I can read your lips when I kiss you I can see you in my eyes Does your heart hurt When I don't call you Do I have you Stuttering your words
Max And Me	Yes I can read your lips When I kiss you Yes, I can see me in your eyes Yes my heart hurts When you don't call me Yes, you have me Stuttering my words
Duet With Max	It takes a lover to know one Our twin souls are Perfect for each other Hot passionate love That explodes when we touch A desire that I've never known
Max	Yes darling, I can read your lips
Me	Yes I can read your lips

I lay in bed thinking how they just do things. Max tells Tony every step I take. Rex ran his mouth about this trip. Not that I'm not grateful, I thought smiling. Telling myself to be quiet, shut my mind off and rest. I did rest but I couldn't go to sleep. I got up and started picking out my clothes for the night. I chose a beautiful short light gold dress and champagne colored shoes. I took my time putting on my makeup and doing my hair.

Both Rex and Max came to pick me up. Both had spit shined shoes and had every hair in place.

I said, "Boy do you two look delicious. Isn't it against the law for you two to look so good?"

Rex said, "Would you want us to show up with our straddle hanging to our knees? Having to hold our pants up with one hand?"

I burst out laughing. We first went to look over the beautiful resort. Just killing time until the band started playing. We danced every dance putting on a show for all the other people. The boys told me joke after joke. I laughed until I cried. Then Rex went one joke too far.

Rex said, "One night Max was bouncing around and he told his penis that they were going to a party. The balls knew it wasn't their party. The penis goes in and leaves them knocking at the door."

Max said, "That's enough of that. Don't tell Drucilla another joke of that kind."

Rex said, "What about it, Drucialla? Tell him you love jokes."

Max said, "I know she does, but you best remember what I said."

Max got up and took me to the dance floor. As the song ended he said, "Doll it's late, let's just dance right out the door."

I didn't have time to answer him; we were already out the door. Max walked me to my door. Gave me a light kiss on my cheek and said goodnight. He turned and hurried away.

The next morning I heard water, at first I thought it was raining. Then I looked at the clock it was nine o'clock. The shower! I grabbed my robe but I don't think my feet even touched the floor.

Tony's kiss, our naked bodies entwined, I was in pure heaven.

I said, "Wait, wait Tony. I've only been with you, like once."

Tony said, "No, no, you've been with me for a life time. This is not a bad thing Dru. We were meant to be together and you know that."

I said, "Yes Tony, I know it. I just want God to know, to know it."

Tony said, "God put our minds together. He'll never take us away from each other."

All the while Tony was soaping me down with body wash, every inch of me.

Tony said, "Now it's your turn. Don't miss a thing."

I said, "Well it would be impossible to miss that thing."

We laughed the whole time in the shower like two teenagers. He poured baby oil all over me, then grabbed the towel and dried my hair, my body, himself and picked me up in his arms and carried me to bed.

Lying naked with him, entwined in each other's arms, so sensual and passionate, so comfortable, I wanted this feeling for the rest of my life. The uneasiness I had felt before was gone, gone forever. I was fully focused on Tony. My dream has come true. He had turned me into a sensual, romantic person.

The hate, the fear that I have lived with for so long, was gone, gone forever.

Tony's eyes were all over me. He said, "Our minds are working in perfect harmony. The worry I once saw in your eyes has disappeared. Now I can see me in your eyes."

I said, "Yes Tony, you have made me a different person. I feel so warm and so free."

Tony reached for my foot. He kissed it and rubbed my ankle. Tony said, "I have something for you this morning."

He reached under his pillow and pulled out a gold ankle bracelet and placed it around my ankle.

He said, "Now you have something from me next to your skin. You have an incredible psychic sense about things and I know you're in tune with me."

I said, "Yes, I knew you would show up again soon and with something in hand."

I reached beside the bed and handed a box to Tony. He said, "My goodness! Where did you find this? I know it must be a one of a kind."

Tony slipped the ring on. It was a cougar standing on a gold rock band with black accents. It looked as if the cougar was watching over something.

Tony said, "This ring is beautiful."

I said, "Yes, just like us."

Tony reached for my foot as his hand rubbed up my leg. He kissed me; he kissed from my toes to my lips. Tony could touch me and send waves of pleasure pulsing though out my body.

I said, "Stop Tony, you don't know what you're doing to me."

Tony said, "Oh yes! I know. A lady down on love, no sex for thirteen years."

I whispered, "But this is wild. Tony you were so right, you do make me nervous. Like now, move your hands."

Tony said, "No Dru!"

His fingers from my hips to my thighs I gasped aloud.

Tony said, "Don't say, baby just let me."

My eyelids opened wide. Tony parted my legs with his hands. Dipped his head to taste my warm willing flesh. I thought if I'd died and went straight to hell. In the next moment I wouldn't give a damn if I did because I was so close to heaven as a mortal could get. My knees buckled and my body swayed. I have never dreamed it could be like this. My thighs tingled, my muscles quivered, seeking more, more of the wonderful sensations.

I said, "Don't ever shave that mustache."

Tony worked his way up and down my inner thigh purposefully letting his mustache trail against my skin.

I said, "Once more, more I want more."

Tony's whiskers had my body jerking upward nearly off the bed.

Tony said, "Easy"

Then his tongue soothed the chafed surface on my thighs.

I said, "Stop! And I mean now!"

Tony lowered his head and his mouth covered me again tasting my wanting loins. Waves of pleasure went though me.

"**Stop Tony,** you're embarrassing me!"

"Now stop screaming. Stop before you awaken everyone."

I said, "But there's no one here."

He said, "I know that baby. I am talking about the neighbors a mile away."

Tony's eyes twinkled with mischief.

I said, "I don't want you to teach me this way. I'm really a case of nerves you know."

"I know, but not for long."

I was telling myself to grow up and welcome him with open arms. I was buried in his strong arms and solid body. As I stared into his dark eyes, desire struck me again. I lifted my pelvis at the same time he grabbed my hips with his hands and joined our bodies with a smooth easy thrust. I let my body stretch to accommodate him. My insides were alive with pulsating desires. A tear ran down my face and Tony kissed it away. He lifted my hips drawing himself deeper. I cried out with pure delight. I wanted more, more penetration, more perfection. God I loved Tony. I lost the ability to hold a part of myself back. I found myself giving in to let Tony teach me everything. Things I didn't want to know about.

Tony said, "Dru, you have beautiful fun bags."

As he was kissing my nipple we both climaxed causing me to shake with passion. My body was weak as Tony held me in his arms.

I said, "I've never known love like this before and now I can't seem to get enough of you."

He said, "You will baby. I'll see to that."

I said, "I feel so loved and lucky. I had forgotten how much I love to kiss.

Thirteen years is a long time to wait for sex. Tony you were sent from God. I'm going to be loved by my new family."

He said, "Don't ever doubt that your new family loves you. Baby I have to leave you, but you know we are magical, pure dynamite. I know without a doubt we were destined to meet. I have never felt capable of the love that I feel for you."

"Yes, Tony, and every second away from you is filled with longing and emptiness."

"Not for long Dru."

Tony took a quick shower and with a passionate kiss he was out the door.

Two hours later Rex was ringing the telephone telling me we must go home. The plane leaves at three p.m. The sunset cruise had been forgotten.

Rex was in the cab when I got out front.

I said, "Boy is Max in trouble. He forgot about the cruise."

Rex said, "He didn't forget. Tony didn't have time this trip, but said he'd make it up to you someday."

I said, "Then get Max on the phone and tell him I want him to get us tickets to see 'Brooks and Dunn'."

"Drucilla, you're spoiled."

"Yes, and you're a smart ass. But when Papa Perricotti gets though with you, you won't be so smart to me."

Rex said, "I haven't been a smart ass to you. Besides I'm going back to Michigan. All you need is Max and even he knows you're an army all by yourself. You're very prissy. You smell too good. You love that make up. Damn, you make me crazy."

"**Yes! Hell yes!** I love being a woman. I'm soft sometimes I get weak and cry. I want to be loved. I don't want to be mean, people just get to me."

Rex said, "Drucilla, you don't have to be mean. You have that Southern charm, charisma. You have confidence. Max said you could charm the Lord off his throne. But you best know what you're doing Missy, especially with Tony Tortomasi. When he takes over he gets very serious. Milano or Pleramo, Italy nor Juliano Sicily has never and you better not defy or betray him."

I said, "You let me worry about that. Rex, I do know the three powers that rule, the Church, the landowner and the Mafia. Until now there were only three then Mr. Williams' pronounced himself the fourth. You listen little boy, if anything should happen to me, even Tony couldn't dig in deep enough to keep Mr. Williams from taking him apart. I love Tony, you fool but if I had to choose, Mr. Williams' would win."

Rex asked, "Girl, are you saying you love Williams?"

I responded, "Hell yes! I love him. He's the first person I ever loved. Rex don't look so gloomy. I swear you're a cross between a bulldog and an Indian. When you aren't sitting on your ass growling you're on the war path."

Rex didn't have much to say on the flight home. As I was getting off the plane I could see Max waiting for us.

Rex said, "I just don't want to be sent back home Drucilla."

I said, "Tony got you here. Just wait and see what plans he has for you."

I ran right into Max's arms saying, "I love you, I love you."

Rex threw his suitcase down with a loud bang and everyone looked at him as if to say what's happening.

Rex looked at me and asked, "Just who in the hell do you love woman?"

There stood and old man next to me. I threw my arms around him and with a kiss I said, "I love everyone."

With a smile from ear to ear, the old man said, "I do to."

Max nudged my shoulder saying "Someone waits for you."

Max got us a limousine at the airport and we were on our way to meet this someone.

I asked, "Are we going to meet Tony?"

Max said, "No, it's Mr. Young. He's very impressed with you and wanted to see you again."

I said, "Oh! Now I remember. He's the Chinese man Tony was talking to."

I had only seen him once. He was a small frame man about fifty-five years old, about five foot seven and he looked rich. Tony told me not to let his appearance fool me. He was head of Chin Chow, that the Chinese equivalent of a Sicilian. Albert Young had tough guys. I had asked about the beautiful ring on his finger. He said it was given to him by his mother.

Albert got up and poured me some wine and asked me to dance with him. That's when he told me I'd never be afraid again. He was Tony's friend and he'd keep me safe.

Later Albert asked for another dance with me. As we danced, I thought Albert was a wonderful dancer, he told me he knew I had seen some tough times, but no more. He wanted me to believe him and I did. I couldn't conceal my delight and neither could he. I asked him if he thought I looked dangerous. With a mischievous laugh he said, "I do and in your last life there was a duel fought over you."

I said, "Albert you are a wonderful dancer but a terrible liar."

Albert danced me out to his white limousine. I said "My friends have been investigating you for some time. They tell me you're just a fun person. They all fell in love with you."

He made me promise to never be afraid again. Then before he left he asked, "Do not ever speak of me again and take care of Anthony that Anthony loved me very much."

He got into his limousine and drove way leaving me standing there alone, but not for long. A brown limousine pulled up, the back door opened and Max pulled me in. Max wanted to know where I wanted to go.

I said "Hong Kong, someday. Albert must be a general."

Max told me never to speak of Albert, not even to Tony. I reminded Max that Tony already knew because he's always in my mind.

We pulled into the back lot of a Chinese restaurant. Max and I went inside and there was Albert. Albert dresses like a multimillionaire. His shoes were Gestoni, the cost start at two thousand a pair, fine silk suits with shirt and tie to match.

Albert said, "Hello Drucilla, how have you been?"

I said, "Fine, but you knew that before you asked."

Albert said, "Beautiful and smart too. Tony is one lucky man."

I said, "I remember what you told me. You know the answers to all questions before you ask them."

Albert said, "Yes I do. It pays in my business to know how others will react in any given situation. Which brings me to why I asked you to see me."

I said, "I must say, I was surprised to hear from you again."

Albert said, "You wouldn't but I was asked to take care of a situation and I know you would want to know how it was handled."

I said, "I just took for granted that Tony was behind it."

Albert said, "That's half right but he asked me to handle it so it couldn't come back on him because of you. Anyway, I took care of the ship. I paid off the Captain and my men were the crew. Everything else was easy. The Captain was instructed not to make a log entry after six hours at sea. He sailed from the Bahamas to the southwest tip of Cuba where I had a freighter waiting. The freighter sent out a distress call and when the Captain stopped to help my men took over the cruise ship. Your list of names was separated from the rest. Then everyone else was moved aboard the freighter. The freighter went through the Panama Canal and on to Hong Kong; there they were sold as slaves in Communist China. Those on your list were moved to another freighter where they were sent though a wood chipper. The freighter stopped over the cannon trench which is three thousand feet deep and the chipper was thrown overboard after the last one. Meanwhile the cruise ship sailed back to where it was found abandoned. I had diesel oil pumped into the ship so only six hours is missing."

I asked, "What about the Captain? You can't trust a man that sells his soul."

Albert said, "Well, Tony told me about that mind thing you two have so I guess you'll know someday. I'm not just a gangster. That's a sideline that I find useful. I'm a high-ranking general in the Chinese Army. Our Captain, as it turns out, had a brother who was a prisoner of war in Vietnam. The Captain was pressuring the congress to investigate prisoners of war being sent to China. I paid him his money but he will find it hard to spend in Communist China. I arranged for him to be reunited with his brother. We still have American soldiers in China from the Korean War. You don't have to worry about our Captain."

I thanked Albert for telling me. He knew I'd never tell because of Tony.

On the way home Max asked, "How did you know about Mr. Young's shoes?"

I said, "Well my Anthony has taught me a lot about the computer over the last few months."

Max said, "He sure has his head in that computer. Anthony said it's time for you to come home. I assure you, there will not be any intimidation or any feeling of imprisonment. You come and go as you please and I'm yours."

I asked, "Does Tony know that?"

We both laughed.

Max said, "I've talked to Amanda and Courtney. They know to help you get packed up and I'll see the movers do it right."

I said, "I just want the things I have from Tuesday Morning and Princess House, well all my crystal. I have seven sets of dishes. Will you drive me down in my car? As my niece Kamron would say, we can let the top down and let the wind blow through our hair."

Max asked, "You're really not afraid of our family are you?"

I said, "No, no no! I'm not as long as I know where Mr. Williams is. I'll never be afraid of anything again. I feel safe for the first time in my life. Remember me; I'm the girl that survived the counterfeit man for all those years. I'll sing you the song."

Have you ever tangled

With a counterfeit man
Have you ever put your heart in
Counterfeit hands
A man that looks real
But he's really fake
Just like the funny money
That the counterfeiters make
My world just came down crashing
Destroying all my hopes and plans
Cause I found out I got myself a
Counterfeit man

I've lost all my illusions
He can't fool me anymore
He kept me in the dark
But now I know the score
He's every woman's man
He just can't be true
And what he did to me
He'll try to do to you

Deceit Deserves Revenge II

A lot of guys will try to tell
You little white lies
But this man starts out
With stories twice that size
He seems so genuine
But he was just a phony
The promises he made
Were all just pure bologna
He led me on with promises
Of a golden wedding band
But I found out I got myself
A counterfeit man

I've lost all my illusions
He can't fool me anymore
He kept me in the dark
But now I know the score
He's every woman's man
He just can't be true
And what he did to me
He'll try to do to you

Have you ever tangled
With a counterfeit man
Have you ever put your heart in
Counterfeit hands
A man that looks real
But he's really fake
Just like the funny money
That the counterfeiters make
My world just came down crashing
Destroying all my hopes and plans
Cause I found out I got myself a
Counterfeit man

"No Max, I'm not even a little bit frightened. The bear I once knew has gone. I know that Brandon will stay with Harriet. It's not my wish but its what he wants. I could persuade him to leave, but I want it to be his choice. I want him to know he can come and go as he pleases."

Max said, "You have Anthony wrapped around your little finger. I'm sure he'll keep you busy. Only this morning he had a masseur waiting on you. He has made sure there are strawberries and blueberries in the freezer. He said you have your own four wheeler."

"Yes, but it stays with Brandon. Anthony knows everything about me. I'll tell you I cherish him and he knows it. I cherish Brandon too, but I have given up. Some things you just can't change, unfortunately. So Anthony has me a masseur. He'll see that I'm toned up, as if all that dancing wouldn't do it."

Max said, "He placed an order for a dozen jars each of lavender therapy and the healing garden all day moisturizer. It's a whipped soufflé body cream, whatever that is."

I said, "Listen Max, in my dream Anthony was a young boy. When I saw him in the hospital he looked to be about twelve years old."

Max said, "He is twelve, but he's the smartest young man you'll ever meet.

He speaks Mandarin dialect of Chinese. He's as high as he can go in Karate belts. He dances, as you know. He does his own financial business and has his own tailor."

I said, "You have got to be kidding!"

Max said, "No, Papa Perricotti has made sure that he was never idle. I'll tell you something else. Anthony met a young lady on the beach from Birmingham. He said she was an angel. Her name is Blakelee and he is letting her draw up the plans for you a nightclub. Anthony said she does magnificent work besides being beautiful with long blond hair. But he did say she was too old for him and he'd never be as tall as she is. So see, you have all kind of arrangements made for you. Anthony knows all about your Amanda being artistic. He set her up a studio you won't believe. Big glass windows with what he believes to be the best lighting. He has found Amanda an art teacher, if she wants one."

I said, "My God! Anthony has thought of everything, has he not?"

Max said, "If not, he will. Well I got you home safe and sound. You want me to come in?"

I said, "No! You go get some rest. I'll be unconscious before I get out of the shower."

Max said, "Maybe I better come in."

I said, "Go home! Wishful thinker."

Max said, "I'm going home and telling Anthony about your Counterfeit Man song."

I asked, "Do you tell him everything about me?"

Max said, "Yes! But most of it he already knows. Good night doll."

I got into the shower and sat on the floor. I just let the water run warm over me. I couldn't help but think, I'm way too dumb to be with these people. I could still hear my friend, Mr. Williams say, 'Don't go there Dru, but if you fall face first, I'll pick you up'.

Just hearing that calmed me down. I rubbed down with lavender crème while praying.

"Dear Lord, You must mean for me to do this or you surely would have sent me in another direction. Because if I'm supposed to have better sense than to get involved with the mob, I don't. I love Tony and his family. Many years ago one of the Forestdale Sheriffs told me it was better to be carried by twelve on a jury than by six in a box. Lord, you know Richard and his bunch have almost killed me. Forgive me if I'm wrong, but I'm leaving this place. I know my Daddy will forgive me. Brandon can have it. Please watch over him. You know Harriet is a pain in the ass to live with. I even believe that when I'm gone, his life will be easier. Thank you Lord for all You have done for me. Amen."

I must have fallen into a deep sleep as soon as I hit the bed. When I awoke things were different.

Thinking back to all I've gone through to get Richard off my mind. The doctors, paying as much as one hundred dollars an hour.

Listening to tape after tape, like Free to be, Instructions to the Levels of the Mind, Opening Unconscious Doors, Subconscious Release of Fear, and Inner Direction for Release of Fear, Self Acceptance, Building Self Confidence, and The Awakening series, Healing Journey, The Answer to Overcoming Anxiety, Stress and Depression and Freedom from Stress. I can't think of anything I didn't try to make myself hate Richard. Well, I'm here today to tell all women that finding someone else to love you is absolutely the only way out of a situation like mine. I'll advise all to give up and get on with life. There are worse things than being alone. After giving myself a sermon I stretched like a cat and climbed out of bed.

I called Courtney and asked her to come over and help me pack some of my most precious things. All my adult life I have collected dishes with the Desert Rose pattern by Francisean. The Fantasia dishes, the Princess Heritage dishes and stainless steel cookware and the Barrington flatware with all the serving pieces had to be packed first. Then we packed all my quilts, my pictures and a large collection of records and CDs.

I have looked in the mirror many times asking myself, what's more important, all I have or my life. I would tell myself, life is not worth a damn if I didn't' have what I needed and wanted. If I was not able to be with the people I love.

The doorbell ringing brought me back to the real world. Peace of mind I thought as I opened the door. Courtney had brought boxes from a moving company. The two of us set into wrapping glass to pack.

Courtney asked, "Don't you think you're taking memories with you?"

I said, "Hell yes, the memories of how hard I had to work to have them and all the BS I've gone through to have it."

Courtney asked, "So using these same dishes with Tony's family is going to be ok?"

I said, "You're so right and if I could pick up this house and take it with me, I'd live in it with Tony. I can't so the hell with it. I'm going to Tony and I'm taking my things with me. Not to give you a short answer, but no, I don't have any qualms about anything. I know you may not understand, but I swear its Tony I need. I should have been with him all my life. Richard hated me from day one. Listen, if you fall into a hole today, most people would have fun throwing dirt over you instead of pulling you out. Mr. Williams was the only person I could ever count on. Richard had his fun, playing his crazy games with me. He almost destroyed me. He almost killed me and my family let him. I've always been in hell. Courtney, I've put Richard's puzzle together and I can go now. I want you to be happy for me. I need to be happy or die. I feel like I'm well qualified to ask you and all young women for that matter to ask what are you hiding that makes your life so miserable. I want to scream out to them to get it in their brains, it's just a brain thing. Get help! Get someone to love you. In reality it's not love that keeps us with a man like Richard. It's a fear of depending on yourself to work and pay the bills. Courtney, you and I knew my family thought I was just the rich bitch that had it all. I could never get it across to them that Mama Marcella should have aborted all her children or at least have given us away. Maybe she should have been fixed so she couldn't have children in the first place."

Courtney said, "Drucilla, I agree with you that insanity keeps running in families. But look at you today."

I said, "Hell yes! Girl, look at me today. It took just thirty years to be as smart as a third grader. Anthony has taught me more in the last few months than I've learned in my whole life. This child made learning things simple. Things I thought were too hard for me to ever learn."

"But Drucilla, I don't know of anything you can't do. I don't know of any other woman that can do fifteen things at one time."

I said, "You're talking about around the house and yard type things. I couldn't get a job with insurance that would take care of me. You know as well as me that I'm in a trap, a prison. Courtney, once I fell in love, deep in love but the man was just teasing me. It hurt me so bad I prayed to die. I almost grieved myself to death. I told Richard I was just sick and he made me sicker. That's when he gave me that rat poison. I think back and I do wonder if I was crazy. It was a druggist that told me to get myself to a doctor. Well

I stopped drinking the coffee Richard had ready for me and I drank water, water, and more water. I did not eat anything he gave me, I made an appointment but by the time I saw the doctor he didn't find anything. Remember, I did tell Richard what he was doing. I saw the little green pellet by the coffee pot. He ran and got the rat poison and threw it under the floor to get rid of it. Also remember this is my house. I wasn't about to leave. So I stayed in my trap with my trap shut."

Courtney said, "As far as a job goes that's right, but you have potential to make money in the arts."

I said, "I'd like to sue the State Board of Education for every child that's been turned out of school that can't read. They can't fill out an application for a job because they can't read it. It's a crime against these kids and I can't stand it."

Courtney said, "Yes, but it's also the parents' fault."

I said, "The Governor of the State would be astonished at the stupidity of his citizens. By the time the State paid each person a yearly salary they could have made if they could read, there wouldn't be any money left to pay their large salaries. That would be one sobering wake up call. Not being able to read makes one a social outcast. It's a disability in my opinion. But I think the federal government is doing it on purpose. Dumbing down of the people makes them easy to control. These liberals think they're so smart, but they're too stupid to know that a nation's worth is the sum of all its citizens. If all your citizens are dumb then you have a dumb nation. The teachers and administrators should be sued for promoting a child that couldn't do the work. Take me for instance. I could have been the President of the United States if I wanted to be. What does that pay, one ninety to two hundred ten thousand dollars a year? I could write my own speeches so that job could be done away with. I can dress myself, do my own hair and makeup and still be as sassy and sissy as Bush. I would even vacuum the white house for that kind of money. As President I'd get free eye lifts and butt tucks."

Courtney said, "Yes, I'd like that myself."

I said, "I've lived in a pressure cooker type of atmosphere for so long that all political parties seem like a joke to me. Take this war in Iraq. We're fighting three different groups of people that hate each other as much as they hate us. Instead of letting our boys' die, I'd wipe out all of them. We need our boys over here to take care of our streets, free our towns of drugs. Courtney, I'm self-educated, but I have more brains than what's been running this country in the past twenty years. Richard always said I didn't know what I was talking about. But when men don't have any more self-control than Clinton did, well they impeached him, but didn't have the guts to put him out of office. It's no wonder the assholes in Washington pay four hundred dollars for a haircut. They have someone to shine their shoes and I wonder how much they pay someone to wipe their ass. I would have found Ben Laden by now. By the time I got through with that place we wouldn't have a Ben Laden."

Courtney said, "Maybe you do need to be President."

I said, "You know I have forty two on my list and can't get rid of them for fear of going to jail."

Amanda stormed into the house screaming at me. Amanda said, "Mama, you said for me to call Mr. Williams' office and he would tell me that Daddy was guilty of all you said. Well, he didn't. Mr. Williams didn't know what I was talking about."

Courtney seized the day. She stepped up to Amanda and said, "If that's true, it's because his secretary didn't show him all the proof your mother left with her. Just maybe she didn't even keep them. Your Mother has detective's reports. Signed notes from people who saw you're Daddy, papers from Richard's own hand and she has never lied to you about your Daddy. For that matter she has never told you the whole truth."

I was in shock, never in my life had I heard Courtney be so out spoken. She really startled me. She went on to tell Amanda that she had stayed out of my life before but now she was here to stay."

I said, "Don't look so confused Amanda."

Amanda was shivering she was so mad. I stepped forward to take Amanda in my arms but she pushed me away.

"First let met tell you about the telephone. Remember I said I had meter-calling put on the phone bill? This cost I'll say, 1 cent a minute. It tells the day the call was made and to where and how long the parties talked. I know this is nuts, but I am always in a hurry, even when paying bills. You know the water bill is about the same. I only order gas for the house when I need it and for a few months Richard paid them. But when my mail started disappearing I had to get in the know. I knew it was past time to pay them so I called and was told yes, they had been sent out of town to a new address. I got out all the last months statements and paid my bills. I put the account number on the checks and put in a note that I didn't receive my mail. Then I looked a last month's bill from Bellsouth. I've got the paper with me so you can see for yourself. I do not know these places and no one was coming to my home to make these calls. I knew it was Richard."

I got the bills from months back.

"Now look at this, the numbers ran from October of one year through December of the next year."

"Then there is Christina Rossett, Angela Beckman, Mary Bathe in Florida. I took all this and more to the Sheriffs office. They said it looks like someone's tracking a trucker or playing with whores on a computer. They said today there are computer sex houses just like shot houses years ago.

Now Amanda, remember I said Richard helped two honey pots get their CDLs, well, this is true because I have the test papers with the answers. So, now while I'm in my locked box I tell you about some other papers I have. Like a letter from Mr. Frank stating, the Stereo unit, caller ID unit, microwave, and phone answering system that were repaired were not hit by lightning.

Mr. Grady wrote, 'Drucilla is a joy, my four grown children love her and will tell you she can do twenty things at one time. You all better look elsewhere for the trouble in her home because you'll never find anything wrong with her.

Richards very own Doctor said 'Mrs. Hallmark had her appointment with me. She discussed her problems with her husband coherently and sensibly'.

Now Amanda, seven car tags and many other things led me back to Marklund Rd in Sumiton. The phone calls didn't stop. Don't you remember that Mr. Perry, he is a queer that moved from Fairfield and

Richard took us there to buy brass from his yard sale? I tell you, I almost died. Remember the black and white Camero with gray tape on the tag that I told you about? There was also the Postmaster of Brookside that told me about the two men that had rented a trailer one block up on the left. The more information I gather up, the more frightened I got. Being accused of harassing people was just a lie. I begged Richard not to let anyone have me arrested because to me the worse thing in this world would be to have to call Mr. Williams to get me out of jail. Sister Harriet and my own niece was hell bent on me going to jail. I had given Mr. Williams' Secretary many papers that proved things on Richard and she was supposed to have given them to Mr. Williams just in case I did need him, even the deeds to my home even my car title. Amanda, you told me Mr. Williams said he didn't know what I was talking about. So, what did his Secretary do with all the things I gave her? I called Johnnie; she gave me a letter that said,

'To all concerned,

During the months of August, September and early October, I rode in Drucilla's car with her to several locations to see if she could find a certain car. She told me about following a small white car down Marklund Road. On one of our trips she took me down Marklund Road to show me where she had been. She told me that her sister Harriet and her niece Red took her there to see if that was where Red's Aunt and Uncle lived. Drucilla met the daughter of this family. But the girl had no children and no light blue Camaro, besides she never thought for one minute it was their daughter from the beginning. Furthermore, while I was with Drucilla, she never stopped at a place of business that I thought was a feed store and I have never seen her harass anyone'.

But see Amanda, Richard sent some thugs to Johnnie's house to rob her and threaten her life. I was going to get the truth even if I did get killed. And here we are with forty-two whores. I've said it, and I am going to say it again, I saw more drugs running up and down the big Warrior River then was ever on the 78 Highway.

Anyway, I finally did have to see Mr. Williams about some of this. Today I know who's who and where and Richard has been the cause of everything that's happened to me. Like I said, he wants me dead and now that I've lived past all he's done, he will look you in the face and say, 'I don't know what you're talking about'. I will say, 'But, Richard, why would so may people lie about you?'

Amanda asked, "What do you want Mama? Do you want God to send him back into the world as a whore with a mean ass pimp or cut his tongue out, and his dick off."

I said, "Amanda, I don't want anything to happen to Richard, but I do want the forty two on my list to be gone. Remember me Amanda; I went to Sumiton to take lessons to be mean and powerful. But I'm not married to any of them. It was just Richard that made all this happen to me.

Father Cross talked to us for 45 minutes and said to Richard, 'I gave Drucilla the rights to go get you out of her home and get on with her life. Amanda, Richard never did a thing to help me feel better about anything that was happening to me. The Valley Trailer Park on Cherry Avenue is where he moved into.

I had the lock changed on the doors and got screws put on all the glass doors and made sure the windows couldn't be opened. What is love, Amanda? I'll tell you.

> 'Love is sweet Wine and Candlelight
> Love is a hot bath, a soft bed in the arms you love.
> Love is being able to read between the lines
> Love is having you near me on good days or bad, happy or sad
> Love is pure romance
> Love is having babies with no regrets
> Love is trusting

Love is intensive care
Love is a phone call for no reason at all
Love is being cherished and adored
Love is a rose garden that wasn't promised
Love is a miracle
Love is I can't live without you
Love is a sick brain thing; it has nothing to do with your heart
Love is not a fear that Billie McCarty will call him today'

Mrs. Rhonda Barns was killed in a wreck after telling me that Richard was at Gooch's trailer every day. The telephone man that looks like a cowboy.

The note I found in his pocket.

'1112 2 St No over the hill to the store
11 Court turn right second door on the right'

The names William Shore called he rents trailers. Finding him at the Knot's house in Republic, backed up to the door with a little blue car there with tag 1ANN belonging to the Granges. This was the woman that came out on the porch with Richard in a see through gown and a new baby in her arms. I took pictures and left after Richard asked 'Can I help you?', as if he didn't know me at all."

Amanda said, "I'm sorry Mom."

She turned and walked out the door without saying another word.

It wasn't but a minute until Rex was knocking at the door. I told about Amanda's visit and told him to check on some things for me.

I said, "Rex, don't forget Heather and Jeff Jones, drug heads for sure, that came to the corner and just set there watching my home. But no matter what, it all goes back to McAdams, Nibletts, and Becky Stillwell. This story goes from trying to hold onto the love I've wanted all your life, to a hate that will make me crazy.

One more thing Rex, I want you to know everything about the people that live on Shoemaker in Center Point, Kelly Hancock and Kellie Cranford. Kay Sellers in Gardendale, June Johnston, Adamsville, Sherrie Melvin, Red Cross worker, and she works for the Phone Company. Oh, let me tell you about Larry, he owns a well-known plumbing company here in town. The first call from their family was Larry's ex-wife Karen Wade, looking for Richard. The next call was from Larry, I answered the phone and he said, 'Hi, how are you?' I said, 'Ok I guess.' Then I asked, 'Who are you?' He said, 'Larry so & so. He asked, 'Don't you know me?' I said, 'No! I don't.' He said, 'You must want to know me; you left your number on my cell phone 2 or 3 times.'

'Well, I am sorry Sir, it wasn't me, and I don't even know your number.' Then I asked him if he was married, he said, 'No'. 'Where is she?' I asked. 'Well, she went to Tennessee to live and I live with my mom. Do you like Auburn?' I replied, "Yes I do.' He asked, 'Are you blond and little?' I said, 'I am. Now Larry, cell phones don't talk. Where do you know me from?' Larry responded, 'Well, it was your husband that took my wife from me. Mrs. Hallmark, will you meet me sometime just to talk?' I said, 'I don't think so. I need to think about this.' 'He replied, 'You know Mam, there's not much to think about, they had fun and you and I didn't. They will go to hell and I won't. I don't go off at night very much, but if you're out this way, you call and I'll come see you.' I said, 'I tell you now, Richard has had many women that it's unbelievable. I don't care about him anymore. I can tell you, you get past the anger and the hurt. This won't keep you from wanting to know the whys but finally you just don't give a damn. Please don't try to hunt me because of what my husband did. I have been tormented to death and the truth is, I don't care anymore. We stay in this same house, and we put on a good front to the outside world. He doesn't have sex with me. Not in years.' Larry said, 'I won't hurt you, thanks for talking to me.'

Now Rex, I told Richard about this call, he said it's just some man trying to get me out. So help me, Larry called that night. I made Richard get on the other phone. I told Larry everything that had happened to me; we talked for over an hour. Richard never said a word, never said don't call my wife or this house; never said he didn't know his wife. I asked Richard why he didn't say something. He said

'It's your party, what should I say.' I walked away from him and went to bed.

Rex, I really do hate these people, it's their character, their personality, their sickness, the harm they are doing to good people that matters to me. My question is, are they gay or not? I heard on the radio the other day that 70% of the married men are gay.

I'll tell you about Richard he's not as smart as I am. He's not as handsome as I am pretty. He has no morals. A whore is like a gossiping woman, if she talks to you about someone, she'll talk to someone about you. Look at him, I bet you he has licked more poo off his whores crack than I have flushed. I see him as a piece of shit. Ms. Linda, you fooled around with her, you took her dancing, ate her mig pie. She has that daughter with her doped up husband and her little granddaughter. That makes three on this earth. Linda's daughter, she's tall and slim but Linda looks like a Mama Ameson thing, a hop of hair with beads and braids trying to look like your Indian squaw."

Rex said, "You're crazy Drucilla."

I said, "I know Richard has been with her. I'm the one that sat on the telephone with her daughter while he took her out dancing. She clawed his back up for me to see. He smelled of, licked up till all 350 lbs of this thing, Fo ha Fo ha cornbread feet, with lice in her hair is as sorry as he is and talked about worse.

Linda's daughter had never called my house before. Her excuse was to tell me about a singer she saw on TV. Like Richard has said many times, I wouldn't know the truth if it hit me in the face. His squaw had let me know in many different ways, like calling my home when she thought Richard was alone. Anyway, this bitch left town after getting through her nurse training. Believe it or not Richard has helped three whores become nurses and one get her CDL license.

Can you imagine the danger I have been in, while in the hospital where his sluts work? Not to mention the restaurants, remember the BBQ place I told you about, that we ate at and I was almost too dizzy to get into the house. It's not just me being paranoid its real danger. So I don't go out to eat in this State and I have told my doctors about the nurses. Which reminds me of the female doctor Richard went to a few times, the last time as I sat in the examination room. I had been in there with him several times. She asked me, 'Do I know you?' I said, 'You should, I've been to see you a few times.' Rex let me tell you this while it's on my mind. Richard and me went to Muscle Shoals to a weekend song writing retreat. Later we met two friends and road with them to get their phone fixed. A jewelry store was next door. Richard said, 'Come on, lets go in there, maybe I'll buy you something.' We walked in the door of the shop and this sales man said, 'Well, Drucilla knows what she wants.' I asked him 'Do you know me?' He said, 'No.' I asked 'Were you at the song writers meeting last night?' He said, 'No.' I said, 'But you know my name.' This is when he leaves to the back of the store and a woman comes out. She asked, 'Can I help you?' I said, 'No.'

Now, Richard didn't know that we were stopping at that shop. But that salesman knew us and I'd bet this house that he is gay. They are running this country; they are doctors, nurses, talk show hosts, and teachers. They are setting this example for all the young to see. They're in all walks of life. It's not like you can just cut the TV off. I want to scream from the top of the world. Lady's, Men, are you safe? Who's waiting around the corner to knock you off? There's something wrong, when you have to ask your husband who is your whore, is it another man or woman? Telling her husband I'm in love with Deb. This world today is run by human species that have turned animal, built by divine hands that have turned on him."

Rex asked, "Do you know what you're saying?"

"**Hell, yes I know!**" I replied. It's ok Rex. It's really ok if you don't believe me. It's taken me many years to believe all this myself. It's because we don't want to believe it. Mr. Williams has handed me my freedom on a silver platter. It's simple; I'm just tired of Richard. I'm tired of it all. All these years it's just been a brain thing."

Rex bid his good-bys and left.

Courtney said, "Drucilla, I don't know how you stand it. You're like a shock absorber."

I said, "I'll tell you one thing. Never pray for patience for God will just keep putting things on you until you can't deal with it. Well I have dealt with it all. Now I'm going to dance for the rest of my life in the arms of Tony, or someone."

Courtney said, "So-o-o let's stop packing and cook a steak. I think we've worked nonstop for over six hours."

I said, "I'm going to call Rex to come back. I need a laugh or two."

Courtney put the steaks on the grill while I poured us a glass of wine. As I walked around the kitchen I remembered the sugar jar. I had told Courtney about finding the lid half off the sugar jar. I removed the lid to find the rim of the jar all chipped up and glass all in the sugar. I showed it to Richard and he asked whom I had let into the house. I didn't even bother to answer him. I took it out for safekeeping and bought all new canisters. It was just another way for Richard to torment me. I never told anyone about it because it made me look real crazy. He pulled buttons off my clothes and the shoulder pads out. Do you now see I'm very careful of what I eat or drink? I don't mind telling you, this house that I love so much is so full of evil memories that it keeps me sick.

Courtney asked, "Did you see the woman on the talk show the other day? She got so mad at her husband for divorcing her that after he married his whore, she went into their bedroom and shot them to death. She's now in prison for years away from her children."

I said, "Yes, I cried through the whole show. Do you know how many times I've killed Richard in my mind? She should have been set free."

Rex came in and said, "Let me tell you this joke."

I asked Rex, "Have you told it to Max yet?"

I looked at Courtney and we laughed out loud. Rex put on a pouting face.

I said, "Did you hear the one about the boy Roy that got married? Before he got married he had beautiful blue eyes and a red pecker. He came back from his honeymoon with beautiful red eyes and a blue pecker."

Courtney screamed, "**Drucilla!!**"

I said, "Rex, if you tell Max I told you that joke, he'll put your lights out."

Things quieted down while we ate. I was so tired and the wine made me sleepy so I asked both of them to stay while I took a bath.

Rex said, "I'll scrub you down."

I said, "No thanks, I'll wait for Tony to do that."

Before Courtney left I asked her to come back the next day. She said she'd be here about ten. By ten I had things in different piles to give to the family. A truck came and loaded up everything that we had packed. All the furniture was left for Brandon. Rex came and I told him to leave the trunk. I'm giving it to Mr. Williams soon.

I was just saying that it would take three men to get it out of there. To my surprise Max came in.

Max asked, "Are you ready, My Lady?"

Before I could answer him, Max scooped me up in his arms and into my car. He handed me a box of Kleenex. I threw the box out the window and said, "Drive on!"

We drove for five hours. Max drove me to his home in Foley. I looked around his home.

I said, "Nice, very nice!"

Max said, "Yes, and it's your home away from home. Like, if a storm comes."

Max after looking at his watch said, "Its seven now and Tony will be here at eight thirty. Your home will be ready with all your things put away by two pm tomorrow. That's when I turn you over to Anthony."

I spotted a newspaper on the kitchen table. The front page had the story about the missing cruise ship headlining another Bermuda Triangle Mystery. It listed all the people that were missing. They had submarines checking the bottom of the ocean and airplanes searching a fifty-mile radius of where the ship was found. They didn't find anything. I made a mental note of each name. Knowing they would never find anything I silently thanked Mr. Young. I folded the newspaper and laid it down. I kicked off my shoes and picked up the drink Max had made for me. I wondered if he changed the name on the freighters as he went back to Red China, but I can't think about him.

I said, "Max, we have a lot of living to do, but tonight I want to be quiet."

I no more got that out of my mouth before the front door flew open and in came Anthony, Papa Perricotti and Tony. Anthony was all over me.

Anthony said, "Mama! I got so much to tell you and you're all mine."

Anthony sat in the floor at my feet. He took off my shoes and started rubbing my foot. Papa sat on one side of me and Tony on the other side.

I said, "Max, this is no dream. I feel like I've died and gone to heaven."

We all laughed and Anthony asked, "Mama, when are you going to marry Daddy?"

I said, "Very soon, we will all go back to Birmingham and I'll ask my friend Judge Case to marry us in the courthouse courtyard. You will get to meet a lot of my friends. Anthony will be the one that gives me away?"

Anthony said, "Oh yes! I'm your man. Max can be Daddy's best man. Papa is your Godfather so he can just hang loose."

I was thinking this boy is full of bull. Then he surprised me when he said, "Well I've rubbed your feet and let you relax."

Anthony turned to Max and said, "If you'll turn on the music, Mama and I will show Papa what kind of teacher I am."

Anthony took a pair of my dancing shoes out of a box and put them on my feet. What could I say? Three dances in perfect step, I couldn't believe Anthony or myself for that matter.

Tony said, "OK young man, you can't have my woman. She's tired and we must go home so she can rest."

Max let them out and locked up for the night. He showed me my bedroom. It was decorated in pink and cream colors and he had placed a dozen pink roses beside my bed.

Max said, "If you need anything at all, just look for it. I've got to go to bed. You have me crying uncle."

I said, "Hey Boy, it wasn't you that danced three dances just now."

Max standing in the doorway asked, "When are you getting married?"

I said, "Well, I did say the fourth of July, but the courthouse won't be open so we'll make it the second or third of July."

The roses from Max had a note with them. It read;

> State certified, insured, licensed and bonded
> I would keep you safe.
>
> Love Max.

It was eleven thirty and as tired as I was, I couldn't go to sleep. I lay there thinking of the mind games Richard had played on me. He would hide my car keys and I would give it back to him. I would move his eyeglasses or move his coffee cup. I had him thinking he was crazy. That would stop him for a while. Richard was born without a soul. He couldn't care less about any of my family or me.

One of my nephews told me that Richard would leave the house for a few hours in the middle of the night. I was taking an Ambien sleeping pill and was dead to the world. Richard could have jumped up and down on the bed and I'd never know it. It was Jerry's son. I tried to pay him to follow Richard, but he's afraid of his shadow and wouldn't do it. I knew he was telling the truth because many a time I'd fill up my car with gas and the next day it would be on one half a tank. I was also told that someone in my house was shinning a flashlight out our bedroom window. There were only the two of us in the house. When he shined the light, a car would turn on its lights and pull into my driveway. This tells me Richard was letting someone into my house. I quit taking the sleeping pill and this stopped. This was crazy, but I was sick in body, heart and mind. But now it's over and his sorry ass is gone. It's nice not having to deal with his stupid ass.

I wonder how many women are living this kind of life. I wonder if it's true that seventy percent of married men are gay. What do these wives have to do to make the government stop this? God will come and clean up his world someday and it won't be too soon for me.

I asked myself what does this spot I'm in make me. I've made love to Tony. My wish was for these forty-eight people to be removed from this earth. Me, the lady that prays every night. Me, the lady that knows that God is real without a doubt in my mind. Me, the lady that wouldn't hesitate to tie some bastard, that has hurt me, to the bumper of my car and drag them up and down a gravel road. Me, the lady that carries a twenty-five caliber automatic pistol in my bosom and a thirty-eight in my hip pocket. Me, the lady that's going to marry a gangster. Well somebody makes us the people we are, and Richard, Mama Marcella and DeRoy made me who I am. I just pray the Lord will forgive me. I've been asked what I think God thinks about me. God loves me. He knows what's in my mind. God destroyed the cities of Sodom and Gomorrah. He parted the Red Sea and let the good people through and closed it on the bad. He can be as mean as I am. He can send a gentle breeze to cool you and a tornado to uproot the trees. He can be pissed off just like me.

I got out of bed at eight am and left Max a note telling him that I was going back to Courtney's house and for him to tell Tony to come to Birmingham to the courthouse on Wednesday. I'd have everything ready for him on the second of July.

I pulled into Courtney's yard at one pm and at two pm Tony, Michael, Max Papa Perricotti, Anthony and Rex pulled into Courtney's yard.

I answered the door and asked, "What took you boys so long?"

Tony said, "Get your shoes on and go pee. We are going to be married today. You will never get away from me again."

I could tell that Anthony was as mad as Tony.

Max said, "Drucilla, you are a hellion."

I said, "You can call me a chair, but that don't make me have four legs. So you're all mad at me. I don't give a damn. I wanted to drive, to be by myself. I couldn't sleep. I love you Tony. I wasn't running away from you."

Tony said, "Well, I'm here, so get your chin in your hand and your ass in the wind. Call your Judge Case, Mr. Williams and anybody else you want at your wedding."

I said, "You're full of hot air. I hope you're full of hot spit."

Courtney was sitting in her rocker with a blanket wrapped around her legs.

I looked at Courtney and said, "Get your ass up and help me."

I looked in the mirror. I had on white jeans, a red shell with a white blouse, red high heels and my makeup was fine.

I said to Tony, "I'm ready."

Rex asked, "Are you going to get married in what you have on?"

Tony said, "I'll take you As Is."

We stood in line to get a marriage license with Judge Case standing close by. Judge Case stood about six foot two and with his flat cappie he had a commanding look. Mr. Williams with those lion eyes, he was five foot eleven and very handsome. I could read his mind. He'd say 'Go on Drucilla. If you fall on your face I'll be there to pick you up. Just don't kill anybody.'

My brother Jerry, all he could say was 'Damn, damn, damn; deceit deserves revenge.'

Courtney was beautiful with her bushel of hair if she would only stop biting her lip.

Amanda, my beautiful little girl, came flying in. I could hear her tires squalling; I know she flies in that Mustang. She came running down the hallway hollering, "Mother have you lost your mind?"

I said, "No Amanda! I'm going through the change of life."

I was nose to nose with Amanda. I was looking into the eyes of Drucilla number two.

She asked, "Did you know that my Daddy and Jeff were on that cruise ship?"

I said, "Yes, and I didn't give it a second thought. He invited me and I said No!"

Amanda asked, "How did you know."

Before I could answer Judge Case saved the day. He said, "Let's get this over with."

I replied, "Yes sir, this has been the longest three days of my life."

In four minutes Tony had papers on me. I now belonged to him. He owned me.

Max said, "Anthony, you go with Papa and Rex. Michael and I will drop Mr. and Mrs. Tortomasi off at the airport."

I said, "Oh my God! I'm now Drucilla Tortomasi. Tony, where are we going?"

Tony stated, "Fort Myers, Florida. Will that do?"

I answered, "Oh yes!"

Tony said, "I think I owe you a sunset cruise."

I said, "Yes, anything you say. But when we leave there I'd like to go to Hawaii."

Tony said, "We could do that."

It was a short flight to Fort Myers. We checked into a motel. I watched as Tony walked across the room, a confidence to his stride that would be hard to miss. I sighed thinking this is a man with presence a man with enough sex appeal to make a woman feel alive and cherished. I have always known I'm a woman with strength and love, but he breaks down all my shields.

Tony said, "I want you to know that you're the only woman I've ever brought here."

Before I could answer, he brushed a kiss over my soft lips. Tony meant to reassure me, but he caused a fire to flare fast and without warning. Desire throbbed inside me as fast as my rapidly beating heart.

I said, "When I see you, I know we have faith, trust and longing. Tony you know I get into trouble when I'm near you."

Tony said, "You're just on target so do what you please."

My hands pulled his shirt out of his pants before I could think about it. My palms were hot against his back.

Tony said, "We need to move this someplace else. At least let me close the door."

Tony closed the door and I pulled him to the bed.

Tony asked, "Any regrets?"

I said, "No! No regrets."

All my feelings came rushing to the surface. I don't know who reached for the other first. His arms were around me and his mouth came down on mine hard. I could feel the firmness of his lips and the sweeping thrusts of his tongue. Oh, the pleasure, I've been deprived for too long. Tony's hands moved, and then cupped me intimately. He's knowing and anticipating my every need. Somehow, I found the strength to part our hips.

Tony said, "I feel your dampness. Dru, tell me, what is it you want?"

I wanted the ache to ease, the throbbing to stop.

I said, "I want you, Tony."

Tony pulled me close to him. He was hard, full and throbbing. Hot liquid heat pooled inside me and trickled down between my legs. A warm flush rose to my cheeks.

Tony said, "Your perfume makes me crazy."

As if by magic, off went my top and my fun bags were in his hands. He teased them with his tongue, and then his teeth until my hips rocked insistently against him until he had lost control.

Tony grabbed for me once more and lifted me off the floor.

Tony said, "Wrap your legs around me."

I did and as he lowered me onto his waiting erection, my body took him wantonly, deep inside. I was wet and hot. To slide into slick heat was as easy as it was sweet. A tear went down my cheek as we broke through pure ecstasy.

Chapter 15

I said, "Tony, I'm so thankful for the rain. We better call Anthony. He will be waiting on the dance floor for me."

Tony said, "By now my love, he'll need a boat to get out. I'll call him to tell him where we are. He will understand."

Anthony didn't understand, I could hear him scream from across the room.

Anthony screamed, "In Honolulu! You two come home at once."

Tony said, "As soon as our honeymoon is over."

Tony hung up the telephone and walked back to the bed and said, "Now let's get back to those fun bags."

Tony nudged my legs apart with his legs and while I watched he entered me slowly as he said, "I need you. I need you!"

I responded, "I need you the most."

He thrust deep slow strokes. I took all of him, milking him with my tight wet nest.

I swear I could see fireworks going off. I went into the shower as Tony was coming out.

He said, "I rented a boat for a moonlight cruise of sorts. It's a paddleboat, just for the two of us."

I said, "Please Tony, let's stay here for three nights. I have an overpowering need for you, just you. You know I have a lot of love making to catch up on. I want to make up for lost time."

Tony said, "Three days here then on to Oahu, then Kauri, then Hawaii and back here, then home. We could have stayed home if sex is all you want."

"Tony, you know it wouldn't be the same."

The rain had stopped and as we lay in bed listening to the waves slap the shore. We slept in each other's arms. I have never slept so good in my life. I awoke early the next morning and stretched like a tiger. I had a desire and sensation sweep through me. As I straddled Tony, he opened his eyes and said, "You sure do know how to wake a man up."

Tony's eyes never left mine as I lowered myself. I took him inside me, inch by inch. The further in he went the more he swelled.

Back to the shower, but this time we got dressed.

Tony said, "I do believe you could be the death of me. Dru, every time I get near you, those green eyes are full of passion."

I said, "Yes, and it comes from my soul."

Tony asked, "Is that an invitation?"

"No, no! Uncle!"

Tony said, "I can tell you one thing. That beautiful naked body of yours makes me nervous. You don't know how bad I've wanted you. The innocent joy you bring to my life. Mixed with a fierceness I've never known."

"Tony, you were so right. You do make me nervous sometimes. Like now, Tony, move your hand!"

"No Dru!"

His fingers slipped from my hips to my thighs and I gasped aloud.

Tony said, "Don't say a word baby. Just let me."

My eyes opened wide. Tony parted my legs with his hands. In the next moment I didn't give a care. It was as close to heaven as a mortal could get. My knees buckled, my body swayed, I had never dreamed it could be like this. My thighs tingled, my muscles quivered and I was begging for more, more of that wonderful sensation.

Tony said, "Easy!"

Tony let his tongue soothe the chafed surface on my thighs.

After an hour, we finally got out of the room.

I asked, "Tony, do you know that poinsettias grow wild in Hawaii. The green plants in our homes, Philodendron, it grows like kudzu over here with leaves as big as elephant ears."

Tony said, "No, really? I bet that's a sight to see, I can't wait."

We spent three days in Honolulu, then to Oahu for three days, then Maui and Hawaii and back to Honolulu for that long flight home.

Tony asked, "Have you had a good time Dru?"

"Read my mind Tony. Didn't you read my lips?"

Tony said, **"Oh yes!** Hotter than the volcanoes and sweeter than the pineapples."

As I elbowed Tony I said, "Not so loud, I get you Tony, very good."

The water was beautiful but the beaches I didn't like at all. To be such a beautiful place it's very sad. All the industry is gone and all the people have is the tourist's money to live on. The houses were run down because the government leases them to the natives for one dollar for one hundred years and his son picks it up for another hundred years for a dollar. They will never own it and won't take care of it. I came to find out that the pearls came from Nashville, Tennessee.

I said, "All in all, it was beautiful but it's a poor place. I wouldn't trade one square foot of Gulf Shores for all of Hawaii."

Tony said, "I'm a strong man, but the Arizona Memorial brought tears to my eyes. Our own government has let our country go to hell."

I said, "Let's not talk about the sad. The flowers were beautiful, the orchids, the plumeria have a cluster of beauty, the trees and the tree ferns, the hanging jade vines and the waterfalls.

It was funny about the chickens having the right of way over a car. I loved the restaurants being open so the birds can land on the tables and eat out of your hands. I knew Anthony wouldn't like sharing with the birds or shooing away all the flies."

Max and Rex were waiting for us at the airport when we landed.

Rex being Rex said, "Well, is your skirt tore, your tits sore and I bet you think you can't pee anymore?"

Max was like a flash of lighting, one punch and Rex was lying on the ground, out cold. Max took out a note pad from his pocket and wrote a note and pinned it to Rex. The note read, don't come back around us until you have cleaned up your mouth.

Max said, "Drucilla, you tell me if he ever talks bad in front of you again. I'll put him under the ground."

People stood in stony silence around us looking at Rex lying on the ground. Max looking at the people said, "He must have had a long flight."

I walked away as if I didn't know anyone, thinking, oh yes! This is my Max.

Outside was Ross helping with the luggage. Tony introduced me to Ross as his new bride. What a character this chauffeur is, I thought. As we drove, he was pointing out all the good places to go. We got to Bama Ice Cream Bar.

Ross said, "They make the best banana split in the world."

I said, "Please stop. I'd love to have one to take home, if that's all right?"

Tony said yes and we drove into the parking lot.

Max asked, "What about a sundae for us?"

Without a word he was gone and back in minutes with me a banana split and everyone else a sundae.

I felt a new pleasantness with my new family. A feeling of cheerfulness then it dawned on me, I felt safe. No one other than Mr. Williams had ever made me feel safe. The fear was gone.

We turned into a driveway and drove for three blocks before I could even see a house. The estate and grounds were manicured. We stopped by a huge old oak tree.

Ross opened the door. Max took my banana split in one hand with me holding his other, as we exited the car. Max gave my banana split back to me as Tony came around the car for me.

We walked over to a swing. Tony said, "Dru, sit here, look over your yard and enjoy your ice cream."

We finished our ice cream and we walked around the most beautiful home I'd ever seen.

I said, "Tony, this reminds me of an antebellum home in Mississippi, much larger than in my dream."

As we walked up the front steps Tony said, "Dru, this home will only have the memories we make."

As we entered our bedroom Ross and Max had already placed our luggage there. We changed clothes and went down stairs. Papa and Anthony were playing a game of Chess. Both stood up as I entered the room. Anthony with joy saying, "So, you're finally home, and now you're my mom, my best girl, my sweetheart!"

Papa said, "Drucilla, this is your dream home isn't it?"

I said, "Yes Papa, right down to Anthony's tree house, fire pole and all."

Tony laughed saying, "And, with no curtains."

Anthony said, "No, no, no!! It's my office! It's equipped with a computer, bookshelves and everything else I need. So, Mama, when you need me just email me."

I said, "Anthony, do you live there?"

Anthony said, "No, no, I just run in and out from time to time."

The next morning I sat there looking at Tony's luscious lips.

His eyes opened and he said, "Come to me baby."

I said, "No, no, no! The paper just came in with the morning coffee. The front page is about the cruise ship."

Tony said, "Bring it to me. Let me read it."

I asked, "Should I feel frightened?"

Tony responded, "No, only a coward feels fear."

I said, "I don't think so. When I'd go hunting with my Daddy sometimes I was afraid we might run across a snake."

Tony said, "Well I assure you, everyone knew where you were, and where I was. We have nothing to fear. There is no sin in tomorrow, only happy memories. It was a legitimate business that sent that bunch of lazy asses the tickets. They couldn't buy a ticket for a merry-go-round but would jump aboard anything for free."

I said, "You're right Tony, and this ride took them to hell. Now we all are going to have a mental block about the past."

Tony said, "Amanda will come to you. She will meet Michael and they will fall in love. Just like in our dream. You will have your night club, and your friends Phillip and Sergeant Stone."

I said, "I'll never have Fritzie. He passed away December 28, 2007. He's one of the best friends I ever had. I loved him. Old Aunt Bessie died and I drank a bottle of wine. Then I pissed on her grave."

Tony said, "Speaking of good memories, Charles Perricotti is coming Friday for a late lunch."

I said, "Wait Tony, don't tell me, we'll have fried red snapper, fries with hush puppies and every Sunday we have spaghetti and salad with fine wine and Italian bread. Oh my, I remember Charlie, he's a ladies' man, tall, dark black hair and very handsome. In my dream, I went with Charlie and Anthony to Our Lady of Sorrows Catholic Church in Homewood and met the Ross family. I realized with nostalgia that earlier generations of Italian Americans were fast disappearing and their younger children had little knowledge of their ethnic heritage. They had no first hand experiences of their pioneering fore fathers, even worse few Alabama people realize that Italian immigrants moved to the deep South during the early part of the twentieth century, just as they had moved to New York, New England, Chicago, San Francisco and Seattle. When told that Sicilians settled in Birmingham and the Deep South people invariably asked were there many, that migrated to Birmingham and were they Mafia. I know later Dothan and Mobile had Mafia and much later Jasper wanted people to think they had mob connections. My thought on that is Jasper people are mean and crazy as hell, but don't have the brains to be in the Mafia.

Tony, I remember Anthony telling me that most Birmingham Italians were Sicilians from the small villages of Biscquineo, Compofronco, and Sutera, Sicily. It's the largest island in the Mediterranean Sea. The poverty stricken area known as the Mezzogiorno, which includes the southern part of the Italian boot around Naples and Calabria. I think the Mezzogiorno was identified as the Kingdom of the Two Sicilia by the Normans. They invaded the island during the crusades, even before the so called invasion of England in ten twenty six. The English heritage of which Birmingham's Anglo-Saxons are so proud of may very well be more closely linked to Sicilian heritage than most Southerners won't admit. Anyway, get this Tony, Anthony told me that the first one hundred years of life for Italians in Birmingham was torn strife, turmoil, bigotry and prejudice. The infamous title for Birmingham was the murder capital of the world. Well I was born seventeen miles from downtown Birmingham and I've been there all my life. When I was seventeen years old, Bull Conner was chief of Police in Birmingham. It was the sixties and all hell broke loose with the blacks. It was blacks against whites, not Italians. They didn't have enough sense to go back to Africa and build themselves a world. They think that we hate them and they hate us. They have taken over Birmingham and it's nothing but a hellhole. All the businesses have shut down. Blacks don't know how to run a big hotel or department store so the city buys the empty buildings and they stay empty. They placed blacks in every school and over night they became all black schools. The whites either home schooled or sent their kids to private schools. The blacks take over and destroy everything and I do mean everything on this earth. Pretty soon it will be Africa right here in the South. Gangs will be roaming the street with machetes, hacking each other's heads off. They will destroy the South after the Italians came here and built up Ensley, Birmingham, East Lake and East Thomas. Tony, take the Bruno family for instance and the Bianca family; no better people have ever lived. As a little girl, I shopped with my Mama at the Bruno's Grocery store in Pratt City and I grew up watching store after store being built in Alabama. I know of the Big B drug stores. Mr. Joe Bruno received achievements and rewards from the drug businesses.

I'll tell you this; the Italians will be the first to tell you that Americans have too long relied on government agencies for handouts. In my eyes the Bruno families have been giants among men. Their good deeds would reach for miles and miles. The Italians take care of their people. Tony, I may look like a dumb blond, but I am an Italian at heart."

Tony said, "Oh yes, I know! And Anthony said you are going through classes with him at the St. Patrick Catholic Church. He said my Mama is a Catholic at heart even if she is the only blond at mass."

I said, "I can only be me. Remember, I like myself just like I am. I'm not going to apologize for my Confederate soldiers, all twenty-three of them. I will not apologize and no one can apologize for me. I even wrote a song to honor not only my twenty-three, but for all Confederate soldiers. I'll sing it for you . . .

Lucy B. Williams

Proud

Living in Dixieland
Yes, I'm a Southern man
I'm a Rebel through and through
My Confederate flag is flying high
I've got pride in my eyes.
Yes, I'm a Rebel and I'm proud
I'm proud of my heritage
I'll never let it die
I'll keep that flag flying high.

Be proud you're in Dixie land
Be proud you're a Southern man
Be a Rebel though and trough
Keep that flag flying high.

Kept Papa's rifle hanging on the wall
Confederate flag standing in the hall
I have the rebel hat that Papa use to wear
I have a lock of Granny's hair
They just fought for their state
They were Rebels like you and I
Be proud of your heritage
Never let it die
Keep that flag flying high.

Be proud you're in Dixie land
Be proud you're a Southern man
Be a Rebel through and through
Keep that flag flying high

It may not fly from the capitol dome
But it will be flying from my home
Against the background of the blue sky
My confederate flag is flying high

I challenge you as of today
To stand for the motto of your state
We dare defend our rights
We dare defend our fights
Keep that flag flying high

Be proud you're in Dixie land
Be proud you're a Southern man
Be a Rebel through and through
Keep that flag flying high

It may not fly from the Capitol dome
But I keep it flying from my home
Yes, keep that flag flying high"

Tony said, "Dru, that is beautiful. I'm sure my Grandfathers would have been right beside your Grandfather if they had been here."

I said, "I know they would have. My heritage goes all the way back to the Revolutionary War. I came from a long line of Rebels. The Father of this country is a Rebel from Virginia. My Great, Great, Great, Great Grandfather William Brown was a hero at the Battle of Cowpens, South Carolina. He was a Private in Captain Bethel's Company of Colonel Kennedy's Regiment assigned to General Nathaniel Greene's Army. They fought General Cornwallis' Army to a standstill. Captain Bethel's Company was down to sixty two percent strength, having fought at Eutaw Springs, Cross Creek and Georgetown. Colonel Kennedy placed Captain Bethel's Company on the far right flank because that was the less likely place for a battle. They were to be held in reserve.

General Greene's Army had eight thousand soldiers while General Cornwallis had eighteen thousand soldiers. General Cornwallis sent four thousand to rout the left flank and four thousand to rout the right flank while sending ten thousand on a frontal attack. The frontal attack started first. Cornwallis wanted General Greene to think that was the main attack so he would pull up his reserves.

General Greene held his own and didn't call up his reserves. By this time the British hit the right flank. But Captain Bethel had his men well entrenched and held his own against enormous odds. The British breached his line with hand-to-hand combat. Bethel's line was breaking and Captain Bethel noticed Private William Brown charging the enemy. Captain Bethel immediately sounded the charge call. His action stunned and confused the British. The British retreated and Private William Brown saved the day.

In 1782, General Washington first awarded the Badge of Military Merit to Sgts. Daniel Bissel, William Brown and Elijah Churchill in recognition of their unusual gallantry, extraordinary fidelity and essential service. These were the only men awarded the heart shaped patch made with purple cloth, better known today as the Purple Heart.

In eighteen o' three the President signed into law giving land to veterans. William Brown Jr. received his father's land grant in Jefferson County. He received five thousand acres in what is now known as Fairfield, Hueytown and Bessemer. He named it Lost Creek, as it is still named today, because while riding the boundary of his land, he was following the river and when he went over a hill, the river was running in the opposite direction. He thought he was lost but upon finding out it was a different river he named it Lost Creek.

William Jr. built his house here in eighteen fifteen. He founded the town of Jonesboro and built a Methodist Church before Alabama became a state. He was friends with Davy Crockett and invited Davy to stay with him and offered him land to build a house, but Davy opted to go to Texas and the rest is history.

William Junior raised cotton and corn for a cash crop. Alabama became a State in eighteen nineteen. William had six sons and three daughters. His sons grew up to become lawyers, judges, mayors and preachers. They founded several small towns around the county.

I had twenty-three soldiers in the Confederate Army, each one a hero in his own right. I've already told you the story of Great Grandpa Ike Brown at the Battle of Nashville. We were winning until Grant figured out he was fighting the same men over and over again. Then Grant stopped the exchange of prisoners. Our prisoner of war camp became over crowded. Then Sherman went through Georgia burning our farms and salting our field so we couldn't feed our solders. If we couldn't feed our families and soldiers, we couldn't feed our prisoners. Jefferson Davis offered to send them back anyway, but Grant wouldn't accept them. Many died from sickness and hunger. When word got back up north about our camps; the first thing the Yankees did was to cut rations to Confederate prisoners of War. It didn't matter that they had food and we didn't. Our guards ate what the prisoners ate. After the war, to cover up his mistakes, Grant had Henry Worth hanged for war crimes. Grant should have been tried for war crimes but the victor never is. After the war carpetbaggers came down South and stole what their army didn't destroy. The carpetbaggers were still running rough shod over us when your people came to Alabama.

I love your people Tony. I love them all. They did what had to be done at the time after the damn Yankees ripped us apart. Your people came in and built their stores and put out merchandise. They built food stands and vegetable stands and were doing fine. Then came the Kennedy's and then Johnson with the war on drugs. That brought attention to the drugs and it went wild and the dope made our country crazy. But our Southern heritage will stand firm in my heart forever, just like yours.

You know Tony; I do know your driver Ross. His parents and Grandparents owned a store in East Thomas. Right next door to Saint Marks Church and his mother and father retired from their own store in Pratt City and moved from Forestdale to Gulf Shores. His mother, Frances, was one of my friends. I don't think Ross has put the two of us together yet. I'll bet as time goes by we will know a lot of the same people. I may have told you once before that an Angel has put our minds together. I think it was Frances, Ross' mother. I know she loved me. She tried to get me to buy a house in Gulf Shores years ago, but I had to stay with my family."

Tony said, "Well, you're here now and here you are going to stay. We must go over to Papa's house. He wants to see if you can show him the layout of his place."

I said, "Oh! I sure can, Tony. I'll ask Papa for the card that opens the elevator to take us to the casino. I'll take him down to where the incinerator is and to where his boat is. And while I'm at it, I'll bring Mama and Papa Perricotti's picture home with me and hang it up in our study. I can tell him how he lost her and that she was with your wife in the plane."

Tony's eyes looked sad.

I said, "I'll not talk about that Tony. I'm sorry; I wouldn't have you hurt for the world. I love you Tony. Let's take a nap before we go to see Papa."

Tony said, "What a deal!"

Tony's eyes brightened up and he swept me up into his arms and up the stairs we went. Tony laid me on the bed and began taking my clothes off.

I asked, "What are you doing? Do I have to have my clothes off just for a nap?"

Tony asked, "Don't you love me?"

I remarked, "Oh yes, I do love you, but it's daytime."

Tony said, "Here, take my hand."

I could feel the heat as I lay beside him looking into his eyes and being wrapped into his arms.

I said, "Oh Tony, you're so warm."

Tony said, "And my lady, you're so soft, I love you."

I asked, "But, Tony, where is everybody?"

Tony replied, "I don't know, but they won't come in here. Dru, I desire you more every day. I love you and I'll treat you like a queen. You're so petite and I love to feel your excitement when I know I've satisfied you."

I said, "We are perfect for each other."

Tony said, "I'm going to want you every time I'm near you. I would almost ask you not to wear panties. You don't have to be bad, just naughty sometimes. Damn, you have me excited and nervous all at the same time."

Tony was on his feet and I was thinking, that I was the most ethical person that I know. I am a professional businessperson. I keep a super-energized enthusiasm. The unfolding evening would underscore this truth. Eighty-three people here for dinner. It went well and I entertained. Always full of excitement. After the party was over, I only had Tony to entertain. Tony said, "The room is so nice, just look around."

I said, "I'll freshen up and change into something more comfortable."

I closed the bathroom door behind me, confident that his excitement was maximized. I think we were both thinking of ravishing each other. Our passion was dual. My bedroom opportunity was to enjoy. I have him, hook, line and sinker. He was about to fly me to the moon. My energy had pushed me beyond control, both in thought and action. I removed my make-up, showered and perfumed. I stretched like a cat saying to myself, 'I am a goddess of beauty'. I then slipped on my thick, pink, towel robe, right side folded over left side. I left it untied and held it together with my hand.

I opened the door and watched Tony turn to face me. He was actually holding some of my drawings for my club. I stepped through the door. Tony stood up. While halfway across the room, I caught his eye. With my right hand, I swung open the right side of the bathrobe revealing the right half of my nude body. In a flash his eyes began to survey, but before he could focus I had recovered myself.

Tony's attention was maximally focused saying, "You are one beautiful lady; nothing in my life has matched this. You are one wide-open hot, lady."

This night would be etched indelibly into our memory banks. I was a goddess of beauty, a goddess of love.

As Tony came out the bathroom door, I stepped to him into his arms. Our lips talked to each other, my robe fell, he picked me up taking me to our bed, and our passion was like magic.

Tony handled me like a china doll. Our lips were telling each other that for sure it wasn't just a dream. We had found the one person that we thought would never exist.

We were both used up. Tony fell asleep, our warm bodies holding each other as if the other would be gone if one awakened.

I had found that satisfying sex like this was like a good glass of wine, it helped me sleep. Tony lay sleeping as I wiped his face and body off. I stepped into the shower to wash the lovemaking off. With Tony, I was experiencing the most fantastic sex of my life. Back in the bed, I snuggled up to Tony thinking I had exhausted him and I have tons of energy! As I awoke at six thirty a.m., I looked over Tony's face, how peaceful he looks. He awoke not from a dream but to a dream, he is my love, the golden god that an angel had given me.

I started to get out of bed.

Tony said, "Come back to me. I love your personality. I love you. I could eat you up. You're the sugar in my tea, the peaches in my cream. You're . . ."

I said, "Keep talking and I may give you everything."

Tony kissed me from head to toe. I had found my soul mate. Tony was so tender and loving.

Tony said, "Dru, just feel this."

I said, "This is what I've missed all my life but never again. Just hold me Tony. Please don't let anything happen to us."

Tony said, "Not in this life time baby. You are loved and safe."

I started to get up again and Tony slid his arms around me and pulled me close.

Tony said, "I'm not quite done here."

Tony sent my blood swimming with a wet and hungry kiss. The taste of him, the feel of him pressed against me. The need we created in each other, time after time erupting inside me, making me beg for more, but we were both panting hard and Tony said, "Now let's run to the shower and go see Papa."

I said, "You really are a sweet heart Tony, but I do know your game, always leave her wanting more."

As we were going out the front door, Max was coming in.

Max said, "Our Anthony said to tell you, dance lessons start for you and Tony on Thursday at six thirty. He has entered both of you in competition."

I said, "Competition! My God!"

Max said, "Don't say it Drucilla, if he didn't think you were good enough, he wouldn't have signed you up."

I said, "But I just got here. I'm not even settled in good. I don't know anybody."

Tony said, "Well, I like that. You know me and by the time Anthony is through you'll know everyone."

Max said, "Drucilla that's not all. Anthony has you all set up to race in the modified division at Six Flags in Pensacola, Friday night week. Then Saturday you are to sing at Papa's club. He has a band lined up just for you."

I asked, "My Lord, and who's car will I race?"

Tony said, "It's your own car and it's a beauty. It's maroon with white striping and has number sixty-six on her. Anthony has your seven sponsors lined up. He didn't want you to worry. Anthony said racing is like dancing you can only think about your next step. Anthony told me that you told him that racing was so wonderful because when you go through the window of the race car you think of nothing but winning."

I said, "Oh yes, you can't think of anything but the sound of your motor. Your ears get to know every sound that car makes and for sure you're out there to win."

Tony said, "Now Dru, you don't have to do this."

I said, "Oh yes, yes I do! I wouldn't let my Anthony down for the world and all that's in it."

Max said, "This is another way to introduce you to more people."

I said, "I don't want to know more people."

Max said, "Well there is one more that Anthony has you lined up for."

I asked, "And what's that?"

Max said, "Golf, golf lessons on Monday afternoons."

I said, "Now, you better be telling me this is all. I'll do this for Anthony to learn, but I don't give a rat's ass for this deal. I know how to play golf and he'll see. You tell Anthony that I said if he had tits I'd braid them."

Tony was still laughing when we went in Papa Perricotti's door.

Papa asked, "What's so funny?"

Tony said, "Papa don't mess with this lady, she just might braid your tits."

I said, "Shut up, Tony! Papa I'm so excited to be home."

Looking around it was just like my dream; Papa put his card in the elevator control and the doors opened. We went to Papa's club. I saw Papa's office and remembered Papa's present.

I said, "Oh! Papa, this box I've been carrying around is yours. It's the very best cherry smoking tobacco."

Papa took me in his arms and said, "Come my doll. I have something for you."

We walked through the club and there was a large dance floor and a beautiful stage.

I said, "Papa, this wasn't in my dream."

Papa said, "No my child, Anthony has worked on this for months."

The thrill of excitement sent chills all over me. My emotions were running overtime. I stepped up onto the stage and turned one of the microphones on.

I asked, "Can I sing now Papa?"

Papa said yes and I sang 'The Rose' acappella.

Papa said, "My dear, you are as wonderful as Anthony said you were. Remember, there's a time for helping and giving and there's a time for slowing down and pulling back. You don't let Anthony push you too fast. I think it's time to remind yourself just how special you really are."

I said, "I will Papa. Being here is like taking a vacation from hell."

Tony said, "Well this vacation will never end."

Papa said, "Let me put my tobacco in this office and then I'll go mix us a drink."

I said, "I . . ."

Papa cutting me off said, "I know, you drink Canadian Club with lemon and Royal Crown Cola."

I asked, "And you know because Anthony told you, didn't he?"

Papa said, "That's right! He knows you pretty well."

Tony said, "Dru, you have been bewitched by him."

I said, "Yes! He gives me strength and he is so persistent. I must ask you two, do you know how wonderful it is to have your husband's son as your best friend?"

Papa said, "Well, wait just a minute. He may have to stand in line on that matter."

I said, "No Papa! Anthony comes first."

Tony teasingly asked, "What about your Mr. Williams?"

I said, "He and Anthony run neck and neck with Papa, Max and you. Then let's see, there's Charles Perricotti, Michael, Roger Tommynacker, Sgt. Stone and Phillip Jimez."

Papa said, "Don't forget Ross, my driver."

I said, "Tony, I hope you're not a jealous man."

Tony said, "Now, where there's not a little jealousy, there's no love."

I said, "Well, maybe I can deal with just a little. And Papa, for the record, you being my God Father. No one comes before you or loved more. You must know that."

We finished our drinks and went back upstairs. Papa let it slip that Max had come over last night and made arrangements to send Rex back North. I had all day to think about Rex. I didn't want him to leave. They were all coming for dinner tonight and I'd get it straight with Papa.

I had told Papa to bring the picture of Mama to be hung behind his smoking chair at my house.

Everyone had arrived but Rex and I heard footsteps in the next room. It had to be Rex.

Max said, "When Rex gets here I want to talk to him."

I said, "I believe that's him now."

Max said, "I'll talk to him after dinner."

I asked, "How much excitement can one girl stand?"

Max said, "It's according to who the girl is."

Later that night after dinner, I met Rex coming down the stairs as I was going up.

I said, "That's a beautiful dinner jacket and tie you're wearing."

I grabbed his tie as if to swing on it, but I pulled him down seven steps.

I asked, "Have you ever heard of Loki?"

Rex said, "No!"

I said, "Loki is the Goddess of Evil. That would be me, or that you've never known. You can't leave me."

I ran up the stairs and into my room and back out. Rex was still standing where I left him. As I ran down the stairs I said, "Damn you, Rex! I don't want you to leave. Tell Max I said to find you a job. You're not going back North, you're not leaving me."

Rex went to find Max. I knew Max would do as I asked.

After everyone had left, as I laid on my bed, my bath was ready and the wonderful radiance of candles reached from my bath to my bed as if calling me. Tony had lit pink candles and placed pink roses all around my bathroom. I wondered what kind of mood Tony wanted me in. The bath was filled with Rose water. I guess he knows lavender puts me to sleep. Leaving my bath in a pink satin gown, I slid between pink satin sheets. They were so cool and tension free I fell into an uninterrupted sleep as I prayed. My prayer was answered and when I awakened, Anthony was sitting at the foot of my bed.

He smiled and said, "You are the real sleeping beauty Mama. Dad has been out of here since seven this morning. Oh! Oh! I should have warned you about the cameras in this house."

I said, **"Cameras!!"**

Anthony said, "Yes Mam, they're hidden from view. Now Dad turns the ones in here off when you two come home. But I was watching the monitor when you pulled Rex down the stairs last night. Papa may have a broken rib, he laughed so hard. Max was beside himself saying, 'That's my blond bomb shell' and Dad said, 'I'll be damned.'

I said, "Ok, but you can't be cursing."

Anthony said, "Mama I almost broke my neck to find Papa, Max and Dad."

I said, "Well, there's a good possibility that I may break something else if you tell anyone else about that."

Anthony said, "Well now Mom, you can't take all the fun away from me. I've got to tell my friends that I have a Loki for a Mom. Goddess of Evil! Max told me that you are an army of one, but you sure don't look like Rambo. Rex has been very good to you. Please don't let Rex leave. He's sorry for what he said."

I said, "I don't want Rex to leave either. Tell Max to make him a gardener. Tell him to have Rex landscape our new yard. I want a rose garden. What about a vegetable garden, even if he had to bring in the right kind of dirt, or an herb garden. I want a fence put up with pink running roses. I want the large purple azaleas and I want lots of flowerbeds, yes, lots of flowerbeds. I know what I want between the house and the garden, I want a Golf Green to practice chipping and putting. I want four pecan trees, six peach trees, six apple trees and two fig trees. I want a birdbath on each side of the house. I want Rex to go to my Daddy's old place and get many water oaks and plant them on both sides of the driveway. Baby, do you need a pen to write all this down?"

Anthony said, "No Mam, I'll remember it all. I'll tell him everything. Now I must go and let you get up. Tonight is your dance class. Do you need to go shopping for anything?"

"No Doll, I do want to thank you for all you have done to make me happy. Some little Charlie you are, remember? The Charlie that taught me dancing and how to use the computer, you have done a lot for me and I'll never forget it."

Anthony said, "Your heart is safe in my hands Mama. Remember, I loved you first."

My dance lesson was good.

Race day came and I was there to face only sixteen cars, not as bad as I thought. I couldn't believe Tony had let Anthony do this, but I knew why. I had told Anthony that I wished Sgt. Stone would close down the Seventy Eight Highway from Jasper to Birmingham and just let me speed as fast as my car could go. Well, here I am, remember be careful what you wish for. Over the public address speaker, I heard an announcement. Ladies and gentlemen, we have a new driver tonight, Mrs. Drucilla Tortomasi in car number sixty-six. Let's give her a big six flags welcome. This is a one half mile oval track and I was used to a quarter mile track. My last run I came in sixth of eighteen. Now I have a better car, but I also know it isn't only the car, it's up to me.

The engines roared, the flag dropped and I was out like a bolt of lightning to third position and on the bumper of the number two car.

He wasn't going to let me by, so just into the third turn I bumped his bumper. He went off the track and over the bank. That put him to the back of the pack. We started back to green with five laps to go. I was closing in the last car with one lap to go. I pressed him hard on the forth turn and he went high and I went under to win by half a car length. The people were all on their feet. The announcer said, he couldn't' believe that a new car and a woman driver has won the race and has beaten the hometown favorite.

The guy I'd put off the track was mad and coming over to tell me off. Max stood ten feet tall in front of me when he saw him coming.

I said, "No Max, I'll do my own talking."

I stepped out all five foot two of me and before he could say a word I reached out my hand and said, "Hi, my name is Drucilla. I'm glad to be running with you boys. I'm sorry you didn't see me in time to move. Maybe next Friday you'll have better luck."

He said, "You damn right I will."

I said, "We should have some fun out there. When I have a race to run, I run to win so give it your best."

He looked at me, then Max, then back to me; he turned on his heels and walked away without a word.

Tony said, "You can bet they will all have a new engine next week."

I grabbed Anthony and said, "You just gave me the time of my life. I had forgotten how much I love the races."

Anthony said, "Well Mama, they will be ready for you next week."

I said, "Don't you worry, I'm ready too."

I finished good all season and then I asked Tony to get Anthony to give the car to Rex. Rex needed the car and all I wanted to do now was sing and dance. Tony is the best dancer in the world. He could make any woman look good. Definitely he was the best lover in the world.

Amanda came to see Tony and me dance. But she was so sad. She couldn't find her Daddy.

I said, "Amanda, stop your worrying. He will drag his ass back someday. He always did."

I couldn't help but laugh when I told her a UFO got him and he is under the sea somewhere. I couldn't stop laughing so she went out mad at me.

Michael met her in the hall and they sat in the swing forever, talking. The next thing I knew, she was moving in with him. The next thing I heard she was planning a wedding. Max and Anthony kept me up to date on them.

I got to thinking about my dream wedding; this is what I'll do for Amanda.

Talking to Max about it he said, "The two of them are going to elope and I want you to be ok with that."

"Ok!"

I know the blood drained from my body. I know what you're thinking; Tony took care of her divorce two months before Jeff got on that cruise ship.

I said, "Please bring Amanda to me; she may need to go shopping. Max, where do you think they will go?"

Max smiled, saying, "Ok, ok, Las Vegas."

I said, "I'm going to see Papa, I'll be back in an hour."

Papa was sitting in his easy chair overlooking the Ocean.

I kneeled at his knee taking his hand. He asked, "What do you need baby?"

I replied, "Papa, I need you to tell me that my Amanda will be fine."

Papa said, "Dru, you don't realize what a tough little girl you have. I tell you it's a miracle that Michael has been able to get her for himself. Amanda is an Earth Angel."

I said, "Well, I must go Papa, Max is bringing her to me. I may need to go shopping with her."

Papa said, "You need any money or want a charge card; there's no limit?"

"No Papa, but thank you for being so precious."

Max came in smiling, rushed to me, picking me up in his arms saying, "Amanda can't come today, she will call you. But your Mr. Williams called and he's here at Fort Morgan, he said to meet him for dinner at the Wolf Bay Lodge at seven o'clock."

I was kicking, pushing, trying to get loose from Max, but he just held me tighter.

I said, "Let me down! Damn you, you better not let me see you with a tie on."

He dropped me on the couch saying, "I'll be faster than you baby!"

Max spun out leaving the room, my shoe hit him in the butt. I smiled saying, "You weren't fast enough Baby!"

He ran back picking up my shoe, he came over to me, lifted up my foot and put my shoe on.

He said, "You just remember, I'll be fast when you need me to be."

He pulled me off the couch onto the floor with my leg. We both laughed.

I screamed saying, "Hey you! Mr. Williams will take you on a trip to Africa and tie your ass in a tree for lion food, you remember that! Now, get out, I must get beautiful to see my Mr. Williams, my life line. He reminds me 'Life is not measured by the number of breaths you take, but by the number of moments that takes your breath away'."

I wiped tears from my eyes thinking of how much I love Mr. Williams. I remember everything he has ever said to me.

All of us go through life with an increasing number of hurts that we carry with us in our hearts. Some of these come to us when we are very young. A very few fade from our memory.

But these scars from hurts are forever with us to give us sorrow and unhappiness.

The important, fact about life is, that it is very deep, full of things to be explained, full of mysteries and beauties that each one of us must hunt out and solve alone.

I came across a sentence one time that read, 'Such brain as mine was located in my heart, and that all roads, as far as I am concerned leads out of my heart'.

And that's where hurts always lodge. A difference of opinion between two people amounts to nothing. It only serves to stimulate and broaden each. But when you send a poisoned arrow of bitterness or falseness into the heart of your friend, you have caused a hurt that will leave its mark forever. How very wonderful to arouse a thrill of love or beauty in the human heart! A man grows by something more than inches when he has done kindness or made this world a bigger, happier place for someone else.

The man who starts a lawsuit, as a rule, carries a shrunken soul around with him. Fine beings are not in that business.

They say to count to ten before you lose your temper, or say something you may regret. I would say count to ten a thousand times before uttering something that may leave a hurt in a heart.

You must be a friend to have a friend and you must love to be loved. And remember there is no sin in tomorrow. I'll not think about yesterday just the happy days that God has for me to deal with. Mr. Williams said to draw a circle around your life and don't reach out to anything that you can't do anything about, and don't let anything in your circle to cause you trouble. Be happy. Oh! How I thank God for him. Thinking I've got to stop this and go have a good joke for Mr. Williams. The last star I see before I close my back door, the first light I see when I open my eyes, Mr. Williams is my life line and I hope he will never forget that I absolutely love him. I feel so certain that he was put on this earth for me, the best friend a person can have.

Going to the arms of Tony, knowing I'm loved and safe. Knowing I live in that circle with Tony's family, knowing that Mr. Williams is a call away. My life will be happy and hopefully the bad I've been through will fade from my mind. May God bless my friends. I know I must love those who have torn my heart out so many times. I also know that God doesn't expect me to like them. None of those people matter anymore. Neither Richard nor any of his devils can hurt me again. My love for Tony is too strong. He sure lets me know he'll play no games with me. I am his.

Getting ready for dinner with Mr. Williams, I put my hair up; put my pearls on with a beautiful pink sundress and white pumps. As I was doing my makeup I couldn't help but think of last night. The ocean waves rolled in from the horizon and pounded on an endless beach, roared and foamed and clapped against my chair.

As Tony strolled through the sand, I knew I was deeply in love and I had never felt so optimistic in my life. So strong, he bent down picking me up, sitting me in his lap, holding me so close, and the kisses, he was everything I had hoped for in a love. He was clever and playful, he had a sense of humor, he is warm and giving, he cares deeply about my feelings. There was a sincerity about him that was tremendously appealing to me. I knew he would always tell me the truth.

Thinking, My God, I have fallen madly in love for the first time in my life. He makes me laugh, makes me concentrate on what is really important. Sitting on the beach with Tony, the sky was filled with very large stars. 'We must go,' I said. He kissed me with such tenderness, sparkle, there was no escape. I was locked in his arms and his lips were locked on mine. Oh, I thought, I enjoy his kisses, the way he holds me, the way his touch makes my heart skip in an uneven kind of way. I like talking to him; I have fallen in love with a tough tender man.

Tony had carried me across the sand to the walkway, from there we walked hand in hand to the car, then we went home and into our room for a night of love.

Max and I drove up to the Wolf Bay Lodge about the same time as Mr. Williams. I'm thinking, what a doll, khaki pants, pink shirt, cream sweater, and sleeves around his neck shinning from head to toe, as always, smiling.

I said, "Oh! Are you a breath of fresh air, and you're so handsome. I have to tell you something, my mouth runs ninety miles an hour most of the time, but when I come to your office, I, lose all thoughts. Today I'm telling you that my love for you ranks with Tony's."

Mr. Williams turned red saying, "Why Drucilla, you're going to embarrass me."

I said, "I didn't think I'd ever let myself say that."

We sat at a nice table placing our orders. Max went in a different direction.

Mr. Williams said, "You know Drucilla, you must come to Birmingham often to see me, I worry about you."

I said, "You have no reason to worry about me, and besides, I would call you if I needed your help."

Mr. Williams said, "Yes you would, but I want you to understand, I would like to see you on some happy days, not just when you're in a panic."

"Ok, but you must tell Tony this, because he doesn't want me out of his sight. I'll never be anywhere but the bedroom and bath without Max."

Mr. Williams said, "Well Drucilla, when you come to see me, your Max can find something else to do. You will be in good hands."

After dinner I asked, "Are you ready to get out of here? Let's just sit in the car and talk."

Mr. Williams, "Yes Drucilla, I have something to ask you. Why did Richard buy that tractor? You know you told me about all your home canned food being taken away and the Sheriffs came to you and locked your home to see if anyone could get into it without a key and they couldn't. Richard said Harriet got it all. You said that wasn't true and you wouldn't cann food ever again. Then the very next summer you found nine boxes of jars, most all were quarts, written on the boxes were bedroom, living room, bath, kitchen and this and that. You had been to Harriet's house and the rest of your family's. So you knew without a doubt that Richard took your food off and brought your jars back."

I said, "Yes, Mr. Williams, and he never has had a good garden and even if he did I would not put up his food. That tractor was just to rub it in my face. You can be sure; I do know what he did to me. One thing, I shouldn't have ever taken a sleeping pill. Well, I'm not crazy; I'm just mad and mean. Hopefully I'll get over it all. I know Tony's family loves me and how I came through all I did, I'll never know. He tried everything he could to take my life, or make me nuts so he could send me off. Nothing worked because I had you and I had the Sheriff's office. I also know you didn't want me to marry him back, but I thought I could find the answer to it all, what a joke! After eight years what I found out was that he had cut me off from his pension. No woman will ever get his pension. Had I known this, I wouldn't have married him back. Richard has tormented me so badly, that I hope they never find that ship."

Mr. Williams asked, "Drucilla, did you have anything to do with that?"

I said, "No! But I should have killed him the night he screamed and screamed at me that he would cut my throat screaming 'G-D you, I'll turn into OJ and kill you', using the F word screaming he hated me. That was the night I should have killed him. He pushed the door in on my hands and arms. I wore a brace for three weeks. He pushed me down breaking my collarbone. Yes, Mr. Williams, I know what a fool I've been. My home is my home, not his, but he wouldn't leave and I've been too ashamed to tell you about all this. Well, now Tony and his family will take care of me. I don't live in fear anymore."

Mr. Williams said, "Drucilla, Richard has changed you, you once were so tender and loving, now you're more of a colder person."

I said, "Yes Sir, I'm sure it will take some time for all the hate to get out of me. Just think how many women are living with counterfeit men. Outside our home people would think that Richard was a Saint. I remember one time I broke my foot and Richard got mad at Amanda and Brandon, I didn't know he was cursing at them like dogs, for that matter I didn't know about it until the next day, sister Harriet told me. I asked her why she didn't take a ball bat to him. I now know that they were afraid of him. She reminded me of the day he shot a dog in the front yard three times, telling me if I didn't leave him alone, this is what he'd do to my family. I didn't believe he would hurt my family because he had them all on his side. It was always, 'Poor Richard, he has to live with her'. And I tell you for a lady that prayed to die every night, I now want to live, I want to sing, dance and take care of Anthony and Tony. Ok, here comes Max, I hate to leave you, but I must go. You call me every time you come to the Gulf and I will come see you."

Mr. Williams said, "Come to me Drucilla, let me hug you. You remember, I'm only a call away."

I said, "I know you are, and I love you."

Max opened my car door saying, "Let's go baby." We waved our good-byes.

Max said, "Drucilla, we are going to stop at the ice cream bar. I need to talk to you."

I said, "Oh my, spend time with you plus an ice-cream!"

Max said, "Yes, plus a surprise, I'm sure you remember Malviene the slut. I have been saving her for you, she is tied to your four-wheeler and I have everything fixed for you to taker her fat ass to the tree you hollowed out for her."

I asked, "Max, is she alive?"

Max said, "Yes Drucilla!"

I said, "Well, what are we waiting for, but you will have to wait on me to do this. I won't let you see me do it."

Max asked, "Can you do this by yourself?"

I said, "Yes Max, I can't believe you saved her for me."

Max said, "Ok Drucilla, she is tied at her wrists, elbows, knees and ankles. There is a chain from her shoulders to her feet and then it meets at her waist and the winch on the four-wheeler is hooked to the chain. All you have to do is open the log, then pick her up with the winch and put her over into the log. Let the top of the log down and back your four-wheeler out and kick the leaves and limbs over and around the log. Kick your way out so no one can tell it was ever touched.

Drucilla, we go to Birmingham on Wednesday because the people around there will be at church. I want us in there and gone. We can bring the four-wheeler and your black truck back with us."

I said, "Yes Max, and all my wicker, maybe a few other things. Max, I can't believe this, I owe you big time boy. Is it you or Tony that knows what I think? I didn't think anyone knew how bad I wanted to put her in that log. I tell you Max, she is use to eating cardboard fish sticks, so she will find a way to eat the rotted wood and I hope she stays alive till she loses down to ninety pounds. I pray a copperhead gets in there, gets up her ass and into her stomach leaving behind nineteen babies. Worms crawl in and worms crawl out.

Max said, "Shut up Drucilla, you can't sing that. I am getting sick."

I said, "You shut up Max, I know you don't get sick. I'll tell you this Max, this is the last thing I'll ever do. I hope God will forgive me, because I am sorry but I don't think I'd ever have piece of mind with her on this earth. Nasty, Nasty, she has been the nastiest person I have heard of. And for her to teach younger people her way of life. When do we leave Max?"

Max said, "What about 4:00 am, this should get us there about 9:00 am. Your people will be at church; I can wait on you in the boathouse. You do what you have to do, but get back to me as soon as possible."

I said, "Ok Max, sounds fine to me. I will be up and ready."

Max said, "As far as anyone knows, we are going after your four-wheeler and a few things you thought of."

The days pasted fast. We drove up to the boathouse. I pulled the four-wheeler from behind the boathouse. I poured water on the sluts face, I wanted her to see me and to know god and well who I was and to know she was going to the log; she had been told about her resting place. I took off on the four-wheeler with the slut in tow. As I put her in the log I covered my tracks, knowing in my heart she wouldn't ever be found.

I asked, "Malviene, Malviene, do remember saying that I looked like a hooker with my blond hair and long red nails? Oh! And my high heels. If you come back into this world twenty times, you'll never be as beautiful as I am, and you'll have to climb a twenty foot ladder to be white trash." As I left her I said, "Sleep well, for I feel so good."

I drove up the ramps onto the trailer telling Max to make sure everything was tied down good and we left.

I said, "Thanks Max, I wouldn't want to live without you."

Max said, "Hopefully you never will. Drucilla, just get your pillow and lay back and go to sleep. I'll have you home in time for dinner. Pull your tennis shoes and socks off and throw them out the window about ten miles apart You can put your heels on when we are getting out."

I said, "Max, you think of everything and I love you so much. Gosh! I wish I could have had her stuffed and mounted so I could hang her on the wall with an apple in her mouth. I wonder what the ACLU can do for her now. One thing is for sure; she won't be spreading her herpies ass around anymore. And I can surely say, she was alive the last time I saw her."

Max said, "Drucilla, your Mr. Williams should take you to Africa so you can get the hate out of you. You can put a name on everything you kill."

I said, "You know Max, that's why I loved golf so much. I put a name on that ball and knocked the hell out of it, but the only thing that makes me feel better is to know they're down under. Max, its over, I never want to talk about any of it again. What I don't know is what Anthony plans to do with the rest of his life. I know he is at the bowling alley every Saturday morning. He out dances anyone I've ever seen. He plays golf like a pro. He can work that computer, finding out anything you can think of."

Max said, "Drucilla, have you been in Anthony's room?"

I said, "No, but I thought it would be like any other young boys room."

Max said, "Well no, you're wrong my girl, Anthony's just been taking a break from his real love. Anthony's been racing from the time he could walk, almost. In his room he has trophies after trophies, and you can bet this will be his life. So Drucilla, you haven't been into Tony's office either?"

I said, "No Max, I feel so stupid. I've been all about me, me, me and you tell me that my baby plays golf, baseball, football, dances, is a champion bowler and is a winning racecar driver. He just turned thirteen years old! My Lord Max, get me home so I can get to know my little man. Max, just Saturday I walked through the den and Tony, Papa and Anthony were watching the Daytona race. Someone was interviewing one of the drivers. He didn't look more than fifteen, sixteen years old. I believe his name was Kasey K. Just a doll, Lord knows I know Tony will make sure that Anthony's car is well built."

Max said, "Wait till you see, Anthony has his own trailer for his car and a motor home. Drucilla, you just don't know how much Tony and Papa love Anthony, and for Anthony to choose you to be his Mom, I tell you, to him you are the Queen."

I said, "Max, this young man is brilliant. What a healthy brain, he makes me feel like a nut. He built me my very own car and I gave it to Rex. I wonder if that upset him."

Max said, "No Drucilla, Anthony was testing you to see just how well you would do. And you satisfied him. I'll tell you one thing, when turkey season opens up, he'll want you to go with him and Papa."

I said, "Max, I can do that. I bet that Papa Perricotti is waiting to show me my roosters. Oh me! I've got a lot to do and I'm so happy. Max, I'm going to need a lot more dancing clothes, and shoes. I see right now, if I don't keep Tony on the dancing floor as much as I can, I won't have his arms around me."

Max said, "That's OK Drucilla, you can have my arms."

I reached for my pillow and pretended to be going to sleep. We drove up to the house with the four-wheeler and Rex came out to help us. I asked him to wash it real good and put it in the garage with Tony's vintage cars and trucks. Rex, the yard is looking wonderful and I want to tell you, you take care of that race car, I want to drive it every once in a while."

Rex said, "I will Drucilla, and Mr. Perricotti said for you to call him or come over, and Anthony said he needs to see you."

Max had propped himself up against the car smiling. He said, "Well, you wanted to be busy, so you've got your wish."

I ran for the house and to my room turned on some bath water and just as I was putting my foot in, Tony grabbed me from behind, my elbow got him in the ribs, I turned and kicked his legs out from under him getting him in the throat with my fist, he got my arm just in time.

I screamed, "Tony, are you OK? My God don't ever slip up behind me again."

Tony said, "Don't you worry, you could have killed me woman."

I laughed and I could not stop laughing. I asked, "Would you want me to do any less to any other man?"

Tony said, "Well, No! Hell, I'm glad Anthony can't see that on camera. I'd never live it down."

Tony then pulled the stopper and we both got into the shower. After dinner I asked Anthony if he would show me his trophies and tell me about his plans for racing. Later I told Max that he was right, someday Anthony would be a top driver. Tony's office was covered in trophies and pictures of Anthony.

I asked Tony, "Are you one proud father, or what?"

Tony said, "I am. My boy is a champ at anything he wants to do. I'll be with him for all he wants to do, too."

I said, "So Tony, you can't love him anymore than I do."

Tony said, "Papa has been calling you. He wants to give you Mama Perricotti's jewelry."

I said, "I'll go see Papa in the morning, but I'll call him now."

The next morning Tony had sore ribs. The boys asked him what was wrong with him. Tony said, "All I'll say is NEVER slip up behind Dru. She will kill you."

Rex said, "You mean, you weren't in her mind?"

Tony said, "No, she must have had Max on her mind."

We all laughed, time flew by. We were in one thing after another. I had never been so happy.

Papa gave me the most beautiful jewelry that could be bought. Amanda and Michael had married.

Mr. Williams called he said, "Hello Drucilla, your Mr. Starr from Savanna has come looking for you. Do you want me to send him there?"

I said, "Lord No! Don't you dare send him here! I hope you didn't."

He said, "I didn't send him, but I just may bring him."

I started to say don't you dare, but Mr. Williams said teasingly, "You know I wouldn't do that Drucilla. Besides my child, this is a small world, Mr. Starr knows your Tony very well."

I said, "Please don't tell me that."

Mr. Williams said, "It's true, I told him to leave you alone, that you married a gangster. I told him who and he said, 'I know him very well, you have no worry, I wouldn't touch that family'. I have got to go now Drucilla, talk to you soon."

I sat with my cup of tea thinking, Tony has two farms, hundreds of cattle, he runs himself to death and I've got to find a way to get Tony to slow down, but he said he lost a lot of time getting me here. I know that's true and I'll just fall in and help do what needs to be done and keep things going.

How could I be so lucky, Brandon got married I hope I don't have to kill her. I do have bad feelings about her. Just look at Anthony, he ran his races every weekend. He is a champion. He calls me everyday with a joke or a dance date. Max is sweet on Courtney and I'm jealous.

Max came to the patio and sat with me. I said, "Tony and I are so in love. I can't help believe that this is just a dream, but I know it isn't."

The Fourth of July is coming and we will have tubs of drinks, melons, every pie and cake, fresh veggies from the garden. All the guys will be BBQing. This is what my Daddy did. He loved the Fourth of July better than any other day maybe because there was plenty to eat and a five-gallon churn of lemonade. Rex has a beautiful garden with everything. He is about to work Sandra to death. Papas in hog heaven and so am I. Anthony loves that his friends can come here to party and to see him and his new Mama dance.

Finally I have a real man, a real family, love I've never known. All the fear I ever had is gone. I now have new friends, one being Lori, I love her and her family. With her I can just be myself. Did you hear that, I can be my **real** self. I now have piece of mind.

The men in my life are not counterfeit men. I ask women all the time, do they know if their man is counterfeit, they all need to know.

Max said, "Well you damn well know I'm not a counterfeit man."

I said, "Oh yes baby! I well know."

The phone rang. It was Brandon crying. I didn't wait to hear what he had to say. I threw the phone down. I was on my feet running but Max grabbed the back pocket of my jeans stopping me in my tracks.

Max asked, "What's wrong?"

I said, "I just had a bad feeling about that thing Brandon married and now he's on the phone with a one hundred six temperature and she won't take him to the hospital. Max, I must go to him, call Tony. I'll call Harriet."

I called Harriet on the telephone and said, "You go get Brandon and take care of him. I'll be there as soon as I can and she better be gone when I get there."

Tony had a jet plane waiting for Max and I at the airport. He also had a rental car waiting for us when I arrived. I made record driving across town.

Brandon saw me as I burst in the door. He was crying and said, "Ma Maw, I didn't want to tell you about her but she has almost killed me."

To see Brandon hurt this much, it brought the Koki out. I thought I had done away with the killer in me.

Max turned to me and asked, "What's next?"

I said, "Call Two Men and a Truck moving company and tell them to be here within a hour."

Within thirty minutes they were backing up to the door. I told what to load and the address to deliver it to and to dump it in the front yard. That night her Mama's car burst into flames. It burned the car, everything in the yard and spread to the house and by the time the fire department arrived there wasn't a bush left standing.

Brandon recovered from a kidney stone and a broke heart.

I said, "Brandon, I'm going home now baby."

Max said, "Baby! He's thirty-one years old."

I said, "You bastard, he'll be my baby when he's ninety-nine years old. Do you get that?"

Max said, "I do Drucilla. What's next?"

I said, "Drive me home."

On the way out of town I stopped off at the law office and started divorce papers for Brandon. When we arrived home Tony was so mad he was screaming at Max. Come to find out we were supposed to wait for Tony.

Max calmly said, "Now you listen. You! Gave me to her, and said do what ever she asked. That's what I did."

I said, "Now Tony, I'm sorry but I haven't had time to realize that I have people to take care of me. I got the call and I took care of the problem."

Tony said, "Yes, Dru, but you could have called Mr. Williams."

I said, "I know you're a wise man Tony, but you better get wiser."

A week later the law office called telling me that she refused to sign the papers and we would have to go before a Judge. At the hearing Brandon gave the Judge some pictures showing what a nasty wife and housekeeper she was. The Judge signed the divorce papers.

On the way out of the courthouse the lawyer said, "I know some of her people and they seem to be nice people."

I said, "Sir, those people would have to climb the tallest ladder, in the world, just to be called white trash."

I told Harriet and Brandon good-bye. Max and I drove back to the Gulf. This let me know I'll always be an Army of one. Maybe it's not meant for me to be a good girl. Some of us know, you have to take care of family and business, that's just life.

Chapter 16

Friday night came fast. Everyone was ready for the race. Drucilla had made up her mind that she was going to win and she did. Then all hell broke loose. As soon as Mr. Williams received word that Drucilla had been shot he called the telephone number that Tony had given him several months ago. He wondered who would answer as he dialed the number.

It was a man's voice on the other end and he said, "Hello Mr. Williams. What has happened to Drucilla?"

Mr. Williams said, "She has been shot."

The stranger asked, "How bad?"

Mr. Williams said, "All I know is that Max called me and said she had been wounded and he was bringing her to me."

The stranger said, "I'll make the arrangements and call you back."

Without another word the stranger hung up the telephone. Max was due in town in four hours. Mr. Williams could only sit and wait. He didn't have long to wait.

\The telephone rang and Mr. Williams picked up the receiver and said, "Hello!"

The same voice said, "Rent a medical jet under the name of Sally Jane McDougal and send Drucilla to the Mobile International Airport. I'll have someone meet you at the charter terminal."

Mr. Williams asked, "Where are you going to take her?"

The voice said, "It's best that you don't know."

Mr. Williams said, "Thank you Mr. Young."

The stranger said, "You're smarter than I thought." He hung up and Mr. Williams called the airport and had the medical jet placed on standby. Max drove up at Mr. Williams' office within thirty minutes. Max and Mr. Williams put Drucilla into Mr. Williams' car.

Max drove off in one direction as Mr. Williams and Drucilla headed for the airport. The medical jet was waiting at the terminal gate and in one hour they had landed at the Mobile airport. Waiting at the terminal gate was an ambulance to take Drucilla to the Alabama State Docks. The ambulance stopped at a seventy-five foot yacht named Crimson Tide registered out of Mobile. As soon as Drucilla was aboard all lines were cast off. No one noticed that Mr. Williams was still on board. About an hour in open seas when Captain John Bear went to check up on Drucilla, Captain Bear was not happy to find Mr. Williams still in her cabin. He took one look at Mr. Williams and left without saying a word. He returned in ten minutes. During that time neither Drucilla or Mr. Williams noticed the course change.

Captain Bear said, "Mr. Williams you have fifteen minutes before you leave this boat."

Mr. Williams asked, "Where am I going?"

Captain Bear said, "You will be told when you disembark."

The Captain said no more. He turned and walked out of the cabin.

Mr. Williams turned to Drucilla and said, "I wonder if they will put me into a row boat in the middle of the gulf."

Drucilla said, "I don't know Captain Bear but I do know where he gets his orders and I can guarantee you that you will not be hurt."

The boat was slowing down and when Mr. Williams looked out of the porthole they were pulling up to a dock. The boat docked and a crew member came to escort Mr. Williams off the boat. Drucilla looked out of the porthole and saw three men dressed in military uniforms escorting Mr. Williams off the dock and into a car. Drucilla watched the car until it went out of sight. Then she saw the sign. It read 'Welcome to the Port of Havana'.

The boat started moving again and in no time they were in the open sea again. After cruising at full speed for two hours the boat slowed and came to a dead stop. The boat was one hundred miles south southwest of Cuba.

Captain Bear knocked on Drucilla's cabin door. He came and said, "This is where we part company. A seaplane will be here in five minutes to take you the rest of the way."

Drucilla asked, "And where would that be?"

He said, "I don't know. This is where I get off."

There was a knock at the door. Drucilla said, "Come in."

The door opened and there stood Mr. Young. He said, "My dear, are you ready?"

Drucilla said, "Yes! And what happened to Mr. Williams?"

Mr. Young said, "He is on his way home to see that Tony, his son and the rest of them are taken care of."

Drucilla said, "Oh! My God, it took me years and more years to find me a family and now, they're, they're all gone. Mr. Williams can't be on his way home. I need him! Mr. Young, have those bastards been taken care of?"

Mr. Young said, "Yes, Drucilla, we are in the cleanup stage now and Mr. Williams is fine and well taken care of. I'll tell you about it later. Right now I need to get you to a hospital."

They boarded the seaplane and it seemed as if the gulf was cooperating with them as it was unusually calm. They took of heading North into the wind and as they circled back South Drucilla took one last look at the yacht. The name had been changed to "El Presidente" out of Havana. As they flew south Mr. Young told Drucilla that he had arranged for Mr. Williams to fly commercial from Havana to Reo de Janeiro and then to his home in Mozambique.

Drucilla was on the seaplane for ninety minutes and it landed on an airstrip in the middle of nowhere. An ambulance was waiting to take Drucilla to an Army hospital. She was checked out thoroughly an the next day was taken to a beach home. Later she would find out that she was on the gulf side of the Panama Canal Zone.

Mr. Young took her to the beach house. He said, "You need to rest now. I have arranged for Max to come and get you in six weeks. You will be safe here and no one will know where you are."

Drucilla said, "But they couldn't be after me. They just got mad because our car was faster than theirs. The other drivers tried to knock me off the track but I was too fast for them. I got out around him and won the race. That's when all hell broke loose. This wasn't about me. I heard there was big money being bet on the favorite and

I beat him. There must have been big, big money on that race. Just tell Mr. Williams to take me or send me to his beach house. I have a cousin named Leonard King that would fight an army for me. He would burn the tires off his car to get to me. Leonard and his friend would leave them in the Cardiff Cemetery, in the back woods, in a heartbeat. When I said I didn't have a family, I was wrong. I do know better. Leonard is my family and he loved my Uncle Louie. I have my nephew Ricky, we call him Squirrel, because he's so fast. And then there's Jerry, he's just sick and too old, I wouldn't want anything to happen to him. I know it would just kill me."

Mr. Young asked, "Drucilla what your plans for Tony and Anthony?"

Drucilla said, "Oh, please don't make me think about that now. I know Rex will take care of it all. Plus there's Amanda and Michael. One thing you can do for me. Get Courtney to come here. She will help me get a bath and get well. Please let me rest for now. I'm so tired."

Drucilla was devastated she had cried herself sick. She had screamed over and over, please God wake me; let this be a dream. She had screamed I hate this world, it's hell. I want to die if I can't have Tony.

Mr. Young was gone about an hour when Drucilla heard a knock at the door. Drucilla walked over and opened the door and there stood Mr. Williams.

Drucilla said, "But!!"

Mr. Williams put his finger to his mouth to let her know to be quiet and came and shut the door. He said, "I slipped by them. I paid another man to take my place in Reo and here I am."

He picked Drucilla up in his arms walked over to the bed and sat on the edge of the bed and rocked her back and forth. He took out his handkerchief and wiped the tears from her eyes as he said, "Please don't cry."

Drucilla said, "I can't help it. I hurt so bad. I've lost Tony, Anthony and Papa."

Lifting her chin he said, "But you haven't lost me. Papa has the house on the beach and when you get better I'll take you there. You are not alone you have Amanda."

Drucilla said, "If you love me you'll throw me overboard on the way home."

A servant girl brought in a tray of food and Drucilla asked her to bring another tray of food. Within two minutes another tray was there and so was Mr. Young.

Mr. Young asked, "How did you manage this?"

Mr. Williams said, "I was just lucky."

Mr. Young said, "We all have been lucky. I just received a telegram from Pensacola. Tony and Anthony are alive. It seems everybody was confused, things were a mess, they're in bad shape but alive."

Drucilla went limp in Mr. Williams' arms. She had fainted. He laid her on the bed and washed her face with a cold wash cloth.

Drucilla opened her eyes and asked, "Was I dreaming or did someone say that Tony is alive?"

Mr. Williams said, "No, it wasn't a dream. Tony is alive. See you have Tony, Me and God. Your new life is going to be fine after all. Drucilla don't cry, we are going to be fine."

Drucilla said, "Please hold me. Don't let this be a joke."

Mr. Young said, "It will only be a few days and you will see for yourself."

Drucilla said, "I wouldn't want to live without you, or you, Mr. Young."

Mr. Young smiled and walked out. Mr. Williams made Drucilla eat her lunch.

Drucilla asked, "Please don't leave me until I'm back home. Thank God, I'm going to have my Tony, my Anthony, my Rex and my Max. God is so good to me and you promise me that you will never leave me."

Mr. Williams said, "I didn't, did I?"

Drucilla said, "No sir! And I know you never will. I want to know if they have arrested the ones that shot us."

Mr. Williams said, "Yes, some of them. From what I hear the ones that started it are at the bottom of the gulf."

Drucilla said, "Well good, because I'm taking my car back to the track if I don't people will say I'm chicken and that will never be."

Mr. Williams said, "Well Drucilla you will have a fight on your hands. Cause Anthony said my Mom will never go back. All she's going to do is dance and sing. I promised I would help her."

Drucilla said, "If only he knew how hurt I was to think he was dead."

Mr. Williams said, "It took me many years to get you to come alive, and now you have a lot to do."

Drucilla said, "You mean I can't play ball with Nick Saban."

Mr. Williams said, "Well, I'll ask Tony and if he says yes, well I'll still say no. But I know I have my Drucilla back and she's going to be happy from now on."

Mr. Williams kept his word and stayed with me until I was back with Papa and all my family. But Anthony nor all the rest of my family couldn't stop Drucilla from going back to the race track and there had never been so many at Six Flags in Pensacola; and, yes, she won.

Tony threw a big dinner party to celebrate and Drucilla made the toast.

"I love fast cars and handsome men but that was my last race. All I want to do now is take care of my family, Tony, Anthony, Papa, Max, Perricotte, Tommynocker, and most of all Michael, Amanda and all my grandbabies to be.

Amanda asked, "Mom, did you forget anyone?"

Drucilla said, "No, no, my Mr. Williams never leaves my mind, and yes, Tony knows I would trade him for my Mr. Williams. I can be talking to him and I lose my mind, can't spell candy."

Amanda said, ""OK Tony you best know Mr. Williams is fox."

THE END

CPSIA information can be obtained at www.ICGtesting.com
Printed in the USA
LVOW08s1351011113

359488LV00001B/1/P